W9-CUT-736

". . . those interested in space flight in general will find THE ENDLESS FRONTIER exceptionally worthwhile."
—The American Library Association *Booklist*

"Pournelle is infectiously optimistic about solutions to the Earth's problems. Entertaining and exhilarating. Highly recommended."
—*Science Fiction and Fantasy Book Review*

"If more people would only listen to Pournelle (and the rest of us), we could mobilize the national/international will and put an end to worries about energy crises, resource shortages, pollution, crowding, and all the rest of the doomster fears."
—Tom Easton, *Analog*

# THE ENDLESS FRONTIER

edited by

## JERRY POURNELLE

with *JOHN F. CARR*

### VOL. II

SF

ace books

A Division of Charter Communications Inc.
A GROSSET & DUNLAP COMPANY
51 Madison Avenue
New York, New York 10010

THE ENDLESS FRONTIER VOL. II

Copyright © 1982 by Jerry Pournelle

All rights reserved. No part of this book may be reproduced in any form or by any means, except for the inclusion of brief quotations in a review, without permission in writing from the publisher.

All characters in this book are fictitious. Any resemblance to actual persons, living or dead, is purely coincidental.

An ACE Book

First Ace printing: January 1982
Published Simultaneously in Canada

2  4  6  8  0  9  7  5  3  1
Manufactured in the United States of America

"The Insurmountable Opportunity" by Jerry Pournelle, Copyright © 1982 by J. E. Pournelle. A substantially different version appeared in *Destinies*, Copyright © 1980 by J. E. Pournelle. Published by special arrangement with the author's agents, Blassingame, McCauley, and Wood.

"The Moon Goddess and the Son" by Donald Kingsbury appeared in *ANALOG SCIENCE FICTION* 1979, Copyright © 1979 by Conde Nast Publications, Inc. Published by arrangement with the author.

"Space and the Longevity of Man" by Stefan T. Possony and J. E. Pournelle appeared in *ISSAC ASIMOV'S SCIENCE FICTION MAGAZINE*, Copyright © 1981 by Davis Publications, Inc.

"Down & Out on Ellfive Prime" by Dean Ing appeared in *OMNI*, Copyright © 1980 by Omni International Publications, Ltd. Published by special arrangement with the author.

"The Study Syndrome" by Jerry Pournelle Copyright © 1982 by J. E. Pournelle. A substantially different version was first published in *ANALOG 'SCIENCE FICTION*, Copyright © 1980 by Davis Publications, Inc.

"Three Poems: NASA, Elegy, and Inner Space" by Helene Knox Copyright © 1979 by Helene Knox. Published by special arrangement with the author's representative Richard C. Hoagland and Associates.

"Our Lady of the Sauropods" by Robert Silverberg appeared in OMNI, Copyright © 1980 by Omni International Publications, Ltd. Published by special arrangement with the author.

"Two Poems: Lighting the Colony, and Seeding the Last Freedom," by Steve Rasnic Tem, Copyright © 1980 by Steve Rasnic Tem. Published by permission of the author.

"How To Build a Beanstalk" by Charles Sheffield was first published in *DESTINIES*, Copyright © 1979 by Charles Sheffield.

"Sky Stalk" by Charles Sheffield was first published in *DESTINIES*, Copyright © 1979 by Charles Sheffield. "Sky Stalk" and "How to Build a Beanstalk" are published by special arrangement with the author.

"Invisible Encounter" by Dan Girard, Copyright © 1982 by Dan Girard Crayne. Published by permission of the author.

"Bellerophon" by Kevin Cristensen was first published in *DESTINIES*, Copyright © 1980 by Kevin Cristensen. Published by permission of the author.

"Highlifter Trilogy" by Robert Frazier, Copyright © 1982 by Robert Frazier. Published by special arrangement with the author.

"Designing a Dyson Sphere" by Jack Williamson was first published in *GALAXY SCIENCE FICTION*, Copyright © 1978 by Universal Publishing and Distributing Corporation. Published by special arrangement with the author.

"Conservation of Mass" by Karl Pflock, Copyright © 1982 by Karl T. Pflock. Published by permission of the author.

"The Quiet" by George Florance-Guthridge, Copyright © 1981 by George Guthridge. Published by permission of the author.

"Psi-Rec: Of Anabasis and Bivouac, the Swarmcantor" by Peter Dillingham, Copyright © 1982 by Peter Dillingham. Published by special arrangement with the author.

"Our Many Roads to the Stars" by Poul Anderson was first published in *GALAXY SCIENCE FICTION*, Copyright © 1978 by Universal Publishing and Distributing Corporation. Published by special arrangement with the author.

"Exploring Infra-Stellar Space" by Dr. Robert L. Forward was first published in *ANALOG SCIENCE FICTION*, Copyright © 1977 by Conde Nast Publications. Published by special arrangement with the author.

"Shapes of Things to Come" by John F. Carr, Copyright © 1982 by John F. Carr. Published by special arrangement with the author.

"The Endless Frontier and the Thinking Machine" by Hans P. Moravec, Copyright © 1978 by Hans P. Moravec. Published by special arrangement with the author.

"Songs of a Spacefarer" by Judith Conly, Copyright © 1982 by Judith Conly. Published by special arrangement with the author.

"Redeemer" by Gregory Benford, Copyright © 1982 by Gregory Benford. Published by special arrangement with the author.

# TABLE OF CONTENTS

INTRODUCTION: The Insurmountable
Opportunity    1

THE MOON GODDESS AND THE SON,
Donald Kingsbury    18

SPACE AND THE LONGEVITY OF MAN,
Stefan T. Possony and Jerry Pournelle    82

DOWN & OUT ON ELLFIVE PRIME, Dean
Ing    96

THE STUDY SYNDROME, Jerry Pournelle    124

THREE POEMS, Helene Knox    131

OUR LADY OF THE SAUROPODS, Robert
Silverberg    137

TWO POEMS, Steve Rasnic Tem    157

HOW TO BUILD A BEANSTALK, Charles
Sheffield    160

SKY STALK, Charles Sheffield    182

INVISIBLE ENCOUNTER, Dian Girard    204

HOW TO BECOME A SPACE COLONIST,
Jerry Pournelle    210

BELLEROPHON, Kevin Christensen    227

HIGHLIFTER TRILOGY, Robert Frazier    276

DESIGNING A DYSON SPHERE, Jack
Williamson    280

CONSERVATION OF MASS, Karl T. Pflock    289

THE QUIET, George Florance-Guthridge    295

PSI-REC: OF ANABASIS AND BIVOUAC,
THE SWARMCANTOR, Peter Dillingham    312

OUR MANY ROADS TO THE STARS, Poul
Anderson    321

EXPLORING INFRA-STELLAR SPACE,
  Dr. Robert L. Forward                          339
SHAPES OF THINGS TO COME, John F. Carr    358
THE ENDLESS FRONTIER AND THE
  THINKING MACHINE, Hans P. Mouravec    374
SONGS OF A SPACEFARER, Judith R. Conly   399
REDEEMER, Gregory Benford                     404
DEAR MR. PRESIDENT, Jerry
  Pournelle                                        419
AFTERWORD                                       428

# Acknowledgements

This book is dedicated to the L-5 Society, 1060 E. Elm, Tucson, AZ 85719; and particularly to those who have undertaken the onerous task of presiding over such stormy but important work: Keith L. Henson, Carolyn Meinel Henson, and Gerald Driggers. It is also dedicated to Barbara Marx Hubbard, whose generous support kept the Society alive in its time of troubles.

Research for this book was supported in part by a grant from the Vaughn Foundation. Responsibility for opinions and conclusions remains with the authors.

Jerry Pournelle
Hollywood, 1982

# INTRODUCTION

# THE INSURMOUNTABLE OPPORTUNITY

## Jerry Pournelle

In spring of 1980 I had an astonishing experience: one of the highest officials of NASA solemnly informed me that the United States could not put a man on the Moon within ten years.

"But," spluttered I, "we did it in eight, starting from a lot less in 1961. Surely we can do better now?"

"No."

Now I know what you're thinking. I was asking about technical ability, and the NASA official must have folded in his opinions about national priorities and budgets and the like, and thus answered a question I hadn't asked. I wish that were true, but I fear it isn't so. Let me start from the beginning.

In early 1980, Marvin Minsky, one of the really top experts in the field of Artificial Intelligence (AI), called to tell me of an upcoming NASA conference on future missions. The participants would be a dozen or so of the brightest and most creative people in the space sciences. Would I be interested in attending?

At first I thought he meant that I should come as a journalist, but no, the steering committee had offered me a seat as a participant; my early work in the aerospace community had found me out. Thus in due course I found myself working to a schedule for the first time in more than a dozen years. The conference was intense: up in the morning, breakfast with the other participants, conferences until lunch, conferences after lunch, dinner with the other participants, and then "informal meetings" until sack time.

The Chairman, Dr. Bob Cannon of Stanford (who incidentally looks startlingly like screen actor Arthur Hill), did an excellent job of cajoling this gaggle of temperamental, opionionated characters into working together instead of cutting each other's throats. We were on a tight schedule because Robert Frosch, then Administrator of NASA, would be joining us at the end of the week.

The meeting task was "Given advances in Artificial Intelligence and Telefactor capabilities, what bold new missions can we perform in the 25, 50, and 100 year time frame? And what technologies must we begin developing now in order to perform those missions?"

Aha, thought I, maybe a science fiction type belongs in this group after all.

About that word "telefactor": old time science fiction readers will be more familiar with the term "Waldo". A "teleoperated system" is one controlled by a remotely located human operator, with or without computer assistance. As an example: if we want to do lunar strip mining, we need not have the bulldozer operator on the Moon. He (or she) can just as easily be in Houston—or in Hollywood, or Dubuque, or Resume Speed, Michigan for that matter.

We were also given a conceptual model: suppose we could put a large package into an environment rich in raw materials. Could that initial package make factories without human assistance? Ideally, could it make factories which would in turn make robots which could make more factories to make more robots, etc., thereby achieving something like exponential growth? Because if so, we're on the track of untold wealth.

Thus a lot of the conference was devoted to the problem of "self replicating systems": machines that make copies of themselves. Ideally they'd also make something useful as well, but it's obvious that any machinery capable of duplicating itself without human assistance would also be capable of making all kinds of valuable stuff. In the worst case we could simply harvest factories and robots.

Well, it's a terrific idea. Moreover, people who ought to know see no reason why it can't be done. *When* is another matter. On the one hand, the Japanese certainly are trying to make completely automated automobile factories, and most experts expect them to succeed a lot quicker than the United Auto Workers would like. On the other, doing that with no humans at all, and using, say, lunar materials, will take a bit longer.

Since we don't need anything as complex as an automobile factory, perhaps we can design a simpler self replicating system (SRS)? After all, the Moon is rich in useful materials. Iron wire isn't as efficient as copper, but there's a lot of iron, and who cares about efficiency when intense sunlight is free and you're after exponential growth? So a lot of very bright people (from graduate students to Roy Smelt, retired Chief Scientist for Lockheed) worked on simplifications. Minsky thought hard about *very* simple technologies, such as Erector Sets (as a boy he'd built a pretty good mechanical hand from a Meccano set, and with smart computers to drive it, might it not be able to assemble another?).

A lot of thought was given to how to eliminate bearings, and must you have hinges, and can you do without the wheel.

We looked at ways to use direct process heat instead of electricity. Danny Hillis, one of Minsky's graduate students, suggested a lunar "sunflower" which focusses solar heat on the lunar surface to fuse the regolith into a mirror, then, using bi-metallic flexure, walks off to do the same job over again. Controlling the mirror doesn't look impossible, but getting the neonate "flower" erect isn't easy. My own suggestion was that another "sex" of the machine comes up to process the "embryo".

There were a number of interesting ideas, but the bottom line was that while we surely would be able to build a lunar (or asteroidal) SRS some day, it won't be soon. We can design systems to minimize dependence on human beings; we might even get down to needing only one person; but eliminating that last man looks to be at least ten times as hard as eliminating the next-to-last, and it won't happen in the next twenty years.

So far, then, the study has negative results. It was not, I hasten to add, a useless exercise. One of our missions was to identify problems we ought to be working on: what aren't we doing that we ought to be? What does NASA's technology research office fund tomorrow morning? We identified several worthwhile projects, and that was worth more than the price of the conference, even if we can't put a self replicating factory on the Moon by 1995.

Or can't we?

Now for the minority report. I think we can. Our journey into the endless frontier can begin sooner than most people think.

* * *

Query: can humans be part of a "system"? Because if so, it's very clear we know how to build a technologically sophisticated SRS. It consists of people plus tools plus raw materials.

To be precise, a lunar settlement.

I don't mean a base. I mean a settlement, or, to use a word in bad repute just now, a colony. The difference should be clear: settlers don't expect to come home. They're going to live on a new frontier; to make a New Beginning. Plans for settlements need not include much payload for bringing people home. At most you need a lifeboat, an emergency means rescuing for survivors in case of disaster. Perhaps you don't need that. It depends on who you ask. Those sending the colony might want to salve their consciences, but the settlers could well prefer that payload go to more equipment.

A lunar settlement would be quite valuable. It's an obvious springboard to really large space operations. For example, there's lots of oxygen on the Moon, and it's not so hard to extract from the rocks. A lunar establishment could fling that into Earth orbit for use by construction crews for space industrial satellites.

Lunar refineries could extract iron and aluminum for Earth orbit operations. For that matter, any mass, including random lunar rock, is valuable if you can put it in Earth orbit—and there are several ways to get material from the lunar surface into space. It can be flung up by "electric cannon" or even by a Kevlar slingshot; once in space you can use low-thrust ion engines fueled with lunar materials for maneuvering.

The lunar settlement would give Earth a new resource base. A whole planet of untapped wealth. And when people *live* on the Moon we will finally and forever have escaped the dangers of "Only One Earth". We would truly live in space, in the endless frontier.

There are some problems with a lunar settlement. Finding settlers isn't one of them. A random example: a local commercial electronics firm was hired to video tape part of the conference final report. I asked the two camera technicians if they'd be willing to settle on the Moon, even though there'd be no way to come back. "Like a shot," said one. And he meant it.

The economic problems are more difficult. An early lunar settlement—say one put up in the next ten years using Shuttle as the primary launch vehicle—would be expensive, and thus must be kept to a minimum survival level. (My preliminary analysis—wild guess?—would be 12 to 20 people.) Most of their initial effort would go to survival effort and living space expansion. They wouldn't have much time for efforts primarily useful to Earth, such as manufacturing solar cells for the Solar Power Satellite, or just putting lunar material into Earth orbits. It would take a while to get any payoff from the kind of colony we could send right now.

Suppose, though, that we could *amplify* their efforts? That each settler could do the work of ten to fifteen skilled people? Then things would change dramatically.

And of course that's possible. Minsky has described the

concept in previous publications. When you send up the colony, you send up a number of Waldoes. A lunar colonist doesn't drive the bulldozer; that's done from Earth. The colonists needn't even do most of the repairs; leave that for experts who've never left the ground and who're working in shirt sleeves. Oh, sure, sometimes things will go wrong in a way that requires human intervention; that's what the colonists are for, after all; but we can try to drive that number of jobs to a minimum as time goes on. We can redesign our Waldoes as we learn what unexpected jobs have to be performed.

At this point you're thinking "time delays". How can you run a lunar bulldozer from Earth when it takes 1½ seconds for your command to get up there, and that long again for you to see what's happening?

It's a special case of what's known in the trade as the "Rover Problem", namely, how can we keep a lunar (or Mars!) roving probe from running over a cliff.

Notice, though, that our problem is much simpler; we're running our Waldoes in an explored environment, and if we want to use the Waldo to look into strange terrain, then we'll control it from the Moon on the first pass. Thus my bulldozer won't run over a cliff because I'll keep it a long way away from cliffs.

Second, notice that many tasks (especially those in a thoroughly known environment) don't need constant attention. The bulldozer in a strip mine: assume we need to see what each shovel-full of stuff looks like before we dig it. This means that we pause a few seconds at the end of each dig and load cycle; not a very hefty burden, and in return we run it three shifts and from Earth.

Now we want to move it, at, say, 10 miles per hour, which is about 15 feet per second; then I need to see 45 feet plus the stopping distance. If we're taking the 'dozer through crowded areas, we don't drive it from Earth; but for across-country transport there's no real problem.

Now consider a more delicate operation such as machining small parts.

What you need is a computer on board the Waldo, and another at the operator's console. Each computer has in its memory a "model" of the task to be performed, and what it expects to happen at each stage. Now the operator gives a command. This goes simultaneously to the Waldo and to the operator's computer. The operator's computer automatically builds in the time delay, then acts as if it has executed the command. Using the model as its information source, it tells the operator what it thinks the Waldo is doing. It is also comparing its latest information on reality with what it *thought* the Waldo was doing 1.5 second ago.

Up on the Moon, the Waldo's computer *knows* what is happening; but since it also has a copy of the operator's computer model, it also knows what its boss *thinks* is happening. It continually compares truth with reality, *and* if the discrepancy goes beyond previously set limits, the Waldo executes a previously designated fail-safe sequence, and tells the operator, "Boss, I'm confused. Here's what things look like to me. What do I do next?"

In fact, by putting smart but ignorant computers on board the Waldoes, we can teach them to become robots. Suppose an Earth operator has just taken a Waldo through a complex task. He then asks the computer, "Remember how you did that?"

"Yeah, boss."

"Put it in permanent memory."

It all looked good to me, and I proposed that we try to design the colony. Not in gory detail, because we weren't that kind of group and we didn't have that kind of mission; but we could, thought I, take a very hard look at just what we'd like the Waldoes to do, and what we have to know in order to construct Waldoes that can do it.

Which may or may not turn out to be a lot. AI and telefactor technology have progressed enormously in the past few years. I recall that about five years ago John McCarthy of Stanford's Artificial Intelligence labs bought a Heathkit color television with the firm intention of having it constructed by a machine. Moreover, it wouldn't be a teleoperated machine, either, but one controlled by a computer; in other words, a true robot. And of course he didn't manage that, and indeed wasn't even able to get the box opened.

Also, I recently talked to one of the people who operate the research sub *Alvin,* and discovered to my horror that *Alvin* 's "hands" are two-fingered clumsy things actuated by toggle switches. Meanwhile, Vic Scheinman, one of McCarthy's graduate students, brought to the conference a small robot which can draw and write and do fairly amazing things under computer control, and is really only limited by its very clumsy mechanical two-fingered hand.

Vic has built a very sophisticated arm, and devised excellent computer programs to control it. Not only does the arm know where it is at all time, but it can shift from the universal x,y,z coordinates to coordinates oriented about the hand/ wrist. It can grab its specially modified (inserted in a block of wood to let the two-finger "hand" grasp it) ball point pen. and it can set objects down precisely where you want them—and, if they haven't moved or fallen over, get them again.

But it couldn't turn pages of a normal book, and it couldn't open a packing crate; not because Vic can't tell it how with the Heathkit H-89 that runs the system, but because the hand on the end just isn't good enough.

In other words, the brains are ahead of the hands, and there's got to be a lot more research on hand/actuator technology, with considerable cooperation between the AI computer types and trained mechanical engineers. At the moment, when AI people need something done, they're so underfunded that if they need a power supply they generally can't just go buy one for $750; instead, a mathematician assembles a kit bought for $300. It's a tragic waste of scarce brainpower, and not much of a way to save money; and we need the development too much to leave it to chance.

But isn't industry developing "hands"?

Yes and no. Yes, of course there's a lot of money going into automation technology; but most of it tends to be for special purpose systems. One of Marvin Minsky's favorite laments is that instead of designing general purpose hands for Waldoes, industrial designers keep trying to "improve" things. If you need a screw turned, why not have an arm with screwdrive built in? Why have a hand, when the special purpose arm does so much better? And indeed it does much better—for the job it was designed to do. What it can't do is a job you didn't expect—such as opening a relief valve inside the reactor containment at, say, Three Mile Island . . .

The general purpose/special purpose fight won't end soon; indeed we had a replay of it every day. John R. Pierce of Cal Tech and JPL (you may know him better as the science fiction writer JJ Coupling) was another conference participant, and he is still convinced that the special-purpose route is best. His convictions are important; after all, Cal Tech and JPL design and build space probes. He may be right; but I know damned well that we can't build the Waldo-augmented lunar colony without at least *some* general-purpose actuators, and the five-fingered hand is still likely to be needed because most of the tools we'll send for use by the colonists require them— and after all, what we're looking for is ways to let Waldoes do jobs that would otherwise use up the settlers' time (or be beyond their ability).

Until we try to build mechanical hands we won't know what we can do; and thus it seems worth considerably more effort than is going into it now.

* * *

We were supposed to look for "bold new missions", and also identify technology requirements. My thought was that the lunar colony concept was ideal for the purpose. First, it was universally agreed among the participants that the only self replicating system we could build before the year 2000 would have humans in it. Secondly, having designed the colony, we could start work on minimizing the need for people, thus identifying tasks we want AI/Waldoes to perform.

Thus I advocated that the study team do preliminary design

work on the only extra-terrestrial self replicating system we can build beore the year 2000. Doing that design would point up critical technology areas we ought to study; and my first cut at the problem doesn't identify any "show stoppers", i.e. capabilities we can't have before, say, 1990, meaning that we could, if we wanted to, actually put up a lunar colony by the year 1992; possibly earlier if we're willing to give the mission enough priority.

That's where it hit the fan.

* * *

By golly, you'd have thought I was advocating treason. Now, here I have to be careful. We were, after all, a study group with limited resources. This was one of the first intensive interactions between space science people and the Artificial Intelligence community, and we were, after all, supposed to look at what automation and AI could do for space. The conference was funded by NASA for a definite purpose, and manned space wasn't really the purpose.

So: many of my colleagues didn't want to devote a lot of time to lunar colonies.

The counter argument is this: if we wait a while, machines may be able to do all the lunar work, and, moreover, do it much more cheaply. Thus, isn't it really better to wait fifty years? Why take chances? Why send settlers to an untamed wilderness when we can, eventually, send up machines to prepare them a Hilton Hotel?

And that is no longer a technical discussion. That one involves philosophy, and national purpose, and economic priorities, including a very serious answer to the question "Why waste all that money in space when there are so many things we need it for right here on Earth?" And yes, there are NASA engineers who ask that question.

Worse, there are NASA officials who say we simply can't do it. We cannot put up a lunar colony by 1992. We can't even put a man on the Moon by then. Not that we won't, not that Congress won't pay for it, not that the people won't stand for the expense, but that we CANNOT do it no matter how hard we try.

"But," spluttered I, "but we *did* it—"

"Things are different now."

And if that isn't bad enough, try this one: when I proposed lunar colonies, one of the very highest NASA officials asked me, quite seriously, "Why would anyone want to live on the Moon?"

That floored me. It's as if a provincial bishop, after working all his life for the Church, went back to the Vatican and discovered that the Curia is filled with atheists.

\* \* \*

"Heretics," I muttered to myself. "Invite 'm to be guests of honor at an auto-de-fe. Let 'em get jobs in broom factories."

Which is an understandable first reaction, but it's also wrong.

"I funded the Sagan Committee," one of the heretics told me. "And my office funded this study, and we invited you, so dammit, how can you say we don't believe in space?"

And that's all true. Me, I can afford to be a true believer. I know there's growing support for space and spectaculars and national achievements. I don't have to face a Congress that believes the public bored by space. I spend most of my time among other True Believers, while these poor chaps in Washington end up thinking there's nobody but them to keep the dream alive.

And they have kept it alive. Whatever happens, they deserve well of us, and if I can persuade a few NASA officials to come to a World Con I expect my fans to cheer them wildly. They haven't had an attaboy! in a long time, and they've got one coming; and when the True Believers do get some influence one day, it would ill suit us not to reward the faithful who've labored in Washington's barren vineyards.

But there do have to be some changes made. Let me tell you a true story.

Consider a scientific satellite. It's all self-contained, and only needs to be put into Earth orbit. It could be launched with Scout, but the Scout production lines are being closed to build missions for Shuttle. This, incidentally, is an administrative judgment call I'm not competent to second-guess. After all, Shuttle's the only big game we have, and if some things have to be done inefficiently to keep Shuttle going, then I suppose that's a price we just have to pay.

But putting our satellite on Shuttle has some penalties. For one thing, the Shuttle managers are scared stiff that someone will muck up the ship. To prevent that, users have to deliver their payload many days in advance of launch—and cannot have access to the payload after it has been handed over to the Shuttle people. Our satellite can't survive many days without power, so we'll need juice from Shuttle until just before launch.

Fine. We design the satellite to take standard ship's power, and now we're ready to interface with Shuttle. What we need is electricity, some means to disconnect the satellite once it's been delivered to orbital speed and altitude, and some way to get it out of the Shuttle bay. That latter doesn't seem much of a problem; a spring would do it, or a small soda-water cartridge, or indeed, a crewman could go back and shove the darned thing out.

It all seems simple. Of course things in space aren't always as simple as they look. We can accept that there are additional systems integration costs. Now. I invite you to take the wildest, most outlandishly extravagant guess you can make as to what those systems integration costs will be. Go on, think about it. Think big.

I've had estimates go from a couple of hundred thousand dollars to Larry Niven's guess of three million. No one has even come close to the true cost: forty million dollars. But what, on Earth or in the universe, can you possibly get for the forty million bucks? Who knows? That's the cost, which is why a number of users aren't exactly thrilled by Shuttle.

I think, I just suspect, that number could be trimmed a bit. I keep remembering the old days, when we didn't have a space budget, and we did our space research in off hours and spare time with surplussed equipment; and I recall how much we got for very little expenditure. Of course we were True Believers, and this wasn't just another job, this was Space; and perhaps that's my point. We've got to inject more believers into the system. We've got to recover the "can do" attitude that once dominated the space business; because if we don't we're out of business.

*  *  *

But—now you see why there's so much crepe hanging. If it costs forty million bucks just to push a dumb satellite out of Shuttle, how can we even consider something like a lunar colony? The costs would be quite literally astronomical.

It's also why there's so much skepticism about Solar Power Satellites.

Just now, SPS is our biggest potential quick payoff from space. A 5 gigaWatt Solar Power Satellite replaces 210,000 barrels of oil per day, 76.7 million barrels a year; if oil costs $40 a barrel, that's over 3 billion bucks a year we don't have to ship overseas. A significant savings.

The SPS program has some of the most sophisticated cost models I've ever seen. Their estimate is about $100 billion for the first SPS (this includes building a new fleet of launch vehicles). Thereafter, each 5 GW satellite costs about $11 billion—and, like a dam, requires no fuel.

Unfortunately, the system costs are dominated by the cost of material delivered to orbit. Those are hard to project—and some people simply don't believe we can bring them down. If we can't, we're stopped. SPS simply cannot be built if we have to absorb present expense per kilogram launched.

Or can it? Comes now David Criswell, formerly the Director of the Lunar and Planetary Institute of Houston. He has studied the Apollo-returned Moon rocks for years, and concludes, startlingly enough, that we can build SPS with Shuttle at today's prices—provided only that as part of the program we establish a Moon base, and we make a lot of our power satellite from lunar materials.

Criswell has done some detailed investigation of industrial

processes on the Moon. He's looked at melting tanks, and large plate vibrators for separating lunar ores (the best model of Moon rock is talcum powder, not sand), and ballistic separators. He's examined some wonderful ways to use energy for building structures. Consider this trick: take a long metal spike, heat to above the melting point for glass, and insert into lunar soil. The lunar materials melt and fuse. When you withdraw the spike, you have behind a ceramic pipe. Now imagine an arched comb of such spikes placed so that the glass fuses together all along the length of the comb. Insert, heat, withdraw—and you have an arched glass cave or tunnel, suitable for making airtight and using as living quarters.

Lunar processes can be very energy inefficient; there's lots of energy up there. Perhaps you can make inefficient photovoltaic cells by the square kilometer. They just lie there on the lunar surface, ready to deliver electric power as needed.

Then there's silane, $SiH_4$, the silicon analog of methane. It burns in oxygen with a specific impulse of 350, plenty good enough for rocket fuel; and although there's precious little hydrogen on the Moon, there's billions of tons of silicon. Hydrogen-oxygen rockets are "better", but by using silane you get a "mass multiplier" effect.

And so forth. It isn't clearly demonstrable that we could build SPS cheaply from the Moon—but it does look possible. It's not wild dreaming.

And there we have the basic conflict.

Some people see opportunities. Others see only problems. Example: one NASA official told me of a recent conference at Woods Hole, where a number of biologists were entirely negative on the concept of extra-terrestrial colonies.

The smallest self-sufficient ecology we know of, say they, is the entire Earth. There's no proof that anything smaller can survive. We can solve the problems we can think of, but we won't think of all the problems, and a lunar colony is just taking too big a chance.

The counter argument is obvious. Ingenuity overcomes a lot of difficulties. Biological isolation has advantages as well as disadvantages—if we didn't take it along, it won't be on the Moon. I'd think isolation for the syphilis spirochete and the cold virus and the cholera germ would be a positive benefit. And we're not proposing to cut off the colonists entirely and forever. If they discover they need vitamin pills, or, God save us, the common cold, we can send the stuff up. Most of it can even be hard landed.

True, we need some studies to show just how many kilograms per colonist per day of biological interaction is required. My guess is that after you establish lunar "farms" you'll find it's more likely to be milligrams than kilograms, but leave that; the colony I propose would assume about a kilo per person per day. Three years supply of expendables comes to only 22 metric tons for the whole colony.

I didn't dream up those numbers. SKYLAB, with essentially no recycling at all, operated on about 1.2 kilograms/day for each crewman. Given lunar conditions—plenty of free cold, free heat, and free vacuum—recycling of water and inert atomspheric gasses should be simple and very efficient; and presumably the colonists can grow *some* of their own food.

The doomsayers don't see it that way. "We've never done it, and thus we can't try it . . ."

So perhaps we need a demonstration; what engineers call "proof of principle". Take a box of rats, and biologically isolate them. Now see what interaction is required; how many grams per kg. of rat must be introduced into the system to keep them healthy. It would even make a good high school Science Talent Search project. It's unlikely that a high school lab would be able to recycle gasses (no cheap cryogenic source) but that could be simulated by using sterile aviator's oxygen, or even highly filtered air, since it's biological isolation we're interested in.

In fact, the lunar colony concept could generate a number of high school and undergraduate and graduate research projects, none of them very expensive, all aimed at proving the principle that extra-terrestrial colonization is possible.

Such demonstrations would be useful. For every problem

I've heard of, there seem to be several solutions. As to problems you haven't thought of and didn't think of—why, there are also going to be advantages and opportunities you didn't foresee. You either trust human ingenuity or you don't.

I point out that frontier societies are usually far more vigorous than their parent civilizations. I even think I know why. Perhaps the characteristic excretion of Western Civilization is bureaucratic structure, and once in a while you have to move off the manure pile to get things growing again.

But for the moment, the high echelons of NASA, and of the Congress, and all of Washington, are dominated by people who see the problems and discount the opportunities. This is more an attitude than a reasoned position; and of course I hold the other view, that we should look for the opportunities and have some confidence in human ability to solve problems.

When I said that in the conference, the chairman told the following story. If you ever knew General Curtis LeMay, former Commander in Chief of the Strategic Air Command, you'll know it could quite possibly have happened.

A colonel ran into LeMay's office. "General," he said, "we have an insurmountable problem."

LeMay hit his fist on the desk. "Colonel, in this Command we don't have problems. We have opportunities."

The colonel looked thoughtful. "Yes, sir. General, we have an insurmountable opportunity."

Now that's a funny story, and everyone in the conference laughed, and I had no answer to it at the time. I've been thinking about it ever since.

First, it seems clear that they didn't have an insurmountable problem. That is, SAC still exists, so they got around the problem somehow.

Second—who in history really did have an insurmountable opportunity? And the name drops out immediately. Christopher Columbus.

Friends, we have an insurmountable opportunity.

* * *

# AUTHOR'S NOTE

I have a confession: the essay wasn't written as the introduction to this book. I wrote it in the summer of 1980, before the elections, as a column in *Destinies*.

Now things are different. The new administration has a positive attitude toward space. They've even asked me—along with many others, of course—to draft a national space policy. We space enthusiasts—and who else would buy this book?—have a lot to cheer about.

Except for one problem: there are those who say we must reduce the national budget, and "we cannot fight inflation on the backs of the poor." The space budget is expendable; while one cannot trim welfare costs and other income-equalizing transfer payments.

If you believe that, you'll believe anything. Society isn't a zero-sum game, and redistributing poverty solves no problems for anyone. The only real way to help the poor is to produce so many goods that everyone can be rich.

Space can do that for us.

EDITOR'S INTRODUCTION TO:

THE MOON GODDESS
AND THE SON

by Donald Kingsbury

*Some people don't want to go to space. That's hardly astonishing. I suppose I shouldn't be surprised to find that some planetary scientists don't want to go Out There. But—*

*Not long ago we had the Voyager encounter with Saturn. Whenever this happens, Cal Tech's Jet Propulsion Laboratories—which built and operated the spacecraft—hosts a panel discussion on the significance of planetary exploration. The original panel was formed years ago before the first Pioneer went to Mars, and was composed of the New York Times' Walter Sullivan; Carl Sagan; Bruce Murray; Arthur C. Clarke; and because Mars was involved, Ray Bradbury. The topic was called "Mars and the Mind of Man" and the panel discussion was so successful that it became a book—and a tradition.*

*Things have changed in the intervening years. For "Jupiter and the Mind of Man" the panel hadn't changed, but Arthur Clarke had become Rector of the National University in Sri Lanka (once called Ceylon) and participated by satellite TV. That didn't work so well—the technical implementation wasn't up to the conception—so for "Saturn and the Mind of Man" they reluctantly replaced Arthur with MIT's Phil Morrison. Meanwhile, Bruce Murray took leave of his position as Professor of Planetary Sciences at Cal Tech to become Director of the Jet Propulsion Laboratories; and Carl Sagan became a super-star spokesman for the Cosmos, with his own TV series.*

*It remains a panel of space enthusiasts—*

Yet a good quarter of the discussion was devoted to a savage attack on the Apollo program, and despite Ray Bradbury's eloquent dissent, the scientists aboard seemed agreed that man has no real place in space. Black boxes and robots will be quite good enough: indeed, much better than men, because you can get so much more information for the dollar. Look at what Voyager brought back from Saturn.

And when the discussion turned to L-5 Colonies, to life in the Endless Frontier, there were chuckles. Before man would live in space or on the Moon, they said, we would first have to cover the seas and Antarctica and the Sahara. No one would want to live up there—

Walter Sullivan didn't get into that discussion, and Ray Bradbury dissented vigorously; but two key planetary scientists, plus Phil Morrison, didn't understand why anyone would want to live in space.

* * *

Don Kingsbury was in the audience for that panel. Spacecraft encounters are rare enough that science fiction writers try to attend them—they make a great occasion for a party—and Don was here from Montreal, where he is a professor of mathematics. Like me, he didn't quite understand that panel.

Kingsbury is one of the new crop of scientifically trained science fiction writers; a man qualified to do science as well as write about it. Indeed, some of his best work is non-fiction presenting new concepts for space travel.

For all that, Kingsbury's stories are not dry engineering treatises. Far from it. Kingsbury gives us some of the most memorable characters you'll meet in modern fiction.

He also knows why people want to live in space.

# THE MOON GODDESS
# AND THE SON

## Donald Kingsbury

### 1

Diana's ambition to get a job on the moon really started the day she found out that her namesake was the moon goddess. She was six and she crawled out her bedroom window onto the porch roof so she could stare at the full moon in the sky where she belonged. Her father caught her. He was furious because she could have fallen off and hurt herself so he stripped her and tied her to the bed and beat her bleeding with his belt.

The pain blotted out this man, blotted out even the pain itself. She saw a wild boar and she cast an arrow into his heart from her perch safe behind the shield of the moon. But in time the trauma evaporated, leaving only the pain of being touched by a bloodstained bed in Ohio that refused to stop torturing her body with its prodding fingers. When the moon rose so high that her round eyes could no longer see it through the window, she felt abandoned.

On her seventh birthday a high school boy showed her his portable tracking telescope. The cratered mountains of the moon stunned her with their beauty—*her* mountains, *her* craters, *her* plains, *her* rills and streamers. Meticulously she located each of the old Apollo landing sites. In a moment of astral travel she imaged herself in a crater full of trees with lots of nymphs to take care of.

He showed her Jupiter and the Pleiades. Another evening they followed the bright thread of the half built spaceport as it arrowed through the southern sky in those few minutes before it faded into the Earth's shadow. When it was gone he explained that they could see the spaceport this far north only because it hadn't yet been towed into equatorial orbit.

At eight Diana had a temper tantrum and stoically endured five beatings until her mother papered her wall with a photo-montage of the moon's surface. At nine she took up archery in school and worked at it until she became the regional champ for her age. When she was ten she ran away from home to visit a space museum but the police brought her back. After the police were gone her father beat her until even her mother cried. At twelve she ran away from home with her arm in a cast, broken by her father when he found her collection of newspaper stories about families who murdered their children in the night.

She fixed her hair like the March cover girl of *Viva Magazine* and she wore one of her mother's bras stuffed with an extra pair of socks. People gave her rides. She told them she was going to visit her mother in California because her father was out of work.

The best ride she got was from a truck driver whom she targeted at a diesel station in Newton, Iowa, mainly because his rig carried a Washington license plate and she knew vaguely that spaceships were built in Washington. He wasn't supposed to take passengers but she flaunted her spare socks and he broke down and got to liking her over the steak he bought her. She chattered to him about a historical novel called *Diana's Temple*.

An endless ride later, through farmland and broken hills and over decaying interstate highways, they pulled into a rest stop near Elk Mountain to sleep in the cab for the night. Diana tried to seduce her driver because she thought girls were supposed to reward nice men. The cast on her arm got in the way and a sock fell out of her bra.

He laughed, holding her by the chin in a vice grip between thumb and fingers. "Diana was a virgin."

"Yeah, I know." She cringed out of the vice to a position back against the door of the cab.

He didn't want to hurt her feelings. He reached out and

pulled her shoulders into his large arm tenderly. "Your virginity is the most valuable thing you have right now. Hang onto it. Grow up a little bit and when you throw it away make sure he's the nicest guy in the world."

"How do you tell the nice guys from the mean ones?"

"Did you ever have any trouble with that?"

"My father always beat me. For *nothing!*"

"Then you know what the bad ones are like."

"What are the good ones like?"

"Me," he laughed.

For a year Diana stayed in a small town near Seattle where they assembled feeder spacecraft for the spaceport as well as cruise missiles for the military. The tiny nine-meter long automatic lighters rocketed to the spaceport from an equatorial base and flew back on stubby delta wings. Diana was excited at first. She did housework and cared for the children of one of the foremen whose wife was recovering from an auto accident. But this sleepy Earth town was just as far away from the moon as Ohio.

She stole some money and caught a bus for L.A. It was scary panhandling in Hollywood. She got picked up by a pimp she didn't know was a pimp and had to crawl out a window in the middle of the night and sleep under a car like a cat. After three days alone she found a family of runaways and slept on the floor. They were all into stealing and hustling and one of them was into heroin but she found a job as a waitress from which she got fired because she didn't have any papers.

Twilight was panhandling time. Afterwards she took her addict friend to a crowded basement dive so she could have company being depressed. The smoke coiled through the dim light, choking at life. She sat there crazying and suddenly darted toward the ladies' room where she knew they had a little open window where she could breathe for a minute, alone.

A large hand clamped on her shoulder. "You got holes in your head, spending time with that buzzhead? He'll take you for everything you've got."

She whirled on the scruffy young man who had a 1950 hairdo. "What have I got to take? I haven't even got a job."

"Lots of jobs around."

"I don't want to be a whore, smartass."

He smiled sardonically. "A waitress, then?"

"I got fired as a waitress because I don't have any papers."

"How about that!" He shook her hand. "I'm a forger." He escorted her into the ladies' room and, after locking the door, hung his head through the window. "What name you want to be known by?"

"I can change my name?"

"Yeah and you get a birth certificate and an L.A. high school record and a social security number. I figure if we stretched it a bit you could pass for eighteen."

"What do you get out of it?" she asked cynically.

"A girl to ferret around records offices who doesn't arouse suspicion. I need new faces all the time." He laughed. "I'm square. My side lady would kill me if I didn't give every thirteen year old an integrity deal."

"Could I get a job on the moon with your papers?"


2


Charlie McDougall was an only child with thickly lashed eyes. He first learned to roll his eyes at his parents when he was thirteen—behind their backs. His whole memory of life was of two giants giving him orders that had to be executed on some strict schedule if he didn't want to be driven crazy by shouting directed into his eardrum.

Mama wanted him to become the world's greatest violinist or maybe a dancer who would wow them in Moscow. Papa wanted him to become the greatest space engineer who ever lived, the cutting edge of the Last Hope of Mankind.

During those crucial years when most babies discover the first spark of individuality by playing with the power of the word "no," Charlie had been broken. He learned to obey. He hated the violin and he hated dancing and he hated space but he hated screaming parents even more. Obeying was the only peace he had.

Still while he became a fine violinist, his strings had a perpetual habit of snapping. He was invariably the best dancer in his class but he was always being thrown out because of his incurable habit of peeking into the girls' dressing room.

For his father he devised even more diabolical tortures. Though he slaved dutifully over his physics and chemistry and math and model building, he refused to read science fiction. On his fifteenth birthday his father tried to seduce him with a luxury hardbound copy of *Dune* with a facsimile Frank Herbert signature.

"You'll love it."

"Hey Papa, that's a great gift. This evening I have some spare time and maybe I'll take a crack at it." When his father went out for a beer, he rolled his eyes.

That evening the old man peeked into his room on tiptoes to see how the first chapter of *Dune* was going, just as Charlie knew he would. Charlie was engrossed in the eighth chapter of Robert's *Differential Equations* setting up the ninth problem.

"Have you had a chance to look at *Dune?*"

"Tomorrow. I got myself hung up on the breaking mode of long cylinders and I don't want to sleep on it."

The coup had kept Charlie happy for weeks. *Dune* was still on his shelf, unopened.

It was only when he was seventeen that he discovered the perfect shelter from his parents, digital music. Electronic instruments frightened his mother. She had a Ph.D in musicology from Mills but couldn't tell a fourier compact series from a quartet concert series; a resistor had something to do with the draft, and a chip was what an uncouth person carried on his shoulder. As for Charlie's father, who polished off textbooks like most slow readers polished off light novels, engineered music was in the same category as purple smells or painted cooking.

Waves, repetitions, pulsations, rumblings, the rise of a

violin taking off can all be described by a fourier series—an amalgamation of sine and cosine waves of different frequencies and amplitudes. A frequency is a number. An amplitude is a number. Charlie composed by choosing those numbers and deciding when they were to change. His computer executed the commands.

He created his own computer language for simulating instruments. It was a simple matter for him to write a subroutine for oboe or violin or harmonica. He had ten violins on file, four of them matching in sound the finest violins ever crafted, the other six of a haunting timbre that could never come from a material violin, wood lacking the proper resonant qualities. He doodled up new instruments in pensive moments and gave them frivolous names like the pooh and the eeyore and the kanga.

By using his world of numbers as an open sesame to the trance underground, he burrowed assiduously into this dark world his parents couldn't understand. Once when he was twenty and deliriously celebrating the end of his junior year by smashing out in the popular Boston Trance Hall where the show was continuous and the waitresses sported silver pantsuits with cutout buttocks, all seven of his friends became dazzled by the nubility of the singer. She was wearing a golden necklace from which her dress flowed, cupric green, so slashed in a thousand ribbons that one both saw all and none of her body as she sang.

Charlie noted the ordinary voice—slightly brassy with a tendency to slurring—and rashly bet his friends she would date him. Gleefully they put $200 in the pot, impelling him to keep pace by taking her hand as she left the stage.

"You have a zorchy voice—a lot could be done with it."

She smiled coolly and let him hold her fingers just long enough to appear unrude. It gave him time to press his card into that hand, a hand so cold his must have seemed tropical.

## ELECTRONIC MADMAN
## DIGITALIZED MUSIC

Her eyes widened slightly when she read it—DM was a controversial thing on the pop music scene; one loved or hated its sounds and argued endlessly about the awesome scope of its territory. DM projected mystery and resentment. Few musicians could handle its technical demands. But an ambitious woman with an ordinary voice would know what a DM magician could do for her.

She sat down and the cupric cloth rippled, sometimes revealing, sometimes hiding, always teasing. "What do you hear in my voice?"

"You'll have to come to my place and listen. It's beautiful."

"It's not. I don't think my mouth is the right shape."

"But you don't hear what I hear."

"Do you do real time or augmented?"

"Both. I can feed your mike right into the shoebox if that's what you want."

She took his palm and read it silently. Then she looked into his face with the eyes of a judge. "What sign are you?"

"Aquarius."

Her face broke into a smile of relief. "Fantastic!" And she wouldn't let his hand go. Charlie's friends, conceding, shoved a money-filled envelope into the other hand.

Betty worked with him. He showed her many versions of her voice. He washed her car. He rushed her clothes out for dry cleaning to give her extra sleep. When she had a new gig, he set up for her. He worked late into many nights decoding the structure of her voice until he was able to customize a shoebox that transformed her into a siren at the wave of a mike.

Charlie's new life thrilled him. He spent all his time thinking about seducing Betty. Devious plans grew out of dreams and finally he convinced Betty to let him move into her place in what had once been the maid's room back in the century when Irish labor was plentiful. He promised to cook and do the dishes and not molest her. His theory was that the way to a girl's heart was through her stomach and after a month of being taken care of by a man who loved her, she would melt.

In a mailgram that gave him great pleasure to write he told his father that he was not returning to MIT. Within a week his father arrived in Boston from orbit and charmed Betty off to Mexico City for a vacation. She sent him a card from Xicotencatl wishing he was there. The card was forwarded to New Hampshire where his mother had taken him by the ear, screaming at him all the time, insisting that if he wasn't going to continue his engineering he had to sign up for the Berlin Conservatory. In self-defense he reregistered at MIT, all the while plotting perfect murders.

It took him only two months to utterly crush his mother. He digitalized a secret recording of one of her screaming rages. Slowly he added harmonics. He mushed the words until their content was lost against a pure emotion. Here he amplified the rage, there he added piteous undertones. Violins played at dramatic moments. Sobbing children filled the silences. He had the tape cut and sold the pressing to a company that pushed it up to thirty-second place on the hit parade.

Charlie figured it would take longer to crush his father. His father was tough. He would have to bide his time and strike at an unexpected moment with overwhelming force.

3

It was a nice name. *Diana Grove*. She could go anywhere and do anything with it. Mostly she went to Texas and Arizona because John the Forger's main business was manufacturing new identities for Mexicans. When she became too well known he let her go and she became a waitress.

Rooming with older girls taught Diana how to imitate adult behavior. Her manners became flirtatious. She was a sassy summertime flower to the bees, little caring whether the men she attracted were young or old or handsome or married—but she never dated the same man twice. She had a perfect excuse whenever an admirer wanted a second date.

"But that's the day I'm seeing Larry."

"How about Saturday then?"

"I always go out with George on Saturday."

When too many people wanted her, she changed jobs or roommates. Eventually she began to move up the coast, carefully picking only the most expensive and popular restaurants. Once in Coos Bay, Oregon, a drunk wacked her around and that so frightened her she flew to San Francisco the very next day.

Not having a job was unimportant. At the airport she bought a paper and answered a classified ad demanding an exceptionally attractive and experienced waitress to work at Namala in the Pacific. Diana was a long time space buff and knew very well that Namala was one of the equatorial stations that supplied the orbiting spaceport.

The secretary of Ling Enterprises smiled and Diana reciprocated. It helped her nervousness that the secretary was sitting down and she was standing. She could pretend that she was just earning a five-dollar tip.

The speaker beside the video camera spoke in a gentle voice. "Send her in. She's expected."

Diana instantly turned her smile on the camera. It was President Ling speaking. That was very suspicious. Presidents of restaurant chains did *not* interview waitresses. She felt faint and, what was worse, she felt fifteen years old.

When she peered around Mr. Ling's door she found him to be Chinese and ancient. His office was Contemporary American except for the paintings—a battle between Earthmen and beastoid in a jungle under a large red sun, the other a desolate landscape somewhere in the galaxy near a star cluster. The fear went out of her.

"You're another space cookie," she said relieved, all her poise back.

"It's a comfortable disease."

"Do you remember when they landed on the moon?"

He laughed. ''I'm so old I remember when they thought landing on the moon was impossible.''

''Do you own a restaurant on the moon?''

''No, but when they build one, I'll be running it.''

She loved him already. She was his slave. She sat down on the couch and couldn't take her eyes off his face, lined and old and frail and the most fascinating face she'd ever seen.

He moved closer to her, sitting on the desk top. ''Are you wondering why a president is interviewing waitresses?''

''Yes,'' she grinned. ''I'm ready to run out the door screaming.''

''I have six space related restaurants and I take a personal interest in them. The frustrated astronaut in me.''

''What's Namala like?''

''Hard work for you. Too many men.''

''I'm a good girl and surprisingly self-reliant.''

''Sometimes you'll need advice. Madam Lilly, who runs my Namala franchise, has large skirts for hiding behind when it is necessary.''

''I never need help,'' said Diana defiantly.

''An unwise consideration.''

They talked. He found out all he needed to know and she found out all she needed to know. He offered her the job. She accepted. There was nothing more to say but she didn't want to leave just yet.

He watched her silence as she moved her fingers and played with a ring. ''Ah, I've finally caught you when you're not smiling.''

''I'm hungry and I want to invite you for lunch,'' she said with frog's legs in her throat.

He smiled a thousand wrinkles.

''Would your wife mind?'' she then asked awkwardly.

''I'm a widower.''

''We could go to the Calchas. I've worked there. It's beautiful and I miss their food.''

She made him talk about himself over too much wine. He was the rebel in his family. His father wanted him to take over the restaurant business and he wanted to be an engineer. He had edited a science fiction fanzine called *Betelgeuse* which went to fourteen issues but when he became engaged to his illustrator who was a Caucasian, his family disowned him. He didn't do well enough in school to get a scholarship and ended up as a city bureaucrat, married, with three lovely mongrel children while he tried to write at night.

Finally his father died and his brothers expanded and took the family fortune into a close brush with disaster and he made a pact with his mother to run the family business. He was good at it. Later he made his breakthrough by discovering how to franchise variety in a world of McDonald's, Johnsons, and Colonels.

Diana had fun. They ran up quite a bill at Mr. Ling's insistence (he thought he was paying) and she had the best fight of her life taking the bill away from him. To make up for it he bought her beautiful luggage. She sighed and told him she had nothing to put in it, so he bought her clothes. She sighed and told him she had no place to take them because she hadn't rented a hotel room yet, so he gave her the key to his place.

She cooked Mr. Ling a gourmet dinner in his kitchen after making many phone calls to the office to find out what he liked and when he would be in. They spent the whole meal and three liquors discussing the history of Jerusalem. She discovered his wicked sense of humor. He convinced her that there had been a whole order of Chinese Knights who fought in the crusades.

"Don't laugh so hard!" she complained. "You're just lucky I didn't bake a lemon meringue pie for supper or you'd get it right in your kisser!"

Ten o'clock was his bedtime. He excused himself gracefully and escorted her all the way to the guest room where he put an arm around her shoulder and thanked her for a lovely evening before he left her.

Diana peeked. She waited until the light went out under his door and then, dressed only in a candle flame, entered his room. "I've come to kiss you goodnight." It was easy to pretend you were twenty years old when you were nude.

His smile in the candlelight was wistful. "Goddess Diana, I am much too old for such escapades."

"That makes us even. I'm much too young for such escapades." She blew out the candle and slipped under the sheets with him. "Don't die of a heart attack just yet. I want my job on the moon." She snuggled up beside him, deciding that she liked to sleep with men. It was the sleep of innocence.

The next day a great aircraft flew her over the ocean to the equator.

## 4

The rocket-supplied lunar base was an improbable cluster of forms on Mare Imbrium which had lately grown a spider web rectenna farm to receive microwaves from a small twenty-five megawatt solar power station that had been built in low Earth orbit and towed up to the Lagrange 1 position 58,000 km above the moon. Each new addition was part of a single-minded plan. The sole purpose of the base was to build an electromagnetic landing track so that access to the moon might be made cheap. This deep out in space, rockets fueled from Earth were not cheap.

When Byron McDougall took the assignment to construct the initial lunar base he was given one-fourth of the money originally allocated for that task. He was a military man from a military family. He thought like a soldier who could still fight when his supply lines had been cut. McDougall's base had shafts without elevators. He used cast basalt instead of aluminum. Eighty percent of the parts by weight of all imported machines were made of lunar metals and glasses. All food was raised locally. The lunar day was given over to energy intensive tasks such as metals production. The lunar night was given over to effort intensive tasks such as design work and machining.

From his tiny office Byron called Louise. "Sweetheart, you have a bottle of champagne tucked away?" He knew she didn't.

"Champagne? You're mad. All I have is a liter of Ralph's turnip rotgut."

"Too bad. How can we celebrate on that? Any last minute hassles with the SPS?"

"No. We should have power exactly on time."

"Good."

"Your son has been trying to reach you. We'll have the connection set up in fifteen minutes. Do you want to take it there or here?"

"I'm hopping right up to the control room."

Byron switched off, smiling slyly. He took out a half bottle of champagne he had hidden, all he could afford to smuggle in by rocket, but enough to give them a taste of victory. It wasn't really victory: getting the SPS power so they weren't energy starved at night was just another milestone, but one certainly worth celebrating.

Maybe there never would be a final victory. Byron sometimes despaired. Maybe in two years this effort might be a ghost town in spite of all the billions that had been invested in it. Risk funding was so damned erratic. Support waxed and waned in Congress. It had been waning now for years, even though the pay-off was a certainty.

He slipped out of his office, soared up the shaft, caught himself, and made his slow leap into the control room with the bottle high in his hand. "Who's got strong thumbs?"

"How did you get that!" Louise's nature lent itself to exclamations.

"False bottomed suitcase."

One of the men turned to Byron from the console display with a smile. "The SPS is powered and checking through beautifully. We should get the first beam down soon."

"Is your son as handsome as you?" asked Louise dreamily.

"Why should you care?"

"Braithwaite was telling me he's coming up here to work on the track as soon as he graduates from MIT."

"No, I'm much better looking than my son. You should try older men once in awhile."

"Not a chance. You see through all of my tricks. I *might* get away with batting my eyes at your son. He's six years younger than I am."

"Actually you might have a chance. When he gets here I'll set you up. He chases older women—but I've never seen him chase one as bright as you. I once took a girl friend of his off to Mexico City. She was a great lay, but I was bored to death with her chatter."

"Byron! You stole your son's girl friend? How could you be so cruel? And I always thought you were such a *nice* man!"

"I did him a favor. She was using him," he said bitterly.

"He probably needed her!"

That stung Byron's anger. "Like hell he needed her. She didn't have enough sense to send him back to school when he quit to take care of her. For that I could have killed the bitch. I shipped her off to Paris with enough bread to keep her amused."

Louise was grinning. "What was your wife saying about all this?"

"She divorced me."

"Byron!"

He laughed. "Something else to celebrate."

The phone rang. Louise took it and chatted with the operator. "Byron. It's your son."

"Hi Papa."

"Charlie!"

Two second pause.

"I'm calling you up to congratulate you. I hear you're not going to need candles at night anymore. Hey, pretty soon you'll have hot running water in the trenches."

"It's pretty good. We'll be powered except for six hours once a month at eclipse."

Two second pause.

"I just got your comments on my last batch of homework. You're two days faster than my profs. I'm glad I'm getting clever enough with my mistakes so even you can't see them."

"While you're on the line I want you to talk with Braithwaite. You'll be working with him on the lunar track. He's anxious to get you after all he's heard about you."

Byron motioned frantically for Braithwaite to come over while his voice travelled to Earth and his son's came back.

"You still want me to get involved in that thing, eh?"

"You bet. When we get it built this place is going to start to pay for itself. She'll mushroom. We've been tooling up for the track and now that we have the power, we're ready to roll."

The lunar track was an electromagnetic cushion to take fifteen-ton ships in for a horizontal landing at lunar circular velocity. Or shoot them off.

"Say Papa, I'm calling to tell you not to bother to come back to Earth for my graduation."

"But of course I'm coming. I need the vacation."

Two second pause.

"Yeah, but I just quit school."

"You're at the top of your class!"

Two second pause.

"I don't want your job. I just want to play around and listen to the birds sing. Why put myself in the position where I need a vacation when I can have one all the time?"

Byron thought frantically. "It's the chance of your lifetime! It will make your career! From this job you can go anywhere!"

Two second pause. There was no real way to argue over this distance. He had caught a barracuda and the line was too light.

"I never liked engineering. Good luck in your log cabin. I'm hanging up, now."

The line went dead. Byron waited for two seconds, stunned, then he smashed his bottle against the bulkhead wall. Gracefully the champagne foamed as it arced in a slow motion spatter.

"She's ready," said the operations man, as calmly as if he had witnessed a christening. "There she goes. The grid is powered."

Louise was rushing over to Byron. "It's all right."

Byron was frozen, his hand outstretched where it had grasped sudden defeat from victory. "No," he said in pain.

"Are you going back to Earth to talk to him?"

"No." Byron paused for two thoughtful seconds, his hand slowly sinking. "I had to push him and push him and push him, the little bastard. He did so well, I couldn't resist. If I didn't push him, he didn't move. So I pushed him. God, how I wanted him here under my thumb where I could make a man out of him." He shrugged bitterly. "It's no use. If you have to push a man, he's not going to move anywhere."

"He'll settle out."

"Yeah, he'll settle out. He'll settle out as a third rate musician."

## 5

Namala was the tropical sea, blue water and a sometimes billowy clouded sky and green islands that, to Diana's airborne eyes, seemed to sleep in the vast moat of the Pacific like a drowsy crocodile. She arrived at sunset while the water was deepening to purple. Never in her life had she been so exhilarated. She was here—part of a base that was shipping goods to the moon to make a home for her that would be there when she found a way to go.

While she waited on the airfield terrace for Madam Lilly, the drowsy crocodile woke. A barrage of delta winged lighters began to lift in roaring flame from the launch area. Then Diana saw to the west the silver thread of the spaceport rising majestically out of the ocean. At first it was only a small thread, a wavering glimmer. On the horizon the spaceport's 150-kilometer length was foreshortened to hardly more than a degree of sky, but, within minutes, as it rose to the thunder of the lighter launches, it grew to stretch its gossamer strand over almost a sixth of the sky—before vanishing into the shadow of the Earth, leaving only stars. She remembered a spider riding a filament of web over the cornfields of Ohio.

Soon another fleet of lighters, electromagnetically ejected

from the spaceport as it passed overhead, began a screaming drop out of the blackness, swooping into the floodlamps of the lagoon to be received with the efficiency of a squadron returning to the deck of its aircraft carrier. Some of the lighters were laden with goods manufactured in the factory pods that lined the spaceport's length like factories had once sprung up along a railway spur line. Some of the lighters came down empty.

The ground crews ran a standard maintenance check on each vehicle, inserting a new 500 kilogram payload module, pumping kerosene and oxygen into the tanks, recooling the superconducting coils that would electromagnetically accelerate the lighter once it had been swallowed by the spaceport's electromagnetic intestine on its next spaceward trip. Finally the fresh readied lighter was rolled to the launch site and pointed at the sky on its own gantry, there to await the return of the spaceport. Every ninety minutes, day and night, this cycle repeated at all of the equatorial stations.

Madam Lilly was standing behind Diana, unwilling to intrude on the girl's rapture. She turned out to be a hard taskmaster. Her restaurant carried the Ling symbol but like all Ling restaurants it supported its own name, the *Kaleidoscope*, which meant that it was constantly changing its atmosphere. Madam Lilly was a theater person. She could do miracles with a few props and backdrops and screens, but her main focus was on the girls. She costumed them perfectly and taught them gesture and emotion and expression and dialog.

When Diana arrived they were doing World War II. There was a Rosie the Riveter in slacks and a Sultry Pinup in black negligee. Diana served the veranda in shorts with a tray over her head as a Hep Carhop. Sometimes she chewed gum and she always said "swell" to the customers. The music was "Deep in the heart of Texas . . ." or "Kiss me once and kiss me twice and kiss me once again, it's been a long long time . . ."

Namala was a paradise for a girl scared of men. The ratio of single men to women was four to one and she had so many dates that she could easily play one against the other for safety. If that failed, Diana pleaded work. She had to re-hearse the movements of a Burmese dancer, or walk like a Persian lady, or catch the subtle way a geisha presented a plate of raw fish. You could find her laughing with her arms around two men, or alone on the beach in the moonlight watching the fireworks supply the spaceport.

The beach could be fun. During the *Kaleidoscope*'s twen-ties' stint Madam Lilly strictly forbade her girls to wear their monokinis and instead had them splashing about in the latest daring flapper bathing suit that exposed the knees. It caused a riot and was very good for business.

Time and the smallness of the Namala community was her enemy. She met a boy named Jack in her martial arts class. He always spoke to her; she consistently ignored him. Their Japanese instructor repeated that the greatest perfection was to defeat an opponent with the minimum of force. Diana was having none of that. She was there to learn how to *demolish* men with the thrust of her heel or the back of her hand. She believed in a safety factor of ten. Break their skulls and then ask questions.

But Jack survived. Smitten, he arranged a surprise birth-day party. There were twenty-one candles on the cake even though she was only turning sixteen. She had a fabulous time hugging everyone for their gifts and singing and fooling around. She successfully avoided Jack for three hours know-ing how dangerous a man in love can be.

Her fatal mistake was to need a Kleenex. Jack kept some in his study which had remained off limits to the party because of the delicate model of the lunar base he kept there. She caught a glimpse of its detail and fell heels over head. Long after the revelry had died she was still in the study, her arms wrapped around Jack kissing his nose and asking him ques-tions about the lunar electromagnetic landing track.

The affair lasted two weeks, a miracle of involvement for Diana. She went everywhere with him. She haunted the launch site when he was at work. He spent all his money at the *Kaleidoscope*. They went surfing together and kissed at every opportunity. He hinted that he wanted to sleep with her. She hinted that she wanted to wait but to herself decided that he was the nicest guy in the world and she was going to throw her virginity away on him and live happily ever after.

In time they found themselves alone. Unhurriedly, gently he began to undress her. Diana only noticed that he was between her and the door. Since she had been a small girl she had learned to keep herself always between her father and a door. For awhile she tried to suppress her silly need, but the anxiety didn't go away—it became worse. It became imperative. Smiling at her insanity she took Jack in her arms hoping to roll him away from the door, toward the wall, without having to say anything. He chose that moment to be assertive.

Suddenly panicked, Diana threw him off the bed. When he looked up in anger, still commanding the doorway, she was so terrified that she struck him with a reflex karate kick to the head, and ran, not remembering that she ran. The next day he apologized when he found her. She turned away without speaking.

He flew in flowers from the States. He sent her letters. He papered love declarations on the corridor walls of her apartment. He slept on her steps. His intensity frightened her. She stayed awake with images of him murdering her. When he came to the *Kaleidoscope*, the other girls waited on him. Madam Lilly soothed her and told her that it was normal for men to go crazy, that it was nothing to worry about, but Diana worried. Jack persisted. He even sent one of the female mechanics he worked with to talk to her. Diana became so upset that she wrote Mr. Ling a mailgram pleading for a transfer.

The reply bounced back via satellite and was printed up immediately. "Spend a week with me. Ling."

6

At the emergency meeting in the main control room of the lunar base Zimmerman told a joke about a congressman that ended with the punch line: "I got no luck at all, nohow. Jist as I was gettin' my ass trained to work without eatin', she has to up and die on me!"

It wasn't a funny joke when you were the ass. They poked at the budget cut and they went over their own expenses from five different angles. No sane way of handling the cut emerged.

During the next shift out on the lunar plain, Byron chewed over his anger in one of the construction trucks along the half built track. His mind kept wandering off to Earth, that goddess of inconsistency.

One year you had Congress convinced that what you were doing was in the economic self-interest of the United States. You'd ask them if they were *sure* because you wanted them to be *sure* before you went ahead. Yes, they were sure. They backed you to the hilt. They made laws. But the next year they were convinced of something else, riding some new fad.

Back at the base Byron took dinner in his room. He cut off the intercom and tended his climbing vines, still seeking a solution to this latest sudden change in the rules. Adam Smith was wrong; men were not motivated by self-interest—they were too myopic to perceive self-interest farther than an inch away. A man would grab for that cigaret because the pleasure was immediate; the surgeon's knife cutting out his cancerous lung lay an unreal fifteen years in the future.

Byron's eyes blurred and for a moment he beheld a religious vision. A luminous hand was reaching out for the stars and that hand was a mosaic of little men held together by little hands in the pockets of the men above. Each little man was complaining about somebody else's greed. The conquest of space was not, at the moment, a gloriously cooperative venture. It was a war of pickpockets. But war gave him an edge. He smiled. Byron was an old fighter pilot.

His fingers switched off the lights so that he was in total darkness, the bed easy under his body. What did a soldier do when he was cornered? He remembered one of the favorite maxims of his father. "There is no such thing as losing," said that very stern man. It was an absurd maxim, parochially American, but one his father could imbue with a peculiar vitality.

As a ten year old Byron had been no fool. "That's what Hitler said at Stalingrad," he argued hotly.

"Ah, but Hitler confused winning with being on the offensive. You and I would have retreated and won."

"We retreated all over the place in Vietnam and lost!"

"Son, recall that you and I were in Germany during that disgraceful affair. Real soldiers aren't so clumsy as to defend something by destroying it."

"What's a real soldier?"

"An ordinary soldier fights well when he is grandly equipped. A *real* soldier can still fight after his supply lines have been cut. A real soldier doesn't even need any help from Congress!"

Once on a 300-kilometer hike with his father he had crumpled, refusing to go farther. The pain was overwhelming.

"A man inured to hell cannot lose."

"He can die," Byron remembered himself whining.

His son-of-a-bitch father had then lifted him up by the hair. "No. You forget. Death comes first. Then hell. Get moving. McDougalls are tough enough to walk out of hell. You're that tough. We make camp in two hours."

Byron walked out of his father's hell into an Air Force recruiting office on his eighteenth birthday. The Air Force groomed him, disciplined him, toughened him, and then sent him to Saudi Arabia to train Bedouins to fly the F-15. It was hell. He found himself drawing upon his father's wisdom about coping with hells because it was all he had. He used that empty time in the desert like a good commander might use a lull in the fighting—to build up his striking power. He sweated out an engineering education by correspondence course.

In those days few Americans cared about space, not even Byron. NASA's program had collapsed to a dismal four shuttle fleet with no solid funding in sight. Russian space ventures began to show signs of life again and Congress frantically authorized the building of the spaceport, giving Rockwell a contract for 70 modified space shuttles. Byron found himself flying one of them above the Earth, above a vision that shattered his isolation.

He resigned from the Air Force and transferred easily into a spaceport construction crew, engineering with love where no men had built before, 275 kilometers above the silly wars in Africa and Afghanistan and Argentina. That was a boom time. Today it was bust.

*Yes, it is like war,* he thought there in the dark. This was a battle to take the high ground. You won some and you lost some. The battle up the slope always cost more than you wanted to pay. Sometimes the home front got tired of the war. Still you kept on fighting your way higher in the hope that once you reached the peak you could dig in and hold it cheaply.

The first low orbital spaceport had to be built on the money of incredibly expensive orbital rockets, but once in place the 150 kilometer long, double barreled spaceport could swallow, and electromagnetically accelerate cheap suborbital rocket freighters and spew the unloaded freighters back down again to maintain momentum equilibrium. But that wasn't the end of the battle. That was only a ridge, a defense line, a trench.

The 275 kilometers wasn't high enough. As long as more mass was rising than falling, momentum balancing of the spaceport required a net energy input into the spaceport's mass drivers. That assumed an expensive auxiliary orbiting power plant which tended to limit spaceport capacity. And so the astronautical strategists began to covet the really high ground, the moon. If lunar mass could be delivered to Earth through the spaceport, momentum balancing of the spaceport would cease to depend upon auxiliary power. Capacity would go way up and costs down. If more mass was going down that coming up, the spaceport would generate a net surplus of power. A kilogram of moon delivered to the Earth contains eight times as much energy as a kilogram of the most powerful chemical rocket propellant.

The dust at the bottom of a minor lunar crater holds more energy reserves than in the whole of the Arabian peninsula. The potential energy of the moon is enough to power the wildest space program for millions of years. Damn the cost! Capture the high ground! Economics demanded it!

And so the war went on. Byron McDougall was chief field engineer when the second spaceport was built parallel to the first. It was designed to accelerate vehicles to high orbit beyond the Van Allen belts and to receive the vehicles back from high orbit. He did the job in three years.

By then congressional support was disintegrating. The Russian tortoise had fallen behind again. Wars are not fought on the battlefield alone. They are backed up by a whole support structure. and a loot-hungry populace is impatient with long sieges.

His father had something to say about long wars. "When the enemy's line is solid, endure, survive, and observe. Do not expect a break to appear at an enemy strong point. The breaks appear where *no one* expects trouble. When they appear victory goes to the swiftest. A place which has no strategic importance may achieve importance simply because it is not being defended."

7

Every civilization contains eddies of its past, sometimes within walking distance of its major centers. An eddy of the nineteenth century lay tucked away between two mountains of the California Coast Range, below the grasslands where the topography traps enough ocean fog to water a redwood stand. A Chinese family has long owned a log cabin there beside a dammed stream. There is no electricity. The road is dirt. Legend has it that every time a land developer comes this way, the wood nymphs call up a fog from the sea to sift through the redwood forest until it becomes invisible.

When Diana was with her Chinese friend she was all woman. At night she lay cozy with him under heavy blanket, by day she cooked over wood for her sage—flapjacks with sweet fried tomato syrup, and eggs and beans and bacon, even bread from flour and yeast. She kissed him and swam with him behind the dam and massaged him and flattered him.

But when she was by herself she reverted to girl. Deep in the forest she built a shrine out of stone to the goddess of moon and glade so that Diana might properly be worshipped. She tracked animals but they got away. She practiced archery for hours. Once she saw a deer and they both stood frozen, staring at each other in awe in that cathedral of trees.

On their last day she splashed in the cold pool behind the dam and toweled herself sassily in front of her boss because she knew he liked to look at her body even if he couldn't do anything with it. A wondrous evening light sneaked through the redwood needles.

"I have a job for you," he said, lighting the coals for a barbecue.

"You just sit down," she smiled. "I'll take care of everything. What do you want me to cook?"

"I meant a job *opening*. One of my places needs a new girl."

"Are you ever nice to me. Where?"

"You might not want it. It's a costume place. It involves playing up to some crazy men."

"What other kind is there?"

"Put this on," he said, giving her a shining package.

She held it out. "Brass bras!" she hooted. "*Mr. Ling*, I didn't know you ran a skin dive."

"Try it on."

Modestly she held it in front of herself. "I'll show through."

"You'll look beautiful, if slightly kinky."

So she stepped into what there was of it. Her hair spilled out of the helmet, a simple brass band around her forehead that supported oval headpieces which might or might not have been earphones. Her breasts spilled out of their immodest cups and her hips spilled out of their hardly adequate metallic banding. "Where do you get your outrageous ideas?"

He took her by the hand into the cabin and pulled his old copies of *Planet Stories* from a shelf. "Treat them like gold. They are from the forties and early fifties and fragile."

Diana shrieked at the cover of an issue he handed her. "That's me! Brass bras and all! And if that monster goes with the job, I'm quitting yesterday! Where is this restaurant?"

"On the spaceport."

Her heart jumped. "How high is that thing?"

"Oh hundred sixty-five miles."

"In kilometers! I didn't go to school in the dark ages like you."

"Two hundred seventy-five."

"And how high is the moon?"

"Too high for the restaurant business at the moment. They have to make do with a cafeteria."

"Damn," she said. "Don't forget me when you get your first lunar franchise. I'm going to send you vitamin pills every week. I want to make sure that you'll live that long."

"You haven't said yes to the spaceport yet."

She squeezed his hand. "When have I ever said no to you? I'm so thrilled I'm speechless. What's the name of your restaurant?"

"*Planet Stories.*"

8

For sixty kilometers the raised track swept across the surface of the Imbrian plain. Since the lunar horizon was only three kilometers away, the track stabbed to the edge of the universe like God's knife separating the light from the darkness.

*If* they were allowed to finish it, within four months graceful ships would be skimming in tangentially at orbital velocity, to be picked up by a travelling platform equipped with superconducting coils, and braked on the maglev track. Right now Byron's staff was installing auxiliary systems, a series of flywheels near the track to soak up the energy of a landing, or feed out energy in the case of a take-off. A fifteen-ton ship moving at 1680 m/sec and decelerating at two Earth gravities generates 500 megawatts of electricity which has to go somewhere.

The flywheels were housed in huts which could be pressurized during construction and maintenance and evacuated during operation. They rotated on magnetic bearings in a vacuum. Their basic frame was built on Earth but the bulk mass for the wheel was made of lunar laminates. It was those laminates that were giving trouble.

Byron was with one of the flywheel crews when he got a call from the main base. "McDougall. Braithwaite here. Louise hasn't been able to find you. She has an urgent call from Earth."

"Goddamn that phone! I've got enough to do seeing if you and Anne are on schedule and under budget without having to listen to every gripe from Earth."

"Louise said it was a panicky message from Seattle. You're going to be recalled."

"I just got back! Oh for Christ's sake. I suppose they aren't satisfied with the deal I made in Washington. I know damn well it was a stopgap, but it was the best I could do. It has *got* to do for the next four months."

"I think the call was about the crisis," said Braithwaite.

"Which crisis? An old one or a new one?"

"You vac-head. *The revolution.*"

"What revolution?"

"In Saudi Arabia."

"Yeah, yeah, Saudi Arabia is going to revolt when hell freezes over. I know those sand eaters. I know Abdul Zamani, the defense minister. I taught him how to fly the F-15."

"Abdul Zamani is dead. The last I heard the refinery complex at Dhahran was in flames. And God alone knows if the new leaders will continue to sell us oil. We don't yet know which freak Marxist heresy they belong to. Old Poker Face raced in from Camp David and seems to be trying to gather support to send in the marines—but hell, it's already way too late. The Royalists who were yelling for help are already dead.''

"You're kidding me?''

"You didn't scan the news this morning? We saw rows of Royal Bodies hanging headless by their feet from the lampposts in Riyadh. The King was murdered three hours ago.''

"My God! And you didn't tell me!''

"I automatically assume you know everything.''

"I'm coming in. Sweet Jesus!''

Back in the huts of the main base Byron replayed the late news on his console screen. It had been a stunning coup. The battle was over before the Pentagon had even received orders to organize an airlift. And the CIA had heard the news via CBS. Modern Arab coups evidently weren't the clumsy affairs of yesterday.

*Swat, just like that.*

He felt disoriented, remembering the tough men he had trained. Those Saudi fighter pilots had been Royalist to the core. He couldn't imagine a coup succeeding without them and he couldn't imagine them siding with the Palestinians and the Pakistanis and the other immigrants who chafed under Royal rule. But he didn't let his disorientation stop him from sensing that here was an extraordinary battlefield situation to be exploited *immediately*.

Zimmerman came into his office with a worried look. "That's bad news. You heard the news?''

"Yeah. I still don't believe it.''

"Look, no American should try already to understand an Arab intrigue.''

"You sound upset.''

"The House of Saud supported *moderate* terrorists. Me, I'm thinking the new government will maybe support *extreme* terrorists.''

"I have a simple philosophy about terrorists—shaved ones and unshaved ones," said Byron. "Give any one of them a buck to do in your blood enemies, and they'll use it to buy a gun to do you in for the *rest* of your money. Bank rolling hatred is a risky line of work.''

''You think the terrorists are behind the coup?''

''Zimmerman, I haven't got a clue. Money is power and power is a double-edged sword, that's all I know. There is no denying that the Royalists have been feeding murderers. Maybe that money was used to kill Jews, maybe it turned into graft, maybe it flowed backwards to water the plots in Jidda. Who will ever know? Whatever the basis for the coup, somebody just lost a queen in a big chess game. The USA is up the creek. And we on the moon have been dealt an ace.'' Byron glanced at his watch. ''Hungry?''

''It's cucumber salad today,'' said Zimmerman disconsolately.

''I'm going to have to crack that whip to get that landing track finished so we can ship in some beef.''

''With whose money?''

''You think money will be a problem after today?''

''I see a depression,'' Zimmerman said gloomily.

Byron was grinning as they drifted off toward the cafeteria. ''I see gas rationing in the States, and I'm dying laughing. I'm seeing the pipes bursting in the middle of winter and I'm rolling in the aisles. I'm seeing the Russians trading weapons for Saudi oil and I'm grinning from ear to ear.''

''That bad you see it?''

''I used to like Americans,'' said Byron with amused savagery. ''I'm an American. It used to feel great to go to them and say, 'Here's a solution to a problem that hasn't happened yet.' So how do they react? They sniff daisies. Even my son. Zimmerman, if an American jumps out of an airplane, you can't sell him a parachute until *after* he hits the ground. I don't even flap about it anymore. Americans are manic freaks who slack off suicidally between crises and then work their asses to a bone to meet a crisis *after* it has bashed them in the face—all the time bitching bitterly that no one ever told them that the fist was on the way. Well, *I* told them. *I* was on my knees begging them, for Christ's sake. That's the whole story. It's a mania that will kill us all dead one day, and our Constitution besides, that one last crisis too many, but in the meantime it is no use yammering to deaf ears about how to prevent a coming crisis, you just have to be cool and work quietly until you know exactly what to tell them to do *after* the crisis has them screaming in pain—and hope to God they can get their silly asses in gear as fast as they always have before. Don't have the parachutes ready! Know all about splints!''

"Well done!" exclaimed Zimmerman. "I haven't heard you rant that well for three days.''

Braithwaite appeared from behind the potted plants and joined them at their table. "Have you phoned Seattle yet?''

"Why should I call Seattle? I know what they are going to say. They're going to send me back to D.C. to try to sell Congress on putting up the risk capital to set up a production line that will crank out one ten-gigawatt solar power satellite per month. I'll go; I'll make salvation noises, and our politicians will stand there with their knees shaking, those Georges who have cut us colonials down to the bone, and they'll kiss my ass and they'll buy it. Eight years ago I would have kissed *their* asses.''

"You're so happy it depresses me," moped Zimmerman. "The State Department is having a morbid nightmare, and you're happy.''

"Give us a smile, Zim.''

"How can I give you a smile? My son is in Israel. I'm worried.''

"Arabs are killing each other and he's worried. Give us a smile. This is the break we've been praying for. Now the bureaucrats need us in a bad way.''

"You really think D.C. is going to buy anything? With our luck they'll revoke our return tickets and turn off the air. We'll starve. Here, maybe have some cucumber salad before it is gone already.''

## 9

The pods were attached all along the sides of the spaceport. Floating down the central corridor of Pod-43 a customer faced the logo of *Planet Stories* set into a glass rectangle above liquid crystal credits for the waitresses such as:

## MOON CRAWLERS

### by Diana Grove

Framed by this layout was the control room of a 1940s class rocketship battle cruiser. The busy "captain" could be seen in free fall, perhaps with his hand on the Pressor Beam Rheostat mixing a whisky sour. Beyond him was a porthole and an awesome view of the Earth filling half the sky.

Beside the porthole sat a surly Bug Eyed Monster deep in his cups. He was so lifelike that the unwary frequently approached him to see if they couldn't detect a defect left by the artist and got the shock of their lives. The BEM turned with a cat's suppleness, bared his teeth and snarled at people who came too close. His electronic innards were, of course, made on the spaceport.

Diana was late for work, the first time in many weeks. It wasn't her fault. There had been a minor malfunction on the maglev transport line that carried passengers and freight and empty lighters along the 150-km length of the spaceport. Her apartment, which she shared with another girl employed in large-scale integrated microelectronics, was 20 km from *Planet Stories*.

She popped through the airlock entrance—a real emergency airlock—whispered hurried words to the "captain" and scooted to the ladies' room where she slipped into her brass scanties and emerged ready to serve. Serving in free fall was freaky but she already knew how to do it with grace.

"Diana!"

She turned. A man with pepper hair and blue eyes was smiling lazily at her. He wore lunar togs. He had a strong aura about him and she thought she saw in his face a gentle fondness for women. That strange heady feeling of love at first sight struck. She let the emotion tingle through her mainly because he was an older man and that made him safe. Three other men hovered with him at a service booth. She glided over, her willingness to serve at a level above and beyond the call of duty.

"What's a Moon Crawler?" he asked.

"How do you know I'm Diana?"

"I've kissed all the other bylines."

"And they rejected your clever pass so you're trying me as a last resort?"

"Byron," said one of the others, "she's armed."

"And beautiful arms they are," said Byron undiscouraged.

"A Moon Crawler," replied Diana, "is a slimy worm from outer space who telepathically poses as an irresistable woman. All that's left of the man in the morning is his toenails."

"Ouch," said Byron. "Let's hug and make up."

"You wouldn't survive. Now what do you want to order?"

He was amused. "I'm rich and charming and experienced, a classic winner. What did I do to deserve you?"

At the first opportunity Diana asked the "captain" in his Tri-planet Rocketforce uniform, "Who is that distinguished one with those accountant types? He's a regular here, isn't he?"

"McDougall."

"Thanks. That tells me a lot."

"He has a few interesting stories to tell. He's an old fighter pilot. He's an old Rockwell shuttle pilot. He built half of this bird we're flying on. I think he is a close friend of Arnold." Arnold had designed the spaceport. "He's top dog of the moon base construction crew."

"He's really been to the moon?" Her eyes darted to the corner.

"He *commutes* to the moon."

She leaned conspiratorially over the battle cruiser weapons control array. "Is he married?"

"Divorced."

She shivered at that news. "He likes me, did you notice?"

"Diana sweetheart, listen to me. You have a superlative bod. He's a make-em and leave-em man. He's out of your class."

"What do *you* know about trapping men!" she flared and left with their dinners.

One thing she liked about her job, the girls were supposed to entertain intellectually as well as serve and be sexy. Ling never sent a woman to *Planet Stories* who wasn't a good conversationalist. It was easy to wedge into this group and dominate the chat. She made her points by touching them lightly with excited hands—except McDougall. She let the men fondle her body—except McDougall. But while his companions caressed her brass armor, she flirted with those flecked blue eyes.

Duties called her away, yet she made special trips back to *his* corner. Only as they finished their after dinner drinks did she tousle Byron's hair and whisper in his ear, "I'm off at 2 A.M. Why don't you pick me up then?" She was trembling with embarrassment.

He smiled. "Too bad I'm not on vacation. This Saudi mess has a stake up all our asses." He scribbled something and handed her a note. "Drop by when you get off. You may have to watch me work."

Diana didn't look at the note until he was gone. It was his Hilton hotel room, the executive suite. She had a flash of anger. *I won't go.* He wanted her to chase him. It was humiliating. *I'll go home and chain myself to the hammock.*

She stared at the wall. On it hung an original *Planet Stories* illustration of the Princess of Io, wearing a World War II hairdo and burlesque costume, racing between the moons of Jupiter on her rocket sled and being pursued. *Some women have all the luck!*

It was a long ride to the Hilton on the maglev. If you were

close to the tubes, you could hear the lighters coming in or being shot out, a kind of humming swoosh that came through your feet, but in the maglev bus, suspended in vacuum, you could hear nothing. She did catch an occasional glimpse of an unloaded lighter, its delta wings retracted, moving along the central transport line in electromagnetic suspension where it was being taken to maintenance or loading or to the ejection breech at the leading edge of the spaceport.

Tremulously, at two-thirty, she was at McDougall's door, knocking. He opened. He seemed confused to see her. Behind him papers were maglocked to the walls and the combination info-computer console that went with the executive suite was alive with readout.

"Didn't you invite me?" She clutched his note, unsure of herself on his territory.

He shook himself. "I wasn't expecting you."

"I thought you invited me."

He eased her inside. "And I thought you were pulling my leg. You pulled my leg all evening. So I pulled yours. If I'd known you were serious I would have been after you with roses. I hate being stood up."

Slightly mollified she said, "Where would you get roses in space?"

"There are ways, my little Moon Crawler."

She watched the tension lift from his face. A lined face could not hide tension as easily as a young face. *He's happy to have me.* He took her in his arms and held her warmly. She let him. *What am I doing here? He's going to try to lay me. I've got to get out of here.* "Did I interrupt something?"

"You most certainly did."

"I'm sorry. I won't bother you. I'll just watch. I love to watch men work. They're so involved."

"Give me another hour or so. I'm making up a presentation for a congressional committee. Looking at energy alternatives with Saudi oil knocked out."

"I thought we weren't importing as much oil from Saudi Arabia as we used to." *Always get a man to talk about his work.*

"We're not. But try turning off ten percent of your oil supply when you're all geared up for it. That new crew of camel-smelling sister-beaters are throwing out their American oil men and importing Soviet technicians to put their oil fields back into production. They killed more than 20,000 of their own American-trained men in the battle. And we can't do a damn thing about it."

Her eyes were glowing. "Will they have to build solar power satellites now?"

"There's a good chance."

"They'll just dig more coal," she said disdainfully. "Where I used to live in Ohio, everything was done with coal."

He snorted. "Coal has been having problems for a long time. Do you know how many billions of dollars the government spends on coal related disabilities every year? I could buy a lunar colony for that budget." He called up a display on the screen. "And look at that. Hydrogen fusion is still 3000 times as expensive as fission. That leaves breeder reactors and solar power satellites. And *we* are clean. It will take a mix of both. It is a pain in the ass figuring out the trade-offs. Time is the factor now. We've got to move *fast* and that changes the trade-offs."

"Is there anything I can do? Sort papers or something?"

"Diana," he said warmly, "you've had a hard day. You've done a whole shift for God's sake. Get to bed. I'll join you later."

"I'd rather watch." With a cringing fascination she watched the terror that was beginning to rise in her.

"And I'd rather see some rosy cheeks in the morning." He took her behind the room screen and pulled out the bed netting and casually began to undress her.

She froze.

He backed off. "We've made different postulates?"

She was panicky. She didn't know how to explain. "I have to be between you and the door. I'm crazy."

He changed positions with her, careful not to touch her, instantly willing to put her at ease. "Is that better?" He was puzzled, and half amused.

She nodded.

"Have you ever made love in space?"

"No."

"You'll enjoy it."

"I'm getting out of here."

"Stay." It was a command. He did not raise his hands.

She stared at those blue eyes which held her, knowing that he would let her go if she had the strength to leave. "I can undress myself." She did so, swiftly, awkwardly, and slipped into the net. "Kiss me goodnight."

Quietly, at six in the morning, he woke her. His body was comfortably warm. That part was like Mr. Ling and she enjoyed it. But Byron's fingers were hungry. That part confused her. She tried to be like the girls in the movies. It didn't work. It was like trying to take control of a runaway horse.

He stopped. "How old did you say you were?"

"Twenty-one."

"You're a virgin."

"Is that bad?"

"Holy Jesus."

"I'm sorry. It's not my fault I was born that way."

"I'm rattled. You aren't in the space I thought you were in, and I'm astonished that I missed it."

"You don't want me?" She was ready to cry.

He didn't stop making love to her, but he was slower and carefully gentle, less intense, more propitiative, and he took contraceptive precautions because he didn't trust her innocence. The pleasure of it astonished her and she clung to him and wouldn't let go.

"My father used to beat me. I've had a hard time liking men. You're a good lover."

"How would you know? I'm a lousy lover."

"You're so delicious that all that's going to be left of you is toenails."

"Maybe it is just space. The first time you try it on Earth, you'll be shocked—especially if you are stuck with a 200-pound man like me."

"I'm never going back to Earth!"

"I am. In three days."

She began to cry. "Are you going to marry me?"

"Sweet Jesus. I could be your father."

"It doesn't matter. I love you. I remember everything you said. In *Planet Stories* you said you'd never met a woman who could love both you and space. Well, I love you and I love space and I want to settle down on the moon just like you do."

"Wench, we will discuss this later when you are sober."

Diana called up one of the other girls and arranged an exchange of days off. She did her best not to let Byron out of her sight. He didn't seem to mind. She let Byron work. She helped him when she could. But the minute he showed signs of relaxing, she seduced him with every wile she knew. Sex, for two whole days, was her entire universe.

The door slid open. Byron's eyes blazed with blue fire. "Get dressed!" Terrified she slipped into her blouse but his anger couldn't wait and he gathered the collar of the blouse in his fist and shoved her against the wall. "You lied to me!"

She loved him too much to hit him or struggle.

"There is no Diana Grove." He shook her like a dog shakes a rat. "Your name is Osborne and you are sixteen years old. You are jailbait!" He let her go. "Do you realize how much trouble you could get me into?"

"Don't hit me! Don't hit me!" She was cringing.

"You slipped up in some of your stories. I got to thinking. And the company has ways of checking up on people. We can't tolerate fools in space. Sixteen. My God. Sixteen! You should be home with your parents!"

"My father beats me," she said piteously. "That's why I ran away when I was twelve."

Byron remained angry. "Kids always blame their fathers. A favorite sport. Fathers happen to be nice guys. Maybe you just never understood what your father was saying. Maybe you are headstrong and willful and don't see the dangers a father sees. You're young. Fathers know, kid. They *know*."

Her face twisted into agony. "You don't love me any-more."

A single tear rolled out of his eye. "Jesus, what a damn fool I am. Yes, I love you. And I'm responsible for you. I'm leaving tomorrow and you're coming with me."

Sometimes the sun breaks through the clouds. "You're going to marry me?"

"I'm going to take you home to your family."

The sun can disappear again behind a thundercloud. "I *hate* my father!"

He took Diana in his arms and soothed her. "Can you remember something nice about him?"

"Why should I?"

"For me."

She paused, wanting to please Byron. "He bought me a rug when I wanted one."

"Did you like the rug?"

"Yeah."

"Remember something else nice."

She thought a long time, her eyes staring off in the direction of Arcturus. "He always made lemon and honey for my mother when she was sick."

"See. He's a nice man. It's been a long time. Our minds don't remember some things well because we are committed to proving that our decisions were right. You'll like him. You'll see."

"Mr. Ling will never forgive me," she said petulantly.

"I'm buying your contract."

"You can't make me go!"

"Oh yes I can," he said grimly.


10


The snow in Ohio was dirty with coal dust. Coal smells were on the air because the wind blew from that direction. Diana was surprised to see her father smiling, surprised to see him contrite, surprised at the warmth of the welcome he gave to the distinguished Mr. McDougall whose power awed him.

She arrived back in her familiar rat warren of factories and dry cleaning stores and chunky houses on tiny lots with potholes in the streets, a prisoner of the man she loved, determined to be emotionless—instead she cried with her mother. Both her parents lavished her with affection.

It was weird to go back to school with kids who hadn't changed since they were twelve because they hadn't done anything since they were twelve. The boys giggled when they said "boobs" and the girls were all virgins who thought SPS was a new thing to put in face cream to keep your pores clean.

Diana introverted into thoughts of Byron, suppressing all the evidence that might tell her she had been abandoned. He had hairs on his chest like Samson and she had some of them in an old perfume bottle. He was a hero angel who built stairways to the stars for men who were as yet too savage to understand. His fingers were pleasure, his eyes an ultimate beauty.

In her loneliness she began a letter to him. She wasn't sure she was going to mail it but the poetry of her love ached on her tongue. "Dearest Byron, I had a dream that there was nothing left of you but toenails and woke up in my bed nude (and beautiful as you well know) and imagined sweet touches. . . ." She redrafted the letter again and again, hiding it under the leather blotter on her desk.

One day when she came home from an errand to buy milk, her father chased her up the stairs raging against the depraved McDougall and against his daughter's dirty pornographic mind. He cornered her in her room, crumpling the letter in his fist.

Karate habits told her to take a defensive posture. She found herself cringing instead but when his arm lashed out to hit, her reflexes took over. A precisely placed foot smashed into his elbow, breaking it. She never looked back. She grabbed her Diana Grove papers from hiding and leaped through the window onto the porch roof and down onto the ground, rebounding in a run, unprotected against the winter cold.

A man and his wife found her on the highway, half frozen

to death, thumbing a ride. They wrapped her in a car blanket
and turned up the heat. She told them she was trying to go to
her mother in New Hampshire. Only after she said New
Hampshire did she remember that Byron's home was there.

The couple were active Christians and though they gave
her endless advice about God and finding Jesus they were
also practical. They insisted on taking her home, feeding her
and finding winter clothes for her from their friends. They
insisted on paying her bus fare and when she protested, they
merely smiled and told her she could pay them back by
helping someone else someday.

On the bus she prepared the scathing lecture with which
she intended to axe-murder Byron.

(1) You are a monster!

(2) You seduced me and, not content with just rejecting
me, you ruthlessly destroyed the whole wonderful life that I
was building up for myself.

(3) And once you smashed my life, you weren't satisfied;
you had to deliver me to a sadist for safekeeping, just so you
could walk away without any burden.

(4) How am I ever going to get a job like that spaceport job
again?

(5) It's not my fault that I had to pretend to be five years
older than I really am. The government is stupid. They won't
let me work and they won't take care of me.

*I'll strangle him. He better give me some money. He better
give me a job on the moon.*

Halfway to New Hampshire she realized she didn't have a
mark on her body and she wouldn't have a story to tell Byron
that he would believe. At one of the hour long rest stops she
went out to a brick wall and bashed her head against it until
the side of her face was bloody and swollen. When some
friendly passengers tried to ask her what had happened she
queered them by talking up the joys of head pounding.

Looking like an accident victim and in a state of confusion,
she stepped off the bus, penniless, at a roadside terminal in a
little New Hampshire town. It was madness to think that
Byron would be home. He would be in D.C. or Seattle or

anywhere but New Hampshire. She was going to a shuttered home buried in snow. His ex-wife, she knew, was in Florida.

She had a cry in the ladies' room before she went over to the post office and asked about Mr. McDougall. The woman told her he wasn't home, but that his son was, and a no good drifter he had for a son. Diana panhandled a quarter for a phone call and when she heard the son's voice, hung up without saying a word. She walked in the snow, ten kilometers, until she reached the McDougall place.

A dark haired young man with Byron's blue eyes answered the door. "You've been walking. Your car is stuck? I have a truck."

"No. I'm your father's mistress."

He tried to say seven things in reply and only a squeak came out. She walked past him, hugging herself. He rushed after her. "Hey, you're cold."

"Take me to your radiator."

"You've had an accident."

She touched her face. "The swelling is down. The black eye is pretty awful, isn't it? My old man beat me up for sleeping with your old man."

"My father abandoned you?"

"Yeah."

"Didn't he give you a free year in Paris?"

"He gave me a free year in an Ohio coal town."

"You could have asked for more."

"You don't ask for things when you're in love."

"You're too young for him."

"I *don't* think *that* is *any* of your *business!*"

"Are you pregnant?"

"*No* I'm *not* pregnant," she said through gritted teeth.

"I'll have some hot tea ready in a minute."

She sat down in the kitchen by the radiator and took her boots off. Her feet were white and numb. "Where is he?"

"I just got a check from Houston, but that was a week ago."

"A lot of good that does me." She started to cry.

"Aw, hey now. It can't be that bad."

"If you come over here with your big blue eyes and try to comfort me, I'll slug you!"

## 11

Diana sulked in the master bedroom except for meals. Across the veranda she had a view of snowed-in farmlands, the kind of rolling landscape rich people purchase when they are bored by the city. The room had a handcrafted look with walnut trim and carved walnut doors. It was wholly a woman's room. Perfume bottles were on display, but things like heavy brass hairbrushes were neatly placed in drawers. Two portraits hung over the bed: a woman lit by sun reflected from spring leaves and a man glooming beneath some autumnal overcast in a fighter pilot uniform. The portrait of Mrs. McDougall, Diana hid under the bed. *His* portrait she launched upon the bed, a raft for a lonely girl to cling to in a king-sized ocean of softness.

Sulking made Diana restless. She had never tried it before and didn't like it. After three days she took a couple of hours off to bake a chicken casserole and that was such a relief she began trying on Mrs. McDougall's clothes, modifying the ones she liked on the sewing machine. A timid knock interrupted her concentration sometime during her fourth day of sewing.

"Like to come to the village? I'm going for groceries."

"Thank God! Did Byron finally send you more money?"

"Naw. I did some electrical work at the Hodge farm."

"You worked?" she exclaimed incredulously.

"Yeah, you're eating me out of house and home."

"And here I thought I was starving!"

"So today we'll have steak. I figured that if my father can keep *my* girlfriend in Paris, I can at least buy *his* girlfriend a steak."

In the village she noticed that the highway restaurant needed a waitress and she went in and took the job. It was a drag to live with a wastrel like Charlie who ate macaroni every night, sweet as he was. She was used to money.

Sometimes she hitchhiked home after work. Sometimes Charlie was waiting for her if she paid for the gas. Once he arrived to pick her up and found her being hassled by three toughs who wanted to give her a ride. The leader blew smoke in his face.

"You being bothered by these lung disease cases?" he asked.

"Stay out of this, Charlie. I know karate."

"It's not a job for a lady." He assumed the stance of a battle-tried colonel. "Leave!"

They left.

"How did you do that?" She was amazed.

He laughed. "Ordering men around and saving women and children runs in the family. Old military tradition. I'm considered the sissy of the McDougalls."

Diana decided to become independent of Charlie and bought a fifty-dollar car and pay-by-the-week insurance policy after she had wangled some gas ration tickets. The car got her halfway home.

"Charlie," said a plaintive voice over the phone. "I'm stuck on the Stonefield road at the hairpin. Would it be too much trouble for you to come and get me? Bring a chain."

"A chain?"

"To pull my car."

"Your car!"

"I bought a car."

"How much did you pay?"

She muttered an answer.

"Good God! You can't buy an unrusty hubcap for that!"

"It made noises and quit. Can you fix it?"

He sighed. "Maybe it's the spark plugs. I'll be right down."

The engine had seized. "How much does a new engine cost?" she whined.

"Oh, maybe a thousand dollars."

She cried all the way home. He tried to console her by telling her he could get something for the tires, and maybe sell a few other parts, but she was unconsolable. He began to feel so sorry for her that the next day he towed the car off to a friend's garage and spent all day doing an engine job. That evening he picked her up.

"Where's the truck?"

"I brought the car."

"I didn't know you could fix cars."

"I can't but I used to repair obsolete jet engines at MIT."

"Where did you get the money for parts?"

Charlie grinned like a man who has just won somebody else's gambling money. "My father is a millionaire. I have a kind of credit around here. He grumbles like hell, but he pays the bills."

"I don't understand you. Why do you loaf around when you could get a job as a mechanic?"

"Diana! That's work! I only did it for you."

"You're my nice sweetie pie. How can I sacrifice myself for you?"

"Entertain me in bed."

"I belong to your father!" she said indignantly.

"What kind of garbage is that?" he snarled.

"A girl belongs to the man who took her virginity."

He groaned. "You believe that drivel?"

"I certainly do!"

"You sound like my grandfather."

"Are you in love with me?" she asked warily.

"An inch, going on an inch and a quarter."

As they were thrown around the hairpin turn on Stonefield Road she kissed him. "If I hadn't met your father first, I'd love you an inch and a quarter, too." She kissed him again.

"Watch that stuff. You'll get dirty. I couldn't wash all the grease off."

"I don't care. I want to be nice to you. What was the nicest thing that ever happened to you—besides sex?"

"When Betty let me give her a bath."

Diana screeched. "I'll give you a bath!"

She sudsed him carefully, in no hurry to finish caressing away the black grease. It made her lonely to touch him, and happy at the same time. He tried to convince her to join him in

the tub but she refused. When she was toweling him afterwards, he tried to kiss her and she hit him and they had a
fight. She ran to the master bedroom and locked the door but
hugging Byron's angular portrait proved to be no way to go to
sleep. She kept thinking about crazy Charlie.

At four in the morning she wrapped a sheet around her
body and shuffled to the kitchen for a glass of milk. She
returned by way of Charlie's study, curiosity driving her to
rifle through his papers. It was mostly schoolwork—
equations, printouts, drawings, projects, experiments.

Charlie appeared at the door in his pajamas. "You're not
asleep." He paused. "I'm sorry."

"I'm not mad at you. What are all those things?"

"I used to go to MIT."

"What are you?"

"A lunar engineer. It's not that really; I didn't specialize in
lunar construction problems until my last year."

"Is that what these diagrams are?"

"Yeah."

"You never told me."

"It's not important to me."

Like a dash of hot tobasco the old excitement was in her
body as it sauced her blood with adrenalin and a pinch of lust.
"Did you flunk?"

"I was the top of my class."

"Why aren't you building houses on the moon? It would
be fun."

"Fun? It would be like New Hampshire in January with the
air missing. Why take the moon when the worst that can
happen to you on Earth is to be staked to an anthill in
Nevada."

"But you could go if you wanted?"

"My father would love it. Staking me to an anthill isn't
good enough for him."

A small adjustment of her shoulders let one curious nipple
peek over the sheet at his blue eyes. "And what's all that
electronic junk?"

"My music."

"Is that the weird stuff I hear once in awhile?"

"No, the weird stuff is when I'm composing. That's just experiments and subthemes. Sometimes it's a foundation sound on which I'm going to build." Then he added shyly, "I've been composing a piece for you."

"Oh, you *are* in love with me!" she teased. "May I hear it?"

"You sing this wild stuff in the shower. I built it on that. You'll have to forgive me for bugging your shower."

"But I have a slug's voice!"

"Ah, but it's all filtered through my electronic ears and I hear the most beautiful things when I listen to you."

"If you weren't so lazy you could work as a queen's flatterer."

"It's called 'Diana in the Rain.' "

Nothing larval was left in the voice he had transformed with his silken touch. Mostly it wasn't even human. Perhaps a nymph bathing in a mountain waterfall would sing that way. The sound folded and unfolded wings of joy so startling even she failed to recognize herself as the music gripped her with her own emotion. Background instruments fluted in tonal patterns no wooden intrument had ever emitted. Her mind, captured by his net, remembered mythical worlds she had never seen.

He stood breathless, anxious, watching her reaction. Slowly becoming aware of what his metamorphic magic had done to her, she worked out of her percale cocoon with little jerking cries of pleased embarrassment.

"Golly."

He was drugged with happiness, just watching her.

"Don't stare at me like that or I'll turn you into a stag and your own hounds will hunt you down!"

Gently he carried her off to bed but, when responding to his memory of her earlier anger, he withdrew, she would not let him go. What is true one hour is false the next.

"Stay with me and cuddle. As long as I get the door side of the bed. You can make love to me in the morning."

When she woke she found him staring at her with his blue

eyes. She rubbed noses with him. "Hi," he said. "Is it morning yet?"

Their sexing was an awkward disaster. The gravity threw her off and he was a virgin. Alternately they swore at each other and laughed. Finally they decided that at least they knew how to hug.

"It reminds me of a story that my grandfather loves to tell," he sighed. "Once upon a time there was a new recruit for the 43rd Cavalry Regiment and the commanding officer asked him, 'Have you ever ridden before, my boy?' 'No, sir,' said the boy. 'Hmm,' replied the colonel, 'I have just the horse for you; she's never been ridden before, either.' "

"Let's have breakfast and try it again," she said.

For three days Diana ran around in a daze, baking, washing his clothes, laughing at his jokes, buying him presents with her tip money and hugging him every time she met him. The second time she found herself scrubbing the kitchen floor in one week, she frowned. Did sex always make a woman feel this way? Byron had given her goosebumps, too. Were men similarly affected? She peeked out the kitchen window and saw Charlie freezing his fingers off changing a bearing on her right front wheel and that was reassuring.

By Friday she was enough in control of her emotions to begin the Great Plan. (1) Get Charlie a job. (2) Get him to finish school. (3) Get him a job on the moon. (4) Marry him. (5) Have children. She wasn't going to do it by nagging. She hated nagging a man. She'd rather leave a man than nag him. She was going to do it by worshipping him when he moved in the right direction and with patience and humor.

A driver's mother died and he trucked potatoes for three days; Diana let him make love to her for three evenings and three mornings. A neighbor's pipes froze and he joined the plumbing crew; she cooked him a four course meal. Slyly she began to encourage him to be more ambitious. He took a weekend gig in Concord with his music. But spring came and he was still only doing odd jobs. Happiness gave her patience. They went walking in the woods when the buds sprouted. They splashed nude in the ice cold brook.

She began to read to him from the papers about the big new push into space. Money was flooding into the effort. Overnight the high frontier had become a business almost half as big as the American cigaret, dope, and cosmetics trade. Charlie was never interested. She hid her hurt.

The Saudi Arabian situation improved. Escaped Royalists had money in America and Europe with which to influence politics at home. Intrigues prospered. Assassinations were frequent. The new leaders found it easier to conquer than to rule, and found some appeasement of the western capitalists necessary. Still the oil situation was grim and as reserves were depleted the United States imposed draconian gasoline rationing. Syntigas plants were pushed to full capacity in spite of a coal strike, suppressed by the Army. But sabotage continued to decimate coal tonnage.

Red tape was cut so that breeder reactors could be put on line in four years but nuisance protests continued to mount. A new tar sands plant was financed for Alberta. Hydrogen fusion power was brought down to $100 per kilowatt hour. A new gas field was discovered at great depth in the Gulf of Mexico. Mainly the economy was gearing up for solar power satellite production.

She read to Charlie the fabulous job offers in the *New York Times*. He wasn't interested. She sulked.

One day like a bolt from Jupiter the father called and Diana listened on the upstairs phone, tears rolling out of her eyes. *There* was a man. He could build. He could fight. His very voice called forth loyalty. He was on the cover of *Time* magazine. He could even be tender to virgins. His kind forged the glory of man. She ached to hold him. Could a woman ever forget her first man?

That noon Diana cooked pies and a mouth watering lasagna. She made a fresh spring salad of new asparagus tips. She adjusted Charlie's collar. She teased him and in all ways was free and easy with her love. When she went to work she left a note in the truck's windshield wiper. "I have a job on the moon." Which wasn't true. "I'll *always* love you." Which was true for the moment. "Keep in touch."

She stopped at the restaurant only long enough to collect her pay and buy a packet of black market gas stamps which got her as far as Montana. In Butte she abandoned the car and took a bus to Seattle, curled over two seats with her head pressed against her wadded jacket, dreaming that she was asleep next to Byron's facial stubble.

## 12

For three hours a nervous girl waited in the hotel lobby where that flighty secretary said he was staying. It stunned her when he sailed by, his weathered eyes scanning over her like a reef to be avoided, his wake washing away the hell in her throat. She buttoned the décolleté she had arranged to remind him of her womanhood, and followed him into the waiting elevator, ignoring him while they touched shoulders.

He left the elevator. She followed silently. He stopped and took out his key card. She waited.

"Diana! For the love of God!"

"So you finally noticed," she said petulantly.

"I had you pegged as one of the convention girls," he apologized, somewhat untactfully, switching on the light and walking over to the telephone. "What'll I order for you?"

"Poison darts!"

He spoke into the phone. "A double whisky for room 412. Also an extra glass, a bucket of ice and three bottles of ginger ale." Carefully he cradled the receiver. "So you ran away again?"

"He beat me up the minute you left! I mistook myself for a gong. I escaped by jumping two stories into the snow. A couple of good samaritans found me frozen to death at the end of a trail of blood. I learned about fathers what I already knew."

He was gazing at her with quizzical amusement. "Any scars?"

"No sir!" She snapped her heels. "Regrouped, re-supplied, rested, and ready for active duty, you son-of-a-bitch, sir!" A clipped salute finished her report.

*"Now* I remember you," he said amiably. "And how have you been spending your AWOL?"

"Living with your son."

His face crumpled like a piece of paper being prepared for a bureaucrat's wastebasket. "You've seen Charlie?"

"We're lovers."

"Did he send you here for money?"

"Oh Byron! I heard your voice last week on the phone. I became nostalgic. I came here to marry you. We're going to have three children and live on the moon."

"A minute ago you were ready to kill me with poison darts."

"That was a minute ago. I'd be a good wife."

"I'm tempted," he said.

"Yeah?" She unbuttoned her décolleté.

"But my good sense remains. I'll give you a choice. I'll argue with you or I'll send you to an orphan asylum."

"Argue with me."

"You laid Charlie, eh?"

"What's it to you! The last I heard from you, just before you abandoned me to that prick father of mine, you wanted me to live in the coal dust and be virtuous."

Byron was trying to visualize being married to her. "I was thinking that you are young, even for Charlie."

"Yaah! Charlie's young, even for me."

"It wouldn't work between you and me," he said decisively.

"Why not!"

"I'm more than thirty years older than you are. I'm dying. You are beginning to flower."

She undid another button and rummaged around under the bed for his dirty socks which she angrily threw into a plastic bag. "Corpses make good fertilizer for flowers. Your power and my youth; it's a fair exchange. Jesus, Byron," she turned to him with regret, "I swooned when I saw you on *Time*. I was horny for a day."

"You'd tire of an old man."

"But it's *men* who are fickle. Women aren't like that.

They're faithful. When they love a man, they *love* him. I'd be faithful to you. I'd forgive you anything.''

He was settling into his decision. ''That's what they all say when they are seventeen. When they are twenty-seven it's a different story.''

''Already you're complaining about ten glorious years?'' she stormed. ''I'll bet you think you deserve fifty!''

There was a polite knock on the door.

''Young girls tend to bore experienced men,'' he reminded her.

She flung open the door and took the double whisky from the bellhop's cart before he had fully entered the room. She set the glass on the dresser, imperiously tipped the man, and poured Byron a ginger ale. ''For your liver, old man. So I bore you, do I?''

''You started me thinking about those fifty years.''

She half finished the whisky in one slurp.

''Can't I even have a sip of my whisky?'' he complained.

''I've decided to blackmail you instead of marry you,'' she answered calmly.

''Blackmail me!'' She had his attention. ''We're not even married yet and you're being a bitch. I hope your lawyers are cheaper than my lawyers! You've stolen my whisky. What else do you want?''

''A job on the moon.''

His humor left him. ''No. That's final. What's your counter-move?''

''You damn fool!'' she flared. ''Your son is in love with me! He'll follow me to the moon! That's where you want him!''

''And do you love Charlie?''

''No! I can't *stand* drifters. Yes. He's very kind.''

Byron gripped her arms in the iron curl of his fingers. ''Diana. He *won't* follow you to the moon.''

''Yes.''

''*No*. I know my son.''

''You've seen him lately with my legs around him?'' she lilted sarcastically, not even trying to escape his crushing hold. "I've watched him butter my toast. I've watched him scatter men who were trying to molest me. I've seen his eyes in the morning. You know *nothing* about your son. You're a dried up old man, remember, who has forgotten what it's like to be driven by his juices. Charlie would follow me to hell. I planned it that way." She started to cry. "At least he will if we move fast enough before he has time to sober up and get another girl."

"He could follow you and refuse to work."

"Then I'd let him die. No man of mine is a suck." She smiled through her tears. "But for me he'd work. He's a sweet guy, Byron."

He began to march around the room, shaking ice from the ginger ale glass he had exchanged for her arm. "And you think I give a *damn* whether he goes to space? I don't give a *damn* anymore. I used to care. Now I'd be happy if he did anything. *Anything*. Wash cars even. How is his *damned* music going?"

"Like his engineering. He piddles at it."

"Is he healthy?"

"He's fine. I took good care of him. He's probably very unhappy right now."

"Suffering, eh?" Byron was smiling again. "A couple of months in the trenches will do him good. Finish your whisky and let's go. You've earned a dinner in Seattle's only real French restaurant."

At dinner he refused to gossip about his son. He ordered the best meal on the menu, the third most expensive. "It's good to eat like this again. For awhile I didn't even have an expense account."

"I'm on your expense account?"

"You're goddamned right. This year the Saudi Arabian Royal family lucked out and I'm enjoying every minute of their agony. We're tripling the size of the lunar colony. I wouldn't have believed that last year. And you should see the assembly line we're setting up for the solar power satellites; subcontracts all over the nation. It is going to be a boom year for the economy even though oil is short."

Her eyes were grinning. "I heard rumors that next year hydrogen fusion prices will drop to one cent a kilowatt hour."

Byron almost didn't laugh. "How could I let my son marry a girl with such a macabre sense of humor?"

He took her walking along the night beach, barefoot, sometimes on the sand, sometimes over the great driftwood trees, his shoes tied by the shoelaces over his shoulder and hers stuffed in his jacket pockets. The Pacific wind was cold and she sheltered herself behind his body, wondering at his silence that lasted for miles, not daring to invade his thoughts. The waves came and broke and went. Their feet were alternately drowned by foam and then free to make wet tracks in the moonlit sand.

"I'm not sure you'd like it up there. There is no moon in the sky for lovers."

"We can make poems about the Earth."

"You still have your Diana Grove papers?"

"Sure."

"They need to be made more solid. I'll spend some money."

She hugged his arm, thanking him silently, the glory and the triumph rising in her bosom to shout down the Pacific wind.

"I'm shipping out in two weeks. I'll take you with me. Not because of Charlie. Charlie can go to hell. For you. If Charlie follows, well, there'll be a job for him. We're building a second electromagnetic track to separate the takeoffs from the landings."

*Blackmail works!* She was amazed. "What will I be doing?"

"Who knows."

"May I stay with you tonight?"

"No!"

"My hotel by the bus station has cockroaches!"

They were halfway back along the beach before he answered. "Zimmerman tells this story about some New York cockroaches that followed him to the moon. He claims to have spaced them and that they didn't die but are running around the crater Aristarchus to this day.''

## 13

Rockets were still used to carry passengers and large freight to orbit. The electromagnetic interaction of a vehicle and the spaceport involved momentum transfer and large lighters would have required a more massive spaceport. Since the material of the original spaceport had to be carried to orbit by rocket, cost demanded that, once built, it would be supplied by a swarm of midget freighters which were intrinsically unsuitable for passenger transport.

Diana felt like a veteran. A mere year ago she had first been thrown into space by a rattletrap Rockwell Mark VI transport, a much modified version of the original Rockwell shuttle but still launched essentially by the means pioneered during the 1980s. Today she was aboard a modern impact rocket fresh from the factory at San Diego, its very design younger than her "Grove" identity. Even the upholstery smelled clean.

"How do you like this imp?" asked Byron cramped beside her, not a patch of their bodies unsupported. Imp was the name by which impact rockets had become known.

"It's super."

"You're not scared?"

"I'm going to heaven!"

"I'm scared to death. I get nervous out of the cockpit."

There were no stewardesses. A robot seat monitored each passenger, checking that regulations were complied with during the countdown. ". . . three. . . two. . . one. . ."

Blast off crushed them. The imp was, among other things, an oxygen-hydrogen rocket of mass ratio four, carry-enough propellant to reach slightly more than half orbital velocity. The roar cut off. A button tumbled in free fall in front of Diana. Then, as the imp found the apogee of its orbit among the blaze of stars, they met the spaceport, an express to hell passing under them so fast that its linear bulk was already perspective lines piercing infinity at the very moment the four gravity acceleration hit them.

The imp's magnetically suspended arms had reached down and were receiving oxygen from precision valved nozzles set into a perfectly straight feed pipe laid along the spaceport. The oxygen was hurtling at circular velocity as it entered the imp's ducts. The gas suffered an almost elastic collision against the vehicle, swinging through the ducts, around and out the rear jets with its relative velocity reversed—thus violently thrusting the ship forward without affecting the momentum of the spaceport at all. As the imp began to catch up with the spaceport the impacting oxygen became less and less effective. Then the imp began to inject hydrogen into the reaction chamber, adding fire to the recoil.

Ten percent of the oxygen used by this impact system was already being supplied by the moon. Eventually all of it would be. In the meantime oxygen was imported from the Earth via the hybrid lighters.

"Poor little Byron, we can relax now. We're here."

"Whew! The old shuttle was a piece of cake compared with this sobering ride. I feel like I've just been put up in front of a firing squad and asked to gently kiss a machine gun burst."

"You're such a stick-in-the-mud. You're too old for me."

They ate at the *Planet Stories* with leisurely gusto. Diana got drunk for the first time in her life. She told Shaggy Dog jokes and, when she had the attention of five booths, tried to dance on the tabletop. If you've ever seen a drunk try to dance on a tabletop in null gravity you may understand the extent to which laughing tears convulsed her audience. When she passed out, Byron towed her back to the Hilton.

The next day they caught a ferry to geosynchronous orbit at the construction site of the first ten-gigawatt solar power satellite. For eleven hours the five passengers played poker while the captain distributed sandwiches and made coffee.

There was some more ship maneuvering. When they went into a parking orbit, the captain called Diana into the cockpit.

"Take a look." The matchstick framework of the SPS angled away into the star laden blackness. "It's hard to comprehend how immense it is. Look, see that crane over there? It's a whopping big crane. See the little dot? That's the cabin for two men."

"Wow."

"I'll give you the grand picture. That thing is going to be as big as Manhattan Island. What you see is only five of the eight modules. What's out there would reach from Battery Park to 110th Street at the end of Central Park. The next module, the one that would contain Columbia University off in one corner if it was a piece of New York City, is being assembled in low orbit right now. They bring them up here by pushing hydrogen through porous electrically heated tungsten to get it through the Van Allen belts quickly, and then the rest of the way with ion jets."

McDougall was laughing behind them. "Tell her how to get from the A-train to the Seventh Avenue line."

Within the hour they docked with a lunar lander and exchanged lunar oxygen for terran hydrogen. The captain of the lunar lander stuck his head through the hatch, mainly to get a chance to razz McDougall. Byron didn't introduce him to Diana until the visit was over.

"Maltby and I used to fly in Saudi Arabia under the same command. He'll be taking care of you from here in. But don't depend on him. He's a rascal. Take care of yourself. Write Charlie. And don't let them send your bags to Mexico City. Ciao."

Maltby took her back through the tunnel.

"You sit copilot with me."

"Where's your copilot?"

"He's too fat. I left him home. Where would I put you if he was here? This ain't no taxicab. This here boat is a freighter. You want to fly the beast?"

"You're scaring me."

"It seems complicated to you? Shucks, you just say 'gid-diap' and the beast goes. She has a brain of her own. She knows where home is. The smell of oats."

"Giddiap," said Diana. Nothing happened.

Maltby did a few quick things with his fingers and the ship swung around. Then he yelled "Giddiap!" with an ear piercing Texas drawl and the ship roared to life.

This trip, instead of poker, she learned how to play chess. He gave her a two-pawn-and-a-rook handicap and she won one out of five games in the next three days.

The ship faced backwards for the horizontal landing, its rockets firing in tiny vernier adjustments. Lazily the barren moon flowed by, slowly rising to meet them. Only when they were skimming the plain at crater-rim height did their speed become evident. A mile every second. Nearby features ran together in a watercolor blur. Suddenly the track appeared beneath them and she saw, for a split second, the rocket-catching-cradle racing up the track toward them. She remembered the spaniel who used to gallop from the neighbor's house to chase her bicycle. The cradle positioned itself underneath them, grabbing with gentle jaws until their ship and the maglev vehicle became one.

Maltby was yelling "Whoa!" at the blood curdling top of his Texan voice. Electromagnetic fields cut in to convert fifteen tons of mass flow into an electron flood. Force hit then, two gravities that slowly built to five. The blur beyond the windows resolved into the majesty of the lunar desert, and finally they were moving sedately along a shunt line towards a shed. Maltby was fondly patting the control panel, smiling. "Atta girl."

*I'm here,* she thought and wonder was all within her.

She was assigned to the hydroponic gardens under a scowling beak-nosed boss who went through his chambers constantly tasting tomatoes and carrots and broccoli like a Punch making passes at lady puppets.

"Now that's a strawberry," he cackled. "I have the little buggers fooled that they are living on the slopes of a British Columbian mountain. Taste is everything. To hell with yield. Yield we can leave to the Californians." Slowly his grin grew, showing his upper gums above his jagged teeth.

She decided that her boss was crazy—not that what he *said*

was crazy, but he had papered the wall of the small strawberry room with a fantastic view of a British Columbian valley. It didn't take her long to find out that everyone else was crazy, too. In the cafeteria with the construction workers she listened curiously to a conversation beside her. Billy was sick. He'd been anemic for months. His leaves were drying around the edges. *His leaves?*

Byron's friend, Zimmerman, dropped around after work to play scrabble. Diana asked him, "What kind of fruitcake would name a lemon tree Billy?"

Zimmerman nodded. "I hear Billy is pretty sick about it, too. My tree, I named Hershel Ostropolier and he's never been sick a day in his life."

Then there was the tiny cook who had a redwood tree called Paul Bunyan. Weird. But he was into Bonsai so Diana supposed it might be all right. When she bought her own baby orange tree she decided it was *not* going to have a name, however, one evening in a humorous mood when the conversation came around to the Celtic worship of trees, she toasted her tree with a local version of Irish Mist. "To my true Irish friend!" Henceforth her orange tree was invariably referred to as "the Irishman."

It wasn't easy living on the moon. The corridors were cramped. The rooms were small. There was no place to go. She missed Charlie and hiking through the New Hampshire woods.

Worse, an enormous sense of loss began to plague her. She had no direction, no purpose to her life which had always known a fierce purpose. It was awful. It was like being a compass that had smashed its way through to the north magnetic pole and was now spinning, aimless. One night she dreamed about the truck driver who had taken her to Washington when she was twelve. In the dream he said with an ironic smile, "Better be careful what you want, kid—you may get it!"

Somehow the most important thing in her life became the study of plants. She was going to become a genius and bring life to the moon. She borrowed botany books and began to memorize all the names. She began to read biology books and agricultural texts and every hydroponic book in the library of her boss. Studying became an urgent compulsion. There wasn't even time to socialize, and finally no time to sleep.

One afternoon, looking for a scrabble game, Zimmerman found her wandering around the landing track control room trying to explain a theory of hers that no one could understand.

## 14

Every time when she woke up and tried to get out of bed so she could go back to work, they held her down and shot her full of drugs again. Once she escaped and turned up for work in her pajamas. They brought her back and put her to sleep. This time she was going to be more cunning. She'd pretend to be asleep until the drugs were all worn off and *then* she'd get up and go to work.

She peeked.

"Ah, you're awake," said Charlie.

She opened her eyes in wide disbelief. "Charlie! What are you doing here?"

"The old man called me up. He told me to get off my ass and take care of you. It was like listening to a wire brush cleaning out the hole between my ears."

"Are you on *their* side?"

"I don't know from nothing. I got here an hour ago. Tomorrow I'm out working on the new track. The old man got me a job as a laborer, the rat."

"Get me out of here, Charlie. I have to go back to work."

"You're on a paid vacation and you're complaining?"

"They'll fire me." She was terrified.

"Nobody is going to fire you with my old man backing you."

"What happened to me? They won't tell me."

"You were wandering around passionately trying to convince people that milkweed was going to save the moon. The flowers are edible or something."

"I wasn't! I don't believe you!" She hid under her covers in shame.

"Yeah, you were really around the bend."

"I don't understand," she said through the covers.

"Neither does the doctor. But I do. You ought to see the loonies wandering around MIT during final exam time."

"You'll take care of me?"

"Do you think I'll let you out of my sight again? You gave me the shock of my life. For a week I thought I was strong enough to dismiss you. Then a funny thing began to happen. The sweet flowered fields of New Hampshire dissolved away into the flowered fields of hell. And the moon up there in the sky began to take on a heavenly beauty."

"Can I go back to work? I could finish the afternoon shift if I started now."

"Maybe tomorrow. We have to settle things between us. Like who is this Irishman you're living with?"

"That's not my Irishman! That's my orange tree!"

"I'm competing with an orange tree? Do you think I have a chance?"

She laughed as Charlie tried to walk her home. He needed low gravity locomotion lessons. Once he collided with one of the awkwardly placed potted trees. "Charlie! Excuse yourself to Jezebel." He looked at her askance as she patted the pear tree. "There, there, Jezebel. Everything is going to be all right." Then she burst into tears.

Select friends gave Diana a homecoming party. Her boss arrived with a bowl of strawberries so delicious they needed neither sugar nor cream. Zimmerman leaned against the wall stealing more than his share. Louise was there and Maltby brought his guitar and his regular copilot. The Irishman moved into one corner to make room for them all.

Later Charlie explained to her the profounder truths of the universe as he saw them. "Some unsolved problem starts to push you. A couple of weeks without sleep and the borderline between the real world and imagination begins to fuzz. You fall asleep on your feet. You begin to treat real people as if they were the ghosts of your dreams and that's when the guys in the white coats come after you. Happens all the time at MIT in May. So if you get eight hours of sleep, I'll let you go to work. Otherwise, no.''

"Make love to me. That'll put me to sleep.''

"Thanks.''

"Is that what happened to you at MIT?''

"Naw. I was pushing to get my father's ass. Sweet revenge. Haven't you ever wanted to strangle your father?''

"Oh yes!'' she said brightly.

"I was going to get 100 percent in every course my last year just to rub that martinet's nose in the robot he'd made out of me. But no matter how much I strove I just couldn't make it as a robot. I couldn't get past 98 percent. It drove me crazy. It was like continually jumping in front of my father's Buick to prove to him what a bad driver he was and always coming out between the wheels without a scratch.''

"You're crazier than I am!''

"I owe it all to my father.'' He was smiling.

"I like Byron!''

"That's because you're a girl.'' He sighed. "Maybe one of these days I'll make my peace with the old prick.''

"You could have finished school. It was in your own best interest.''

He shrugged. "I wasn't doing it for me.''

"Why didn't you do more with your music?''

"My music was something they *didn't* want, so it was a reaction, too, I guess.''

"What *do* you want then?''

"You.''

"Oh Charlie! That's not enough and you know it!''

"Maybe it is. Men are more romantic than women. Women only pretend to be romantic because they know men like it.''

"Are you calling me a fake?'' she bridled.

"No. You made it very clear that what you wanted to do was sit on a peak 380,000 kilometers high and look down on the rest of us.''

"Screw you!'' She strode to the furthest corner of the

room, which wasn't very far away, and sat with her arms crossed, confronting him belligerently.

"Don't you think it's romantic that I climbed a peak that high just to ask you to marry me?"

She smiled mischievously, still with her arms crossed. "You haven't passed the other tests yet. You have to learn how to work first. Then *maybe* I'll marry you."

Within two years Charlie worked his way to assistant chief construction engineer. He was known with awe as the 100 percent man; the man who got the job perfect the first time. He lived with Diana and refused to take an SPS construction job because it would take him away from her.

Diana began to write papers on taste in high yield crops. For a lark she sent some tomatoes to a California fair and won first prize. She had seven projects going at once. Some people suspected that she never slept. Then, when necessity moved the command center out of the original Spartan diggings into much larger quarters, Diana made some frantic calls to Byron before someone else could find a use for the space. Charlie did the conversion design work. Zimmerman did the politicking. Ling, her old friend Ling, put up the money.

The place is called *Diana's Grove*. There are trees everywhere, not big trees, but what they lack in size they make up for in lushness. Some of them bear fruit—lemons and oranges and figs. There are vines and bamboo stands, even a brook that flows in too dreamlike a manner to gurgle. The benches are real wood. The food is the best in the solar system—just don't ask for beef. Nymphs with names like Callisto serve the tables wearing Roman hairdos and wispy gowns.

Diana, when she comes, makes her appearance in a white tunic with quiver over her shoulder. She knows everyone. Often she has a dinner party in one of the alcoves and brings people together who should be together, sometimes for major or minor politicking, sometimes because she delights in the clash of disparate views, sometimes because she is a secret matchmaker, sometimes for trivial reasons—an old professor of Charlie's needs company or one of her friends needs to discuss curtains. She is fiercely protective of the girls who work for her.

If you've ever heard the music at *Diana's Grove* you know that Charlie has risen into the league of the greatest. He claims it is just a hobby. The compositions can be as simple as birds chattering in the morning from somewhere beyond the leaves—a heron's cry, a sightseeing flock southbound, a lone warbler—or it can be a conversation-stopping argument between the gods.

Infrequently Charlie still proposes to Diana. She smiles her teasing smile, even though they already have one child, and writes him out a new contract in a flourishing script that promises she will be faithful to him for at least the next fortnight. He grumbles that living with her is like being an untenured professor.

The solar power satellites are winking on all around the equator, half of their mass coming from the moon now. All of the oxygen used by the space fleet is manufactured on the moon. America is prosperous, doing what it has always done best, selling high technology to the rest of the world. Her economy has achieved power independence and resource independence. The investment is considerable but it is, as yet, not well defended. Both McDougalls belong to an unofficial defense ministry which considers problems that Pentagon thinking is too archaic to handle. Serious decisions have to be made to secure the high ground in the face of a Russian resurgence into space. Such duties take Charlie back to the homeworld once a year.

Diana never goes with him. She is a minor Earth deity who worked hard for her promotion to moon goddess and she is well content with her position.

# EDITOR'S INTRODUCTION TO:

## SPACE AND THE LONGEVITY OF MAN

### By Stefan T. Possony and Jerry Pournelle

*Steve Possony is one of the most interesting people I know; and he is so seldom wrong that if I were told I could never again have an opinion of my own, but must accept one and only one person's judgments forevermore, I would very likely choose Stefan.*

*Possony took his doctorate from the University of Vienna in the early 30's, and immediately became one of the leaders of the conservative opposition to the Nazi takeover of Austria. For several years he and his friends kept Austria independent; the result was that his name was on the first page of the Gestapo's list. After many adventures he reached the United States.*

*Dr. Possony is Senior Fellow Emeritus of the Hoover Institution on War, Revolution, and Peace. The Hoover, located at Stanford University, has furnished most of Reagan's team of advisors for the early days of his administration.*

\* \* \*

*The American Association for the Advancement of Science holds annual public meetings at which scientists try to explain their work to each other and to the general public. In spring of 1980, Dr. Possony and I were privileged to co-chair a session of scientists and science fiction writers examining the general subject of science and the future.*

*The session must have been successful: there was an over-*

*flow crowd, and the AAAS informed us later that they counted the largest last-day attendance in the history of their annual meetings.*

*This paper was our keynote presentation to that session.*

# SPACE AND THE LONGEVITY OF MAN

## Stefan T. Possony and Jerry Pournelle

*This paper was presented at the 1980 annual meeting of the American Association for the Advancement of Science.*

Animals, it is believed, live only in the present. Man, the time-binding animal, lives in the future and past as well; and his assumptions about the future will profoundly affect his actions.

Of particular importance is how *long* the future is assumed to be. Actions may be rational or irrational depending on this assumption: it makes sense to spend the nest egg and eat the seed corn if the world must end tomorrow. Much contemporary irrationality may be caused by a sharp reduction in mankind's historical dimension.

For example: many computer models show that our civilization is doomed no matter what we do. Although the purported message of *The Limits To Growth* (1) was a recommended action, namely severe limits to population growth and industrial development, the actual message was taken by many to be the opposite; according to the models used in *Limits* our civilization is doomed within a few hundred years no matter what we do. Why, then, be concerned with preserving such a limited future?

But man's days may be longer than that.

In the past only prophets and mystics tried to determine the time alloted to mankind. The early Christians expected the Day of Judgment within their lifetimes. Some 25 generations later the end was expected at the millenium: sometime in 1000 AD history would end. Nostradamus carried his predictions to 3797 A.D.; and while he seems to have anticipated continuity beyond that date, he warned that "God only knows the eternity of the light proceeding from Himself." He added that we live in the seventh millenary when the eternal revolution will be ended. In the eighth sphere the "celestial bodies" will move again, and their "superior motion" "will make the Earth firm and stable." Whatever this means, survival was conceived as a short-time prospect, for no more than 100 or so generations into the future.

The Etruscans believed that the cosmos would exist for no more than 12,000 years, and they themselves would last only 1200; their end was inevitable and dictated by fate. They did not care to defend themselves against decline, and made little resistance to the Roman conquest which liquidated their civilization.

Prophecy has fallen out of fashion, which is probably just as well. At least the prophets with literary inclinations have largely abandoned the field to those with high speed computers. Decline of religion has brought a corresponding decline in contemplation of eternity. But the unfortunate result of this atrophy of prophecy is that barely anybody now worries about how much future we do have. According to Victor Franke, a prominent successor to Freud, the contemporary world suffers from loss of meaning. Freeman Dyson remarked on this in his paper at the Washington AAAS meeting, quoting Steven Weinberg's *The First Three Minutes* (2) as follows: "This present universe has evolved from an unspeakably unfamiliar condition, and faces a future extinction of endless cold or intolerable heat. The more the universe seems comprehensible, the more it also seems pointless."

And so while we search for meaning, we pointlessly continue our hopeless existence.

Of course evolution has a way of dealing with those who despair. For most of us, meaning is linked to protracted survival. Given longevity it makes no sense to eat the seed corn. What is rational for mayflies is not rational for the longer-lived.

* * *

What are our chances for indefinite survival?

At present there are three cosmological theories, each leading to a different estimate of time remaining: the open and expanding universe—which is the most popular candidate this year; the closed universe whose expansion will be followed by contraction and death by fire; and the steady-state universe during whose existence no major changes are anticipated. At present this latter seems the least favored; but certain steady-state theories, such as the suggestion by Sir Fred Hoyle that there may be continuous creation, lead to very long survival estimates indeed.

Allan Jacobsson, principal investigator for NASA's High Energy Astronomy Observatory HEAO-3 and specialist in gamma ray astronomy, is looking for evidence of nuclear activity in celestial bodies. "There are heavy elements in the universe with half lives shorter than the age of the universe. . . . They must have been manufactured since the creation of the universe. . . . What we are looking for are sites where heavy elements are synthesized." Whereas the infra-red background radiation supports the thesis of the expanding universe, continuous creation would support a modernized version of the steady-state thesis.

All three cosmological theories allow one to assume the earth will remain inhabitable for a billion years or so. Then, eventually, around 1 or 2 billion A.D., *homo terrestris* must embark on Noachian Arks of Space and leave the solar system.

Thereafter he has 100 billion years in the open universe before the stars burn out. For the closed universe the turning point from expansion to contraction will come in some 50 billion years, but by skillfully choosing his habitations man should be able to survive for an additional 60 billion, for a total of 110. In the steady-state universe he should last longer, although most such models show that life there must also end. The open universe gives us some $10^{©}27$ to $10^{©}100$ years, provided that we can extract some of the rotational energy from black holes. In the last phases there might be many civilizations "close" together—a few light days from each other—clustered around the last hole in the universal or one-world galaxy.

Thus life in this planetary system seems limited to some 40-odd million generations, while within the universe itself survival can be stretched by a factor of 100, to 4 billion generations. (Four generations are assumed for 100 years.)

In the end, though, the universe collapses, and is eventually reduced to neutron stars, black dwarfs, black holes, and a few odds and ends. The temperature will sink toward absolute zero. The most distant estimate we have seen for final doom was in Freeman Dyson's Washington AAAS meeting paper: 10 to the 10 to the 76 years, no small time.

But of course that assumes no intervention, human or Divine.

Divine intentions are beyond the scope of this paper; but, barring Divine interference, we see no reason why humanity cannot take part in the evolution of the cosmos. Human direction of galactic events seems no further beyond our present capabilities than space flight would be to an amoeba—and we are closer in time to the amoeba than we are to our descendents 50 billion years from now. Teilhard de Chardin may have underestimated our potential.

Even taking the shortest estimates for the potential end of the universe, Weinberg's lament seems a bit premature. Since for the next billion years we will—or could be—engaged in spreading mankind to and beyond the stars, concern for the end of time may safely be postponed, or perhaps left to Dyson perids and Divine providence.

We thus have one billion years to prepare our departure from this neighborhood, and another billion after that to move to other galaxies.

Two years ago Bell Laboratory's Dr. Wm. Gale added the provision "if no one beats us to them." Fermi's famous analysis took the number of stars, an estimate of the probability of planets, another estimate of the probability of life; finally the time it would take travelling at relatively slow speeds to visit us. He concluded with what may be the most important question ever asked: "Where are they?"

Robert Bussard answers that they are here, and we're them.

But assuming no one successfully disputes possession with us, we have time. The past history of *homo sapiens* extends some 200,000 years; of *homo erectus* and his ancestors 3 or 4 million; and for the hominids, perhaps as much as 10 million. Compared with our potential of 100 billion we have only just begun. It's not quite time to give up.

The billion years we have in this solar system will not give us the entire universe. We may not visit more than one percent of it. Yet given velocities of 0.1 c we can, within a million years, traverse this galaxy—and we could in theory build a .1 c probe with present technology. See Robert W. Forward of Hughes Research for details.

Frank Drake has suggested that "colonization" can be completed within about 10 million years per galaxy: even if he is off by a factor of two, we could colonize 50 galaxies before we must abandon Earth. Parenthetically, by that time we may decide to move the Earth, or bring it a new Sun; Earth will, after all, have sentimental value, and we ought to preserve it as a park . . .

Given our billion years in this solar system we will be able to learn quite a bit about many parts of the universe. A few illustrative examples are in order.

The nearest planet is Venus, some 30 million miles away at closest approach. The furthest planet we know of, and one for which we may have little use, is Pluto at 3 billion miles. This is our backyard.

The nearest stars are some 6000 times as far as Pluto: Alpha Centauri at 4 lightyears. Sirius is some 10 lightyears away. There are also smaller and less interesting stars, such as Barnard's Star, in the 4 to 10 lightyear range.

Within a sphere with radius 60 lightyears from Earth (strictly speaking, from the Sun, but at those distances it hardly matters) there are some 4.5 stars per cubic lightyear, or over 4 million total.

We expect that at least some of those stars will have planets, and a few of those planets may be inhabitable without extensive modification; these are unknowns at present. Note, however, that humanity's longterm survival does not depend on the existence of planets at all; we could, with present technology, construct space habitats, and we can conceive of ways to turn stars into raw materials.

Even though we are well out on the spiral arm of our galaxy, there are very significant star populations within 500 lightyears; and only 30,000 lightyears away is the center of the galaxy. The whole Milky Way spreads across some 100,000 lightyears.

There are distant galaxies, ranging from our near neighbors at distances comparable to the diameter of our own Milky Way through Andromeda—just visible to the naked eye on a clear night—at 2,000,000 lightyears, on up to the Coma cluster of thousands of galaxies at 500,000,000 lightyears. There are more beyond that distance, but probably the point is made. Each galaxy contains some 100 billion stars on the average, and galaxies tend to occur in clusters. Penetration to one "foreign" galaxy brings access to additional galaxies; there may be as many as 100 billion galaxies out there. We are unlikely to run out of stars for a long time.

Or are we? Starting with our present population and assuming a modest 0.05% population growth, by the time we have used up our billion years there will be more people around than our calculators can handle. (Actually that's the case if we start with only 2 people.) We may need all those stars.

Of course that kind of space travel is not analogous to a long trip with the traveler planning to return. It is better compared to the migrations of the American Indians from Asia to America; no one returned, but each generation moved forward by significant albeit limited steps.

But what are our chances of accomplishing these star treks? That is the same as asking what are the chances of competence.

In perhaps 200,000 years we have gone from animal existence to the capability of living in space. We could, with what we know at present, put permanent colonies in orbit, on the Moon, and in the asteroid belt.

Beyond that we don't know. When we consider interstellar flight, we cannot now know whether we are going to detect the resources we need in the places we will require them. But we do know that discovery and usefulness of "matter" are functions of knowledge. We also know that knowledge is a process which is both self-propelled and accelerating.

If knowledge were to grow at a rate of .00083—roughly the rate of our beginnings—it would multiply 4000-fold within 10,000 years. If the growth rate stabilized at 0.1%, the original stock would grow 21,000-fold. Our current growth rate of about 5% would put us in the position of multiplying knowledge each 5000 years by 100 orders of magnitude.

If we survive there seems little question that the store of knowledge will grow explosively as a function of elapsed time; in a period of a billion years any non-negative growth rate produces astounding results. Although much knowledge becomes obsolete or invalid as a result of new discoveries, still more is additive.

If we live long enough, humanity should be able to reach the stars and other galaxies. It is not necessary that *we* know how it will be done.

\* \* \*

What, then, are our chances of survival?

Well, first there are catastrophes. One of us has made a lot of money writing about one possibility: a celestial collision with a large object at high relative velocities. True, this is a low-probability event; but over a long enough period of time it becomes well-nigh inevitable.

And we have the example of Professor Alvarez's speculations on the extinction of the dinosaurs. There is considerable evidence now, all indicating that the dinosaurs starved after a large comet or asteroid struck the Earth and so changed planetary albedo as to kill off most vegetation.

We have survived whatever disasters have happened to

this planet, but perhaps we exist because some predecessor was utterly wiped out.

There are indications that the Sun, and perhaps Jupiter and Saturn, are not entirely stable.

The solar system may be crossed by inter-stellar clouds and dust; by bands of high radioactivity—as an example, Messier 82 seems to be flooded by speedy gas streams resulting from star explosions and formations. Then too there are some 200 globular clusters in our galaxy, with about half of them near the 100 lightyear line. There are some 500 planetary nebulae, with NGC 7293, accompanied by a large ring of gas, a near neighbor at 85 lightyears.

With such troublesome and potentially violent neighbors—and with so little knowledge about what makes supernovae explode—it is not impossible that a nova or supernova might fry us all. Not likely; but what is unlikely over a period of a billion years? We observed one, fortunately at a healthy range of 4500 lightyears, in 1054 AD. Its remains are visible, a shell of gas 6 lightyears in diameter, with plentiful x-rays, gamma rays, etc.

The Chinese are said to have observed supernovae in 1006 and 1181 as well as in 1054. Tycho Brahe saw one in 1572, and Kepler another in 1604. And most such explosions may be concealed by interstellar dust.

Weiler of the Max Planck Institute for Radioastronomy, distinguishes supernova from dying *and* young stars. An explosion in our galaxy takes place every 20 to 30 years; a supernova blow-up within a dangerous range of Earth is likely to impact terrestrial geology and life every 100 million years (7).

Certainly the immense distances of space act as protective shields. Astronomers are not crying warnings. But over the time span of a billion years many things can and will happen. Weiler's paper implies that we will be threatened ten times by supernova explosions before we must leave the Earth.

Are new stars forming close by? Do we have large aging stars within a dangerous radius? This is the type of warning intelligence we ought to procure. We have the potential to live 100 billion years; we shouldn't want to be cut off in our comparative youth. Our permanent departure from this Earth may be required suddenly, and well before 1 billion AD.

\* \* \*

Speculative answers to the Fermi Paradox ("Where are they?") include one fairly chilling possibility: Civilizations reach a certain stage and commit suicide. They blow themselves up, or otherwise alter their development.

Any rational projection of technology gives us that capability within a short time; or alternately, gives us the capability to make our presence known throughout the galaxy.

In other words, there are reasons other than the daily newscasts for believing we are at a critical point in our history.

As we have said elsewhere, this generation has the resources to start man on his journey out of the solar system. The costs have been estimated at various sums, but no estimate exceeds the cost of the Panama Canal: some 5% of the US budget over a period of fifteen years.

We believe we are on fairly safe ground in asserting that a vigorous program of research and development has a beneficial effect on US and world economics. Some economists do not agree; others seem to have ignored the entire matter. We have seen economic models in which investment is no more than a black box; it doesn't matter *what* you invest in, only the amounts are important. We reject that view, and assert the to us not unreasonable proposition that the sustained economic growth of the sixties was due in large part to the vigorous space program—a program which not only served as the cutting edge of technology, but had profound psychological effects as well.

Although this generation has the resources to move the human race upward to what amounts to a new evolutionary plane—space-dwelling man—it is not at all clear that future generations will be able to afford such an investment. We have a choice: we can believe we are mayflies, doomed within generations; or we can believe we have a future measured in billions of generations. Each belief leads to certain actions.

* * *

Assuming we act as a long-lived people, there are many things we can do.

First, we must acquire full knowledge of the solar system. There's a lot of matter out there, and we need to learn how to make full use of it. In part that's necessary for near-term survival; but it's also practice for the time when we'll have to abandon the solar system.

While that's going on, we can study the nearer stars. For example: if we embark on a real space program, something like solar power satellites as an example, then for literally trivial extra amounts we can orbit a telescope capable not only of finding planets at the distances of nearby stars, but also of studying their cloud structure.

We can study the Sun. As MIT's Philip Morrison is fond of saying, it's insane not to study the Sun.

Those are steps we can take. In fact, if we truly believe our racial lifespan is measured in tens of billions of years—and there is no reason to assume otherwise—then we can set down items that must be accomplished. We don't know how to travel between galaxies. We only dimly see how we might reach stars (although with present resources we could get a few of us to the nearer stars if we wanted to badly enough). But we can take steps toward both goals.

1. As stated, we decide to acquire full knowledge of the solar system, and begin study of the sphere within 100 lightyears of Earth.

2. Find optimal orbits of advance.

3. Search for vital resources within the solar system, and evidence of them beyond it.

4. Identify hazards and dangers; threats to future travellers, and threats to our present system and planet.

5. Build up bases and observation posts in space: the

Moon, L-5 Colonies, satellite islands, major asteroids, nearby planets. Support these with transportation and communications. It is clear that within a decade we could, if we wanted to, have a colony on the Moon, supported by minimal shipments of food and biologicals from Earth. Within a hundred years such a colony could be self-sufficient.

6. Learn to use space itself: build industries using gravity gradients, extreme temperature differences, hard vacuum, asteroid and lunar mines; and learn to reap economic advantages from space. At some point the space program must become economically self-sustaining.

7. As we develop our capabilities for industry in space, we will inevitably learn how to build habitations. After all, in only a short billion years we'll *have* to leave the solar system; why not start developing the ability early? We might want to test it before we've no choices. . .

8. While we're at it, we should experiment with artificial atmospheres.

9. Intensify the search for planetary bodies outside the solar system. This comes as a major bonus to the other activities, yet for space-dwelling man it might be thought the highest priority item of all. How many stars *do* have planets? Is Frank Drake's estimate of one star in 20,000 correct? Stephen Dole estimated some 50 inhabitable planets within 100 lightyears. All these estimates depend entirely on guesses. We have suspicions, but no hard data on the existence of any planets beyond our solar system.

The discovery of the first planet at interstellar distances will begin a new phase in man's relationship with space.

*Conclusion*

Our future depends on our perception of the future. If we are convinced that we have but a short time left, then anything we do will be in vain—and we will do little. Yet if we see mankind as a species barely out of the cradle, with an unimaginably long future ahead, we can act to make that vision a reality.

If we want, the stars are no limit at all, but steps toward a long and interesting future.

# References

(1) Donella H. Meadows et. al. *The Limits to Growth*, Signet, 8th edition (first edition 1972).

(2) Steven Weinberg, *The First Three Minutes*, Basic Books, 1977.

(3) Jerry E. Pournelle, *A Step Farther Out*, Ace Books, 1979.

(4) Jamal N. Islam, "The Ultimate Fate of the Universe," *Sky and Telescope*, January 1979.

(5) Harry L. Shipman, *The Restless Universe*, Houghton-Mifflin, 1978. See in particular the estimated probability of each star having planets based on a formula by Frank Drake, p. 423. The formula refers to "communicative civilizations," and is related to the Fermi paradox.

(6) Stephen H. Dole, *Habitable Planets for Man*, American Elsevier, 2nd ed. 1970.

(7) Weiler, "A New Look at Supernovae Remnants," *Sky and Telescope*, November 1979, pp. 414-418.

EDITOR'S INTRODUCTION TO:

## DOWN & OUT ON
## ELLFIVE PRIME

by Dean Ing

*Dean Ing was also here for the Saturn encounter. A former engineering technician, Dean is a tough-looking man who likes backpacking much as I do. Some day we'll have to hike together.*

*I never met a man who looked less like a college professor, but Ing has acquired a Ph.D. in Communications, and writes meaningfully about the influence of media on modern life. Mrs. Pournelle says that Dean has managed the neat trick of bringing rugged individualism, and some pioneering spirit, into the Groves of Academe. After all, how many professors have their own trout stream?*

*Which may be why Dean can construct such believable characters who live in the wild underground areas of an artificial world . . .*

# DOWN & OUT ON ELLFIVE PRIME

## by Dean Ing

Responding to Almquist's control, the little utility tug wafted from the North dock port and made its gentle pirouette. Ellfive Prime Colony seemed to fall away. Two hundred thousand kilometers distant, blue-white Earth swam into view: cradle of mankind, cage for too many. Almquist turned his long body in its cushions and managed an obligatory smile over frown lines. "If that won't make you homesick, Mr. Weston, nothing will."

The fat man grunted, looking not at the planet he had deserted but at something much nearer. From the widening of Weston's eyes, you could tell it was something big, closing fast. Torin Almquist knew what it was; he eased the tug out, watching his radar, to give Weston the full benefit of it.

When the tip of the great solar mirror swept past, Weston blanched and cried out. For an instant, the view port was filled with cables and the mirror pivot mechanism. Then once again there was nothing but Earth and sharp pinpricks of starlight. Weston turned toward the engineering manager, wattles at his jawline trembling. "Stupid bastard," he grated. "If that'll be your standard joke on new arrivals, you must cause a lot of coronaries."

Abashed, disappointed: "A mirror comes by every fourteen seconds, Mr. Weston. I thought you'd enjoy it. You asked to see the casting facility, and this is where you can see it best. Besides, if you were retired as a heart case, I'd know it." *And the hell with you,* he added silently. Almquist retreated into an impersonal spiel he knew by heart, moving the tug back to gain a panorama of the colony with its yellow legend, *L-5'*, proud and unnecessary on the hull. He moved the controls gently, the blond hairs on his forearm masking the play of tendons within.

The colony hung below them, a vast shining melon the length of the new Hudson River Bridge and nearly a kilometer thick. Another of its three mirror strips, anchored near the opposite South end cap of Ellfive Prime and spread like curved petals toward the sun, hurtled silently past the view port. Almquist kept talking. " . . . Prime was the second industrial colony in space, dedicated in 2007. These days it's a natural choice for a retirement community. A fixed population of twenty-five hundred—plus a few down-and-out bums hiding here and there. Nowhere near as big a place as Orbital General's new industrial colony out near the asteroid belt."

Almquist droned on, backing the tug farther away. Beyond the South end cap, a tiny mote sparkled in the void, and Weston squinted, watching it. "The first Ellfive was a General Dynamics-Lever Brothers project in close orbit, but it got snuffed by the Chinese in 2012, during the war."

"I was only a cub then," Weston said, relaxing a bit. "This colony took some damage too, didn't it?"

Almquist glanced at Weston, who looked older despite his bland flesh. Well, living Earthside with seven billion people tended to age you. "The month I was born," Almquist nodded, "a nuke was intercepted just off the centerline of Ellfive Prime. Thermal shock knocked a tremendous dimple in the hull; from inside, of course, it looked like a dome poking up through the soil south of center."

Weston clapped pudgy hands, a gesture tagging him as neo-Afrikaner. "That'll be the hill, then. The one with the pines and spruce, near Hilton Prime?"

A nod. "Stress analysts swore they could leave the dimple if they patched the hull around it. Cheapest solution—and for once, a pretty one. When they finished bringing new lunar topsoil and distributing it inside, they saw there was enough dirt on the slope for spruce and ponderosa pine roots. To balance thousands of tons of new processed soil, they built a blister out on the opposite side of the hull and moved some heavy hardware into it."

The fat man's gaze grew condescending as he saw the great metal blister roll into view like a tumor on the hull. "Looks slapdash," he said.

"Not really; they learned from DynLever's mistakes. The first Ellfive colony was a cylinder, heavier than an ellipsoid like ours." Almquist pointed through the view port. "Dyn-Lever designed for a low ambient pressure without much nitrogen in the cylinder and raised hell with water transpiration and absorption in a lot of trees they tried to grow around their living quarters. I'm no botanist, but I know Ellfive Prime has an Earthside ecology—the same air you'd breathe in Peru, only cleaner. We don't coddle our grass and trees, and we grow all our crops right in the North end cap below us."

Something new and infinitely pleasing shifted Weston's features. "You used to have an external crop module to feed fifty thousand people, back when this colony was big in manufacturing—"

"Sold it," Almquist put in. "Detached the big rig and towed it out to a belt colony when I was new here. We didn't really need it anymore—"

Weston returned the interruption pointedly: "You didn't let me finish. I put that deal over. OrbGen made a grand sum on it—which is why the wife and I can retire up here. One hand washes the other, eh?"

Almquist said something noncommittal. He had quit wondering why he disliked so many newcomers. He *knew* why. It was a sling-cast irony that he, Ellfive Prime's top technical man, did not have enough rank in OrbGen to be slated for colony retirement. Torin Almquist might last as Civil Projects Manager for another ten years, if he kept a spotless record. Then he would be Earthsided in the crowds and smog and would eat fish cakes for the rest of his life. Unlike his ex-wife, who had left him to teach in a belt colony so that she would never have to return to Earth. And who could blame her? *Shit*.

"I beg your pardon?"

"Sorry; I was thinking. You wanted to see the high-g casting facility? It's that sphere strapped on to the mirror that's swinging toward us. It's moving over two hundred meters per second, a lot faster than the colony floor, being a kilometer and a half out from the spin axis. So at the mirror tip, instead of pulling around one standard g, they're pulling over three g's. Nobody spends more than an hour there. We balance the sphere with storage masses on the other mirror tips.''

Restive, only half-interested: ''Why? It doesn't look very heavy.''

''It isn't,'' Almquist conceded, ''but Ellfive Prime has to be balanced just so if she's going to spin on center. That's why they filled that blister with heavy stored equipment opposite the hill—though a few tons here and there don't matter.''

Weston wasn't listening. ''I keep seeing something like barn doors flipping around, past the other end, ah, end cap.'' He pointed. Another brief sparkle. ''There,'' he said.

Almquist's arm tipped the control stick, and the tug slid farther from the colony's axis of rotation. ''Stacking mirror cells for shipment,'' he explained. ''We still have slag left over from a nitrogen-rich asteroid they towed here in the old days. Fused into plates, the slag makes good protection against solar flares. With a mirror face, it can do double duty. We're bundling up a pallet load, and a few cargo men are out there in P-suits—pressure suits. They—''

Weston would never know, and have cared less, what Almquist had started to say. The colony manager clapped the fingers of his free hand against the wireless speaker in his left ear. His face stiffened with zealot intensity. Fingers flickering to the console as the tug rolled and accelerated, Almquist began to speak into his throat mike—something about a Code Three. Weston knew something was being kept from him. He didn't like it and said so. Then he said so again.

'' . . . happened before,'' Almquist was saying to someone, ''but this time you keep him centered, Radar Prime. I'll haul him in myself. Just talk him out of a panic; you know the drill. Please be quiet, Mr. Weston,'' he added in a top-polite aside.

"Don't patronize me," Weston spat. "Are we in trouble?"

"I'm swinging around the hull; give me a vector," Almquist continued, and Weston felt his body sag under acceleration. "Are you in voice contact?" Pause. "Doesn't he acknowledge? He's on a work-crew-scrambler circuit, but you can patch me in. Do it."

"You're treating me like a child."

"If you don't shut up, Weston, I *will*. Oh, hell, it's easier to humor you." He flicked a toggle, and the cabin speaker responded.

" . . . be okay. I have my explosive riveter," said an unfamiliar voice; adult male, thinned and tightened by tension. "Starting to retro-fire now."

Almquist counted aloud at the muffled sharp bursts. "Not too fast, Versky," he cautioned. "You overheat a rivet gun, and the whole load could detonate."

"Jeez, I'm cartwheeling," Versky cut in. "Hang tight, guys." More bursts, now a staccato hammer. Versky's monologue gave no sign that he had heard Almquist, had all the signs of impending panic.

"Versky, listen to me. Take your goddamn finger off the trigger. We have you on radar. Relax. This is Torin Almquist, Versky. I say again—"

But he didn't. Far beyond, streaking out of the ecliptic, a brief nova flashed against the stars. The voice was cut off instantly. Weston saw Almquist's eyes blink hard, and in that moment the manager's face seemed aged by compassion and hopelessness. Then, very quietly: "Radar Prime, what do you have on scope?"

"Nothing but confetti, Mr. Almquist. Going everywhere at once."

"Should I pursue?"

"Your option, sir."

"And your responsibility."

"Yes, sir. No, don't pursue. Sorry."

"Not your fault. I want reports from you and Versky's cargo-team leader with all possible speed." Almquist flicked toggles with delicate savagery, turned his little vessel around, arrowed back to the dock port. Glancing at Weston, he said, "A skilled cargo man named Yves Versky. Experienced man; should've known better. He floated into a mirror support while horsing those slag cells around and got grazed by it. Batted him hell to breakfast." Then, whispering viciously to himself, "God*damn* those big rivet guns. They can't be used like control jets. Versky knew that."

Then, for the first time, Weston realized what he had seen. A man in a pressure suit had just been blown to small pieces before his eyes. It would make a lovely anecdote over sherry, Weston decided.

Even if Almquist had swung past the external hull blister he would have failed to see, through a darkened view port, the two shabby types looking out. Nobody had official business in the blister. The younger man grimaced nervously, heavy cords bunching at his neck. He was half a head taller than his companion. "What d'you think, Zen?"

The other man yielded a lopsided smile. "Sounds good." He unplugged a pocket communicator from the wall and stuffed it into his threadbare coverall, then leaned forward at the view port. His chunky, muscular torso and short legs ill-matched the extraordinary arms that reached halfway to his knees, giving him the look of a tall dwarf. "I think they bought it, Yves."

"What if they didn't?"

Zen swung around, now grinning outright, and regarded Yves Versky through a swatch of brown hair that was seldom cut. "Hey, do like boss Almquist told you: Relax! They *gotta* buy it."

"I don't follow you."

"Then you'd better learn to. Look, if they recover any pieces, they'll find human flesh. How can they know it was a poor rummy's body thawed after six months in deep freeze? And if they *did* decide it's a scam, they'd have to explain how we planted him in your P-suit. And cut him loose from the blister, when only a few people are supposed to have access here; *and* preset the audio tape and the explosive, *and* coaxed a decent performance out of a lunk like you, *and,*'' he spread his apelike arms wide, his face comically ugly in glee, ''nobody can afford to admit there's a scam counterculture on Ellfive Prime. All the way up to Torin Almquist there'd be just too much egg on too many faces. It ain't gonna happen, Versky.''

The hulking cargo man found himself infected by the grin, but: ''I wonder how long it'll be before *I* see another egg.''

Zen snorted, ''First time you lug a carton of edible garbage out of Hilton Prime, me lad. Jean Neruda's half-blind; when you put on the right coverall, he won't know he has an extra in his recycling crew, and after two days you won't mind pickin' chicken out of the slop. Just sit tight in your basement hidey-hole when you're off duty for a while. Stay away from crews that might recognize you until your beard grows. And keep your head shaved like I told you.''

Versky heaved a long sigh, sweeping a hand over his newly bald scalp. ''You'll drop in on me? I need a lot of tips on the scam life. And—and I don't know how to repay you.''

''A million ways. I'll think of a few, young fella. And sure, you'll see me—whenever I like.''

Versky chuckled at the term *young fella*. He knew Zen might be in his forties, but he seemed younger. Versky followed his mentor to the airlock into the colony hull. ''Well, just don't forget your friend in the garbage business,'' he urged, fearful of his unknown future.

Zen paused in the conduit that snaked beneath the soil of Ellfive Prime. ''Friendship,'' he half-joked, ''varies directly with mutual benefit and inversely with guilt. Put another way,'' he said, lapsing into scam language as he trotted toward the South end cap, ''a friend who's willing to be understood is a joy. One that demands understanding is a pain in the ass.''

''You think too much,'' Versky laughed. They moved softly now, approaching an entry to the hotel basement.

Zen glanced through the spy hole, paused before punching the wall in the requisite place. ''Just like you work too much.'' He flashed his patented gargoyle grin. ''Trust me.

Give your heart a rest."

Versky, much too tall for his borrowed clothing, inflated his barrel chest in challenge. "Do I *look* like a heart murmur?"

A shrug. "You did to OrbGen's doctors, rot their souls—which is why you were due to be Earthsided next week. Don't lay that on *me, ol*' scam; I'm the one who's reprieved you to a low-g colony, if you'll just stay in low-g areas near the end caps." He opened the door.

Versky saw the hand signal and whispered, "I got it: Wait thirty seconds." He chuckled again. "Sometimes I think you should be running this colony."

Zen slipped through, left the door nearly closed, waited until Versky had moved near the slit. "In some ways," he stage-whispered back, "I do." Wink. Then he scuttled away.

At mid-morning the next day, Almquist arranged the accident report and its supporting documents into a neat sequence across his video console. Slouching behind his desk with folded arms, he regarded the display for a moment before lifting his eyes. "What've I forgot, Emory?"

Emory Reina cocked his head sparrowlike at the display. Almquist gnawed a cuticle, watching the soulful Reina's eyes dart back and forth in sober scrutiny. "It's all there," was Reina's verdict. "The only safety infraction was Versky's, I think."

"You mean the tether he should've worn?"

A nod; Reina started to speak but thought better of it, the furrows dark on his olive face.

"Spit it out, dammit," Almquist goaded. Reina usually thought a lot more than he talked, a trait Almquist valued in his assistant manager.

"I am wondering," the little Brazilian said, "if it was really accidental." Their eyes locked again, held for a long moment. "Ellfive Prime has been orbiting for fifty years. Discounting early casualties throughout the war, the colony has had twenty-seven fatal mishaps among OrbGen employees. Fourteen of them occurred during the last few days of the victim's tour on the colony.''

"That's hard data?''

Another nod.

"You're trying to say they're suicides.''

"I am trying not to think so.'' A devout Catholic, Reina spoke hesitantly.

*Maybe he's afraid God is listening. I wish I thought He would.* "Can't say I'd blame some of them,'' Almquist said aloud, remembering. "But not Yves Versky. Too young, too much to live for.''

"You must account for my pessimism,'' Reina replied.

"It's what we pay you for,'' Almquist said, trying in vain to make it airy. "Maybe the insurance people could convince OrbGen to sweeten the Earthside trip for returning people. It might be cheaper in the long run.''

Emory Reina's face said that was bloody likely. "After I send a repair crew to fix the drizzle from that rain pipe, I could draft a suggestion from you to the insurance group,'' was all he said.

"Do that.'' Almquist turned his attention to the desk console. As Reina padded out of the low Center building into its courtyard, the manager committed the accident report to memory storage, then paused. His fingers twitched nervously over his computer-terminal keyboard. Oh, yes, he'd forgotten something, all right. Conveniently.

In moments, Almquist had queried Prime memory for an accident report ten years past. It was an old story in more ways than one. Philip Elroy Hazen: technical editor, born 14 September 2014, arrived on L-5' for first tour to write modification work orders 8 May 2039. Earthsided on 10 May 2041; a standard two-year tour for those who were skilled enough to qualify. A colony tour did not imply any other bonus: The tour *was* the bonus. It worked out very well for the owning conglomerates that controlled literally everything on their colonies. Almquist's mouth twitched: *well, maybe not literally* . . .

Hazen had wangled a second tour to the colony on 23 February 2045, implying that he'd been plenty good at his work. Fatal injury accident report filed 20 February 2047.

Uh-*huh;* uh-*huh!* Yes, by God, there was a familiar ring to it: a malf in Hazen's radio while he was suited up, doing one last check on a modification to the casting facility. Flung off the tip of the mirror and—*Jesus, what a freakish way to go*—straight into a mountain of white-hot slag that had radiated like a dying sun near a temporary processing module outside the colony hull. No recovery attempted; why sift ashes?

Phil Hazen; Zen, they'd called him. The guy they used to say needed rollerskates on his hands; but that was envy talking. Almquist had known Zen slightly, and the guy was an absolute terror at sky-bike racing along the zero-g axis of the colony. Built his own tri-wing craft, even gave it a Maltese cross, scarlet polymer wingskin, and a funny name. The *Red Baron* had looked like a joke, just what Zen had counted on. He'd won a year's pay before other sky-bikers realized it wasn't a streak of luck.

Hazen had always made his luck. With his sky bike—it was with young seasoned spruce and the foam polymer, fine engineering and better craftsmanship, all disguised to lure the suckers. And all without an engineering degree. Zen had just picked up expertise, never seeming to work at it.

And when his luck ran out, it was—Almquist checked the display—only days before he was slated for Earthside. Uh-*huh!*

Torin Almquist knew about the shadowy wraiths who somehow dropped from sight on the colony, to be caught later or to die for lack of medical attention or, in a few cases, to find some scam—some special advantage—to keep them hidden on Ellfive Prime. He'd been sure Zen was a survivor, no matter what the accident report said. What was the phrase? *A scam, not a bum;* being on the scam wasn't quite the same. A scam wasn't down and out of resources; he was down and out of sight. Maybe the crafty Zen had engineered another fatality that wasn't fatal.

Almquist hadn't caught anyone matching the description of Zen. Almost, but not quite. He thought about young Yves

Versky, whose medical report hadn't been all that bad, then considered Versky's life expectancy on the colony versus his chances Earthside. Versky had been a sharp hard-worker too. Almquist leaned back in his chair again and stared at his display. He had no way of knowing that Reina's rain-pipe crew was too late to ward off disaster.

A rain pipe had been leaking long before Grounds Maintenance realized they had a problem. Rain was a simple matter on Ellfive Prime: You built a web of pipes with spray nozzles that ran the length of the colony. From ground level the pipes were nearly invisible, thin lines connected by crosspieces in a great cylindrical net surrounding the colony's zero-g axis. Gravity loading near the axis was so slight that the rain pipes could be anchored lightly.

Yet now and then, a sky-biker would pedal foolishly from the zero-g region or would fail to compensate for the gentle rolling movement generated by the air itself. That was when the rain pipes saved somebody's bacon and on rare occasions suffered a kink. At such times, Almquist was tempted to press for the outlawing of sky bikes until the rabid sports association could raise money for a safety net to protect people and pipes alike. But the cost would have been far too great: It would have amounted to a flat prohibition of sky bikes.

The problem had started a month earlier with a mild collision between a sky bike and a crosspiece. The biker got back intact, but the impact popped a kink on the underside of the attached rain pipe. The kink could not be seen from the colony's axis. It might possibly have been spotted from floor level with a good, powerful telescope.

Inspection crews used safety tethers, which loaded the rain pipe just enough to close the crack while the inspector passed. Then the drizzle resumed for as long as the rain continued. Thereafter, the thrice-weekly afternoon rain from that pipe had been lessened in a line running from Ellfive Prime's Hilton Hotel, past the prized hill, over the colony's one shallow lake, to work-staff apartments that stretched

from the lake to the North end cap, where crops were grown.
Rain was lessened, that is, everywhere but over the pine-
covered hill directly below the kink. Total rainfall was unchanged; but the hill got three times its normal moisture,
which gradually soaked down through a forty-year accumu-
lation of ponderosa needles and humus, into the soil below.

In this fashion the hill absorbed one hundred thousand
kilograms too much water in a month. A little water perco-
lated back to the creek and the lake it fed. Some of it was still
soaking down through the humus overburden. And much of
it—far too much—was held by the underlying slope soil,
which was gradually turning to ooze. The extra mass had
already caused a barely detectable shift in the colony's spin
axis. Almquist had his best troubleshooter, Lee Shumway,
quietly checking the hull for a structural problem near the hull
blister.

Suzanne Nagel was a lissome widow whose second passion was for her sky bike. She had been idling along in
zero-g, her chain-driven propeller a soft whirr behind her,
when something obscured her view of the hill far below. She
kept staring at it until she was well beyond the leak, then
realized the obstruction was a spray of water. Suzy sprint-
pedaled the rest of the way to the end cap, and five minutes
later the rains were canceled by Emory Reina.

Thanks to Suzy Nagel's stamina, the slope did not collapse
that day. But working from inspection records, Reina tragi-
cally assumed that the leak had been present for perhaps three
days instead of a month. The hill needed something—a local
vibration, for example—to begin the mud slide that could
abruptly displace up to two hundred thousand tons of mass
downslope. Which would inevitably bring on the nightmare
more feared than meteorites by every colony manager: spinquake. Small meteorites could only damage a colony, but
computer simulations had proved that if the spin axis shifted
suddenly a spinquake could crack a colony like an egg.

The repair crew was already in place high above when
Reina brought his electrabout three-wheeler to a halt near a
path that led up to the pines. His belt-common set allowed

direct contact with the crew and instant access to all channels, including his private scrambler to Torin Almquist.

"I can see the kink on your video," Reina told the crew leader, studying his belt-slung video. "Sleeve it and run a pressure check. We can be thankful that a leak that large was not over Hilton Prime," he added, laughing. The retired OrbGen executives who luxuriated in the hotel would have screamed raw murder, of course. And the leak would have been noticed weeks before.

Scanning the dwarf apple trees at the foot of the slope, Reina's gaze moved to the winding footpath. In the forenoon quietude, he could hear distant swimmers cavorting in the slightly reduced gravity of the Hilton pool near the South end cap. But somewhere above him on the hill, a large animal thrashed clumsily through the pines. It wasn't one of the half-tame deer; only maladroit humans made that much commotion on Ellfive Prime. Straining to locate the hiker, Reina saw the leaning trees. He blinked. No trick of eyesight; they were really leaning. Then he saw the long shallow mud slide, no more than a portent of its potential, that covered part of the footpath. For perhaps five seconds, his mind grasping the implication of what he saw, Reina stood perfectly still. His mouth hung open.

In deadly calm, coding the alarm on his scrambler circuit: "Torin, Emory Reina. I have a Code Three on the hill. And," he swallowed hard, "potential Code One. I say again, Code One; mud slides on the main-path side of the hill. Over." Then Reina began to shout toward the pines.

Code Three was bad enough: a life in danger. Code Two was more serious still, implying an equipment malfunction that could affect many lives. Code One was reserved for colony-wide disaster. Reina's voice shook. He had never called a Code One before.

During the half-minute it took for Almquist to race from a conference to his office, Reina's shouts flushed not one but two men from the hillside. The first, a heavy individual in golf knickers, identified himself testily as Voerster Weston. He stressed that he was not accustomed to peremptory demands from an overall-clad worker. The second man emerged far to Reina's right but kept hidden in a stand of mountain laurel, listening, surmising, sweating.

Reina's was the voice of sweet reason. "If you want to live, Mr. Weston, please lie down where you are. Slowly. The trees below you are leaning outward, and they were not that way yesterday."

"Damnation, I know that much," Weston howled; "that's what I was looking at. Do you know how wet it is up here? I will not lie down on this muck!"

The man in the laurels made a snap decision, cursed, and stood up. "If you don't, two-belly, I'll shoot you here and now," came the voice of Philip Elroy Hazen. Zen had one hand thrust menacingly into a coverall pocket. He was liberally smeared with mud, and his aspect was not pleasant.

"*O demonio,* another one," Reina muttered. The fat man saw himself flanked, believed Zen's implied lie about a weapon, and carefully levered himself down to the blanket of pine needles. At this moment Torin Almquist answered the Mayday.

There was no way to tell how much soil might slide, but through staccato interchanges Emory Reina described the scene better than his video could show it. Almquist was grim. "We're already monitoring an increase in the off-center spin, Emory; not a severe shift, but it could get to be. Affirmative on that potential Code One. I'm sending a full emergency crew to the blister, now that we know where to start."

Reina thought for a moment, glumly pleased that neither man on the slope had moved. "I believe we can save these two by lowering a safety sling from my crew. They are directly overhead. Concur?"

An instant's pause. "Smart, Emory. And you get your butt out of there. Leave the electrabout, man, just *go!*"

"With respect, I cannot. Someone must direct the sling deployment from here."

"It's your bacon. I'll send another crew to you."

"Volunteers only," Reina begged, watching the slope.

For the moment it seemed firm. Yet a bulge near cosmetically placed slag boulders suggested a second mass displacement. Reina then explained their predicament to the men on the slope, to ensure their compliance.

"It's worse than that," Zen called down. "There was a dugout over there," he pointed to the base of a boulder, "where a woman was living. She's buried, I'm afraid."

Reina shook his head sadly, using his comm set to his work crew. Over four hundred meters above, men were lashing tether lines from crosspieces to distribute the weight of a sling. Spare tethers could be linked by carabiners to make a lifeline reaching to the colony floor. The exercise was familiar to the crew, but only as a drill until now. And they would be hoisting, not lowering.

Diametrically opposite from the hill, troubleshooters converged on the blister where the colony's long-unused reactor and coolant tanks were stored. Their job was simple—in principle.

The reactor subsystems had been designed as portable elements, furnished with lifting and towing lugs. The whole reactor system weighed nearly ten thousand tons, including coolant tanks. Since the blister originally had been built around the stored reactor elements to balance the hill mass, Almquist needed only to split the blister open to space, then lower the reactor elements on quartz cables. As the mass moved out of the blister and away from the hull, it would increase in apparent weight, balancing the downward flow of mud across the hull. Almquist was lucky in one detail: The reactor was not in line with the great solar-mirror strips. Elements could be lowered a long way while repairs were carried out to redistribute the soil.

Almquist marshaled forces from his office. He heard the colony-wide alarm whoop its signal, watched monitors as the colony staff and two thousand other residents hurried toward safety in end-cap domes. His own P-suit, ungainly and dust-covered, hung in his apartment ten paces away. There was no time to fetch it while he was at his post. *Never again,* he promised himself. He divided his attention among monitors showing the evacuation, the blister team, and the immediate problem above Emory Reina.

Reina was optimistic as the sling snaked down. "South a bit," he urged into his comm set, then raised his voice. "Mr. Weston, a sling is above you, a little north. Climb in and buckle the harness. They will reel you in."

Weston looked around him, the whites of his eyes visible from fifty meters away. He had heard the alarm and remembered only that it meant mortal danger. He saw the sling turning gently on its thin cable as it neared him.

"Now, steady as she goes," Reina said, then, "Stop." The sling collapsed on the turf near the fat man. Reina, fearful that the mud-covered stranger might lose heart, called to assure him that the sling would return.

"I'll take my chances here," Zen called back. The sling could mean capture. The fat man did not understand that any better than Reina did.

Voerster Weston paused halfway into his harness, staring up. Suddenly he was scrambling away from it, tripping in the sling, mindless with the fear of rising into a synthetic sky. Screaming, he fled down the slope. And brought part of it with him.

Reina saw apple trees churning toward him in time to leap atop his electrabout and kept his wits enough to grab branches as the first great wave slid from the slope. He saw Weston disappear in two separate upheavals, swallowed under the mud slide he had provoked. Mauled by hardwood, mired to his knees, Reina spat blood and turf. He hauled one leg free, then the other, pulling at tree limbs. The second man, he saw, had slithered against a thick pine and was now trying to climb it.

Still calm, voice indistinct through his broken jaw, Reina redirected the sling crew. The sling harness bounced upslope near the second man. "Take the sling," Reina bawled.

Now Reina's whole world shuddered. It was a slow, perceptible motion, each displacement of mud worsening the off-center rotation and slight acceleration changes that could bring more mud that could bring worse. . . . Reina forced his mind back to the immediate problem. He could not see himself at its focus.

Almquist felt the tremors, saw what had to be done. "Emory, I'm sending your relief crew back. Shumway's in the blister. They don't have time to cut the blister now; they'll have to blow it open. You have about three minutes to get to firm ground. Then you run like hell to South end cap."

"As soon as this man is in the sling," Reina mumbled. Zen had already made his decision, seeing the glistening ooze that had buried the fat man.

"Now! Right fucking *now*," Almquist pleaded. "I can't delay it a millisecond. When Shumway blows the blister open it'll be a sudden shake, Emory. You know what that means?"

Reina did. The sharp tremor would probably bring the entire middle of the slope thundering down. Even if the reactor could be lowered in minutes, it would take only seconds for the muck to engulf him. Reina began to pick his way backward across fallen apple trees, wondering why his left arm had an extra bend above the wrist. He kept a running fire of instructions to the rain-pipe crew as Zen untangled the sling harness. Reina struggled toward safety in pain, patience, reluctance. And far too slowly.

"He is buckled in," Reina announced. His last words were, "Haul away." He saw the mud-spattered Zen begin to rise, swinging in a broad arc, and they exchanged "OK" hand signals before Reina gave full attention to his own escape. He had just reached the edge of firm ground when Lee Shumway, moving with incredible speed in a full P-suit, ducked through a blister airlock and triggered the charges.

The colony floor bucked once, throwing Reina off stride. He fell on his fractured ulna, rolled, opened his mouth— perhaps to moan, perhaps to pray. His breath was bottled by mud as he was flung beneath a viscous gray tide that rolled numberless tons of debris over him.

The immense structure groaned, but held. Zen swayed sickeningly as Ellfive Prime shook around him. He saw Reina die, watched helplessly as a retiree home across the valley sagged and collapsed. Below him, a covey of Quetzal birds burst from the treetops like jeweled scissors in flight. As he was drawn higher he could see more trees slide.

The damage worsened; too many people had been too slow. The colony was rattling everything that would rattle. Now it was all rattling louder. Somewhere, a shrill whistle keened as precious air and more precious water vapor rushed toward a hole in the sunlight windows.

When the shouts above him became louder than the carnage below, Zen began to hope. Strong arms reached for his and moments later he was attached to another tether. "I can make it from here," he said, calling his thanks back as he hauled himself toward the end-cap braces.

A crew man with a video comm set thrust it toward Zen as he neared a ladder. "It's for you," he said, noncommittal.

For an instant, an eon, Zen's body froze, though he continued to waft nearer. Then he shrugged and took the comm set as though it were ticking. He saw a remembered face in the video. Wrapping an arm around the ladder, he nodded to the face. "Don Bellows here," he said innocently.

Pause, then a snarl: "You wouldn't believe my mixed emotions when I recognized you on the monitor. Well, *Mister* Bellows, Adolf Hitler here." Almquist went on, "Or you'll think so damned quick unless you're in my office as fast as your knuckles will carry you."

The crew man was looking away, but he was tense. He knew. Zen cleared his throat for a whine. "I'm scared—"

"You've been dead for ten years, Hazen. How can you be scared? Frazer there will escort you; his instructions are to brain you if he has to. I have sweeping powers right now. Don't con me and don't argue; I need you right here, right now."

By the time Zen reached the terraces with their felled, jumbled crops, the slow shakes had subsided. They seemed to diminish to nothing as he trotted, the rangy Frazer in step behind, to an abandoned electrabout. Damage was everywhere, yet the silence was oppressive. A few electrical fires were kindling in apartments as they moved toward the Colony Center building. Some fires would be out, others out of control, in minutes. The crew man gestured Zen through the courtyard and past two doors. Torin Almquist stood looming over his console display, ignoring huge shards of glass that littered his carpet.

Almquist adjusted a video monitor. "Thanks, Frazer; would you wait in the next room?" The crew man let his face complain of his idleness but complied silently. Without glancing from the monitors, Almquist transfixed the grimy Zen. "If I say the word, you're a dead man. If I say a different word, you go Earthside in manacles. You're still here only because I wanted you here all the time, just in case I ever needed you. Well, I need you now. If you hadn't been dropped into my lap we'd have found you on a Priority One. Never doubt that.

"If I say a third word, you get a special assistant's slot—I can swing that—for as long as I'm here. All I'm waiting for is one word from *you*. If it's a lie, you're dead meat. Will you help Ellfive Prime? Yes or no?"

Zen considered his chances. Not past that long-legged Frazer. They could follow him on monitors for some distance anyhow unless he had a head start. "Given the right conditions," Zen hazarded.

Almquist's head snapped up. "My best friend just died for you, against my better judgment. *Yes or no.*"

"Yes. I owe you nothin', but I owe him somethin'."

Back to the monitors, speaking to Zen: "Lee Shumway's crew has recovered our mass balance, and they can do it again if necessary. I doubt there'll be more mud slides, though; five minutes of spinquakes should've done it all."

Zen moved to watch over the tall man's bare arms. Two crews could be seen from a utility tug monitor, rushing to repair window leaks where water vapor had crystallized in space as glittering fog. The colony's external heat radiator was in massive fragments, and the mirrors were jammed in place. It was going to get hot in Ellfive Prime. "How soon will we get help from other colonies?"

Almquist hesitated. Then, "We won't, unless we fail to

cope. OrbGen is afraid some other corporate pirate will claim salvage rights. And when you're on my staff, everything I tell you is privileged data.''

"You think the danger is over?''

"Over?'' Almquist barked a laugh that threatened to climb out of control. He ticked items off on his fingers. ''We're losing water vapor; we have to mask mirrors and repair the radiator, or we fry; half our crops are ruined and food stores may not last; and most residents are hopeless clods who have no idea how to fend for themselves. *Now* d'you see why I diverted searches when I could've taken you twice before?''

Zen's mouth was a cynical curve.

Almquist: "Once when you dragged a kid from the lake filters I could've had you at the emergency room.'' Zen's eyebrows lifted in surprised agreement. "And once when a waiter realized you were scamming food from the Hilton service elevator.''

"That was somebody else, you weren't even close. But okay, you've been a real sweetheart. Why?''

"Because you've learned to live outside the system! Food, shelter, medical help, God knows what else; you have another system that hardly affects mine, and now we're going to teach your tricks to the survivors. This colony is going to make it. You were my experimental group, Zen. You just didn't know it.'' He rubbed his chin reflectively. "By the way, how many guys are on the scam? Couple of dozen?'' An optimist, Torin Almquist picked what he considered a high figure.

A chuckle. "Couple of hundred, you mean.'' Zen saw slack-jawed disbelief and went on: "They're not all guys. A few growing families. There's Wandering Mary, Maria Polyakova; our only registered nurse, but I found her dugout full of mud this morning. I hope she was sleepin' out.''

"Can you enlist their help? If they don't help, this colony can still die. The computer says it will, as things stand now. It'll be close, but we won't make it. How'd you like to take your chances with a salvage crew?''

"Not a chance. But I can't help just standing here swappin' wind with you."

"Right." Eyes bored into Zen's, assessing him. The thieves' argot, the be-damned-to-you gaze, suggested a man who was more than Hazen *had* been. "I'll give you a temporary pass. See you here tomorrow morning; for now, look the whole colony over, and bring a list of problems and solutions as you see 'em."

Zen turned to leave, then looked back. "You're really gonna let me just walk right out." A statement of wonder, and of fact.

"Not without this," Almquist said, scribbling on a plastic chit. He thrust it toward Zen. "Show it to Frazer."

Inspecting the cursive scrawl: "Doesn't look like much."

"*Mas que nada,*" Almquist smiled, then looked quickly away as his face fell. *Better than nothing;* his private joke with Emory Reina. He glanced at the retreating Zen and rubbed his forehead. Grief did funny things to people's heads. To deny a death you won't accept, you invest his character in another man. Not very smart when the other man might betray you for the sheer fun of it. Torin Almquist massaged his temples and called Lee Shumway. They still had casualties to rescue.

Zen fought a sense of unreality as he moved openly in broad daylight. Everyone was lost in his own concerns. Zen hauled one scam from his plastic bubble under the lake surface, half dead in stagnant air after mud from the creek swamped his air exchanger. An entire family of scams, living as servants in the illegal basement they had excavated for a resident, had been crushed when the foundation collapsed.

But he nearly wept to find Wandering Mary safe in a secret conduit, tending to a dozen wounded scams. He took notes as she told him where her curative herbs were planted and how to use them. The old girl flatly refused to leave her charges, her black eyes flashing through wisps of gray hair, and Zen promised to send food.

The luck of Sammy the Touch was holding strong. The crop compost heap that covered his half-acre foam shell seemed to insulate it from ground shock as well. Sammy patted his little round tummy, always a cheerful sign, as he ushered Zen into the bar where, on a good night, thirty scams might be gathered. If Zen was the widest-ranging scam on Ellfive Prime, Sammy the Touch was the most secure.

Zen accepted a glass of potato vodka—Sammy was seldom *that* easy a touch—and allowed a parody of the truth to be drawn from him. He'd offered his services to an assistant engineer, he said, in exchange for unspecified future privileges. Sammy either bought the story or took a lease on it. He responded after some haggling with the promise of a hundred kilos of "medicinal" alcohol and half his supply of bottled methane. Both were produced from compost precisely under the noses of the crop crew, and both were supplied on credit. Sammy also agreed to provision the hidden infirmary of Wandering Mary. Zen hugged the embarrassed Sammy and exited through one of the conduits, promising to pick up the supplies later.

Everywhere he went, Zen realized, the scams were coping better than legal residents. He helped a startlingly handsome middle-aged blonde douse the remains of her smoldering wardrobe. Her apartment complex had knelt into its courtyard and caught fire.

"I'm going to freeze tonight," Suzy Nagel murmured philosophically.

He eyed her skimpy costume and doubted it. Besides, the temperature was slowly climbing, and there wouldn't *be* any night until the solar mirrors could be pivoted again. There were other ways to move the colony to a less reflective position, but he knew Almquist would try the direct solutions first.

Farmer Brown—no one knew his original name—wore his usual stolen agronomy-crew coverall as he hawked his pack load of vegetables among residents in the low-rent area. He had not assessed all the damage to his own crops, tucked and espaliered into corners over five square kilometers of the colony. Worried as he was, he had time to hear a convincing story. "Maybe I'm crazy to compete against myself," he told Zen, "but you got a point. If a salvage outfit takes over, it's kaymag." KMAG: Kiss my ass good-bye. "I'll sell you seeds, even breeding pairs of hamsters, but don't ask me to face the honchos in person. You remember about the vigilantes, ol' scam."

Zen nodded. He gave no thought to the time until a long shadow striped a third of the colony floor. One of the mirrors had been coaxed into pivoting. Christ, he was tired—but why not? It would have been dark long before, on an ordinary day. He sought his sleeping quarters in Jean Neruda's apartment, hoping Neruda wouldn't insist on using Zen's eyesight to fill out receipts. Their arrangement was a comfortable quid pro quo, but please, thought Zen, not tonight!

He found a more immediate problem than receipts. Yves Versky slumped, trembling, in the shambles of Neruda's place, holding a standard emergency oxygen mask over the old man's face. The adjoining office had lost one wall in the spinquake, moments after the recycling crew ran for end-cap domes.

"I had to hole up here," Versky gasped, exhausted. "Didn't know where else to go. Neruda wouldn't leave either. Then the old fool smelled smoke and dumped his goldfish bowl on a live power line. Must've blown half the circuits in his body." Like a spring-wound toy, Versky's movements and voice diminished. "Took me two hours of mouth-to-mouth before he was breathing steady, Zen. Boy, have I got a headache."

Versky fell asleep holding the mask in place. Zen could infer the rest. Neruda, unwilling to leave familiar rooms in his advancing blindness. Versky, unwilling to abandon a life, even that of a half-electrocuted, crotchety old man. Yet Neruda was right to stay put: Earthside awaited the OrbGen employee whose eyes failed.

Zen lowered the inert Versky to the floor, patted the big man's shoulder. More than unremitting care, he had shown stamina and first-aid expertise. Old Neruda awoke once, half-manic, half-just disoriented. Zen nursed him through it with surface awareness. On another level he was cataloguing items for Almquist, for survivors, for Ellfive Prime.

And on the critical level a voice in him jeered, *bullshit: For yourself.* Not because Almquist or Reina had done him any favors, but because Torin Almquist was right. The colony manager could find him eventually; maybe it was better to rejoin the system now, on good terms. Besides, as the only man who could move between the official system and the scam counterculture, he could really wheel and deal. It might cause some hard feelings in the conduits, but . . . Zen sighed, and slept. Poorly.

It was two days before Zen made every contact he needed, two more when Almquist announced that Ellfive Prime would probably make it. The ambient temperature had stabilized. Air and water losses had ceased. They did not have enough stored food to provide three thousand daily calories per person beyond twenty days, but crash courses in multicropping were suddenly popular, and some immature crops could be eaten.

"It'd help if you could coax a few scams into instructing," Almquist urged as he slowed to match Zen's choppy pace. They turned from the damaged crop terraces toward the Center.

"Unnn-likely," Zen intoned. "We still talk about wartime, when vigilantes tried to clean us out. They ushered a couple of nice people out of airlocks, naked, which we think was a little brusque. Leave it alone; it's working."

A nod. "Seems to be. But I have doubts about the maturing rates of your seeds. Why didn't my people know about those hybrid daikon radishes and tomatoes?"

"You were after long-term yield," Zen shrugged. "This hot weather will ripen the stuff faster, too. We've been hiding a dozen short-term crops under your nose, including dandelions better than spinach. Like hamster haunch is better'n rabbit, and a lot quicker to grow."

Almquist could believe the eighteen-day gestation period, but was astonished at the size of the breeding stock. "You realize your one-kilo hamsters could be more pet than protein?''

"Not in our economy," Zen snorted. "It's hard to be sentimental when you're down and out. Or stylish either.'' He indicated his frayed coverall. ''By the time the rag man gets this, it won't yield three meters of dental floss.''

Almquist grinned for the first time in many days. What his new assistant had forgotten in polite speech, he made up in the optimism of a young punk. He corrected himself: an *old* punk. "You know what hurts? You're nearly my age and look ten years younger. How?''

It wasn't a specific exercise, Zen explained. It was attitude. "You're careworn," he sniffed. "Beat your brains out for idling plutocrats fifty weeks a year and then wonder why you age faster than I do.'' Wondering headshake.

They turned toward the Center courtyard. Amused, Almquist said, "You're a plutocrat?''

"Ain't racin' my motors. Look at all the Indians who used to live past a hundred. A Blackfoot busted his ass like I do, maybe ten or twenty weeks a year. They weren't dumb; just scruffy.''

Almquist forgot his retort; his desk console was flashing for attention. Zen wandered out of the office, returning with two cups of scam "coffee.'' Almquist sipped it between calls, wondering if it was really brewed from ground dandelion root, considering how this impudent troll was changing his life, could change it further.

Finally he sat back. "You heard OrbGen's assessment,'' he sighed. "I'm a Goddamned hero, for now. Don't ask me about next year. If they insist on making poor Emory a sacrificial goat to feed ravening stockholders, I can't help it.''

Impassive: "Sure you could. You just let 'em co-opt you.'' Zen sighed, then released a sad troglodyte's smile. "Like you co-opted me.''

"I can unco-opt. Nothing's permanent.''

"You said it, bubba.''

Almquist took a long breath, then cantilevered a forefinger

in warning. "Watch your tongue, Hazen. When I pay your salary, you pay some respect." He saw the sullen look in Zen's eyes and bored in. "Or would you rather go on the scam again and get Earthsided the first chance I get? I haven't *begun* to co-opt you yet," he glowered. "I have to meet with the Colony Council in five minutes—to explain a lot of things, including you. When I get back, I want a map of those conduits the scams built, to the best of your knowledge."

A flood of ice washed through Zen's veins. Staring over the cup of coffee that shook in his hands: "You *know* I can't do that."

Almquist paused in the doorway, his expression smug. "You know the alternative. Think about it," he said, and turned and walked out.

When Torin Almquist returned, his wastebasket was overturned on his desk. A ripe odor wrinkled his nose for him even before he saw what lay stop the wastebasket like an offering on a pedestal: a lavish gift of human excrement. His letter opener, an antique, protruded from the turd. It skewered a plastic chit, Zen's pass. On the chit, in draftsman's neat printing, full caps: I THOUGHT ABOUT IT.

Well, you sure couldn't mistake his answer, Almquist reflected as he dumped the offal into his toilet. Trust Zen to make the right decision.

Which way had he gone? Almquist could only guess at the underground warrens built during the past fifty years, but chose not to guess. He also knew better than to mention Zen to the Colony Council. The manager felt a twinge of guilt at the choice, truly no choice at all, that he had forced on Zen—but there was no other way.

If Zen knew the whole truth, he might get careless, and a low profile was vital for the scams. The setup benefited all of Ellfive Prime. Who could say when the colony might once more need the counterculture and its primitive ways?

And that meant Zen had to disappear again, genuinely down and out of reach. If Almquist himself didn't know exactly where the scams hid, he couldn't tell OrbGen even under drugs. And he didn't intend to tell. Sooner or later

OrbGen would schedule Torin Almquist for permanent Earthside rotation, and when that day came he might need help in his own disappearance. *That* would be the time to ferret out a secret conduit, to contact Zen. The scams could use an engineering manager who knew the official system inside out.

Almquist grinned to himself and brewed a cup of dandelion coffee. Best to get used to the stuff now, he reasoned; it would be a staple after he retired, down and out on Ellfive Prime.

# EDITOR'S INTRODUCTION TO:

## THE STUDY SYNDROME

### by Jerry Pournelle

*Lincoln, Nebraska doesn't sound like much of a place for changing human destiny, even though it is said to have the highest "quality of life" in the US. (I note that quality of life doesn't include getting a drink on Sunday, or after midnight.) Otherwise it's a nice little city with a good convention center, where, this spring, two important events took place.*

*One was the first face to face meeting of the Board of Directors of the L-5 Society.*

*Time for a commercial. If you're concerned about space; if you think we really ought to go Out There, then one way you can help is to join the L-5 Society. It isn't a large outfit, but it has its successes—as for example the defeat of the give-away Lunar Treaty. L-5 helped keep solar power satellites alive during the last days of the Carter administration, and has provided some inputs to the Reagan administration's space policy planning committee. We'd do a lot more if we had more resources; which means more members.*

*You can join by sending $20 to L-5, 1060 E. Elm, Tucson, Arizona, 85719. Dues are $20/year, and we need every nickel (although we do have a $15 rate for students). Join now and go recruit a friend.*

*The other event was a five day formal report by the Department of Energy and NASA on the Solar Power Satellite (SPS) concept. That one* should *have changed the world.*

# THE STUDY SYNDROME

## Jerry Pournelle

In our earlier paper, Stefan Possony and I argue that the human race will be around for 100 billion years.

Roll that number around on your tongue a bit. One hundred billion years. That is our future. Compared to it, our past is miniscule, vanishing, a tiny drop in the bucket. We are so very young, and so much lies ahead of us; our only limit is the limit to everything, our only certain doom is the end of the universe—and who knows, after a hundred billion years, perhaps we will know how to prevent that too. It may be that as a species we have no inevitable doom; certainly 100 billion years is, for those of us here and now, close enough to eternity.

But to realize anything like that potential, we must outlive our planet. We must outlive our sun. Eventually we will outlive our galaxy.

None of this is impossible. We can today conceive of interstellar ships, although it will be some time before we can build them; meanwhile, the first step is within our grasp right now. We can, if we will, make our home not Only One Earth, but in the solar system at large. In this generation, in this decade, we could put a settlement on the Moon. Not a base, or an outpost; but a settlement, a colony; a home. We know how to do this now, with today's technology, for about what we now spend on cosmetics, less than what we spend on tobacco.

It is an idea whose time has come; and SPS gives us another reason to start now.

\* \* \*

Solar Power Satellites are not a particularly new idea.
They've been around in science fiction since the Golden Age,
but they were first seriously proposed by Peter Glaser in
1968. The concept is simple enough: instead of building solar
power installations on Earth, where the Sun isn't up at night,
and weather and season can interfere with the sunlight received, put the solar collectors in orbit and send the power
down to Earth.

The concept may be simple, but there are some tough
technical problems. SPS is *big*, 10 kilometers long by 5 wide
for the solar cells and mirrors. It has an antenna a full
kilometer in diameter, employing 100,000 klystron tubes, to
send the power down as microwaves. SPS requires massive
construction in orbit, which means long-term life support
systems, not only down low under the Van Allen Belt, but up
in geosynchronous orbit as well. It's a bold concept; is it too
bold?

Concepts are easy. Finding out whether something like
SPS is really practical is much more difficult—and very
expensive. Although the SPS idea has been around since
1968, nobody took it seriously; but came the energy crunches
and DOE decided to look at "exotic" ideas. They took a first
cut at SPS—and it survived. They took a second slice, and it
still looked good. So finally they bit the bullet and came up
with $25 million bucks; enough to take a really hard look.
The report of that study was given in Lincoln last spring.

It was a thorough study. Every aspect of SPS was
examined. As an example, the University of California at
Davis exposed honey bees to microwaves, then studied their
social behavior. There were preliminary studies of antenna
sites shosen to avoid migratory bird flyways. Arecibo was
employed to squirt microwaves into the ionosphere, with
Guadeloupe Island's big dish looking to see what effects that
heating might have. Bechtel Corporation (which builds large
structures here on Earth) looked at support structures and
wind loadings on the ground antenna site. Grumman looked
at various control systems for moving around large structures
in space. And so forth.

The results were pretty clear: no show stoppers. There don't look to be insoluble problems. True, there are some unanswered questions. Some environmentalists worry about long term exposure to very low levels of microwaves. The Arecibo experiments didn't send up as much energy as SPS would send down, and that's got to be done full scale. Construction in orbit isn't easy. There probably will be some adverse effects on certain commercial FM radio frequencies—the point where the power beam enters the ionosphere becomes a "radio mirror", so taxi drivers in New York may find themselves tuned in to Los Angeles, which means reassigning some frequencies and changing some radio sets.

And so forth. But *any* energy system has problems, which is why DOE included comparative assessment studies in the package: and the amazing thing is that SPS looks pretty good compared to everything else. Even the dollar costs look reasonable. SPS is quite expensive to install; but there aren't any fuel costs, and it's not much more expensive per kilowatt than nuclear power. The SPS environmental costs are small compared to coal, and if you add into coal the cost of the rail transport system we'll have to build, then SPS may even be *cheaper*.

Furthermore, SPS development money is spent here, not shipped overseas to buy oil; and while DOE will not allow "fallout" technology to be entered as benefits of SPS, we all know there will be some. The SPS program would be big. It would involve building new launch vehicles, and it would make space operations routine. Thus we'd inevitably begin space industries.

And to make it even nicer, the program phases well; of the hundred billion dollars required for SPS, a full $75 billion is *investment* in a fleet of new launch vehicles. All the engineering research and feasibility demonstrations are done with the first $25 billion.

So. We had a $25 million study, and no one found any show stoppers.

We know the country is in a critical energy situation that

isn't going to get better by itself.

So what did the study recommend?

More studies, of course.

\* \* \*

It sounds a reasonable principle. Study a number of competing energy systems, and when you know which is best, then and only then do you invest much in it. Don't spend money on an idea that may come a cropper, and don't spend lots of money on a system that costs too much. Get the right system first shot, and if you don't yet know which one that is, why then study until you do. . .

It sounds reasonable, but it's insane, if you concede that the energy crisis is real.

Look: suppose that today you knew which was the "best" answer to the energy crisis. It would still take years before you could produce kiloWatts. Worse: there is an optimum growth for any big program. Starting with too much money can be worse than not starting at all: there are only so many good people available in any given year. Starting up with too much money means that you're hiring anything that can walk up the steps.

So there are startup lags, and there's a definite limit to the optimum rate of growth of a big program; any big program, whether it's coal, or "heavy oils", or shale, or synthetic fuels, or fusion, or fast breeders. . .

So what should we do? Start them all?

Yes. That is, if you're really serious about the energy crisis, you ought seriously to consider starting a number of projects, with the firm intention of writing off the least promising lines when you know more.

The SPS study included one of the very few comparative assessments of energy systems. It looked at SPS, fusion, coal, synfuels, fast breeders, light water reactors, centralized ground-based solar, and exotics like ocean thermal.

But what they never assessed was the cost of doing nothing.

Yet—aren't the economic, environmental, and public health costs of having no new energy sources quite well known? The public health costs of coal are all too predictable: some 15 to 30 thousand people a year killed by emphysema, not to mention 50 to 100 miners, people killed by train wrecks (by 1998 even with extreme conservation we will be mining and shipping at least 6 billion tons of coal each year), etc. The environmental costs are high: those sludges that come out of stack gas scrubbers take up more volume than the original coal did—where do we put them? And what of acid rains?

Doing nothing commits us to coal and oil.

In fact, if I could make one change in the assessment system, I would mandate that all studies examine the effects of doing nothing. I think you'll find it's cheaper to start a number of programs, cancel those that don't work, and eat the losses.

If they are truly losses. Robert Heinlein said years ago that good research always makes money; and that seems a demonstrable proposition. High technology exports kept the US in a favorable balance of trade for many years, and could again if we could ever catch up. At the very worst, some good R&D programs in energy and space would tempt bright young men and women into science and technology instead of accounting and law. . .

Doing nothing is expensive.

\* \* \*

Instead, of course, we study the problem—if indeed we do that. A bureaucrat named N. Douglas Pewitt took great pains to declare that he had killed any follow up study of SPS. As I write this, the L-5 Society is frantically trying to get Congress to restore the SPS study funds. But DOE is very proud of the SPS "assessment methodology"—as if study methodology were more important than the energy crisis.

I have a better plan.

One unsettled controversy regarding SPS is just how much

of it could be built with lunar materials. David Criswell,
formerly Director of the Lunar and Planetary Institute at
Houston, finds that about 90% of what SPS needs is found in
industrial quantities on the Moon. Now true, we don't know
whether solar cells can be manufactured in quantity, either on
the Moon, or in orbit from lunar materials; but it looks a very
fruitful field for study. Instead of building a fleet of Heavy
Lift Launch Vehicles, Criswell suggests we use Shuttle to
send up a lunar exploration/exploitation team. With any luck
they'll be able to use enough lunar materials to substantially
lower the cost of SPS.

And for that matter, lunar materials are valuable even
without SPS. How valuable won't be known until we invest
more in lunar refining technologies, but we're going to need
raw materials for space industries, and we're going to need
mass for constructing space industrial stations. Both could
come from the Moon.

Which brings us to the bottom line.

We're going to space some day. Why not now? France was
saved from the humiliating defeat of 1870-71 by the Eiffel
Tower: it may not have been a lot of use, but it was a splendid
achievement and a symbol of the vigor of France. Can the
United States not be saved from the humiliations of Viet Nam
and Watergate by building a lunar colony?

A lunar colony would be a national goal that we could take
pride in. It would aid the entire human race, move us all
toward that 100 billion year future—

And it might make a potful of money, too.

EDITOR'S INTRODUCTION TO:

THREE POEMS

by Helene Knox

*These poems come from the time when the first VOYAGER went to Jupiter, and we found four new worlds. Ms. Knox was at JPL for the encounter, and I first read her poems while the data were flowing in.*

*Set the scene. To get to Cal Tech's Jet Propulsion Laboratory (JPL), you drive out the arroyo where a hundred years ago Tiburcio Vasquez and his gang fled from a Pasadena posse. JPL is there because, eons ago, they actually tested small rockets at the labs, and the City Fathers were concerned lest Cal Tech blow up parts of Pasadena and San Marino; the arroyo was considered expendable.*

*Of course since that time others have moved in, so that not far from JPL's fenced and guarded boundary they've built one of the most expensive bedroom communities in the world, but what the hell. JPL still rules the arroyo, and like most such institutions boasts a mixed architecture: ultra-modern glass office tower, lower buildings with vaguely Spanish arches and verandas, interspersed with "temporary" clapboard buildings constructed during World War II. The press facility is in the von Karman Center, a one-story somewhat modernistic structure of severely square architecture at the very boundary of the labs. There are guards everywhere, and you wear badges at all times.*

*Inside the von Karman center there's a large room with raised dais for scientists, a wooden platform for TV camera crews, lots of chairs for reporters and guests—and rather spectacularly, an exact full-size replica of VOYAGER. The walls are lined with magnificent photographs taken by one or another of the JPL-operated spacecraft (there's been a lot of them); just at the moment, of course, the data from VOYAGER 1 dominates. Everywhere you look you can see Jupiter and his satellites in detail orders of magnitude better than the largest earthbound telescopes ever could deliver.*

*The room is reasonably full; not quite as full as it was during the VOYAGER 1 encounter, certainly not packed to the gills the way it was the night VIKING landed on Mars, but many of the regular science press corps are present, as well as a goodly contingent of science fiction writers.*

*Come now the scientists charged with understanding just what VOYAGER is telling us. Frank Bristow, JPL press relations manager, introduces Larry Soderblom. Dr. Soderblom, US Geological Survey, is deputy team leader of the imaging science experiments. (Imaging science means what you think it does: getting pictures we can look at.)*

*He opens rather simply. "We used to think we understood planets."*

*Next time somebody questions the value of spacecraft like VOYAGER, quote that line.*

*                    *    *    **

*Let me set another scene.*

*During an encounter, the von Karman Center at JPL is a madhouse. All over the Center there are TV screens, and every minute or so there's a new picture coming in from Jupiter. Go to the bathroom and the spacecraft has moved another 10,000 miles, and you may have missed something important.*

*There are two press rooms, both overcrowded. Each room has a dozen or so tables, and on each table are two or three typewriters and telephones supposedly reserved for working press types with deadlines to meet. In addition to those hordes (VOYAGER 1 drew reporters from nearly every major paper in the country) there are reps from magazines with short lead time (such as Science News). Add to the* mixture a sprinkling of columnists and book writers. Now stir in over two dozen science fictioneers thoughtfully invited by JPL Public Relations Director Frank Colella, and the rooms are jammed. Moreover, they stay that way. Nobody dares leave because of the nature of the data coming in.

I know that doesn't sound reasonable. Sure, there's a big thrill attached to being there as it happens, but you'd think those of us without short deadlines could with some profit sit back and wait. Unfortunately it doesn't work that way. If you don't see those pictures as they come in, the chances are good that you'll never see them again, and I expect that's worth an explanation.

Start with the spacecraft. They have aboard a good slow-scan TV camera which takes a picture of whatever the science team has decided to look at. The picture is recorded aboard the spacecraft—and now what can you do with it? You certainly aren't going to send it across half a billion miles as a picture! Instead, the image is broken up into little bits of data, mere strings of numbers, which are squirted at 115,000 bits/second through a high-gain antenna towards Earth. Incidentally, the Caltech-designed transmitter sending that data uses less than 100 Watts, which means that receiving the picture is a little like seeing a 100 Watt lightbulb blinking on and off at a distance of 500 million miles.

The string of numbers comes through the Deep Space network to JPL, and is recorded on tape. It is of course totally incomprehensible to humans, so the data must be translated by a computer. The computer takes those numbers and generates an image on a TV screen. Scientists and reporters get to look at the picture at exactly the same time.

The image stays up until another one comes in, then the old one vanishes. Now sure, the data string has been recorded, and the image could in theory be generated again—but the two spacecraft will send back some 40,000 pictures over their lifetimes, and there's nowhere near enough money to make hard copies of all of them. In practice JPL makes black and white photos of the images thought really interesting, color photos of those especially so, and lithographs of the *most spectacular; but all together that's a very small percentage of the total.*

\* \* \*

*Thanks to JPL's recent policy of inviting science fiction writers to their spectaculars, the VOYAGER encounters became a kind of gathering of the clan. The Andersons, the Heinleins, the Nivens, George Scithers, Van Vogt, Gordon Dickson, Hal Clement, Fred Pohl, John Carr, the Goldins, Greg Benford, the Williamsons, Rick Sternbach, Ted Sturgeon, Harry Stine, and a host of others came out for one or the other, and since I live out here it seemed like a great occasion to throw a party. Two parties, actually, one after each VOYAGER went by.*

*There was a slightly different character to each.*

*After VOYAGER 1 we were all keyed up, excited by our first look at not one, but four new planets, as well as the new information on Jupiter himself.*

*After VOYAGER 2 there was excitement, but it was a bit wistful as well. Sure, the VOYAGERS went on to Saturn, and in November 1980 we'll get new looks at the Saturnian system: six more planets, including Titan, the largest "moon" in our neighborhood; and we'll be surprised indeed if there aren't new surprises.* [And indeed there were. The Saturnian system couldn't have been invented by all the known science fiction writers with unlimited supplies of the best possible dope. JEP, December 1980.] *But—we won't see Jupiter close up again until the GALILEO spacecraft arrives there in 1985; and meanwhile, as we partied, SKY-LAB was falling.*

*GALILEO will be a highly ambitious project. If all goes well, it will fly from Canaveral in 1982, the first interplanetary mission to use Shuttle to get to Earth orbit.*

*From Earth, GALILEO will head for, not Jupiter, but Mars: by coming close to Mars, the spacecraft picks up free velocity. And by close, they mean close: GALILEO will come within 275 miles of the Martian surface before heading on to Jupiter in June-July of 1985 (and I know where I'll be then!).*

They'll send down a probe into Jupiter's atmosphere. It won't last long. Once the Probe has died, Orbiter's main engine will send the spacecraft caroming around among the moons. While there it will collect data on Jupiter's magnetic field and the plasmas that permeate the Jovian system: and that information will tell scientists a lot about plasmas and plasma stability in general, allowing better theories on just how plasmas behave.

A good theory of plasma activity is a major requirement for developing practical fusion generators.

Meanwhile, planetary scientists are in a fever pitch of activity. Throughout all of man's history we've had only one planet to study. Theory outstripped data; it's very hard to select among theories about anything if you've only one specimen to examine. Now, though, we've had a good look at all the inner planets plus the four Jovian "moons" plus Jupiter himself. There are new data, and from those data we'll get new and better theories of the planets: all of them, including the one we live on.

[And now, of course, we have Saturnian data: new moons, ring systems, a wealth of data . . .]

As Helmholz observed in the last century, "The most practical thing in the world is a good theory."

The best way to get new theories is to have your old ones shot down by new observations.

We used to think we understood planets. Now, thanks to the spacecraft, we know better.

\* \* \*

So. That's the setting in which I first encountered Helene Knox. And literally while I was reading her poem "NASA", I heard that the GALILEO mission was in trouble.

It's still in trouble; in fact, the Carter administration pretty well killed it. Whether it will or can be restored isn't known as I write this.

Meanwhile, Helene Knox, who has captured an essence worth preserving.

# THREE POEMS

*NASA*

Parapets
   within a spoon.

Speak of truth
   within a lie.

Astronauts
   collect the moon,

then, splash home
   to die.

*Elegy*

I fall away,
   spinning in my sleep.

The inner vortex of a slow dream
   floats sideways past tomorrow.

Three cosmonauts melted in space,
   today, in galactic time.

Measure time from a far star,
   our molten blood.

*Inner*
*Space*

Too many lives
   confuse the body.

The blood is flowing
   a contrary direction:

down and within—
   the orbits of love.

# EDITOR'S INTRODUCTION TO:

## OUR LADY OF THE SAUROPODS

### by Robert Silverberg

*One way I avoid work is by playing with my friend Ezekial, who happens to be a micro computer; and one of his favorite pastimes is to link up with other computers (and their humans) in a nation-wide net through which pours more information than anyone could possibly absorb.*

*Take mail for example: it flashes up on the screen at a rate faster than I can read it, and waits for me to do something with it; and I have many choices. I can, with the touch of a button, put it into electronic "file folders" to be recovered later. Another button lets me reply—I can even include portions of the message I'm replying to if I wish—and send copies to others. And so forth.*

*In late 1979 there flashed into my electronic mailbox a fascinating message: Professor Luis de Alverez, Nobel prizeman at the University of California at Berkeley, had speculated that the extinction of the dinosaurs was caused by an asteroid striking the Earth.* Lucifer's Hammer *had happened for real.*

*And lo, at the 1980 meeting of the American Association for the Advancement of Science (held that year in San Francisco), Dr. de Alverez presented some quite convincing evidence, based in part on, of all things, distribution of the rare element iridium in sea-bottom mud.*

*Since that time there have been other studies, and they all strongly suggest that's what happened: a large asteroid crashed into Earth, vaporizing so much water and dust that the sky became a mirror, reflecting back most of the sunlight; so for several years the lights went out, and plants died, and the large critters which depended on warm tropical jungles died away.*

Lucifer's Hammer *indeed. And fair warning: it has happened before, at about 100 million year intervals; and we have not had an asteroidal impact for about 100 million years. We're due. Not this year or this century or even this millenium, perhaps; but it's going to happen, and when it does, it would be well to have some life boats.*

\* \* \*

*Robert Silverberg is an authentic science fiction super star. He won the first "best new writer" Hugo ever given; he was a prominent adventure-story writer in the golden days of the 50's and 60's; he wrote a half-dozen popular archaeology books that are still in print; and then turned to something so different that the profession coined it "the new Silverberg."*

*"I knew what I wanted to read," Bob said once. "And no one was writing that kind of story, so I thought I would." The "new Silverberg" included* Dying Inside, Son of Man, Nightwings, *and others. Opinions are very mixed: some critics hated* Dying Inside; *others think it one of the few genuine classics in the science fiction genre. No one has ever doubted Bob's ability to tell stories.*

*I first met Robert Silverberg just after I had been elected President of Science Fiction Writers of America. Bob had been the second President of SFWA (that's pronounced seff-wah) following founder Damon Knight. I expected the ex-presidents to be helpful, and they all were. Bob, however, did more: he went out of his way to express confidence in my ability to handle the myriad problems which we faced. That helped a lot.*

*Bob Silverberg periodically "retires" from writing; but then he finds that he has another story which insists on bursting out. This one, combining L-5 Colonies and Alverez's theory on the extinction of dinosaurs, is one of them.*

# OUR LADY OF THE SAUROPODS

## Robert Silverberg

*21 August. 0750 hours.* Ten minutes since the module
meltdown. I can't see the wreckage from here, but I can smell
it, bitter and sour against the moist tropical air. I've found a
cleft in the rocks, a kind of shallow cavern, where I'll be safe
from the dinosaurs for a while. It's shielded by thick clumps
of cycads, and in any case it's too small for the big predators
to enter. But sooner or later I'm going to need food, and then
what? I have no weapons. How long can one woman last,
stranded and more or less helpless, aboard Dino Island, a
habitat unit not quite fifteen hundred meters in diameter that
she's sharing with a bunch of active, hungry dinosaurs?

I keep telling myself that none of this is really happening.
Only I can't quite convince myself of this.

My escape still has me shaky. I can't get out of my mind
the funny little bubbling sound the tiny powerpak made as it
began to overheat. In something like fourteen seconds my
lovely mobile module became a charred heap of fused-to-
gether junk, taking with it my communicator unit, my food
supply, my laser gun, and just about everything else. But for
the warning that funny little sound gave me, I'd be so much
charred junk, too. Better off that way, most likely.

When I close my eyes, I imagine I can see Habitat Vronsky
floating serenely in orbit a mere one hundred twenty kilometers away. What a beautiful sight! The walls gleaming like
platinum, the great mirror collecting sunlight and flashing it
into the windows, the agricultural satellites wheeling around
it like a dozen tiny moons. I could almost reach out and touch
it. Tap on the shielding and murmur, "Help me, come for
me, rescue me." But I might just as well be out beyond

Neptune as sitting here in the adjoining Lagrange slot.
There's no way I can call for help. The moment I move
outside this protective cleft in the rock I'm at the mercy of my
saurians, and their mercy is not likely to be tender.

Now it's beginning to rain—artificial, like practically everything else on Dino Island. But it gets you just as wet as the
natural kind. And just as clammy. Pfaugh.

Jesus, what am I going to do?

*0815 hours.* The rain is over for now. It'll come again in
six hours. Astonishing how muggy, dank, thick the air is.
Simply breathing is hard work, and I feel as though mildew is
forming on my lungs. I miss Vronsky's clear, crisp, everlast-
ing springtime air. On previous trips to Dino Island I never
cared about the climate. But of course I was snugly englobed
in my mobile unit, a world within a world, self-contained,
self-sufficient, isolated from all contact with this place and
its creatures. Merely a roving eye, traveling as I pleased,
invisible, invulnerable. Can they sniff me in here?

We don't think their sense of smell is very acute. And the
stink of the burned wreckage dominates the place at the
moment. But I must reek with fear signals. I feel calm now,
but it was different when I got out of the module. Scattered
pheromones all over the place, I bet.

Commotion in the cycads. *Something's coming in here!*
Long neck, small birdlike feet, delicate grasping hands. Not
to worry. Struthiomimus, is all—dainty dino, fragile,
birdlike critter barely two meters high. Liquid golden eyes
staring solemnly at me. It swivels its head from side to side,
ostrichlike, click-click, as if trying to make up its mind about
coming closer to me. *Scat!* Go peck a stegosaur. Let me
alone.

It withdraws, making little clucking sounds. Closest I've
ever been to a live dinosaur. Glad it was one of the little ones.

*0900 hours.* Getting hungry. What am I going to eat?

They say roasted cycad cones aren't too bad. How about
raw ones? So many plants are edible when cooked and

poisonous otherwise. I never studied such things in detail. Living in our antiseptic little L5 habitats, we're not required to be outdoors-wise, after all. Anyway, there's a fleshy-looking cone on the cycad just in front of the cleft, and it's got an edible look. Might as well try it raw, because there's no other way. Rubbing sticks together will get me nowhere.

Getting the cone off takes some work. Wiggle, twist, snap, tear—*there*. Not as fleshy as it looks. Chewy, in fact. It's a little like munching on rubber. Decent flavor, though. And maybe some useful carbohydrate.

The shuttle isn't due to pick me up for thirty days. No-body's apt to come looking for me, or even to think about me, before then. I'm on my own. Nice irony there: I was desperate to get out of Vronsky and escape from all the bickering and maneuvering, the endless meetings and memoranda, the feinting and counterfeinting, all the ugly political crap that scientists indulge in when they turn into administrators. Thirty days of blessed isolation on Dino Island! An end to that constant dull throbbing in my head from the daily in-fighting with Director Sarber. Pure research again! And then the meltdown, and here I am cowering in the bushes, wonder-ing which comes first, starving or getting gobbled by some cloned tyrannosaur.

*0930 hours*. Funny thought just now. Could it have been sabotage?

Consider Sarber and I, feuding for weeks over the issue of opening Dino Island to tourists. Crucial staff vote coming up next month. Sarber says we can raise millions a year for expanded studies with a program of guided tours and perhaps some rental of the island to film companies. I say that's risky for the dinos and for the tourists, destructive of scientific values, a distraction, a sellout. Emotionally the staff's with me, but Sarber waves figures around, shows fancy income projections, and generally shouts and blusters. Tempers run-ning high, Sarber in lethal fury at being opposed, barely able to hide his loathing for me. Circulating rumors—designed to get back to me—that if I persist in blocking him, he'll abort my career. Which is malarkey, of course. He may outrank me, but he has no real authority over me. And then his politeness yesterday. *(Yesterday?* An eon ago!) Smiling smarmily, telling me he hopes I'll rethink my position during my observation tour on the island. Wishing me well. Had he gimmicked my powerpak? I guess it isn't hard, if you know a little engineering, and Sarber does. Some kind of timer set to withdraw the insulator rods? Wouldn't be any harm to Dino Island itself, just a quick, compact, localized disaster that implodes and melts the unit and its passenger. So sorry, terrible scientific tragedy, what a great loss! And even if by some fluke I got out of the unit in time, my chances of surviving here as a pedestrian for thirty days would be pretty skimpy, right? Right.

It makes me boil to think that someone would be willing to murder you over a mere policy disagreement. It's barbaric. Worse than that, it's tacky.


*1130 hours.* I can't stay crouched in this cleft forever. I'm going to explore Dino Island and see if I can find a better hideout. This one simply isn't adequate for anything more than short-term huddling. Besides, I'm not as spooked as I was right after the meltdown. I realize now that I'm not going to find a tyrannosaur hiding behind every tree. And even if I do, tyrannosaurs aren't going to be much interested in scrawny stuff like me.

Anyway, I'm a quick-witted higher primate. If my humble mammalian ancestors seventy million years ago were able to elude dinosaurs well enough to survive and inherit the earth, I should be able to keep from getting eaten for the next thirty days. And, with or without my cozy little mobile module, I want to get out into this place, whatever the risks. Nobody's ever had a chance to interact this closely with the dinos before.

Good thing I kept this pocket recorder when I jumped from the module. Whether I'm a dino's dinner or not, I ought to be able to set down some useful observations.

*1830 hours.* Twilight is descending now. I am camped near the equator in a lean-to flung together out of tree-fern fronds—a flimsy shelter—but the huge fronds conceal me, and with luck I'll make it through to morning. That cycad cone doesn't seem to have poisoned me yet, and I ate another one just now, along with some tender new fiddleheads uncoiling from the heart of a tree fern. Spartan fare, but it gives me the illusion of being fed.

In the evening mists I observe a brachiosaur, half-grown but already colossal, munching in the treetops. A gloomy-looking triceratops stands nearby, and several of the ostrichlike struthiomimids scamper busily in the underbrush, hunting I know not what. No sign of tyrannosaurs all day. There aren't many of them here, anyway, and I hope they're all sleeping off huge feasts somewhere in the other hemisphere.

What a fantastic place this is!

I don't feel tired. I don't even feel frightened—just a little wary.

I feel exhilarated, as a matter of fact.

Here I sit, peering out between fern fronds at a scene out of the dawn of time. All that's missing is a pterosaur or two flapping overhead, but we haven't brought those back yet. The mournful snufflings of the huge brachiosaur carry clearly even in the heavy air. The struthiomimids are making sweet honking sounds. Night is falling swiftly, and the great shapes out there take on dreamlike, primordial wonder.

What a brilliant idea it was to put all the Olsen-process dinosaur reconstructs aboard a little L5 habitat of their very own and turn them loose to re-create the Mesozoic! After that unfortunate San Diego event with the tyrannosaur it became politically unfeasible to keep them anywhere on Earth, I know, but, even so, this is a better scheme. In just a little more than seven years Dino Island has taken on an altogether convincing illusion of reality. Things grow so fast in this lush, steamy, high-$CO_2$ tropical atmosphere! Of course we haven't been able to duplicate the real Mesozoic flora, but

we've done all right using botanical survivors, cycads and
tree ferns and horsetails and palms and ginkgos and au-
racarias, and thick carpets of mosses and selaginellas and
liverworts covering the ground. Everything has blended and
merged and run amok. It's hard now to recall the bare and
unnatural look of the island when we first laid it out. Now
it's a seamless tapestry in green and brown, a dense jungle
broken only by streams, lakes, and meadows, encapsulated
in spherical metal walls some five kilometers in circumference.

And the animals, the wonderful, fantastic, grotesque animals.

We don't pretend that the real Mesozoic ever held any such
mix of fauna as I've seen today, stegosaurs and corythosaurs
side by side, a triceratops sourly glaring at a brachiosaur,
struthiomimus contemporary with iguanodon, a wild unsci-
entific jumble of Triassic, Jurassic, and Cretaceous, a
hundred million years of the dinosaur reign scrambled together. We take what we can get. Olsen-process reconstructs
require sufficient fossil DNA to permit the computer synthesis, and we've been able to find that in only some twenty
species so far. The wonder is that we've accomplished even
that much to replicate the complete DNA molecule from
battered and sketchy genetic information millions of years
old, to carry out the intricate implants in reptilian host ova, to
see the embryos through to self-sustaining levels. The only
word that applies is *miraculous*. If our dinos come from eras
millions of years apart, so be it: We do our best. If we have no
pterosaur and no allosaur and no archaeopteryx, so be it: We
may have them yet. What we already have is plenty to work
with. Someday there may be separate Triassic, Jurassic, and
Cretaceous satellite habitats, but none of us will live to see
that, I suspect.

Total darkness now. Mysterious screechings and hissings
out there. This afternoon as I moved cautiously but in delight
from the wreckage site up near the roation axis to my present
equatorial camp, sometimes coming within fifty or a hundred
meters of living dinos, I felt a kind of ecstasy. Now my fears

are returning, and my anger at this stupid marooning. I imagine clutching claws reaching for me, terrible jaws yawning above me.

I don't think I'll get much sleep tonight.

*22 August. 0600 hours.* Rosy-fingered dawn comes to Dino Island, and I'm still alive. Not a great night's sleep, but I must have had some, because I can remember fragments of dreams. About dinosaurs, naturally. Sitting in little groups, some playing pinochle and some knitting sweaters. And choral singing, a dinosaur rendition of *The Messiah* or Beethoven's Ninth. I don't remember which, I think I'm going nuts.

I feel alert, inquisitive, and hungry. Especially hungry. I know we've stocked this place with frogs and turtles and other small-size anachronisms to provide a balanced diet for the big critters. Today I'll have to snare some for myself, grisly though I find the prospect of eating raw frog's legs.

I don't bother getting dressed anymore. With rain showers programmed to fall four times a day, it's better to go naked anyway. Mother Eve of the Mesozoic, that's me! And without my soggy tunic I find that I don't mind the greenhouse atmosphere of the habitat half as much as I did.

Out to see what I can find.

The dinosaurs are up and about already, the big herbivores munching away, the carnivores doing their stalking. All of them have such huge appetites that they can't wait for the sun to come up. In the bad old days when the dinos were thought to be reptiles, of course, we'd have expected them to sit there like lumps until daylight got their body temperatures up to functional levels. But one of the great joys of the reconstruct project was the vindication of the notion that dinosaurs were warm-blooded animals, active and quick and pretty damned intelligent. No sluggardly crocodilians, these! Would that they were, if only for my survival's sake.

*1130 hours.* A busy morning. My first encounter with a major predator.

There are nine tyrannosaurs on the island, including three born in the past eighteen months. (That gives us an optimum predator-to-prey ratio. If the tyrannosaurs keep reproducing and don't start eating each other, we'll have to begin thinning them out. One of the problems with a closed ecology— natural checks and balances don't fully apply.) Sooner or later I was bound to encounter one, but I had hoped it would be later.

I was hunting frogs at the edge of Cope Lake. A ticklish business: calls for agility, cunning, quick reflexes. I remember the technique from my girlhood—the cupped hand, the lightning pounce—but somehow it's become a lot harder in the last twenty years. Superior frogs these days, I suppose. There I was kneeling in the mud, swooping, missing, swooping, missing; some vast sauropod snoozing in the lake, probably our diplodocus; a corythosaur browsing in a stand of ginkgo trees, quite delicately nipping off the foul-smelling yellow fruits. Swoop. Miss. Swoop. Miss. Such intense concentration on my task that old T. rex could have tiptoed right up behind me and I'd never have noticed. But then I felt a subtle something, a change in the air, maybe, a barely perceptible shift in dynamics. I glanced up and saw the corythosaur rearing on its hind legs, looking around uneasily, pulling deep sniffs into that fantastically elaborate bony crest that houses its early-warning system. *Carnivore alert!* The corythosaur obviously smelled something wicked this way coming, for it swung around between two big ginkgos and started to go galumphing away. Too late. The treetops parted, giant boughs toppled, and out of the forest came our original tyrannosaur, the pigeon-toed one we call Belshazzar, moving in its heavy, clumsy waddle, ponderous legs working hard, tail absurdly swinging from side to side. I slithered into the lake and scrunched down as deep as I could go in the warm, oozing mud. The corythosaur had no place to slither. Unarmed, unarmored, it could only make great bleating sounds, terror mingled with defiance, as the killer bore down on it.

I had to watch. I had never actually seen a kill before. In a graceless but wondrously effective way the tyrannosaur dug its hind claws into the ground, pivoted astonishingly, and, using its massive tail as a counterweight, moved in a ninety-degree arch to knock the corythosaur down with a stupendous sidewise swat of its huge head. I hadn't been expecting that. The corythosaur dropped and lay on its side, snorting in pain and feebly waving its limbs. Now came the coup de grace with hind legs, and then the rending and tearing, the jaws and the tiny arms at last coming into play. Burrowing chin-deep in the mud, I watched in awe and weird fascination. There are those among us who argue that the carnivores ought to be segregated—put on their own island—that it is folly to allow reconstructs created with such effort to be casually butchered this way. Perhaps in the beginning that made sense, but not now, not when natural increase is rapidly filling the island with young dinos. If we are to learn anything about these animals, it will only be by reproducing as closely as possible their original living conditions. Besides, would it not be a cruel mockery to feed our tyrannosaurs on hamburger and herring?

The killer fed for more than an hour. At the end came a scary moment: Belshazzar, blood-smeared and bloated, hauled himself ponderously down to the edge of the lake for a drink. He stood no more than ten meters from me. I did my most convincing imitation of a rotting log, but the tyrannosaur, although it did seem to study me with a beady eye, had no further appetite. For a long while after he departed I stayed buried in the mud, fearing he might come back for dessert. And eventually there was another crashing and bashing in the forest—not Belshazzar this time, though, but a younger one with a gimpy arm. It uttered a sort of whinnying sound and went to work on the corythosaur carcass. No surprise: We already knew from our observations that tyrannosaurs had no prejudices against carrion.

Nor, I found, did I.

When the coast was clear, I crept out and saw that the two tyrannosaurs had left hundreds of kilos of meat. Starvation knoweth no pride and also few qualms. Using a clamshell for my blade, I started chopping away at the corythosaur.

Corythosaur meat has a curiously sweet flavor—nutmeg and cloves, dash of cinnamon. The first chunk would not go down. You are a pioneer, I told myself, retching. You are the first human ever to eat dinosaur meat. *Yes, but why does it have to be raw?* No choice about that. Be dispassionate, love. Conquer your gag reflex or die trying. I pretended I was eating oysters. This time the meat went down. It didn't stay down. The alternative, I told myself grimly, is a diet of fern fronds and frogs, and you haven't been much good at catching the frogs. I tried again. Success!

I'd have to call corythosaur meat an acquired taste. But the wilderness is no place for picky eaters.

*23 August. 1300 hours.* At midday I found myself in the southern hemisphere, along the fringes of Marsh Marsh, about a hundred meters below the equator. Observing herd behavior in sauropods: five brachiosaurs, two adult and three young, moving in formation, the small ones in the center. By *small* I mean only some ten meters from nose to tail tip. Sauropod appetites being what they are, we'll have to thin that herd soon, too, especially if we want to introduce a female diplodocus into the colony. *Two* species of sauropods breeding and eating like that could devastate the island in three years. Nobody ever expected dinosaurs to reproduce like rabbits—another dividend of their being warm-blooded, I suppose. We might have guessed it, though, from the vast quantity of fossils. If that many bones survived the catastrophes of a hundred-odd million years, how enormous the living Mesozoic population must have been! An awesome race in more ways than their mere physical mass.

I had a chance to do a little herd thinning myself just now. Mysterious stirring in the spongy soil right at my feet, and I looked down to see triceratops eggs hatching. Seven brave little critters, already horny and beaky, scrabbling out of a nest, staring around defiantly. No bigger than kittens, but active and sturdy from the moment they were born.

The corythosaur meat has probably spoiled by now. A more pragmatic soul very likely would have augmented her diet with one or two little ceratopsians. I couldn't bring myself to do it.

They scuttled off in seven different directions. I thought briefly of catching one and making a pet out of it. Silly idea.

*25 August. 0700 hours.* Start of the fifth day. I've done three complete circumambulations of Dino Island. Slinking around on foot is fifty times as risky as cruising around in a module, and fifty thousand times as rewarding. I make camp in a different place every night. I don't mind the humidity any longer. And despite my skimpy diet I feel pretty healthy. Raw dinosaur, I know now, is a lot tastier than raw frog. I've become an expert scavenger—the sound of a tyrannosaur in the forest now stimulates my salivary glands instead of my adrenals. Going naked is fun, too. And I appreciate my body much more, since the bulges that civilization put there have begun to melt away.

Nevertheless, I keep trying to figure out some way of signaling Habitat Vronsky for help. Changing the position of the reflecting mirrors, maybe, so I can beam an SOS? Sounds nice, but I don't even know where the island's controls are located, let alone how to run them. Let's hope my luck holds out another three and a half weeks.

*27 August. 1700 hours.* The dinosaurs know that I'm here and that I'm some extraordinary kind of animal. Does that sound weird? How can great dumb beasts *know* anything? They have such tiny brains. And my own brain must be softening on this protein-and-cellulose diet. Even so, I'm starting to have peculiar feelings about these animals. I see them *watching* me. An odd, knowing look in their eyes, not stupid at all. They stare, and I imagine them nodding, smiling, exchanging glances with each other, discussing me. I'm supposed to be observing them, but I think they're observing me, too, somehow.

No, that's just crazy. I'm tempted to erase the entry. But I suppose I'll leave it as a record of my changing psychological state, if nothing else.

*28 August. 1200 hours.* More fantasies about the dinosaurs. I've decided that the big brachiosaur—Bertha—plays a key role here. She doesn't move around much, but there are always lesser dinosaurs in orbit around her. Much eye contact. *Eye contact between dinosaurs?* Let it stand. That's my perception of what they're doing. I get a definite sense that there's communication going on here, modulating over some wave that I'm not capable of detecting. And Bertha seems to be a central nexus, a grand totem of some sort, a—a switchboard? What am I talking about? What's happening to me?

*30 August. 0945 hours.* What a damned fool I am! Serves me right for being a filthy voyeur. Climbed a tree to watch iguanodons mating at the foot of Bakker Falls. At the climactic moment the branch broke. I dropped twenty meters. Grabbed a lower limb or I'd be dead now. As it is, pretty badly smashed around. I don't think anything's broken, but my left leg won't support me and my back's in bad shape. Internal injuries, too? Not sure. I've crawled into a little rock shelter near the falls. Exhausted and maybe feverish. Shock, most likely. I suppose I'll starve now. It would have been an honor to be eaten by a tyrannosaur, but to die from falling out of a tree is just plain humiliating.

The mating of iguanodons is a spectacular sight, by the way. But I hurt too much to describe it now.

*31 August. 1700 hours.* Stiff, sore, hungry, hideously thirsty. Leg still useless, and when I try to crawl even a few meters, I feel as if I'm going to crack in half at the waist. High fever.

How long does it take to starve to death?

*1 September. 0700 hours.* Three broken eggs lying near me when I awoke. Embryos still alive—probably stegosaur—but not for long. First food in forty-eight hours. Did the eggs fall out of a nest somewhere overhead? Do stegosaurs make their nests in trees, dummy?

Fever diminishing. Body aches all over. Crawled to the stream and managed to scoop up a little water.

*1330 hours*. Dozed off. Awakened to find haunch of fresh meat within crawling distance. Struthiomimus drumstick, I think. Nasty sour taste, but it's edible. Nibbled a little, slept again, ate some more. Pair of stegosaurs grazing not far away, tiny eyes fastened on me. Smaller dinosaurs holding a kind of conference by some big cycads. And Bertha Brachiosaur is munching away in Ostrom Meadow, benignly supervising the whole scene.

This is absolutely crazy.

I think the dinosaurs are taking care of me. But why would they do that?

*2 September. 0900 hours*. No doubt of it at all. They bring me eggs, meat, even cycad cones and tree-fern fronds. At first they delivered things only when I slept, but now they come hopping right up to me and dump things at my feet. The struthiomimids are the bearers—they're the smallest, most agile, quickest hands. They bring their offerings, stare me right in the eye, pause as if waiting for a tip. Other dinosaurs watching from the distance. This is a coordinated effort. I am the center of all activity on the island, it seems. I imagine that even the tyrannosaurs are saving choice cuts for me. Hallucination? Fantasy? Delirium of fever? I feel lucid. The fever is abating. I'm still too stiff and weak to move very far, but I think I'm recovering from the effects of my fall. With a little help from my friends.

*1000 hours*. Played back the last entry. Thinking it over. I don't *think* I've gone insane. If I'm sane enough to be worried about my sanity, how crazy can I be? Or am I just fooling myself? There's a terrible conflict between what I think I perceive going on here and what I know I ought to be perceiving.

*1500 hours*. A long, strange dream this afternoon. I saw all the dinosaurs standing in the meadow, and they were connected to one another by gleaming threads, like the telephone lines of olden times, and all the threads centered on Bertha. As if she's the switchboard, yes. And telepathic messages were traveling through her to the others. An extrasensory hookup, powerful pulses moving along the lines. I dreamed that a small dinosaur came to me and offered me a line and, in pantomime, showed me how to hook it up, and a great flood of delight went through me as I made the connection. And when I plugged it in, I could feel the deep and heavy thoughts of the dinosaurs, the slow, rapturous philosophical interchanges.

When I woke, the dream seemed bizarrely vivid, strangely real, the dream ideas lingering as they sometimes do. I saw the animals about me in a new way. As if this is not just a zoological research station but a community, a settlement, the sole outpost of an alien civilization—an alien civilization native to Earth.

Come off it. These animals have minute brains. They spend their days chomping on greenery, except for the ones that chomp on other dinosaurs. Compared with dinosaurs, cows and sheep are downright geniuses.

I can hobble a little now.

*3 September. 0600 hours.* The same dream again last night, the universal telepathic linkage. Sense of warmth and love flowing from dinosaurs to me.

And once more I found fresh tyrannosaur eggs for breakfast.

*5 September. 1100 hours.* I'm making a fast recovery. Up and about, still creaky, but not much pain left. They still feed me. Though the struthiomimids remain the bearers of food, the bigger dinosaurs now come close, too. A stegosaur nuzzled up to me like some Goliath-sized pony, and I petted its rough, scaly flank. The diplodocus stretched out flat and seemed to beg me to stroke its immense neck.

If this is madness, so be it. There's a community here,

loving and temperate. Even the predatory carnivores are part of it: Eaters and eaten are aspects of the whole, yin and yang. Riding around in our sealed modules, we could never have suspected any of this.

They are gradually drawing me into their communion. I feel the pulses that pass between them. My entire soul throbs with that strange new sensation. My skin tingles.

They bring me food of their own bodies, their flesh and their unborn young, and they watch over me and silently urge me back to health. Why? For sweet charity's sake? I don't think so. I think they want something from me. More than that. I think they need something from me.

What could they need from me?

*6 September. 0600 hours.* All this night I have moved slowly through the forest in what I can only term an ecstatic state. Vast shapes, humped, monstrous forms barely visible by dim glimmer, came and went about me. Hour after hour I walked unharmed, feeling the communion intensify. I wandered, barely aware of where I was, until at last, exhausted, I have come to rest here on this mossy carpet, and in the first light of dawn I see the giant form of the great brachiosaur standing like a mountain on the far side of Owen River.

I am drawn to her. I could worship her. Through her vast body surge powerful currents. She is the amplifier. By her are we all connected. The holy mother of us all. From the enormous mass of her body emanate potent healing impulses.

I'll rest a little while. Then I'll cross the river to her.

*0900 hours.* We stand face to face. Her head is fifteen meters above mine. Her small eyes are unreadable. I trust her and I love her.

Lesser brachiosaurs have gathered behind her on the riverbank. Farther away are dinosaurs of half a dozen other species, immobile, silent.

I am humble in their presence. They are representatives of a dynamic, superior race, which but for a cruel cosmic accident would rule the Earth to this day, and I'm coming to revere them, to bear witness to their greatness.

Consider: They endured for a hundred forty million years in ever-renewing vigor. They met all evolutionary challenges, except the one of sudden and catastrophic climatic change, against which nothing could have protected them. They multiplied and proliferated and adapted, dominating land and sea and air, covering the globe. Our own trifling, contemptible ancestors were nothing next to them. Who knows what these dinosaurs might have achieved if that crashing asteroid had not blotted out their light? What a vast irony: millions of years of supremacy ended in a single generation by a chilling cloud of dust. But until then—the wonder, the grandeur. . .

Only beasts, you say? How can you be sure? We know just a shred of what the Mesozoic was really like, just a slice, literally the bare bones. The passage of a hundred million years can obliterate all traces of civilization. Suppose they had language, poetry, mythology, philosophy? Love, dreams, aspirations? No, you say, they were beasts, ponderous and stupid, that lived mindless, bestial lives. And I reply that we puny hairy ones have no right to impose our own values on them. The only kind of civilization we can understand is the one we have built. We imagine that our own trivial accomplishments are the determining case, that computers and spaceships and broiled sausages are such miracles that they place us at evolution's pinnacle. But now I know otherwise. Humans have done marvelous, even incredible, things, yes. But we would never have existed at all, had this greatest of races been allowed to live to fulfill its destiny.

I feel the intense love radiating from the titan that looms above me. I feel the contact between our souls steadily strengthening and deepening.

The last barriers dissolve.

And I understand at last.

I am the chosen one. I am the vehicle. I am the bringer of rebirth, the beloved one, the necessary one. Our Lady of the Sauropods am I, the holy one, the prophetess, the priestess.

Is this madness? Then it is madness, and I embrace it.

Why have we small hairy creatures existed at all? I know now. It is so that through our technology we could make possible the return of the great ones. They perished unfairly. Through us, they are resurrected aboard this tiny globe in space.

I tremble in the force of the need that pours from them.

*I will not fail you,* I tell the great sauropods before me, and the sauropods send my thoughts reverberating to all the others.

*20 September. 0600 hours.* The thirtieth day. The shuttle comes from Habitat Vronsky today to pick me up and deliver the next researcher.

I wait at the transit lock. Hundreds of dinosaurs wait with me, each close beside the next, both the lions and the lambs, gathered quietly, their attention focused entirely on me.

Now the shuttle arrives, right on time, gliding in for a perfect docking. The airlocks open. A figure appears. Sarber himself! Coming to make sure I didn't survive the meltdown, or else to finish me off.

He stands blinking in the entry passage, gaping at the throngs of placid dinosaurs arrayed in a huge semicircle around the naked woman who stands beside the wreckage of the mobile module. For a moment he is unable to speak.

"Anne?" he says finally. "What in God's name—"

"You'll never understand," I tell him. I give the signal. Belshazzar rumbles forward. Sarber screams and whirls and sprints for the airlock, but a stegosaur blocks the way.

"No!" Sarber cries as the tyrannosaur's mighty head swoops down. It is all over in a moment.

Revenge! How sweet!

And this is only the beginning. Habitat Vronsky lies just one hundred twenty kilometers away. Elsewhere in the Lagrange belt are hundreds of other habitats ripe for conquest. The Earth itself is within easy reach. I have no idea yet how it will be accomplished, but I know it will be done and done successfully, and I will be the instrument by which it is done.

I stretch forth my arms to the mighty creatures that surround me. I feel their strength, their power, their harmony. I am one with them, and they with me. The Great Race has returned, and I am its priestess. Let the small hairy ones tremble!

# EDITOR'S INTRODUCTION TO:

## TWO POEMS

### by Steve Rasnic Tem

*I remember my first meeting with Paolo Soleri. We were to testify to a select Congressional Committee on Non-renewable Resources. First came Herman Kahn; then me; fortunately Soleri came last, because who could follow an act like his? A man who dreams of bridges containing cities larger than Manhattan cannot be accused of thinking small . . .*

*Afterwards we had lunch; and I went away to begin work on what became the fourth collaboration with Niven,* Oath of Fealty.

*Thus, I'm a sucker for anyone who appreciates Soleri; especially when they can capture a mood as well as Tem does.*

# Lighting the Colony

## Steve Rasnic Tem

*"The probe of life into space is ultimately not a technological
or a political or economic problem but a theological ones."*
—Palo Soleri

This sudden flare of light you've become,
   soon to be a tide,
    began like a dying, a final grounding
    in goodbyes to remembered soils.
Rising head-first into the narrowing
   of sky, you're suddenly *outside*
   seeing candelabra in the dark
   yet still looking back
   out of the steel body to ask
*Was it worth it? Are we ready?*
*What have we done?*

Your feet still remember all
   you ever knew, New York to San Francisco,
   the problem of birth, rising up
   on ill-engineered limbs, your mother's
   rocking, in the dark woods
   the dim eyes of your first stranger.
All this light danced-out with feeling,
   all these sparks of a history transferred
   and carried up into the focal point
   within your feet a whole life
   staked on this new step into the stars.

You arrive frightened.
The shuttle descending, you're caught
   by the womb of the spinning mandala
   drawing you back into the world;
   you were not ready to die.
All life seems to smolder.
The solar system is made a village
   a town, then a city evolves.
All kindles into light.

# Seeding the Last Freedom

## Steve Rasnic Tem

Form follows dream;
   eyes, ears, stray thoughts
   wander the hidden topographies of space.

Sails are pushed into Venus
   by the sun's weight.
Stars taken apart, asteroids hollowed
   and pastures sown into the linings.

We grow wings, lengthen bones,
   make new eyes for seeing into the dark.
We become what we think about most,
   new shapes to surround us,
   we become inward and frugal

   to make life everywhere possible
   to habitate, grow into purpose
   to make all creation think.

EDITOR'S INTRODUCTION TO:

## HOW TO BUILD A BEANSTALK

by Charles Sheffield

*Dr. Charles Sheffield is yet another scientist who writes science fiction.*

*Strictly speaking, I suppose, Charles is not a scientist but an engineer. He is vice president of a firm which takes NASA's EARTHSAT observations and refines them, manipulating the imagery in ways that make even JPL's VOYAGER imaging teams jealous; the results are sold to prospectors, agronomists, geologists, and all those concerned with what's going on over large areas of the globe.*

*Charles is President of the American Astronautical Society, a group of hard-headed professionals who believe in space travel; and a member of the Board of the L-5 Society. The AAS thinks Dr. Sheffield somewhat optimistic in his projections of the future of man in space; the L-5ers think him a bit cautious.*

*There's nothing cautious about beanstalks; but they may be an idea whose time is coming fast. Charles Sheffield and Arthur C. Clarke came up with novels on the theme at almost precisely the same time; each was a bit worried that someone might think there was copying involved, but of course there wasn't.*

*Given an article and a story on the same theme I had a problem: which do I put first? Tell the reader how they're built first, or let the story do that?*

*Eventually I put the story after the non-fiction; if you don't care for that arrangement, by all means skip to the story.*

# HOW TO BUILD A BEANSTALK

## Charles Sheffield

*THE AGE OF ROCKETS.*

The launch of a Saturn V rocket is an impressive sight. It is impressively noisy, impressively big and impressively risky. It is also one of Man's outstanding examples of conspicuous consumption, where a few thousand tons of fuel go up (literally) in smoke (literally) in a couple of minutes. And yet it is, in 1981, the best space transportation system that we have.

If we were to sit down and make a list of the properties of our 'ideal' space transportation system, without worrying about whether or not we could ever hope to achieve it, what would it look like? Well, first and most important it ought not to use up any raw materials in its working—no reaction mass, which all rockets need to propel themselves. It ought to allow us to take materials up and down from planetary surfaces, and be equally good at moving us around in free space. And it would be nice if it were somehow completely energy-free. While we are at it, let's ask that it be also silent and non-polluting.

Note that our old friend, the rocket, satisfies *none* of our ideal system requirements. The Space Shuttle, our first reusable spacecraft, is not suited to anything beyond low earth orbit activities, and is, with all its advantages over its non-reusable predecessors, still a very primitive system.

It may sound improbable, but an ideal space system, satisfying *all* our requirements, could be here in a couple of generations. As we shall see, the technology needed is not far from that already available to us.

It is curious that science fiction, which likes to look

beyond today's technology, has remained so infatuated with the idea of rockets. Some people even use them to *define* the field. Look at the 'sf' section in public libraries and you will often see a small drawing of a rocket attached to the spine of each volume. It may be a perverse choice of label for a branch of writing that covers everything from *Ringworld* to *Flowers For Algernon,* but you can see how the logic goes; science fiction means space travel, and space travel means rockets—because they are 'the only way of getting up to space and around in space.' After all, there is nothing for any other sort of transportation to 'push against' in space. Right?

Not quite. We will try and dispose of that peculiar viewpoint here. Our preoccupation with rockets for space travel will probably amaze our descendants.

"Why use something as wasteful and noisy as a rocket," they will ask, "when there are simple, clean, efficient alternatives? Why didn't they use Beanstalks?"

The Age of Rockets may look to them like the Age of Dinosaurs. Let's try and see it through their eyes, beginning with the most basic principles.

A spacecraft, orbiting Earth around the equator just high enough to avoid the main effects of atmospheric drag, makes a complete revolution in about an hour and a half. If the Earth had no atmosphere, a spacecraft in a 'grazing orbit' would skim around just above the surface in 84.9 minutes. At the end of that time, it would *not* be above the same point on the Earth where it started. The Earth is rotating, too, and if the spacecraft revolves in the same direction as Earth it must go farther—about 2,370 kilometers, the distance that a point on the equator rotates in 84.9 minutes—before it again passes over the point where it began.

Now keep the spacecraft in a circular path above the equator, but instead of a grazing orbit, imagine that it travels 1,000 kilometers above the surface. Then the orbital period will be greater. It will now be about 106 minutes: the higher the orbit, the longer the period of revolution.

When the height of the spacecraft is 35,770 kilometers, the

orbital period is 1,436 minutes, or one sidereal day (a *solar* day, the time that a point on the Earth takes to return to point exactly at the Sun, is 1,440 minutes). In other words, the spacecraft now takes just as long as the Earth to make one full revolution in space. Since the spacecraft is moving around at the same rate as the Earth, it seems to hover always above the same point on the equator.

Such a specialized orbit is called *geostationary*, because the satellite does not move relative to the Earth's surface. It is a splendid orbit for a communications satellite. There is no need for ground receiving antennae to track the satellite at all—it remains in one place in the sky. The term 'Clarkian orbit' has been proposed as an alternate to the cumbersome 'geostationary orbit', in recognition of Arthur Clarke's original suggestion in 1945 that such orbits had unique potential for use in worldwide communications. Note, by the way, that a 24-hour period orbit does not have to be geostationary. An orbit whose plane is at an angle to the equator can be *geosynchronous*, with 24-hour period, but it moves up and down in latitude and oscillates in longitude during one day. The class of geosynchronous orbits includes all geostationary orbits.

A geosynchronous orbit has some other unusual features. It is at the distance from the Earth where gravitational and centrifugal accelerations on an orbiting object balance. To see what this means, suppose that you could erect a thin pole vertically on the equator. A long pole, and I do mean *long*. Suppose that you could extend it upwards over a hundred thousand kilometers, and it was strong and rigid enough that you could make it remain vertical. Then every part of the pole *below* the height of a geostationary orbit would feel a net downward force, because it is travelling too slowly for centrifugal acceleration to balance gravitational acceleration. On the other hand, every element of the pole beyond geostationary altitude would feel a net *outward* force. Those elements are travelling so fast that centrifugal force exceeds gravitational pull.

(Every mechanics textbook will point out that there are no such things as 'centrifugal forces'; there is only the gravita-

tional force, curving the path of the orbiting body from its
natural inclination to continue in a straight line. The centrifugal forces are fictitious forces, arising only as a conse-
quence of the use of a rotating reference frame for calculations. But centrifugal forces are so convenient that everyone
uses them, even if they don't exist! And when you move to an
Einsteinian viewpoint you find that centrifugal forces now
appear as real as any others. So much for theories.)

The higher that a section of the pole is above geostationary
height, the greater the total outward pull on it. So if we make
the pole just the right length, the total inward pull from all
parts of the pole *below* geostationary height will exactly
balance the outward pull from the higher sections *above* that
height. Our pole will hang there, touching the Earth at the
equator but not exerting any downward force on it. If you
like, we can think of the pole as an enormously long satellite,
in a geostationary orbit.

How long would such a pole have to be? If we were to
make the pole of uniform cross-section, it would have to
extend upwards a distance of about 143,700 kilometers. This
result does not depend on the cross-sectional area of the pole,
nor on the material from which it is made. It should be clear
that in practice we would not choose to make a pole of
uniform cross-section, since the downward pull that it must
withstand is far greater up near geosynchronous height than it
is near the Earth. At the higher point, the pole must support
the weight of more than 35,000 kilometers of itself, whereas
near Earth it supports only the weight hanging below it. From
this, we would expect that the best design will be a tapered
pole, with its thickest part at geostationary altitude where the
pull on it is greatest.

The idea of a rigid pole is also misleading. We have seen
that the only forces at work are tensions. It is thus more
logical to think of the structure as a *cable* than a pole.

We now have the major feature of our 'basic Beanstalk'. It
will be a long, strong cable, extending from the surface of the
Earth on the equator, out to beyond the geostationary orbit. It
will be of the order of 144,000 kilometers long. We will use it

as the load-bearing cable of a giant elevator, to send materials up to orbit and back. The structure will hang there in static equilibrium, revolving with the Earth. It is a bridge to space, replacing the old ferry-boat rockets.

That's the main concept. What could be simpler? We have—perhaps an understatement—left out a number of 'engineering details,' but we will look at those next.

## DESIGNING THE BEANSTALK.

Let us list some of the questions that we must answer before we have a satisfactory Beanstalk design. The most important ones are as follows:

• What shape should the load-bearing cable have?
• What materials will it be made from?
• Where will we get those materials?
• Where will we build the Beanstalk, where will we attach it to Earth, and how will we get it installed?
• How will we use the main cable to move materials up and down from Earth?
• Will a Beanstalk be stable, against the gravitational forces from the Sun and Moon, against weather, and against natural events here on earth?
• What are the advantages of a Beanstalk over rockets?
• If we can get satisfactory answers to all these questions, *when* should we be able to build a Beanstalk?

We can offer definite answers to some of these questions; other answers can only be conjectures. Let's begin with the first, which is also the easiest.

Suppose that the load-bearing cable is made of a single material. Then the most efficient design is one in which the stress on the material, per unit area, is the same all the way along it. This means there is no wasted strength. With such an assumption, it is a simple exercise in statics to derive an equation for the cross-sectional area of the cable as a function of distance from the center of the Earth.

The result has the form:

(1)        $A(r) = A(R) . \exp (K.f(r/R).d/T.R.)$

In this equation, A(r) is the cross-sectional area of the cable at distance r from the center of the Earth, A(R) is the area at the distance R of a geostationary orbit, K is the gravitational constant for the Earth, d is the density of the material from which the cable is made, T is the tensile strength of the cable per unit area, and $f(r/R) = 3/2 — R/r — (r/R)^2/2$.

Equation (1) tells us a great deal. First, we note that the variation of the cross-sectional area with distance does not depend on the tensile strength T directly, but only on the *ratio* T/d, which is the strength-to-weight ratio for the material. The substance from which we will build the Beanstalk must be strong, but more than that it should be strong and *light*.

Second, we can see that the shape of the cable is tremendously sensitive to the strength-to-weight ratio of the material, because this quantity occurs in the exponential of equation (1). To take a simple example, suppose that we have a material with a *taper factor* of 10,000. We define *taper factor* as the cross-sectional area of the cable at geostationary height, divided by the cross-sectional area at the surface of the Earth. So, for example, a cable that was one square meter in area at the bottom end would in this case be 10,000 square meters in area at geostationary height.

Now suppose that we could double the strength-to-weight ratio of the material we use for the cable. The taper ratio would drop from 10,000 to 100. If we could double the strength-to-weight ratio again, the taper ratio would reduce from 100 to 10.

It is clear that we should make the Beanstalk of the strongest possible material. Note that an infinitely strong material would need no taper at all.

Two other points are worth noting about the shape of the cable. It is easy to show that the function f(r/R) has its maximum value at r = R. This confirms the intuitive result, that the cable must be thickest at geostationary height, where the load is greatest since the cable must support all the downward weight between that height and the surface of the Earth. Second, a look at the change of f(r/R) with increasing r shows that the cross-sectional area decreases slowly above geostationary height. This is why we need a cable with a length that is much more than twice the distance to that height.

## MATERIALS FOR THE BEANSTALK.

The cable that we need must be able to withstand a tension at least equal to its own weight from a height of 35,000 kilometers down to the surface. In practice, it must be a good deal stronger than that. We will certainly want to build in a reasonable safety factor, and we will want to hang other structures on the cable all the way down, to make it into a usable transportation system. So we expect that we will need to work with a very strong material, one with an unusually high strength-to-weight ratio. Of course, if one does not have a material that is quite as strong as needed, one can try and compensate by increasing the taper factor, but we have seen that this would be a very inefficient way to go. Halving the strength of materials would square the taper factor. The incentive to work with the strongest possible materials is very large.

The tension in the cable at a height of 35,770 kilometers, where upward and downward forces exactly balance, is less than the weight of a similar length of 35,770 kilometers of cable down here on Earth, for two reasons. The downward gravitational force decreases as the square of the distance from the center of the Earth, and the upward centrifugal force increases linearly with that distance. Both these effects tend to decrease the tension that the cable must support. A straightforward calculation shows that the maximum tension in a cable of constant cross-section will be equal to the weight of 4,940 kms. of such cable, here on Earth. This is in a sense a 'worst case' calculation, since we know that the cable will be designed to taper. However, the need for a safety factor means that we need to be conservative, and the figure of 4,940 kms. gives us a useful standard in terms of which we can calibrate the strength of available materials.

The definition we have chosen of a cable's strength,

namely, how much length of its own substance it must support under Earth's gravity, is used quite widely. For a particular material, the length of itself the cable will support is called the 'support length' or 'characteristic length'. It is particularly handy because of the way in which the strength of materials is usually described, in terms of the tons *weight* per square centimeter (or per square inch) that they will support. (It would be more desirable, scientifically speaking, to give strength in dynes per square centimeter, or in newtons per square meter. These measures are independent of the Earth's surface gravity. But historically, pounds per square inch and kilos per square centimeter came first and things are still given that way in most of the handbooks. Note also that we are concerned only with *tensile* strength—how strong the material is when you pull it. *Compressive* and *shear* strengths are quite different, and a material may be very strong in compression and weak in tension. A building brick is a good example of this.)

Against our requirement of a support length of 4,940 kms, how well do the substances that we have available today measure up?

Not too well. Now we see why no one has yet built a Beanstalk. Table 1 shows the strengths of currently available materials, their densities, and their support lengths. (The physical data that I am using here is drawn, wherever possible, from the *Handbook of Chemistry and Physics*, 57th Edition. It is one of the most widely available reference texts and should be in any reasonable library.)

Not surprisingly, we won't be trying to make a Beanstalk support cable from lead. As we can see from the table, even the best steel wire that we can find has a support length only one hundredth of what we need. The last entry in the table, Fictionite, would be perfect but for one drawback: it doesn't exist yet. The strongest materials that we have today, graphite and silicon carbide whiskers, still fall badly short of our requirements (for Earth, that is. A Mars Beanstalk has a minimum support length of only 973 kms. We could make one of those nicely using graphite whiskers).

TABLE 1
STRENGTH OF MATERIALS

| Material | Tensile strength (kgms/sq.cm.) | Density (gms/c.c.) | Support length (kilometers) |
|---|---|---|---|
| Lead | 200 | 11.4 | 0.18 |
| Gold | 1,400 | 19.3 | 0.73 |
| Aluminum | 2,000 | 2.7 | 7.4 |
| Cast iron | 3,500 | 7.8 | 4.5 |
| Carbon steel | 7,000 | 7.8 | 9.0 |
| Manganese steel | 16,000 | 7.8 | 21. |
| Drawn tungsten | 35,000 | 19.3 | 18. |
| Drawn steel wire | 42,000 | 7.8 | 54. |
| Iron whisker | 126,000 | 7.8 | 161. |
| Silicon whisker (SiC) | 210,000 | 3.2 | 660. |
| Graphite whisker | 210,000 | 2.0 | 1,050. |
| Fictionite | 2,000,000 | 2.0 | 10,000. |

Does this mean that we have a hopeless situation? It depends what confidence you have in the advance of technology. Table 2 lists the strength of materials that have been available at different dates in human history. There is some inevitable arbitrariness in making a table like this, since no one really knows when the Hittites began to smelt iron, and

TABLE 2
PROGRESS IN STRENGTH OF MATERIALS
AS A FUNCTION OF TIME

| Year | Available material | Tensile Strength (kgms/sq.cm.) |
|---|---|---|
| 1500 B.C. | Bronze | 1,400 |
| 1850 | Iron | 3,500 |
| 1950 | Special steels | 16,000 |
| 1970 | Drawn steel | 42,000 |
| 1980 | Graphite and silicon whiskers | 210,000 |

Note: Years given indicate the dates when the materials could first be reliably produced in production quantities.

there must have been poor control of times, temperatures and purity of raw materials in the Bronze Age and early Iron Age. All these factors have a big effect on the tensile strength of the products.

It is tempting to try and fit some kind of function to the values in the table, and see when we will have a material available with a support length of 5,000 kms. or better. It is also very dangerous to even think of such a thing. For example, consider a fit to the data of the form: Strength = $B/(t-T)$, where B and T are to be determined by the data, and t is time in years before the year 2000 A.D. This fits the data fairly well if we choose B = 525,000 and T = 17.5 years. Unfortunately, such a form becomes infinite when $t = T$. If we were to believe such a fit, we would expect to have infinitely strong materials available to us some time in 1982!

Not surprisingly, extrapolation of a trend without using physical models can lead us to ridiculous results. A much more plausible way of predicting the potential strength of materials is available to us, based on the known structure of the atom. In chemical reactions, only the outermost electrons of the atom participate, and it is the coupling of these outer electrons that decides the strength of chemical bonds. These bonds in turn set bounds on the possible strength of a material. Thus, so far as we are concerned the nucleus of the atom—which is where almost all the atomic mass resides—contributes nothing; strength of coupling, and hence material strength, comes only from those outer electrons.

In Table 3 we give the strengths of the chemical bonds for different pairs of atoms. These strengths, divided by the molecular weight of the appropriate element pair, decide the ultimate strength-to-weight ratio for a material entirely composed of that pair of elements. The final column of the table shows the support length that this strength-to-weight ratio implies, using the carbon-carbon bond of the graphite whisker as the reference case.

Examining the Table, we see that the hydrogen-hydrogen bond has by far the greatest potential strength. In this bond, every electron participates in the bonding process (each atom

TABLE 3
POTENTIAL STRENGTH OF MATERIALS BASED ON THE
STRENGTH OF CHEMICAL BONDS

| Element pairs | Molecular weight* | Chemical bond strength (kcal/mole) | Support length (kilometers)** |
|---|---|---|---|
| Silicon-carbon | 40 | 104 | 455 |
| Carbon-carbon | 24 | 145 | 1,050 |
| Fluorine-hydrogen | 20 | 136 | 1,190 |
| Boron-hydrogen | 11 | 80.7 | 1,278 |
| Nitrogen-nitrogen | 28 | 225.9 | 1,418 |
| Carbon-oxygen | 28 | 257.3 | 1,610 |
| Hydrogen-hydrogen | 2 | 104.2 | 9,118 |
| Positronium-positronium | 1/918.6 | 104 | 16,700,000 |

*Some of these element pairs do not exist as stable molecules, but can exist in a crystal lattice structure.
**We are using the support length of the graphite whisker as the standard of strength provided by the chemical bonds.

has only one!) and the hydrogen nucleus contains no neutrons, which offer added weight without adding anything to the possible strength. A substance that consisted of pure solid hydrogen could in principle have a support length of more than 9,000 kilometers—very similar to the Fictionite of Table 1.

Even this strength is very modest if we are willing to look at a rather more exotic composition for our cables. Positronium is an 'atom' consisting of an electron and a positron. The positron takes the place of the usual proton in the hydrogen atom, but it has a far smaller mass. Positronium has been made in the laboratory, but it is unstable with a very short lifetime. If, however, positronium could be stabilized against decay, perhaps by the application of intense electromagnetic fields, then the resulting positronium-positronium bond should have a strength comparable with that of the hydrogen-hydrogen bond, and a far smaller molecular weight. It will have a support length of 16,700,000 kilometers

—the taper of a Beanstalk made from such a material would be unmeasurably small. This would be true even for a Beanstalk on Jupiter, where the strength requirement is higher than for any other planet of the Solar System.

The positronium cable is likely to remain unavailable to us for some time yet. Even the solid hydrogen cable offers us the practical problem that we don't know how to build it. Rather than insisting on any particular material for our Beanstalk, it is safer and more reasonable to make a less specific statement: the strength of materials available to us has been increasing steadily throughout history, with the most striking advance coming in this century. It seems plausible to look for at least an increase of another order of magnitude in strength in the next hundred years. Such an advance in materials technology would make the construction of a Beanstalk quite feasible by the middle of the next century, at least from the point of view of strength of materials. It could come far sooner.

Something with the properties of Fictionite would do very nicely. The taper ration would be only 1.6, and a Beanstalk that was one meter in diameter at the lower end and of circular cross-section could support a load of nearly sixteen million tons.

## WHERE TO BUILD THE BEANSTALK.

We have talked about what we will make the Beanstalk out of, but we have not discussed where we will find those materials. The answer to such a question is provided when we look at *how* we will build it.

For several reasons, the 'Tower of Babel' technique—start here on Earth and just build upwards—is not the way to go. The structure would be in *compression*, not tension, all the way up to beyond geostationary altitude, and we picked our material for its tensile strength. Worse still, structures in compression can buckle, which is a form of mechanical failure that does not apply to materials under tension.

Clearly, we will somehow begin *at the top*, with materials

that we find up there. But *where* at the top? This is worth thinking about in more detail.

To a first approximation, the Earth is a sphere and its external gravity field is the same as that of a point mass. To a good second approximation, it is an oblate spheroid, with symmetry about the axis of rotation (the polar axis). The third order approximation gets much messier. Not only does the Earth "wobble" a bit about its axis of rotation, but there are fine inhomogeneities in the internal structure that show up as 'gravity anomalies' in the external gravitational field. These gravity anomalies are the deviations of the field from that which would be produced by a regular spheroid of revolution.

The anomalies are small—only a couple of milligals—but they are important. (In geodesy, a *gal* is not something that a male geodesist would like to snuggle up to; it is a unit of acceleration, equal to 1 cm. per second per second. A *milligal* is a thousandth of that. Earth's surface gravity is about 980 gals. If the Earth's gravity field were to change by one milligal, you would weigh differently by about one four-hundredth of an ounce. Even a change of a full gal—a thousand milligals—would not be noticed.)

If we look at these small gravity anomalies in the region of the orbit of a geostationary satellite, we find that they give rise to local maxima and minima of the gravitational potential. Satellites in such orbits tend to 'drift' to where the potential has its nearest local maximum, and to oscillate about such a position. For this particular location (35,770 kms. up, in the plane of the equator) these are the stable points of the gravitational field. At first sight, this looks like the best place to start to build your Beanstalk. You could put your source of materials there, and begin to extrude load-bearing cable up and down simultaneously, so as to keep a balance between the gravitational and centrifugal forces on the whole cable. Doing this, you might expect to be able to keep the cable Earth-stationary, always over the same fixed point of the surface.

Unfortunately, the gravitational potential is not so well-behaved. The positions of the stable points, the places where the potential has its local maxima, depend on the distance from the center of the Earth.

As you begin to extrude cable upwards and downwards, parts of the cable will move into regions where they are no longer at a local maximum of the potential. There will then be a strong tendency for the cable to "walk." It will begin to move steadily around the equator (and off the equator!), adjusting its position to the *average* of the gravity potential maxima encountered at all heights where a piece of the cable is present.

Such behavior is—at the very least—an annoyance. It means that you must allow for such motion in the design and construction, and you must tether the cable at the ground end when you have finished.

Such a tether is not a bad thing. We shall see later that it is an essential part of Beanstalk design if we want a usable structure, one that can carry cargo and people up and down it. However, you can't tether the Stalk until you have *finished* building it. So we have still not answered the question, where do you do that construction? Remember, the geostationary location is full of other satellites—the communications satellites sit out there, and some of the weather satellites. It would be intolerable for the Beanstalk, half-built, to come drifting along through their *lebensraum* until it was finally long enough to tether.

What other options do we have? Well, there is the "bootstrap" method. In this, you fabricate a very thin Beanstalk, tether it, and use that to stop your main Beanstalk from wandering about during the construction.

My own favorite is more ambitious than a construction from geostationary orbit. You build *all* your Beanstalk well away from Earth, out at L-4 or L-5. When you have it all done, you fly it down. You arrange your timing so that the lower end arrives at a pre-prepared landing and tether site on the equator at the same time as the upper end makes a rendezvous with a ballast weight, way out beyond geostaary height. Once the Beanstalk has been tethered, the problem of a stable position for the orbit is not serious—it merely means that the Stalk doesn't follow the exact local vertical on the way up, because it tries to adapt to the mean gravity gradient all the way along its length.

Building the Stalk well away from Earth helps the problem of material supply. We certainly don't want to use Earth materials for construction, since getting them up there would be an enormous task. Fortunately, two of the promising substances that we found in the table of strong materials are graphite and silicon carbide. Coincidentally, two of the main categories of asteroid are termed the carbonaceous and the silicaceous types. They can be the source of our raw materials.

The way to build the Beanstalk is now apparent. We fly a smallish (a couple of kilometers in diameter) asteroid in from the Asteroid Belt and settle it at L-4. We build a solar power satellite or a fusion plant out there, too, to provide the energy that we need. Then we fabricate the Beanstalk, the whole thing: load-bearing cable, superconducting power cables, and drive train (more on these in a moment). And we fly it on down to Earth.

The final descent speed need not be high. We can use the inertia of the whole length of the Stalk to slow the arrival of its lower end.

The demand on the raw material resources of Earth in this whole operation will be minimal.

## USING THE BEANSTALK.

A couple of paragraphs back, I threw in reference to superconducting power cables and drive train. These are the key to making the Beanstalk useful. Let us look in more detail at the whole structure of the Stalk.

We will have a load-bearing cable, perhaps a couple of meters across at the lower end, stretching up from the equator to out past geosynchronous altitude. It will be tethered at its lower end to prevent it from moving about around the Earth. It will be strong enough to support a load of millions of tons.

What else do we need to do to make it useful?

First, we will strengthen the tether, to make sure that it can stand a pull of many millions of tons without coming loose from Earth. Next, we will go out to the far end of the cable, and hang a really big ballast weight there. The ballast weight pulls outwards, so that the whole cable is now under an added tension, balancing the pull of the ballast against the tether down on Earth.

We really need that tension.

Why? Well, suppose that we want to send a million tons of cargo up the Beanstalk. The first thing we will do is hang it on the cable near the ground tether. If the tension down near the lower end is a couple of million tons, when we hang the cargo on the cable we simply reduce the upward force on the tether from two million tons to one million tons. The cargo itself is providing some of the downward pull needed to balance the upward tug of the ballast at the far end. The whole system is still stable.

But if we had used a smaller ballast weight, enough to give us a pull at the tether of only half a million tons, we would be in trouble. If we hang a million tons of cargo on the cable, it will pull the blallast weight downwards. There is just not enough ballast to provide the required upward pull. We must provide an initial ballast weight that is sufficient to give a tension more than any weight that we will ever try and send up the cable.

There is another advantage to a massive ballast weight. We can use a shorter cable. We can hang a really big ballast at, say, a hundred thousand kilometers out, and it will not be necessary to have more cable beyond that point. The ballast weight provides the upward pull that balances the downward pull of the cable below geostationary height. We have to be a little careful here. A ballast that has a *mass* of ten million tons will not be enough to allow you to raise a *weight* of ten million tons up from Earth. The ballast will not pull outwards as hard as the weight pulls downwards, unless it is out at a distance where the net *outward* acceleration due to combined centrifugal and gravitational forces is one gee. This requires that the ballast be more than 1.8 million kilometers out from Earth—far past the Moon's distance of 400,000 kilometers.

We conclude from this that the ballast will be a massive one. This is no real problem. After all, even a modest sized asteroid, a kilometer across, will mass anything up to a billion tons.

Once we have a taut cable, suitably anchored, we need a power source for the activities on the Beanstalk. We put a solar power satellite or a fusion plant out at the far end and run cables all the way down, attaching them to the main loadbearing cable. Superconducting cables make sense, but we will have to be sure that they are suitably insulated—near-Earth space isn't *that* cold. But perhaps by the time we build the Stalk we will have superconductors that operate up to higher critical temperatures. The ones available now remain superconductors only up to about 23 degrees Kelvin.

There is a fringe benefit to running cables down the Beanstalk. We can carry down power from space without worrying about the effects of microwave radiation on the Earth—which is a serious worry with present solar power satellite designs.

Once we have the power cables installed, we can build the drive train, again attaching it to the load cable for its support. The easiest system for a drive train is probably a linear synchronous motor. The principles and the practice for that are well-established, which means it will all be off-the-shelf fixtures—except that we will want fifty to a hundred thousand kilometers of drive ladder. But remember, all this construction work will be done before we fly the Beanstalk in for a landing, and the abundant raw materials of the asteroid at L-4 will still be available to us.

Assuming that we drive cars up and down the Stalk at the uniform speed of 300 kilometers an hour, the journey up to synchronous altitude will take five days. That's a lot slower than a rocket, but it will be a lot more restful—and look at some of the other advantages.

First, we will have a completely non-polluting system, one that uses no reaction mass at all. This may appear a detail, until you look at the effects of frequent rocket launches on the delicate balance of the upper atmosphere and ionosphere of Earth.

Second, we will have a potentially *energy-free* system. Any energy that you use in the drive train in taking a mass up to synchronous height can in principle be recovered by making returning masses provide energy to the drive train as they descend to Earth. Even allowing for inevitable friction and energy conversion losses, a remarkably efficient system will be possible.

In some ways, the Stalk offers something even better than an energy-free system. When a mass begins its ascent from the surface of the Earth, it is moving with the speed of a point on the Earth's equator—a thousand miles an hour. When it reaches synchronous height, it will be travelling at 6,600 miles an hour. And if, from that point on, you let it "fall outwards" to the end of the Stalk, it will be launched on its way with a speed of more than 33,000 miles an hour, relative to the Earth. That's enough to throw it clear out of the Solar System.

Where did all the energy come from to speed up the mass?

The natural first answer might be, from the drive train. That is not the case. The energy comes from the rotational energy of the Earth itself. When you send a mass up the Beanstalk, you slow the Earth in its rotation by an infinitesimal amount, and when you send something back down, you speed it up a little. We don't need to worry about the effects on the planet, though. You'd have to take an awful lot of mass up there before you could make an appreciable effect on the rotation rate of Earth. The total rotational energy of Earth amounts to only about one thousandth of the planet's gravitational self-energy, but that is still an incredibly big number. We can use the Beanstalk without worrying about the effects that it will have on the Earth.

The converse of this is much less obvious. What about the effects of the Earth on the Beanstalk? Will we have to be worried about weather, earthquakes, and other natural events?

Earthquakes sound nasty. We certainly want the tether to be secure. If it came loose the whole Beanstalk would shoot off out into space, following the ballast. However, it is quite easy to protect ourselves. We simply arrange that the tether be held down by a mass that is itself a part of the lower end of the Stalk. Then the tether is provided by the simple weight of the bottom of the Beanstalk, and that will be a stable situation as long as the force at that point remains "down"—which will certainly be true unless something were to blow the whole Earth apart; in which case, we might expect to have other things to worry about.

Weather should be no problem. The Stalk presents so small a cross-sectional area compared with its strength that no storm we can imagine would trouble it. The same is true for perturbations from the gravity of the Sun and the Moon. Proper design of the Stalk will avoid any resonance effects, in which the period of the forces on the structure might coincide with any of its natural vibration frequencies.

In fact, by far the biggest danger we can conceive of is a man-made one—sabotage. A bomb, exploding halfway up the Beanstalk, would create unimaginable havoc in both the upper and lower sections of the structure. That would be the thing against which all security measures would be designed.

## WHEN CAN WE BUILD A BEANSTALK?

We need two things before we can go ahead with a Beanstalk construction project: a strong enough material, and an off-Earth source of supplies. Both of these ought to be available in the next fifty to one hundred years. The general superiority of Beanstalks to rockets is so great that I expect to see the prototype built by the year 2050.

I do not regard this estimate as very adventuresome. It is certainly less so than Orville Wright's statement, when in 1911 he startled the world by predicting that we would eventually have passenger air service between cities as much as a hundred miles apart.

Unless we blow ourselves up, bog down in the Prox-mire, or find some other way to begin the slide back to the technological Dark Ages, normal engineering progress will give us the tools that we need to build a Beanstalk, by the middle of the next century. The economic impetus to deploy those tools will be provided by a recognition of the value of the off-Earth energy and raw materials, and it will be with us long before then.

This discussion seems to me to be so much a part of an inevitable future that I feel obliged to speculate a little further, just to make the subject matter less pedestrian. Let us look further out.

Non-synchronous Beanstalks have already been proposed for the Earth. These are shorter Stalks, non-tethered, that move around the Earth in low orbits and dip their ends into Earth's atmosphere and back out again a few times a revolution. They are a delightful and new idea that was developed in detail in a 1977 paper by Hans Moravec. The logical next step is free-space Beanstalks. These are revolving about their own center of mass, and they can be used to provide momentum transfer to spacecraft. They thus form a handy way to move materials about the Solar System.

Look ahead now a few thousand years. Civilization has largely moved off Earth, into free-space colonies. There are many thousands of these, each self-sustaining and self-contained, constructed from materials available in the Asteroid Belt. Although they are self-supporting, travel among them will be common, for commerce and recreation. Naturally enough, this travel will be accomplished without the use of reaction mass, via an extensive system of free-space Beanstalks which provide the velocity increases and decreases needed to move travellers around from colony to colony. There will be hundreds of thousands of these in a spherical region centered on the Sun, and they will all be freely orbiting.

The whole civilization will be stable and organized, but there will be one continuing source of perturbation and danger. Certain singularities of the gravitational field exist, disturbing the movements of the colonists and their free transfer through the Solar System.

The singularities sweep their disorderly way around the Sun, upsetting the orbits of the colonies and the Beanstalks with their powerful gravity fields and presenting a real threat of capture to any who get too close to them.

It seems inevitable that, in some future Forum on one of the colonies, a speaker will one day arise to voice the will of the people. He will talk about the problem presented by the singularities, about the need to remove them. About the danger they offer, and about the inconvenience they cause. And finally, as a newly-arisen Cato he may mimic the words of his predecessor to pronounce judgment on one or more of those gravity singularities of the Solar System, the planets.

"Terra delenda est"—Earth must be destroyed!

## *BEANSTALK TIME—A FINAL NOTE.*

Beanstalks, originally called skyhooks, are an idea of the 1960's whose time may at last have come. They are used as important elements of at least two novels published in 1979, Arthur Clarke's *The Fountains Of Paradise* and my own *The Web Between The Worlds*. I suspect that they will become a standard element of most projected futures, as a rational alternative to the rocketry that has served sf writers so long and so well.

EDITOR'S INTRODUCTION TO:

## SKY STALK

by Charles Sheffield

*Dr. Sheffield's article describes how a Beanstalk might be built. His story puts you on one. It's an interesting experience . . .*

# SKY STALK

## Charles Sheffield

Finlay's Law: Trouble comes at three a.m.

That's always been my experience, and I've learned to dread the hand on my shoulder that shakes me to wakefulness. My dreams had been bad enough, blasting off into orbit on top of an old chemical rocket, riding the torch, up there on a couple of thousand tons of volatile explosives. I'll never understand the nerve of the old-timers, willing to sit up there on one of those monsters.

I shuddered, forced my eyes open, and looked up at Marston's anxious face. I was already sitting up.

"Trouble?" It was a stupid question, but you're allowed a couple of those when you first wake up.

His voice was shaky. "There's a bomb on the Beanstalk."

I was off the bunk, pulling on my undershirt and groping around for my shoes. Larry Marston's words pulled me bolt upright.

"What do you mean, *on* the Beanstalk?"

"That's what Velasquez told me. He won't say more until you get on the line. They're holding a coded circuit open to Earth."

I gave up my search for shoes and went barefoot after Marston. If Arnold Velasquez were right—and I didn't see how he could be—then one of my old horrors was coming true. The Beanstalk had been designed to withstand most natural events, but sabotage was one thing that could never be fully ruled out. At any moment, we had nearly four hundred buckets climbing the Stalk and the same number going down. With the best screening in the world, with hefty rewards for information even of *rumors* of sabotage, there was always the small chance that something could be sneaked through on an outbound bucket. I had less worries about the buckets that went down to Earth. Sabotage from the space end had little to offer its perpetrators, and the Colonies would provide an unpleasant form of death to anyone who tried it, with no questions asked.

Arnold Velasquez was sitting in front of his screen door at Tether Control in Quito. Next to him stood a man I recognized only from news pictures: Otto Panosky, a top aide to the President. Neither man seemed to be looking at the screen. I wondered what they were seeing on their inward eye.

"Jack Finlay here," I said. "What's the story, Arnold?"

There was a perceptible lag before his head came up to stare at the screen, the quarter of a second that it took the video signal to go down to Earth, then back up to synchronous orbit.

"It's best if I read it to you, Jack," he said. At least his voice was under control, even though I could see his hands shaking as they held the paper. "The President's Office got this in over the telecopier about twenty minutes ago."

He rubbed at the side of his face, in the nervous gesture that I had seen during most major stages of the Beanstalk's construction. "It's addressed to us, here in Sky Stalk Control. It's quite short. 'To the Head of Space Transportation Systems. A fusion bomb has been placed in one of the out-going buckets. It is of four megaton capacity, and was armed prior to placement. The secondary activation command can be given at any time by a coded radio signal. Unless terms are met by the President and World Congress on or before 02.00 U.T., seventy-two hours from now, we will give the command to explode the device. Our terms are set out in the following four paragraphs. One—' "

"Never mind those, Arnold." I waved my hand, impatient at the signal delay. "Just tell me one thing. Will Congress meet their demands?"

He shook his head. "They can't. What's being asked for is preposterous in the time available. You know how much red tape there is in intergovernmental relationships.''

"You told them that?''

"Of course. We sent out a general broadcast.'' He shrugged. "It was no good. We're dealing with fanatics, with madmen. I need to know what you can do at your end.''

"How much time do we have now?''

He looked at his watch. "Seventy-one and a half hours, if they mean what they say. You understand that we have no idea which bucket might be carrying the bomb. It could have been planted there days ago, and still be on the way up.''

He was right. The buckets—there were three hundred and eighty-four of them each way—moved at a steady five kilometers a minute, up or down. That's a respectable speed, but it still took almost five days for each one of them to climb the cable of the Beanstalk out to our position in synchronous orbit.

Then I thought a bit more, and decided he wasn't quite right.

"It's not that vague, Arnold. You can bet the bomb wasn't placed on a bucket that started out more than two days ago. Otherwise, we could wait for it to get here and disarm it, and still be inside their deadline. It must still be fairly close to Earth, I'd guess.''

"Well, even if you're right, that deduction doesn't help us.'' He was chewing a pen to bits between sentences. "We don't have anything here that could be ready in time to fly out and take a look, even if it's only a couple of thousand kilometers. Even if we did, and even if we could spot the bomb, we couldn't rendezvous with a bucket on the Stalk. That's why I need to know what you can do from your end. Can you handle it from there?''

I took a deep breath and swung my chair to face Larry Marston.

"Larry, four megatons would vaporize a few kilometers of the main cable. How hard would it be for us to release ballast at the top end of the cable, above us here, enough to leave this station in position?''

"Well . . .'' He hesitated. "We could do that, Jack. But

then we'd lose the power satellite. It's right out at the end there, by the ballast. Without it, we'd lose all the power at the station here, and all the buckets too—there isn't enough reserve power to keep the magnetic fields going. We'd need all our spare power to keep the recycling going here.''

That was the moment when I finally came fully awake. I realized the implications of what he was saying, and was nodding before he'd finished speaking. Without adequate power, we'd be looking at a very messy situation.

"And it wouldn't only be us," I said to Velasquez and Panosky, sitting there tense in front of their screen. "Everybody on the Colonies will run low on air and water if the supply through the Stalk breaks down. Dammit, we've been warning Congress how vulnerable we are for years. All the time, there've been fewer and fewer rocket launches, and nothing but foot-dragging on getting the second Stalk started with a Kenya tether. Now you want miracles from us at short notice.''

If I sounded bitter, that's because I *was* bitter. Panosky was nodding his head in a conciliatory way.

"We know, Jack. And if you can pull us through this one, I think you'll see changes in the future. But right now, we can't debate that. We have to know what you can do for us *now*, this minute.''

I couldn't argue with that. I swung my chair again to face Larry Marston.

"Get Hasse and Kano over here to the Control Room as soon as you can." I turned back to Velasquez. "Give us a few minutes here, while we get organized. I'm bringing in the rest of my top engineering staff.''

While Larry was rounding up the others, I sat back and let the full dimensions of the problem sink in. Sure, if we had to we could release the ballast at the outward end of the Stalk. If the Beanstalk below us were severed we'd have to do that, or be whipped out past the Moon like a stone from a slingshot, as the tension in the cable suddenly dropped.

But if we did that, what would happen to the piece of the

Beanstalk that was still tethered to Earth, anchored down there in Quito? There might be as much as thirty thousand kilometers of it, and as soon as the break occurred it would begin to fall. Not in a straight line. That wasn't the way that the dynamics went. It would begin to curl around the Earth, accelerating as it went, cracking into the atmosphere along the equator like a billion-ton whip stretching half-way around the planet. Forget the carrier buckets, and the super-conducting cables that carried electricity down to the drive train from the solar power satellite seventy thousand kilometers above us. The piece that would do the real damage would be the central, load-bearing cable itself. It was only a couple of meters across at the bottom end, but it widened steadily as it went up. Made of bonded and doped silicon whiskers, with a tensile strength of two hundred million Newtons per square centimeter, it could handle an incredible load—almost two-thirds of a billion tons at its thinnest point. When that stored energy hit the atmosphere, there was going to be a fair amount of excitement down there on the surface. Not that we'd be watching it—the loss of the power satellite would make us look at our own survival problems; and as for the Colonies, a century of development would be ended.

By the time that Larry Marston came back with Jen Hasse and Alicia Kano, I doubt if I looked any more cheerful than Arnold Velasquez, down there at Tether Control. I sketched out the problem to the two newcomers; we had what looked like a hopeless situation on our hands.

"We have seventy-one hours," I concluded. "The only question we need to answer is, what will we be doing at this end during that time? Tether Control can coordinate disaster planning for the position on Earth. Arnold has already ruled out the possibility of any actual *help* from Earth—there are no rockets there that could be ready in time."

"What about the repair robots that you have on the cable?" asked Panosky, jumping into the conversation. "I thought they were all the way along its length."

"They are," said Jen Hasse. "But they're special purpose, not general purpose. We couldn't use one to look for a radioactive signal on a bucket, if that's what you're thinking of. Even if they had the right sensors for it, we'd need a week to reprogram them for the job.''

"We don't have a week," said Alicia quietly. "We have seventy-one hours." She was small and dark-haired, and never raised her voice much above the minimum level needed to reach her audience—but I had grown to rely on her brains more than anything else on the station.

"Seventy-one hours, if we act *now*," I said. "We've already agreed that we don't have time to sit here and wait for that bucket with the bomb to arrive—the terrorists must have planned it that way."

"I know." Alicia did not raise her voice. "Sitting and waiting won't do it. But the total travel time of a carrier from the surface up to synchronous orbit, or back down again, is a little less than a hundred and twenty hours. That means that the bucket carrying the bomb will be at least *half-way* here in sixty hours. And a bucket that started down from here in the next few hours—"

"—would have to pass the bucket with the bomb on the way up, before the deadline," broke in Hasse. He was already over at the Control Board, looking at the carrier schedule. He shook his head. "There's nothing scheduled for a passenger bucket, in the next twenty-four hours. It's all cargo going down."

"We're not looking for luxury." I went across to look at the schedule. "There are a couple of ore buckets with heavy metals scheduled for the next three hours. They'll have plenty of space in the top of them, and they're just forty minutes apart from each other. We could squeeze somebody in one or both of them, provided they were properly suited up. It wouldn't be a picnic, sitting in suits for three days, but we could do it."

"So how would we get at the bomb, even if we did that?" asked Larry. "It would be on the other side of the Beanstalk from us, passing at a relative velocity of six hundred kilometers an hour. We couldn't do more than wave to it as it went by, even if we knew just which bucket was carrying the bomb."

"That's the tricky piece." I looked at Jen Hasse. "Do you have enough control over the mass driver system, to slow everything almost to a halt whenever an inbound and an outbound bucket pass each other?"

He was looking doubtful, rubbing his nose thoughtfully. "Maybe. Trouble is, I'd have to do it nearly a hundred times, if you want to slow down for every pass. And it would take me twenty minutes to stop and start each one. I don't think we have that much time. What do you have in mind?"

I went across to the model of the Beanstalk that we kept on the Control Room table. We often found that we could illustrate things with it in a minute that would have taken thousands of words to describe.

"Suppose we were here, starting down in a bucket," I said. I put my hand on the model of the station, thirty-five thousand kilometers above the surface of the Earth in synchronous orbit. "And suppose that the bucket we want to get to, the one with the bomb, is here, on the way up. We put somebody in the inbound bucket, and it starts on down."

I began to turn the drive train, so that the buckets began to move up and down along the length of the Beanstalk.

"The people in the inbound bucket carry a radiation counter," I went on. "We'd have to put it on a long arm, so that it cleared all the other stuff on the Stalk, and reached around to get near the upbound buckets. We can do that, I'm sure—if we can't, we don't deserve to call ourselves engineers. We stop at each outbound carrier, and test for radioactivity. There should be enough of that from the fission trigger of the bomb, so that we'll easily pick up a count when we reach the right bucket. Then you, Jan, hold the drive train in the halt position. We leave the inbound bucket, swing around the Stalk, and get into the other carrier. Then we try and disarm the bomb. I've had some experience with that."

"You mean we get out and actually *climb* around the Beanstalk?" asked Larry. He didn't sound pleased at the prospect.

"Right. It shouldn't be too bad," I said. "We can anchor ourselves with lines to the ore bucket, so we can't fall."

Even as I was speaking, I realized that it didn't sound too

plausible. Climbing around the outside of the Beanstalk in a space-suit, twenty thousand kilometers or more up, dangling on a line connected to an ore bucket—and then trying to take apart a fusion bomb wearing gloves. No wonder Larry didn't like the sound of that assignment. I wasn't surprised when Arnold Velasquez chipped in over the circuit connecting us to Tether Control.

"Sorry, Jack, but that won't work—even if you could do it. You didn't let me read the full message from the terrorists. One of their conditions is that we mustn't stop the bucket train on the Stalk in the next three days. I think they were afraid that we would reverse the direction of the buckets, and bring the bomb back down to Earth to disarm it. I guess they don't realize that the Stalk wasn't designed to run in reverse."

"Damnation. What else do they have in that message?" I asked. "What can they do if we decide to stop the bucket drive anyway? How can they even tell that we're doing it?"

"We have to assume that they have a plant in here at Tether Control," replied Velasquez. "After all, they managed to get a bomb onto the Stalk in spite of all our security. They say they'll explode the bomb if we make any attempt to slow or stop the bucket train, and we simply can't afford to take the risk of doing that. We have to assume they can monitor what's going on with the Stalk drive train."

There was a long, dismal silence, which Alicia finally broke.

"So that seems to leave us with only one alternative," she said thoughtfully. Then she grimaced and pouted her mouth. "It's a two-bucket operation, and I don't even like to think about it—even though I had a grandmother who was a circus trapeze artiste."

She was leading in to something, and it wasn't like her to make a big build-up.

"That bad, eh?" I said.

"That bad, if we're lucky," she said. "If we're unlucky, I guess we'd all be dead in a month or two anyway, as the recycling runs down. For this to work, we need a good way of dissipating a lot of kinetic energy—something like a damped mechanical spring would do it. And we need a good way of sticking to the side of the Beanstalk. Then, we use *two* ore buckets—forty minutes apart would be all right—like this . . .''

She went over to the model of the Beanstalk. We watched her with mounting uneasiness as she outlined her idea. It sounded crazy. The only trouble was, it was that or nothing. Making choices in those circumstances is not difficult.

One good thing about space maintenance work—you develop versatility. If you can't wait to locate something down on Earth, then waste another week or so to have it shipped up to you, you get into the habit of making it for yourself. In an hour or so, we had a sensitive detector ready, welded on to a long extensible arm on the side of a bucket. When it was deployed, it would reach clear around the Beanstalk, missing all the drive train and repair station fittings, and hang in close to the outbound buckets. Jen had fitted it with a gadget that moved the detector rapidly upwards at the moment of closest approach of an upbound carrier, to increase the length of time available for getting a measurement of radioactivity. He swore that it would work on the fly, and have a better than ninety-nine percent chance of telling us which outbound bucket contained the bomb—even with a relative fly-by speed of six hundred kilometers an hour.

I didn't have time to argue the point, and in any case Jen was the expert. I also couldn't dispute his claim that he was easily the best qualified person to operate the gadget. He and Larry Marston, both fully suited-up, climbed into the ore bucket. We had to leave the ore in there, because the mass balance between in-going and outbound buckets was closely calculated to give good stability to the Beanstalk. It made for a lumpy seat, but no one complained. Alicia and I watched as the bucket was moved into the feeder system, accelerated up to the correct speed, attached to the drive train, and dropped rapidly out of sight down the side of the Beanstalk.

''That's the easy part,'' she said. ''They drop with the

bucket, checking the upbound ones as they come by for radioactivity, and that's all they have to do.''

"Unless they can't detect any signal," I said. "Then the bomb goes off, and they have the world's biggest roller-coaster ride. Twenty thousand kilometers of it, with the big thrill at the end.''

"They'd never reach the surface," replied Alicia absent-mindedly. "They'll frizzle up in the atmosphere long before they get there. Or maybe they won't. I wonder what the terminal velocity would be if you hung onto the Stalk cable?''

As she spoke, she was calmly examining an odd device that had been produced with impossible haste in the machine shop on the station's outer rim. It looked like an old-fashioned parachute harness, but instead of the main chute the lines led to a wheel about a meter across. From the opposite edge of the wheel, a doped silicon rope led to a hefty magnetic grapnel. Another similar arrangement was by her side.

"Here," she said to me. "Get yours on over your suit, and let's make sure we both know how to handle them. If you miss with the grapple, it'll be messy.''

I looked at my watch. "We don't have time for any dry run. In the next fifteen minutes we have to get our suits on, over to the ore buckets, and into these harnesses. Anyway, I don't think rehearsals here inside the station mean too much when we get to the real thing.''

We looked at each other for a moment, then began to suit up. It's not easy to estimate odds for something that has never been done before, but I didn't give us more than one chance in a hundred of coming out of it safely. Suits and harnesses on, we went and sat without speaking in the ore bucket.

I saw that we were sitting on a high-value shipment—silver and platinum, from one of the Belt mining operations. It wasn't comfortable, but we were certainly traveling in expensive company. Was it King Midas who complained that a golden throne is not right for restful sitting?

No matter what the final outcome, we were in for an

unpleasant trip. Our suits had barely enough capacity for a six-day journey. They had no recycling capacity, and if we had to go all the way to the halfway point we would be descending for almost sixty hours. We had used up three hours to the deadline, getting ready to go, so that would leave us only nine hours to do something about the bomb when we reached it. I suppose that it was just as bad or worse for Hasse and Marston. After they'd done their bit with the detector, there wasn't a thing they could do except sit in their bucket and wait, either for a message from us or an explosion far above them.

"Everything all right down there, Larry?" I asked, testing the radio link with them for the umpteenth time.

"Can't tell." He sounded strained. "We've passed three buckets so far, outbound ones, and we've had no signal from the detector. I guess that's as planned, but it would be nice to know it's working all right."

"You shouldn't expect anything for at least thirty-six hours," said Alicia.

"I know that. But it's impossible for us *not* to look at the detector whenever we pass an outbound bucket. Logically, we should be sleeping now and saving our attention for the most likely time of encounter—but neither one of us seems able to do it."

"Don't assume that the terrorists are all that logical, either," I said. "Remember, we are the ones who decided that they must have started the bomb on its way only a few hours ago. It's possible they put it into a bucket three or four days ago, and made up the deadline for some other reason. We think we can disarm that bomb, but they may not agree—and they may be right. All we may manage to do is advance the time of the explosion when we try and open up the casing."

As I spoke, I felt our bucket begin to accelerate. We were heading along the feeder and approaching the bucket drive train. After a few seconds, we were outside the station, dropping down the Beanstalk after Jen and Larry.

We sat there in silence for a while. I'd been up and down

the Stalk many times, and so had Alicia, but always in passenger modules. The psychologists had decided that people rode those a lot better when they were windowless. The cargo bucket had no windows either, but we had left the hatch open, to simplify communications with the other bucket and to enable us to climb out if and when the time came. We would have to close it when we were outside, or the aerodynamic pressures would spoil bucket stability when it finally entered the atmosphere—three hundred kilometers an hour isn't that fast, but it's a respectable speed for travel at full atmospheric pressure.

Our bucket was about four meters wide and three deep. It carried a load of seven hundred tons, so our extra mass was negligible. I stood at its edge and looked up, then down. The psychologists were quite right. Windows were a bad idea.

Above us, the Beanstalk rose up and up, occulting the backdrop of stars. It went past the synchronous station, which was still clearly visible as a blob on the stalk, then went on further up, invisible, to the solar power satellite and the great ballast weight, a hundred and five thousand kilometers above the surface of the Earth. On the Stalk itself, I could see the shielded superconductors that ran its full length, from the power satellite down to Tether Control in Quito. We were falling steadily, our rate precisely controlled by the linear synchronous motors that set the accelerations through pulsed magnetic fields. The power for that was drawn from the same superconducting cables. In the event of an electrical power failure, the buckets were designed to 'freeze' to the side of the Stalk with mechanical coupling. We had to build the system that way, because about once a year we had some kind of power interruption—usually from small meteorites, not big enough to trigger the main detector system, but large enough to penetrate the shields and mess up the power transmission.

It was looking down, though, that produced the real effect. I felt my heart begin to pump harder, and I was gripping at the side of the bucket with my space-suit gloves. When you are in a rocket-propelled ship, you don't get any real feeling of height. Earth is another part of the Universe, something independent of you. But from our position, moving along the side of the Beanstalk, I had quite a different feeling. We were *connected* to the planet. I could see the Stalk, dwindling smaller and smaller down to the Earth below. I had a very clear feeling that I could fall all the way down it, down to the big, blue-white globe at its foot. Although I had lived up at the station quite happily for over five years, I suddenly began to worry about the strength of the main cable. It was a ridiculous concern. There was a safety factor of ten built into its design, far more than a rational engineer would use for anything. It was more likely that the bottom would fall out of our ore bucket, than that the support cable for the Beanstalk would break. I was kicking myself for my illogical fears, until I noticed Alicia also peering out at the Beanstalk, as though trying to see past the clutter of equipment there to the cable itself. I wasn't the only one thinking wild thoughts.

"You certainly get a different look at things from here," I said, trying to change the mood. "Did you ever see anything like that before?"

She shook her head ponderously—the suits weren't made for agility of movement.

"Not up here, I haven't," she replied. "But I once went up to the top of the towers of the Golden Gate Bridge in San Francisco, and looked at the support cables for that. It was the same sort of feeling. I began to wonder if they could take the strain. That was just for a bridge, not even a big one. What will happen if we don't make it, and they blow up the Beanstalk?"

I shrugged, inside my suit, then realized that she couldn't see the movement. "This is the only bridge to space that we've got. We'll be out of the bridge business, and back in the ferry-boat business. They'll have to start sending stuff up by rockets again. Shipments won't be a thousandth of what they are now, until another Stalk can be built. That will take thirty years, starting without this one to help us—even if the

Colonies survive all right, and work on nothing else. We don't have to worry about that, though. We won't be there to hassle with it."

She nodded. "We were in such a hurry to get away it never occurred to me that we'd be sitting here for a couple of days with nothing to do but worry. Any ideas?"

"Yes. While you were making the reel and grapnel, I thought about that. The only thing that's worth our attention right now is a better understanding of the geometry of the Stalk. We need to know exactly where to position ourselves, where we'll set the grapnels, and what our dynamics will be as we move. I've asked Ricardo to send us schematics and lay-outs over the suit videos. He's picking out ones that show the drive train, the placing of the superconductors, and the unmanned repair stations. I've also asked him to deactivate all the repair robots. It's better for us to risk a failure on the maintenance side than have one of the monitoring robots wandering along the Stalk and mixing in with what we're trying to do."

"I heard what you said to Panosky, but it still seems to me that the robots ought to be useful."

"I'd hoped so, too. I checked again with Jen, and he agrees we'd have to reprogram them, and we don't have the time for it. It would take weeks. Jen said having them around would be like taking along a half-trained dog, bumbling about while we work. Forget that one."

As we talked, we kept our eyes open for the outbound buckets, passing us on the other side of the Beanstalk. We were only about ten meters from them at closest approach and they seemed to hurtle past us at an impossible speed. The idea of hitching on to one of them began to seem more and more preposterous. We settled down to look in more detail at the configuration of cables, drive train, repair stations and buckets that was being flashed to us over the suit videos.

It was a weary time, an awful combination of boredom and tension. The video images were good, but there is a limit to what you can learn from diagrams and simulations. About once an hour, Jen Hasse and Larry Marston called in from the lower bucket beneath us, reporting on the news—or lack of it—regarding the bomb detection efforts. A message relayed from Panosky at Tether Control reported no progress in negotiations with the terrorists. The fanatics simply didn't believe their terms couldn't be met. That was proof of their naivety, but didn't make them any less dangerous.

It was impossible to get comfortable in our suits. The ore buckets had never been designed for a human occupant, and we couldn't find a level spot to stretch out. Alicia and I passed into a half-awake trance, still watching the images that flashed onto the suit videos, but not taking in much of anything. Given that we couldn't sleep, we were probably in the closest thing we could get to a resting state. I hoped that Jen and Larry would keep their attention up, watching an endless succession of buckets flash past them and checking each one for radioactivity count.

The break came after fifty-four hours in the bucket. We didn't need to hear the details from the carrier below us to know they had it—Larry's voice crackled with excitement.

"Got it," he said. "Jen picked up a strong signal from the bucket we just passed. If you leave the ore carrier within thirty-four seconds, you'll have thirty-eight minutes to get ready for it to come past you. It will be the second one to reach you. For God's sake don't try for the wrong one."

There was a pause, then Larry said something I would never have expected from him. "We'll lose radio contact with you in a while, as we move further along the Stalk. Good luck, both of you—and look after him, Alicia."

I didn't have time to think that one through—but shouldn't he be telling *me* to look after *her*? It was no time for puzzling. We were up on top of our bucket in a second, adrenalin moving through our veins like an electric current. The cable was whipping past us at a great rate; the idea of forsaking the relative safety of the ore bucket for the naked wall of the Beanstalk seemed like insanity. We watched as one of the repair stations, sticking out from the cable into open space, flashed past.

"There'll be another one of those coming by in thirty-five

seconds," I said. "We've got to get the grapnels onto it, and
we'll be casting blind. I'll throw first, and you follow a
second later. Don't panic if I miss—remember, we only have
to get one good hook there."

"Count us down, Jack," said Alicia. She wasn't one to
waste words in a tight spot.

I pressed the digital read-out in my suit, and watched the
count move from thirty-five down to zero.

"Count-down display on Channel Six," I said, and
picked up the rope and grapnel. I looked doubtfully at the
wheel that was set in the mddle of the thin rope, then even
looked suspiciously at the rope itself, wondering if it would
take the strain. That shows how the brain works in a crisis—
that rope would have held a herd of elephants with no trouble
at all.

I cast the grapnel as the count touched to zero, and Alicia
threw a fraction later. Both ropes were spliced onto both
suits, so it was never clear which grapnel took hold. Our
bucket continued to drop rapidly towards Earth, but we were
jerked off the top of it and went zipping on downwards
fractionally slower as the friction reel in the middle of the
rope unwound, slowing our motion.

We came to a halt about fifty meters down the Beanstalk
from the grapnel, after a rough ride in which our deceleration
must have averaged over seven gee. Without that reel to slow
us down gradually, the jerk of the grapnel as it caught the
repair station wall would have snapped our spines when we
were lifted from the ore bucket.

We hung there, swinging free, suspended from the wall of
the Stalk. As the reel began to take up the line that had been
paid out, I made the mistake of looking down. We dangled
over an awful void, with nothing between us and that vast
drop to the Earth below but the thin line above us. When we
came closer to the point of attachment to the Beanstalk wall, I
saw just how lucky we had been. One grapnel had missed
completely, and the second one had caught the very lip of the
repair station platform. Another foot to the left and we would
have missed it altogether.

We clawed our way up to the station rim—easy enough to do, because the gravity at that height was only a fraction of a gee, less than a tenth. But a fall from there would be inexorable, and we would have fallen away from the Beanstalk, with no chance to re-connect to it. Working together, we freed the grapnel and readied both lines and grapnels for re-use. After that there was nothing to do but cling to the side of the Beanstalk, watch the sweep of the heavens above us, and wait for the outbound ore buckets to come past us.

The first one came by after seventeen minutes. I had the clock read-out to prove it, otherwise I would have solemnly sworn that we had waited there for more than an hour, holding to our precarious perch. Alicia seemed more at home there than I was. I watched her moving the grapnel to the best position for casting it, then settle down patiently to wait.

It is hard to describe my own feelings in that period. I watched the movement of the stars above us, in their great circle, and wondered if we would be alive in another twenty minutes. I felt a strong communion with the old sailors of Earth's seas, up in their crow's-nest in a howling gale, sensing nothing but darkness, high-blown spindrift, perilous breakers ahead, and the dipping, rolling stars above.

Alicia kept her gaze steadily downwards, something that I found hard to do. She had inherited a good head for heights from her circus-performer grandmother.

"I can see it," she said at last. "All ready for a repeat performance?"

"Right." I swung the grapnel experimentally. "Since we can see it this time, we may as well throw together."

I concentrated on the bucket sweeping steadily up towards us, trying to estimate the distance and the time that it would take before it reached us. We both drew back our arms at the same moment and lobbed the grapnels towards the center of the bucket.

It came past us with a monstrous, silent rush. Again we felt the fierce acceleration as we were jerked away from the Beanstalk wall and shot upwards after the carrier. Again, I realized that we couldn't have done it without Alicia's friction reel, smoothing the motion for us. This time, it was more dangerous than when we had left the downbound bucket. Instead of trying to reach the stationary wall of the Stalk, we were now hooked onto the moving bucket. We swung wildly beneath it in its upward flight, narrowly missing contact with elements of the drive train, and then with another repair station that flashed past a couple of meters to our right.

Finally, somehow, we damped our motion, reeled in the line, slid back the cover to the ore bucket and fell safely forward inside it. I was completely drained. It must have been all nervous stress—we hadn't expended a significant amount of physical energy. I know that Alicia felt the same way as I did, because after we plumped over the rim of the carrier we both fell to the floor and lay there without speaking for several minutes. It gives some idea of our state of mind when I say that the bucket we had reached, with a four megaton bomb inside it that might go off at any moment, seemed like a haven of safety.

We finally found the energy to get up and look around us. The bucket was loaded with manufactured goods, and I thought for a sickening moment that the bomb was not there. We found it after five minutes of frantic searching. It was a compact blue cylinder, a meter long and fifty centimeters wide, and it had been cold-welded to the wall of the bucket. I knew the design.

"There it is," I said to Alicia. Then I didn't know what to say next. It was the most advanced design, not the big, old one that I had been hoping for.

"Can you disarm it?" asked Alicia.

"In principle. There's only one problem. I know how it's put together—but I'll never be able to get it apart wearing a suit. The fingerwork I'd need is just too fine for gloves. We seem to be no better off than we were before."

We sat there side by side, looking at the bomb. The irony of the situation was sinking in. We had reached it, just as we hoped we could. Now, it seemed we might as well have been still back in the station.

"Any chance that we could get it free and dump it overboard?'' asked Alicia. ''You know, just chuck the thing away from the bucket.''

I shook my head, aware again of how much my suit impeded freedom of movement. ''It's spot-welded. We couldn't shift it. Anyway, free fall from here would give it an impact orbit, and a lot of people might be killed if it went off inside the atmosphere. If we were five thousand kilometers higher, perigee would be at a safe height above the surface—but we can't afford to wait for another sixteen hours until the bucket gets up that high. Look, I've got another idea, but it will mean that we'll lose radio contact with the station.''

''So what?'' said Alicia. Her voice was weary. ''There's not a thing they can do to help us anyway.''

''They'll go out of their minds with worry down on Earth, if they don't know what's happening here.''

''I don't see why we should keep all of it for ourselves. What's your idea, Jack?''

''All right.'' I summoned my reserves of energy. ''We're in vacuum now, but this bucket would be air-tight if we were to close the top hatch again. I have enough air in my suit to make a breathable atmosphere in this enclosed space, at least for long enough to let me have a go at the bomb. We've got nearly twelve hours to the deadline, and if I can't disarm it in that time I can't do it at all.''

Alicia looked at her air reserve indicator and nodded. ''I can spare you some air, too, if I open up my suit.''

''No. We daren't do that. We have one other big problem—the temperature. It's going to feel really cold in here, once I'm outside my suit. I'll put my heaters on to maximum, and leave the suit open, but I'm still not sure I can get much done before I begin to freeze up. If I begin to lose feeling in my fingers, I'll need your help to get me back inside. So you have to stay in your suit. Once I'm warmed up, I can try again.''

She was silent for a few moments, repeating the calculations that I had just done myself.

''You'll only have enough air to try it twice,'' she said at last. ''If you can't do it in one shot, you'll have to let me have a go. You can direct me on what has to be done.''

There was no point in hanging around. We sent a brief message to the station, telling them what we were going to do, then closed the hatch and began to bleed air out of my suit and into the interior of the bucket. We used the light from Alicia's suit, which had ample power to last for several days.

When the air pressure inside the bucket was high enough for me to breathe, I peeled out of my suit. It was as cold as charity in that metal box, but I ignored that and crouched down alongside the bomb in my underwear and bare feet.

I had eleven hours at the most. Inside my head, I fancied that I could hear a clock ticking. That must have been only my fancy. Modern bombs have no place for clockwork timers.

By placing my suit directly beneath my hands, I found that I could get enough heat from the thermal units to let me keep on working without a break. The clock inside my head went on ticking, also without a break.

On and on and on.

They say that I was delirious when we reached the station. That's the only way the Press could reconcile my status as public hero with the things that I said to the President when he called up to congratulate us.

I suppose I could claim delirium if I wanted to—five days without sleep, two without food, oxygen starvation, and frostbite of the toes and ears, that might add up to delirium. I had received enough warmth from the suit to keep my hands going, because it was very close to them, but that had been at the expense of some of my other extremities. If it hadn't been for Alicia, cramming me somehow back into the suit after I had disarmed the bomb, I would have frozen to death in a couple of hours.

As it was, I smelled ripe and revolting when they unpacked us from the bucket and winkled me out of my suit—Alicia hadn't been able to re-connect me with the plumbing arrangements.

So I told the President that the World Congress was composed of a giggling bunch of witless turds, who couldn't sense a global need for more bridges to space if a Beanstalk were pushed up their backsides—which was where I thought they kept their brains. Not quite the speech that we used to get from the old-time returning astronauts, but I must admit it's one that I'd wanted to give for some time. The audience was there this time, with the whole world hanging on my words over live TV.

We've finally started construction on the second Beanstalk. I don't know if my words had anything to do with it, but there was a lot of public pressure after I said my piece, and I like to think that I had some effect.

And me? I'm designing the third Beanstalk; what else? But I don't think I'll hold my breath waiting for a Congressional Vote of Thanks for my efforts saving the first one.

EDITOR'S INTRODUCTION TO:

INVISIBLE ENCOUNTER

by Dian Girard

*Dian Girard continues to amaze me. I suppose, given that her man is a scientist/executive with IBM, it was inevitable that she go from being an artist to working with computers; but now she's moved beyond that, changing to a supervisorial position in a new company. Every time she's about to quit work in order to stay home and write, they offer her another promotion.*

*Some idiot once asked me why Cheryl Harbottle stories have become a tradition in my anthologies. The answer is awfully simple. I like them.*

# INVISIBLE ENCOUNTER

## Dian Girard

It must have come in through a docking port. That was the official "best guess" at any rate. It came in from Outside, which was pretty amazing in itself. Not many creatures could stand the cold void of outer space and then seem equally at home in a space station designed for humans. No one knew that it WAS at home, of course, since they couldn't catch it to find out. It moved disturbingly fast. All anyone had been able to report was a blur of movement, like a quick shimmer and ripple in the air.

It didn't seem to be very large, but it was destructive and potentially dangerous. It made holes in wall panels like a hot knife going through butter. So far all of the reports had come from the Agricultural Sectors. There were disquieting stories of odds and ends of assemblies missing, and certain specific tools vanishing without a trace. One thing was sure. Anything that could make four-inch holes in styrene bulkheads could obviously make similar holes in a human being.

The big question was, was it intelligent? If it was, the theft of tools and parts of electronic assemblies might have an important meaning. It could be anything from a shipwrecked sailor to an actively antagonistic opponent. It could be making some sort of apparatus to blow up the space station. It might not even stop at the space station. Some damage had been reported from one of the Communications groups. It could be notifying its home world and planning an all-out war against mankind. The danger could not be overlooked. The xenobiologists were excited, and the Administration was alarmed. If word got around there might be panic, and panic on a space station was like fire on a ship at sea. There was no

205

place to run. The whole matter was strictly hush-hush in an environment where everything was already Top Secret.

Things being the way they were, Cheryl Harbottle wasn't overly alarmed when she saw the hole. She bent down to look at it closer and frowned. Sure enough, a neat quarter-circle was gone from the corner of the bright yellow cupboard door, right where it met the steel frame. The plastic door looked almost like it had been melted away. Humph! Cheap construction. Either it had come from the factory that way, or the plastic was starting to break down. That was what came of jobbing everything out to the lowest bidder. Still, it seemed odd that she hadn't noticed it before.

Cheryl pulled at the knob and swung the small door open. A whoosh of air zipped past her ear with an audible thunder clap—just like a miniature jet fighter. She stood up and looked around confusedly. What the devil was THAT! There were a lot of odd things on the Station, granted, but supersonic anythings weren't part of the overall plan.

She glanced around the small dining area and spotted the second hole. Now really! One hole she might have overlooked, but not two—especially when the second one was smack dab in the middle of the dining room's Genuine Imitation Tiffany lamp.

Cheryl did what any red-blooded woman would have done under the circumstances. She sat down at the dining room table and dialed up a cup of coffee. There was the faint familiar click as her order moved into the microwave unit and a moment later the Autochef panel slid back and a styrene cup of steaming imitation coffee appeared.

She picked it up. There was a rush of air, a tiny BOOM!, and she found herself with a lapful of hot coffee. The cup handle was hanging neatly from her forefinger. The rest of the cup was gone. She swore, loudly.

Cheryl tried again. This time she didn't even get a chance to pick up the cup. It vanished, handle and all, right off of the table. She got up, grabbed a towel, and mopped up the spills. This was like playing fairy chess with a Monster Queen! It rushed out, grabbed something, and vanished. But what on Earth—or in space—was it?

Maybe she could slow it down enough to get a look at it. She rummaged around in some drawers, trying to ignore the clammy feel of her wet clothes, and found a thick plastic box that had originally held some of her husband's scientific instruments. She held it over the Autochef panel, in back of where a cup ought to appear, and dialed up another cup of coffee. The cup appeared, disappeared, and she was left with a bigger pool of coffee and a box with a neat round hole in the bottom. Phooey. Cheryl tossed the box on the floor and flounced into the bedroom to change her sodden pink jumpsuit for a pretty hostess gown. It was one of her favorites. It tied around the neck and had a series of gold-colored plastic fasteners on the front.

She stepped back into the dining room and got caught in what felt like a whirlwind. There was an invisible flurry of activity around her and the gown slithered slowly to the floor. Every one of the dainty fasteners had vanished—along with the bows on her bedroom slippers.

Cheryl was too mad to even swear. She bent down to pull up her ravaged gown and felt a little PLINK! as the back fastener on her brassiere went the way of everything else.

She straightened up, holding her gown and other things with one hand and mentally vowed vengeance. She'd kill it! She'd stomp it into little pieces! She'd tear it limb from limb—if it had limbs.

There was one little problem. She had to catch it first.

She changed clothes again—this time to a fluffy wrap-around robe with no plastic fasteners—and thought about traps. She didn't have anything heavy enough to drop on it, even if she was quick enough to do the dropping. Off-hand she couldn't think of any way to make a spring trap either. A box trap, maybe? She'd seen pictures of little boys with those. You propped up a box with a stick, tied a piece of string to the stick, and put something yummy under the box. Then you jerked away the stick and whatever you were trying to catch got caught. The way this little monster moved she wasn't sure she'd get a chance to bait the trap, but it was worth a try.

She went into the bedroom and pulled a deep drawer out of a wall cabinet, arbitrarily dumping the contents on the bed. A long chain from her jewelry box and one of her violated bedroom slippers made the trigger. She carried the things to the dining room table, tied the chain to the slipper, and carefully set up the trap. Now for the bait.

She yanked open a cupboard that held a bunch of small odds and ends, grabbed a handful of doodads, slammed the cupboard shut, and tossed her booty under the trap. There was an instant's silence, and then that odd flurry of motion. Cheryl jerked the chain. The slipper came loose and the drawer fell. She laughed gleefully—a little too soon.

The drawer was made of light-weight polystyrene. First there was a hole in one side. Then the drawer started to look like a piece of Swiss cheese. Then there was nothing left at all. Cheryl even fancied that she could hear a satisfied belch.

She sat down and stared at the table for a long moment. Then she smiled slowly, evilly. There was one thing in the apartment she knew wasn't plastic. She grabbed up her slipper in one hand and put her other hand flat on the Autochef panel. She pressed down and back, firmly. There was a goodly amount of spring tension, but the panel eventually slid back enough for her to wedge the slipper in place.

There was no way she could dial up a cup of coffee, in spite of her invisible opponent's obvious fancy for coffee cups. The microwave interlock wouldn't let the unit work if the door was open. But how about something cold, that wouldn't activate the oven circuit?

She dialed up a dish of butterscotch pudding. The Autochef made its customary encouraging click. There was a moment of quiet and then that odd little flurry. Cheryl jerked away the slipper and the panel snapped shut. There was a satisfying series of bumps, thumps, and crashes from inside the metal-clad oven.

Cheryl reached for the disposal button, which would wisk anything left in the Autochef off to the recycler—and paused.

Whatever her nemesis was, it was just trying to get along. Sort of like the racoons that her mother had battled in the summer cottage when she was a little girl. Animals couldn't help being what they were, after all. It had only cost her a dress, a pair of slippers, and some little damage to her cupboards. She could get that fixed easily enough. It wasn't very big, and it was probably scared. She reached for the communicator instead and called a friend in Agriculture.

"Hello, Toby? Can you come over? There seems to be a mouse trapped in my Autochef."

# HOW TO BECOME A SPACE COLONIST

## J. E. Pournelle, Ph.D.

It would seem simple enough. With all our experience we must know what makes a good space crewcritter, and thus it remains only to collect the information from the experts and write it up in my inimitably readable manner.

Alas, no. First, there aren't any experts. There are those who must select astronauts, but they aren't experts because no one knows what makes a good space crewcritter. (With respect to the ladies, may I revert to "crewman" in future? I understand that we need women spacers as well as colonists. Alas, I find "crewperson" inelegant and affected, and my humorously attempted substitute no better.)

It was easy enough to select the first astronauts. We (well, those who did the job; I was a consultant to the selection team) knew what we were looking for: hot jet jockeys. Flying the first spacecraft would take skill, and for MERCURY at least the most important—and most difficult—part of the mission was to get back alive. So we wanted test pilots, who were highly motivated, able to endure claustrophobia (as John Glenn once remarked, you didn't ride the MERCURY capsule, you wore it), able to endure boredom (not only the endless training for a single short mission, but the endless waiting in the capsule before launch), phlegmatic, adaptable, and above all, mission oriented.

There were lots of men who fit that description. I say men advisedly: Jackie Cochran was about the only qualified woman test pilot in the US at the time. There were thought to be plumbing problems with women astronauts. The Germans didn't like the idea of women in space owing to some experiences the Luftwaffe had with women test pilots (I remember Konrad Buettner, former chief of German Aviation Medicine, lecturing at length on the subject). Thus the problem was to select among a number of qualified male applicants.

The first cut was simple. Select the best pilots, then pick the best engineers from among them. They would all be in excellent physical condition or they wouldn't be test pilots. This reduced the field considerably, but not enough. There was one name that stood higher than the rest: Iven C. Kinchloe, test pilot with an engineering Ph.D., rated by his peers as a superb aerobatic pilot. Among betting men in the human factors business he was the definite favorite to the first man we'd put on the Moon (assuming that he wouldn't have a grey beard by then: we weren't shooting for any ridiculous date like 1969 back then). But Kincheloe was killed flying a routine acceptance flight-test of an F-104, and no other individual stood quite that high. There was a definite need for an objective method of selecting the very best from among an outstanding group. No easy task.

In fact, there wasn't any way on Earth to do it; and we couldn't get off Earth without astronauts.

Therefore a number of irrelevant tests were devised. They weren't *intended* to be irrelevant: remember that no one knew what the job requirement was. One criterion chosen was heat tolerance: we weren't sure what the capsule interior temperature would be during re-entry. Thus candidates were cooked in labs across the country (including mine). Startle reactions were tested. Physical endurance tests were devised.

One such test, incidentally, was pretty well known by its inventors to be irrelevant: this one involved sticking the candidate's feet in a bucket of ice water and leaving them there for half an hour. It measured nothing relevant to space conditions, but it was thought a good measure of motivation (and probably was; try it sometime).

There were centrifuge tests, shaker-pot tests, and any number of tests of physiological response to stress, usually conducted while the poor SOB was trying to fly a flight simulator. Now true: a lot of these tests were done simply because they *could* be done; it isn't often that human factors scientists get an opportunity like that. . .

Anyway, the final result was the group of super-heroes known as The Astronauts, and judging by their performance we must have done something right: the missions were performed just about flawlessly. We lost no astronauts in space and only three in a ground accident. A few had problems once they returned from their missions, and no wonder, given the pressures they were under—and given the way we kept cutting back the program, so that men who'd trained all their lives for a single job found that no one was going to let them do that job again. By and large, though, the selection program worked.

There were the Seven, and then some others, and more after that, and meanwhile we were learning a bit more about space conditions so that the ground tests bore more relationship to the actual mission; but although the original selection tests were modified, the fundamental philosophy didn't change. We wanted highly motivated hot jet jockeys in splendid physical condition. Came Apollo and some one pointed out that you'd like maybe a real scientist or two on the Moon, so compromise just a little on the test-pilot aspect; but the scientists could learn to fly.

Incidentally, to set the record straight: there was no bias against science in the Apollo program. There *was* bias against compromising the mission, which by Presidential Directive was to land a man on the Moon and bring him home safely. The one present we weren't going to give the nation was a capsule of crispy critters. Thus performance and stamina, not scientific ability, were the qualifications demanded.

Besides, in the early days we—all of us associated with the space program—made a mistake. We assumed that once the nation had gone to the Moon, we would be in space to stay. After all, wasn't that the progression in every science fiction story we'd ever read? Sure: Heinlein had postulated a hiatus after initial space flight, but even he thought that once on *the Moon* we would be in space to stay. . .

Came SKYLAB, and the criteria changed again. You didn't need three pilots. Two and a flight surgeon or even a genuine scientist (pilot-trained, of course) would do, and while we're at it let's expand the education of the pilots; but still the lot fell to men in splendid physical condition; men so highly motivated that they'd train for a very long time; and other things being equal, test-pilot status certainly didn't hurt. And once again it paid off: remember Kerwin and Conrad going outside to fix the solar panel and thus save the mission? And it took a great deal of physical strength; Conrad had to heave up on the stuck panel ("I gave a mighty heave, and the science pilot gave a mighty heave, whereupon everything went black and I shot straight up into the air.") with all his strength, and that was barely enough.

The repair of SKYLAB was one of the most dramatic events of the space program. To the general public it was one more proof of NASA's wisdom: obviously they were sending up the right kind of people. Strong, mission-oriented, motivated, splendid physical specimens: in short, astronauts, a word that roughly meant "hero".

By the time of SKYLAB IV (the third manned mission in NASA's confusing nomenclature) NASA wasn't so sure. First, Pogue threw up; not disastrous or even unusual, but NASA regulations required that the crew freeze the barf and bring it back to Earth. Instead they heaved the gup out the airlock. NASA heard about it (SKYLAB was bugged). The SKYLAB IV crew earned the first ground-to-space reprimand in history. Shortly after that, things got worse. The crew didn't keep up the work schedule. They made errors. They didn't talk to the ground much, and when they did, they bitched. Finally there was a near mutiny as they flatly refused to continue the overcrowded work schedule laid out for them.

Houston's response was predictable: as the astronauts got into difficulties, Hutchinson, the lead flight director, ordered the schedule speeded up; he piled on more work, on the theory that the astronauts were lazy. Eventually Lt. Col. Carr, the SKYLAB IV commander, called a halt, and for a full day the crew did what they damned well wanted to.

Some NASA administrators began to wonder if they'd selected the wrong people.

To make it worse, the astronaut who seemed to be giving the most trouble was a civilian physicist; the science pilot for the mission. Maybe, just maybe, if he'd been a colonel like the other two? If the space program had just kept that gung-ho mission-oriented attitude?

Except that Gibson, the complainer, made more usable suggestions about design of future space habitats than any other astronaut in the history of the program, and Pogue was not far behind; while Carr, a Marine and thoroughly military, was a vehement spokesman against the impossible mission schedule.

And all three worried excessively about staying in shape; in fact, one reason they didn't keep up the science schedule was the time they put in on the exercise machine.

Clearly some rethinking was needed.

\* \* \*

That's history. We come now to the recent past. NASA had to select crews for the Shuttle. Who?

The pressure was on. Not so many Greek gods this time. Maybe that's why the public lost interest in space: they couldn't identify with the hero-astronauts, and couldn't conceive of an ordinary person going up there.

After all, the Apollo follow-on programs (my last professional assignment was to work with the mission-planning team for Apollo Extended Lunar Missions) were cancelled due to the low Nielsen ratings of the final two Apollo missions. The public didn't find space glamorous enough; therefore, it was seriously said by presumably intelligent people, let's put glamour in space: let's put up some beautiful women. And some blacks, while we're at it.

This wasn't the official view, of course; I don't even know how far this Madison Avenue approach to space extended. I was outside by then; but I was at one meeting where some pretty high-up officials talked like characters out of the movie *Network,* and they meant every word of it.

Incidentally, I always thought the whole theory was silly. Leaving out the intellectual wisdom of using sheer popularity as the principal factor for making a decision as important as any in human history—and the space program in my judgment is as important as the invention of agriculture, or fire, or the lung—the TV ratings weren't the proper way to measure public interest. Analogy: people watch the World Series; but even an avid baseball fan may turn to the news instead of an in-season game. Does this mean we should abolish baseball?

And the program's lack of glamour was as much NASA's fault as anyone's; as Ted Sturgeon once remarked, NASA's most astounding achievement was to make mankind's greatest achievement look *dull*. Most of the PR types NASA hired were old flacks; it wasn't until very late in the game that they cooperated with interest dramatists; and they were *always* willing to shunt science fiction writers off into a corner to make room for the "legitimate" press (such as the East Pasadena Shopping News, which got press passes to VIKING while the foremost science fiction writer of our time was refused admission. No, I am not making this up. I was there, having taken the trouble to get a press card. And yes, some quite high officials of NASA were informed, and couldn't understand why the decision was shortsighted.)

But for a number of reasons, the Greek god approach was to be abandoned: some plain folks would be selected. The word went out.

And lo, the applications came thick and fast. Meters-tall stacks of them flowed in. Of these thousands, there were hundreds of applicants qualified under any rational rule you could think of.

It was a hell of a demonstration of public interest in space, but nobody thought of that. What they thought was, My God, what do we do now?

Well, number one, don't change the rules for pilots. Select them from among the best jet jockeys, and insist on physical perfection. No one's going to argue with that, and it makes sense anyway: Shuttle isn't the easiest bird to fly, having the gliding characteristics of a flat rock.

But now we've got to select science types, and we're stuck. We've dropped the Class I FAA pilot's physical. We've dropped the training flights in T-birds. We've dropped the feet-in-cold-water test (which was one of the most efficacious in eliminating applicants, relevant or not). We've dropped the centrifuge tests. So how are we to choose among hundreds of qualified people? What rational means can be employed?

Well, I don't know. Maybe it would help to introduce you to someone who didn't make it.

Meet Dr. Danielle Goldwater. Graduate of Yale University and Yale Medical School. Residency and training at Stanford. Of the woman applicants, one of the very few who could do any chinups. Not obviously inferior in any of the other tests given. Certainly not unintelligent. Able to get around in a full-pressure suit; found it tiring, but so did most of the others, men and women. Not claustrophobic when stuffed into the personal rescue sphere (a sort of enormous plastic beachball with internal life support which will be used to carry personnel without pressure suits through vacuum). Certainly motivated—in fact still works in space research. Willing to go. Why wasn't she selected?

No one I know is certain: but she wears glasses. She doesn't have 20/20 vision; and those selected all seem to be able to see without glasses. The official criterion now is 20/20 without glasses for pilots, and 20/100 correctable for the scientific personnel.

As near as I can tell, those selected in the latest round of tests are Greek gods and goddesses; nearly perfect physical specimens. Given equality in academic and scientific credentials, the ones who don't wear glasses and who are in the best physical condition get the nod.

Sensible, right?

Wrong.

\* \* \*

Once again we're faced with irrelevant criteria. If left to me (which it surely won't be) I'd rather see the old feet in the cold water, which is also irrelevant but does measure pain tolerance and endurance and motivation, and thus has (in my judgment) more power to predict success in space than does the presence or absence of glasses.

Look: the major objection to spectacles in space is that when you're buttoned into a full pressure suit, you can't adjust or wipe sweat off your eyeglasses; and that might be important. Only: present NASA policy is that the non-pilot crew on Shuttle won't even *have* full pressure suits. If the ship loses pressure, they're to use the beach balls.

And general physical excellence isn't relevant either. Sure, if Kerwin and especially Conrad hadn't been in terrific shape, they'd never have been able to endure the early days in SKYLAB and certainly wouldn't have been able to go outside and fix the crippled bird; but so what? The science types on Shuttle couldn't EVA if they had to: no suits. And EVA is the only really physically demanding job.

Maybe health considerations? I think not. The evidence is against it, anyway. Dr. Harold Sandler, who heads a group at NASA Ames studying space physiology has concluded from his tests (and from the SKYLAB data) that "from what we've seen, there are no physiological limits to prevent anyone from going to space. Some may need protection, such as g-suits, but the protection systems are readily available. The only real limit is common sense."

Present data indicates that age isn't particularly important either.

And finally there's this remark from Dr. Heany at the Skylab Life Science Symposium: "I have found myself asking, repeatedly, why there is this quite extraordinary emphasis on physical fitness for function in a weightless environment. Great muscular strength and endurance, which have obvious survival value in the jungle, are all but redundant in a zero-gravity environment . . . We can select individuals already adapted to something closer to zero gravity . . . I refer to sedentary, skinny, small individuals, like myself, who would be better suited than these athletes.''

It's true enough that for *long* missions in zero-gravity, the healthiest jocks who exercised the most came back in the best shape; but that's long missions, and a year after their return there was no physiological evidence that any of the astronauts had ever been in space.

But having said all that: I don't know what criteria NASA ought to be using. There are too many applicants. They have to be weeded out somehow. Since we don't know the relevant criteria, NASA will *have* to use irrelevant. I wish them luck.

\* \* \*

So: if you're looking for a spot on the Shuttle to be paid for by NASA, you've not a lot of chance, and I can't help you much. My best advice is to study an experimental science, get top grades, and in general act as if you're trying to win an appointment to the faculty of Harvard University. In addition, you'll want to be a perfect physical specimen with 20/20 vision (at worst 20/100 correctable to 20/20). It won't harm you to be able to do 100 pushups, swim five miles, run ten, and do 30 chinups.

Not much help, eh? Sorry about that. Wish I had better news. And I do.

\* \* \*

However, my good news requires some optimistic assumptions about the future of man in space (and thus, in my view, optimism about the future of mankind). I must assume that space flight will become routine; that there will be a lot more than quickie scientific Shuttle missions in future.

Let's assume, for instance, that we opt for Solar Power Satellites. How can you get on the construction gang?

Well, alas, the physical condition parameter is *very* important here. The early construction crews will have to endure low to null gravity for periods as long as humans can stand them without permanent physiological damage; and will have to do a lot of EVA work, which we know to be as tiring as any human activity including professional sports or lumberjacking (in the old days before chainsaws, yet).

The skills are fairly obvious. There will be room for power-system engineers, construction workers, riggers, electronics experts, power workers, cooks, physicians, and the whole panoply of talents required to do heavy construction in an isolated environment. Study what kind of people INCO took to the Guatemala jungles to build their power plant, and you'll have a good idea of the skills needed for power stations in space.

\* \* \*

But beyond the initial construction there is another phase: the exploitation of space. We can assume that some kind of station large enough to provide artificial (spin) gravity has been constructed, and various companies are looking for workers who'll go up and make them lots of money—and incidentally get rich themselves, since for a good long while salaries of space-based workers are going to be a pretty small part of the cost of doing business in space. Who will they pick?

Here we get into a myriad of unknowns: not in the sense that we can't predict the personnel policies of GM and Westinghouse and IBM and Upjohn, because we can, and if you're really interested in spaceflight you'll go read up on what they teach personnel managers in business administration courses. No: the unknowns are in space itself.

ITEM: what *are* the long-term effects of low gravity on humans? SKYLAB gave no real answers, just more questions. True, the crew of SKYLAB IV, who stayed up longest, seemed to make healthy physiological adjustments that the SKYLAB III crew weren't up long enough to experience— but IV's crew also had the greatest losses of bone calcium. Would that too have ceased had they stayed up longer? No one knows, although the Russians may find out. (Whether they'll tell us, and whether they'll tell us the truth, is another problem; as I write this they don't know either.)

ITEM: assuming that we'll have to keep the earliest space structures at lower pressures, and thus have to use some gas other than nitrogen to mix with oxygen, is there an interaction between low-gee, low pressure, and different gas mixtures? There certainly is an interaction between gas mixes and tolerance to *high* pressures; SEALAB and other experiments proved that.

ITEM: is diet a factor? It quite likely is, you know. But in which direction?

ITEM: science fiction has long assumed that low gravity makes for longevity. Arthur Clarke assumed it in his Lunar colony stories; so did Heinlein; so have we all. Yet there is not one shred of evidence for this. In fact, the only *evidence* we have points in the opposite direction. I happened the other day to be talking about this with Robert Prehoda (*Your Next Fifty Years,* ACE Books) and he told me of an experiment done years ago in which rats were subjected to high gravity (they lived in a centrifuge). Those kept at 3 gravities developed legs like, uh, superrats; the experimenters said "they walked like little elephants"; and the 3-gee rats lived longer than the normal-gravity controls!

Of course there are a myriad of objections to this experiment. Rats aren't people. Would varying the diet have an effect? And so forth. But it is the only experimental evidence I know of, and it points in exactly the wrong direction.

ITEM: how long is the tour of duty? This is related to the above questions, naturally. But it should be obvious that the longer the term, the cheaper the project (getting people up and down is the most expensive operation in space, requiring flights by man-rated boosters, etc.); and therefore the missions will be made as long as possible.

If the missions are relatively short, you'll get a lot of volunteers. The longer the tour in space, the better your chance, because the fewer you'll compete with. And if it turns out that the only way to build Solar Power Satellites is to build permanent colonies in space? That going to space for a year or more is a permanent decision: that you can't go home again (as Heinlein assumed in *The Moon Is A Harsh Mistress*)—then what? The number of volunteers is going to plummet. In my interview with Dr. Danielle Goldwater I asked if she'd go on a space construction project. Certainly. And if you can't return? No.

She thinks older people might.

I know damned well I can get plenty of volunteers for the one-way mission; but it's unlikely they'll have to compete with recent Yale MD's.

\* \* \*

Now what advice have I for the young person now in college or high school who wants someday to go to space and spend considerable time there? (If you want merely to go for a short mission, write NASA at Houston and ask what they advise; and do that annually, because their criteria are going to change; and be prepared to compete with people like Dr. Goldwater.)

Well, the qualifications break down into three categories.

*Physical:* this is obvious. As time goes on the physical fitness requirements will get less and less attention, perhaps, but given equality in professional qualifications, the best physical specimen will be chosen. Stay in shape.

*Education and Professional:* Not so obvious. You have to make two predictions: skills needed in space, and the number of people who will have that skill *at the time you want to go*. The second is harder than the first: the US, for its sins, allows high-school seniors to allocate a very great part of its educational investment. (Departments get money by enrollment; thus they operate a kind of oriental rug market trying to attract majors; and those choosing the major have vast influence over the department budgets.) Thus there's no rational plan for training skilled personnel; what we're short of this year we may have in overabundance four years later.

What you ideally want to do is choose a skill useful in space that few will have when you're ready to go.

Some pointers: if it can be done on the ground, it will be.

Recall that the more effort we put into space, the better space-ground communications will be. Thus you want to study observational astronomy rather than theoretical if you're determined to become a space-based astronomer. You want to study computer hardware rather than programming. Programming can be accomplished down here, so why send up an expensive man? If you're in biology, you want to be an experimentalist, and get lots of practice in the lab.

In fact, whatever your field, get your hands dirty. Learn how to use, repair, and make the equipment needed for your specialty. Become a gadgeteer. If you go into architecture and design, take a summer off and do construction work. Learn a building trade. In fact, I'd say a good industrial designer with architectural training who can show a year or two of high-steel construction work might be uniquely and evidently valuable.

Pay a lot of attention to articles on space industry, and choose a specialty accordingly. Materials science. Manufacturing/engineering. Biological production work. But whatever you choose, get into the messy end of it; learn to *do,* not just think. And it should be obvious that the more skills you have, the better your chance.

*Psychological:* Here's the tricky one. Recall the situation: you're asking to go up and work in cramped quarters with others. You'll be under stressful conditions, and you won't see many new faces—while you'll get damned tired of the old ones.

Can you handle that? Are you adaptable enough? And if you're not Mr. Nice Guy (or Ms. Nice—O Lord, what term do I use? Fill in your own. I'm in enough trouble already) can you nonetheless manage not to drive insane others who'll have to put up with you? Do you have nauseating habits?

Offhand, I'd say learning old-fashioned *manners* would be worth the effort. I've found by and large that mutual politeness can make tolerable a multitude of stressful situations. (I don't always practice that, as some of you know; but then I'm a bit old to be planning a long-term career in space. Perhaps, just perhaps, I'll get a shot aboard a mission set aside for journalists and bards; and if so, for the duration of that mission a politer person you'll never see.)

Given that you can manage to stay sane and not drive others up the wall, how do you prove it? That, I fear, I'm not going to tell you. I suspect I can figure out a number of the psychological tests they're likely to use in the selection process, but I suspect I'll be doing you no favors—and I know I'll be doing your potential shipmates no favors—by telling you which. It's not easy to study up for that kind of test, but it's possible.

And given the costs of sending you to orbit, any big company is likely to do some checking: talk to your roommates, neighbors, old boy/girl friends, current girl/boy friends, employers, peers, and in general anybody who's had to get along with you. I would.

\* \* \*

So. We've covered NASA missions past and present, construction projects, and early space industries. What about colonies, either Lunar or O'Neill?

*Physical:* requirements relaxed, of course. There'll be fewer applicants. Older people may well be preferred for psychological reasons (as well as skills). All things considered, the healthier you are, and the better condition you're in, the better your chances of going; but it won't be quite so critical.

*Education and Professional:* Again relaxed. More skills will be needed. Agronomists with actual farm experience will be highly desirable. Some entertainers may be wanted, probably as a secondary ability rather than full-time, but there may well be recreational specialists who can direct drama, teach dance, and organize entertainment in general. The more nearly self-sufficient a permanent colony can become, the cheaper it will be to operate; thus there will be a myriad of skills needed. You need only convince the management that it's cheaper to take you up than to import whatever it is you do.

Teachers and child care will be important (but may be left
to families of professionals, or traded off). The general
emphasis will still be on *doers* rather than thinkers, but again
not so stringent: given the 1½ second time lag between the
Moon or the O'Neill colony and Earth, communications
won't be quite so good; it may be better to have an on-board
programmer than to talk by TV to an Earthbound computer
hacker. But do note that if it can be done on Earth, it probably
will be.

I should also mention a fourth qualification here: *financial*.
It is by no means unlikely that colonists will have to buy stock
in the corporation. The governance of a space colony is
beyond the scope of this column—indeed might make a good
column someday—but is in any event likely to be neither
straight corporate nor straight democracy; and I can easily see
the requirement that colonists invest, say, the equivalent of
$100,000 in 1978 dollars as a condition of going. (Those with
particularly needed skills may be excused the investment, of
course.)

*Psychological:* I haven't a clue beyond common sense.
We just don't know enough. It's possible that whoever is
organizing a space colony will insist that most colonists come
as families; it's also possible but unlikely that they'll try to
abolish the family altogether and make the colony one big
commune. That latter is in my judgment unlikely to the point
of near-impossibility: I've seen the horrible outcome of many
and many an attempt at a perfect commune; but it could be.

The colonies will be larger than scientific satellites or
industrial satellites or construction shacks; more screwballs
can be tolerated, for the stress per individual will be less. But
the organizers are very likely to have theories on both organi-
zation and personality type wanted, and frankly I haven't any
better qualifications for guessing those than you do.

Maybe that's not quite true. Were it my problem, I'd do as
I advised you in an earlier paragraph: look carefully at the
personnel practices of some of the largest US (and West
German) corporations. Look especially at how they select
middle management, and what is their attitude toward the
employee's personal life. (Some big companies couldn't care

less what you do when you aren't at work; others want to manage your entire life, and will let you know exactly what they think of, say, living together without benefit of clergy.) You might also take a look at the personnel manuals for the US Civil Service (although God Forbid that we get a Civil Service Colony!) §§ I can't resist: in the old days at Boeing we used to call BOMARC the Civil Service Missile: it won't work and you can't fire it.††

\* \* \*

Which about covers it. If you're seriously interested in how to become a spaceman you'll have joined the L-5 Society and get their newsletters and other information; you'll attend meetings of the American Association for the Advancement of Science, and of the American Astronautical Society; and in general you'll keep up with the literature of your future chosen profession. (For that matter, I recommend the L-5 Society to all my readers.)

I've left one thing off. It is perhaps the most important of all:

IF YOU WANT TO BE A SPACEMAN, THERE HAS TO BE A SPACE PROGRAM.

Elementary, no? And there's a good chance the space program will be Proxmired. Make no mistake, friends: the politicians are out for our blood. I live in California, and I was an ardent supporter of Proposition 13; my property taxes had quintupled in seven years. And many of you know I am no ardent supporter of high taxation of any kind, or of big government.

Leave that: my point is that suddenly it's fashionable to be for tax cuts. You would think from hearing him now that the Governor of California had invented Proposition 13 (when in fact he condemned it roundly up to the day on which it won by a landslide).

What better way for the Fritz Mondales of this world, who have always hated the space program, to win popularity than by killing NASA in the name of lower taxes?

Without NASA we have no space program. It is the historic mission of government to build roads to the frontier and provide access for settlers. Until that is done, there won't be any settlers.

So: if you really want to go to space, tell your Congressman, early and often, that when it comes time to cut government spending, don't cut out the space program; that the last time you felt really proud of the US of A was one July afternoon when through the hiss and crackle came the spine-chilling words: The Eagle has Landed.

Do that much, or there's no point to this article.

*AFTERWORD: Things look a lot better now; we have an administration that's interested in high technology, and wants to make the country look good.*

*However, the new President will be under enormous pressure to cut government spending. Welfare programs have highly organized lobbies. They're vocal. Space and high technology advocates tend to be quiet.*

*So: if you want to be a space colonist, now's the time to let the government know you want a space program.*

*And join the L-5 Society.*

EDITOR'S INTRODUCTION TO:

## BELLEROPHON

by Kevin Christensen


*This one is John Carr's discovery. John has the thankless task of reading all the unsolicited manuscripts sent for these anthologies—and we get a lot of them. Our postman vividly recalls the day he delivered twenty-three linear inches, a two-foot stack. Alas, there wasn't one usable story in the pile.*

*Sometimes, though, it's all worth it, as when he found this gem. It's Kevin Christensen's first published work; we liked it enough that we sent it on to Jim Baen, who bought it for* Destinies.

*Christensen gives us a look at a future strange enough for anyone; and he makes it quite real.*

# BELLEROPHON

## Kevin Christensen

Saturation point arrived with the new Earth Intercorp ambassador. He smiled, clasped my hand and said, "Natalie Schofield? You were there when he fell."

He hadn't garbled the words through an hors d'oeuvre, or slurred them across a cocktail glass; unlike some others among the various diplomats, city VIPs, socialites, party-up-and-comers, and even waiters who had offered up the same words earlier this evening, and on a myriad similar occasions. But damn. Like it had been a privilege.

"Representative Schofield to you." I held my hand straight as a cold mackerel in his grip. "No matter where I was." His hand dropped away in the sudden local silence, the smile gave way to embarrassment. "Excuse me." I turned away and began to thread my way through the host of mingling notables assembled in the open plaza.

"Natalie." I recognized Lyle Sarr's voice and felt his hand on my shoulder. I pulled from his grasp with a shrug. "At least tell me what's wrong." I stopped to let him catch up. He is a portly little man, and has been with me since my first campaign, so I owed it to him not to make him chase me.

"The usual," I said simply.

He wrinkled his forehead, and nibbled his lip.

"And don't apologize for me."

"Okay," he sighed. He glanced overhead. "Bridling Peggy?"

"Yeah."

"Nice night for it." He blends sympathy and sarcasm without real understanding. But he needs me, so we let it go

at that. He went back to the reception. I went and got Peggy
from the stables and led her to the elevators beneath the flight
landing.

My mood is generally rotten to begin with, but with Peggy
along the ascent gets really claustrophobic. Her big feathered
wings seem to overwhelm the compartment. And she's always shifting her hooves about, making great clop-clop
noises, and neighing at odd intervals. Besides all that, the
sensation of weight leaving as we get closer to the axis makes
me nauseous. Then the door opens. Catharsis begins with the
view.

Below me a panel of landscape thirty kilometers long
stretches off to the opposite end of the cylinder. Overhead
and from the sides two other land panels and the three
alternating glass sections reach off, converging in a parasol
horizon. Mirrorshift is nearly complete. Clouds form a
wispy tunnel where nocturnal flyers soar and glide.

Here the centrifugal effect is lessened enough for Peggy's
wings to become more than cumbersome ornaments, to become, in fact, wings. We move forward gingerly, down near
the edge. I tangle my fingers in her mane, and pull myself to
her back. A few more steps, then she leaps and adds the
power of her wings, taking us nearer the axis where flight is
nearly effortless.

Consider the sight and the setting: A winged horse in the
sky of an inside-out world. A moment's pause, and Virgil
Sayer must come to mind, the assumed he of a thousand
conversations.

I think I come up here less to get away from his name, more
to remember who he was, apart from myth and folklore. (You
know how it goes: Take one part amiable rogue. Place in the
casino aboard the Hohmann Queen. Add remarkable success. Allow enemies to gravitate. Spice with a few folk
motifs. Garnish with a few genetic creations from the darkride zoo. Serve up with a tragic romance. Voilà. C'est un
crap.)

Virgil, when not enouraging misconceptions, merely allowed them.

I met him back on the Hohmann Queen, due to a lapse of judgment on my part.

A friend named Iyako pointed Sayer out on my first visit to the Hohmann Queen's notorious casino.

"He's the one with the female entourage," she said. "Why the sudden interest?"

"Cohabing with Dirk turned out to be a mistake," I replied. My ex had neglected to mention a passion for gambling surpassing his passion for me. He managed to put me in debt for an extra hour of intransit labor per day, as well as losing me my guitar. Iyako kept I-told-you-so down to a passing glimmer in her eyes.

Sitting with four other players on the gaming floor a meter below us, Virgil Sayer was dressed in a black frock coat, frilled shirt and vest. His dusty brown hair covered his ears, and was parted to reveal a wide forehead over clear gray eyes. He wore a jawline beard, was tall and possessed an athletic build. He gave an impression of easy confidence.

"Ten years he's been doing this?" I asked, and Iyako nodded. "Where did he come from?"

"No one knows for sure," she replied. Iyako is a little gem of atypical beauty: deep vertical dimples under fine cheekbones, and a cascade of black hair among other attributes. "Sayer has your guitar?"

I shook my head. "A man who can be found playing with him." After breaking Dirk's nose, I'd briefly inquired as to the distribution of my Fleta. "An Emory Titus."

"Titus is the balding man across from Sayer."

I couldn't see Titus' face. He looked shorter and stockier than Sayer, and not so popular with the groupies. I noticed then that a few of the players used hand computers.

"Rumor has it that Titus has been hired to get Sayer off the Queen," Iyako continued.

"Oh? What powers object to clever charlatans?"

"Who else but dull authority types?" As we watched the game, Iyako described a few. Eve Brooks, a Providence Representative, epitomized the Offense to Tradition move-

ment. Her efforts turned up in the form of plaques honoring
pioneering colonists and builders; an attempt to fight Sayer's
romantization, and some anti-gambling legislation. Jerome
Hawthorne represented the Damaged Pride movement. He
headed Truesight Prosthetics R&D at Providence. Truesight
is a large firm claiming total prosthetic capability. Sayer had
taken a lot of money from Titus. Rumor connected Titus with
some of the more unsavory attempts to bring down Sayer.

Sayer's continuing success in the face of such opposition
enhanced his notoriety all the more. I'd first heard of him on
the last trip, when he'd been accused of raping an Intercorp
ambassador's daughter. Despite polygraph and VSA supported testimony from the victim, and supporting testimony
from the girl's personal doctor and bodyguard who found
Sayer drunk and unconscious with scratches on his face, and
a heat picture of the area showing no trace of anyone other
than the principals in the area. Sayer was released with
apologies from Ambassador Widengren and his daughter. No
details were released. Speculation was rampant. Sayer continued on, troubles or no.

A murmur from the table below interrupted our conversation. I looked down to see Sayer make a slight gesture of
acquiescence, and Titus gathering in a stack of chips. Sayer
rose to leave, saying something to his retinue which left a few
of them with pouty expressions.

"His troubles appear to be continuing," I commented.
Iyako frowned after Sayer. The game below began to break
up. "I guess this is my best chance to negotiate with Titus."

"I wish you luck," Iyako said. "He's a story in himself. A
cyborg."

She smiled and retreated before I could frame another
question. So I strode down to the gaming floor and walked up
to Emory Titus.

His face startled me at first. It was completely immobile,
void of any expression, with a slight caricature effect in the
definition of his features; the distinct lines at the corners of
his eyes and across his brow, the sudden black of his eye-

brows and mustache, and the abrupt baldness. After a brief
hesitation I spoke.

"Emory Titus?" He gazed at me from behind his blank
face like a machine waiting for more data. I complied. "It's
about one of your recent gambling companions, a Dirk Jaussen. He lost something precious to me in a game with you; I
want to buy it back." I recognized his left eye as prosthetic by
the aperture—like a camera's rather than an iris. He spoke in
a flat dispassionate voice.

"You're Jaussen's cohab."

"No longer."

"A little late, but a wise move. He's a fool." Titus
scrutinized me further. I felt like a butterfly pinned to a
board. "What was the item?"

"A Spanish guitar."

"I don't have it."

"I was told you did."

"Jaussen didn't explain properly, I'm sure. One moment,
I think I can help you." He made a gesture with his left hand.
His features relaxed and flowed with expression. Then he
screwed up his features and massaged his face with both
hands. "It's easier to talk when I turn off the poker-face," he
explained, his voice now carrying a degree of humor. He
turned and swept his winnings into a purse. "Come with me,
and we can see if no one has taken your instrument from the
Shambles."

I fell into step beside him. "Let me guess. There's a hock
shop."

"Very nearly I suppose. People can exchange credit, or
pledge work or exchange goods for chips."

"I haven't seen many leisure goods up here."

"They accumulate a bit each trip," he said. "People pawn
things they've brought along. The ship imports a few things
to put up for sale in the markets, to go along with the food and
handcrafts. Some colony items are displayed or advertised
here. Real estate. Occasional zoo excess. Enough to spend a
pleasant afternoon browsing, if that's your inclination."

We passed through the gardens and entered the quaint crooked streets of the Shambles.

On impulse I asked, "What do you do?"

"I'm involved with decision-theory. Teaching computers to work with incomplete information. How to guess skill-fully."

"I thought you might be a professional gambler."

"Like Sayer? No," he laughed. "PanSol won't allow that to happen again. With me it's a serious hobby related to my work." He led the way into a little shop. "I'll just be a moment." He stood in a short line at the counter.

There were no goods in this shop to look at, so I waited near the window. Across the narrow way little knick-knacks, the latest beta-cloth fashions, and various gastronomic arti-cles filled most of the shop windows. The shop directly across the way had an eye-catching difference: it showed holo images of a unicorn and a griffin. Providence zoo excess. Titus interrupted my observations.

"Your instrument has been sold."

"Who to?"

His real eye seemed to twinkle.

"Virgil Sayer. I thought he might have gotten it. He's an easy mark for that kind of thing."

I felt my depressed and bewildered look come on.

"I think you can forget about buying it," he continued. "Sayer doesn't need the money just yet."

"What does he need?"

"I can tell you where to find him." He paused and ran his eyes over me. "You may be able to come up with some-thing."

Titus' directions had me waiting outside a gymnasium just the other side of the spoke. Though the day had worn on me enough that I doubted all the hassle was worth it, when Sayer finally strode out, heading for the elevators, I went after him and expressed my wish to talk.

"You caught me at a bad time," he said. "Later, maybe."

Something in his manner brought back a memory of pouty faces. A few clouds of ill-will drifted over the fuse that ran to my temper. I tried to suppress an outbreak. Nearby, an elevator door hissed open.

"It's very important."

He turned a lazy glance my way and ambled through the door. "Aren't you one of Emory's little jokes?" he said.

I flared. "Aren't you being phased out by a machine? I came to gloat."

He sat and strapped in. "I've got plenty of time to handle Emory." He spoke with the defiance a man might use as the edge of his confidence has begun to wear away. Then he smiled and returned to a condescending tone. "Floor please."

I glanced over the long row of buttons, then back to him. I ran my hand over them all. He glared at me as the door closed, cutting off the meeting. I felt anger at losing my chance for negotiation, further vexation at Dirk, and outrage at Titus. He appeared to have used me easily for some petty prank.

"Twenty-seven and still gullible," I muttered. Then I went home.


The designers of the Hohmann Queen had gone to great lengths to avoid the mind-numbing effects of standardization, extending great variety to every part of the ship. The basic housing however, seemed impervious to their efforts. No matter how they arranged the bed, closet, drawers, no kitchen and no bath, it always looked or felt the same. When I got home I threw my stuff all over the room, attempting to break the outlines. All the disarray left a guitar-shaped hole. In an effort to relax, I stepped out on the balcony (labeled patio) to take in the scenery.

Living in the Hohmann Queen is like living in a big doughnut. Overhead the sky is a glass mosaic. Beyond the glass is a view of the central hub, and the stars made gypsy by our rotation. Inside, closer around me, cluster various types of housing, especially dense here near the base of a spoke.

The apartments are stacked in piles, or terraced in irregular rows. Sometimes drawn beta-cloth curtains glow with internal illumination. A family of four plays on a grass patio, unaware of a couple making love in the apartment beneath them. There are no streets, only paths. Cypress trees grow abundantly, and are reaching ages where they begin to be interesting. Not surprisingly, it failed to soothe.

Iyako met me after work the next day.

"How did things go yesterday?"

"Lousy."

"How lousy?"

I told her. Just as I finished, lamenting how I'd never see my guitar again, I led the way into my apartment. My guitar rested in the middle of the floor.

"How lousy?" she said.

On the case I found a delivery slip and a note from my landlord. And a change of ownership affidavit signed by Sayer.

"I thought you said he legally owned it."

"He did." I opened the case, took it out and played a scale. "I didn't even tell him I wanted it."

"No charge?" she asked. "No strings?"

"New strings. I suppose I ought to be grateful . . . . I didn't even tell him who I was."

"Titus knew."

"So Titus told him. Why would he give it back?"

"At least you've got it."

"I guess I shouldn't worry about it."

I played a few bars of Dowland and fumbled.

"I would if I were you," Iyako said.

"I am."

"You said you weren't going to."

"Sayer is supposedly a drone, an athletic hedonist, a drunken rapist, and capable of manipulating PanSol and Intercorp justice. He gives a stranger who insulted him something he paid five figures for absolutely free, and I'm not supposed to wonder why?"

"How are you going to find out?"

"Ask him."

"He didn't seem very easy to talk to."

"Yeah." I fell silent. "Maybe I'll just forget about it."

Maybe not. Two days later I found where he lived and sat on his front steps with my guitar. If I'd cared to look, and if there were enough light, I could have watched him coming from far off. (By Hohmann Queen standards.) Living quarters were spread thin here. An open stream flowed by, winding among adolescent pines and aspens. Here more than anywhere else on the Queen, I felt tranquil spaciousness. So, involved as I was in playing, I didn't notice him approach. He applauded as I finished a piece.

"Very nice," he said. I looked to see him standing a few meters away.

"Thank you." I put my instrument in the case, and set it by my feet. He wore a frock coat similar to the last I'd seen him in.

"You are Natalie Schofield."

"My Indian name is Sitting-on-Stairs."

He smiled and stepped closer.

"I appreciate the gift," I continued.

"I apologize for being rude," he replied.

"And I shouldn't have made that remark about you being phased out."

"Your provocation is understandable." He shrugged. "How did you come across a Fleta, by the way."

"A friend of a friend died."

He nodded.

"I was going to offer to buy it back," I said.

"Emory told me the circumstances."

"Can you afford this?"

"Time will tell," he replied. "I expect so. Good P.R."

"The way I heard it, you weren't the one to win it anyway. It was Titus."

"I've taken Dirk for quite a lot." His tone held regret not for Dirk, but for our relationship.

"You weren't responsible."

He shrugged again, and fingered his beard gently with one hand. "I am sorry though."

Then he moved forward as if to pass me and enter his lodging. I held my place on the stair.

"Wait," I said. "What are Emory's jokes?"

"Emory likes to create a negative environment for his opponents, to take their mind off the game. He sends people to me, telling them they are wanted."

I flushed, remembering. I hoped it was dark enough that Virgil didn't notice.

"I hope you beat him," I said.

"I've got time."

"But you are worried."

"Don't you worry."

"Why not?"

He hesitated a short moment. He glanced around, thought a short time more, then said. "Come in and I'll show you."

I gathered up my guitar, and let him pass in front of me to palm open the door lock. I entered after him. I had imagined more luxury, or at least less austerity. The main features of the room where a visiterminal and a bean-bag chair. Three other doors led off the front room. One to a small kitchen. One to a bedroom in which I saw a conspicuously ordinary bed. The other door was closed. A sliding glass panel opened to a patio under the bedroom window. Virgil went up to the terminal and called up a program called cyborg.

"I don't lose that much to Titus, except in attempts to buy information. The biggest problem is that his winnings cut into what is available for me."

The screen showed an elaborate series of graphs charting betting patterns and winnings of the various players. Virgil explained that Titus had a computer instead of a left lung. Aside from doing the sensory moderation for his prosthetic eye it played the game for him. He input in various ways, and output into the vision field of his left eye. Virgil described his method of figuring the program an opponent ran; mixing the various decision variables—straight odds, risk-profit, betting history and so on—and claimed he could deceive a program once he knew it.

"I think your mind is constipated," I said.

Virgil scowled at me.

"I assume you've played computers before and won. Has it ever taken this long? I think he cheats."

"I can tell when people cheat."

"Do you cheat?"

"No."

"How come you win so much?"

"I'm very talented."

"Maybe Titus is more talented."

"I can't be read."

"What about him and his poker-face?"

"I don't see what any of this has to do with you."

"I don't like Titus. And I owe you. And right now you remind me of Dirk. So sure you're okay and everything falling apart."

He stared into the terminal for a moment. He canceled the program, and walked into the kitchen. He reappeared with something strawberry and frothy which he handed to me. Then he stepped inside the room I hadn't seen and closed the door behind him.

I sat in the chair and sipped the drink. After ten minutes, he hadn't come out, so I went over and knocked on the door.

"Yes," he said from behind me. I spun around. The v.t. screen showed a view of him, apparently in the next room, his back to me.

"What are you doing?" I asked.

"Relaxing," he replied. "I thought you left."

He worked over a table which held some stop-motion figures, two of which intimately concerned him, both thirty centimeters tall. One at first glance looked like an upright bear; the other like a man-shaped figure in dark armor. A hemisphere-front projection screen spread around the rear of the table. He moved each creature slightly, so slightly that I was only intuitively aware that each limb, joint, and facial feature had been shifted. He stepped back. I saw a flash and heard a distinct shutter click. Then he moved forward and began again.

"You aren't a very good host," I said.

"I don't get much practice."

I assumed he was doing a darkride film. Darkride parks are everywhere. They reproduce fantasy or inaccessible experiences in such a manner that the brain perceives them as real. They evolved from amusement parks and movies. A man named Trumball got to asking what would happen if he projected films at faster than the standard twenty-four frames per second. He found that at seventy frames per second, the mind could not perceive between frames at even subconscious levels, and is five times as convinced of the reality. Contemporary rides blend film sound, holography, physical design, and mechanical props to achieve their effect.

As I watched Virgil manipulating the kinetic sculptures, it occurred to me how he could win so much at a game like poker.

"Curiouser and curiouser," I said.

Virgil chuckled. Still he didn't turn. His fingers touched the face of the bear-thing.

"What happens if you don't beat Titus," I asked.

"A couple of things. If I can't pay my fare, I get dumped off at Providence. He's eating into my working capital. Between him and expenses, I'm way behind."

"Could you get work at Providence?"

"Sure." He paused briefly to consider his handiwork. "Eve'd love to have me doing something respectable."

"At the darkride park?"

"No. What exotics and rides are done at Providence use genetic engineering, emphasis on engineering. They don't have nearly the control over the finished product, and they don't have much use for them when they're done."

I remembered the zoo excess I'd seen up for sale in the Shambles.

"I saw where they've got a couple up for sale."

"Killing an exotic is a status thing in certain circles," Virgil commented. "I expect it will continue." He turned his attention back to the armored figure.

"Then what would you do?"

"Something basic. Chasing rock, or picking up cargo." He sighed. "Maybe I am in a rut, though I can't see it," he said, mostly to himself. "If you get any ideas, I'll be glad to listen."

"How long are you going to be in there?"

"Till Zapranoth gets this close to Draffut."

That, I could see, would take a while, and I did have to get up in the morning. I turned off the v.t. and went to sleep.

"What are you doing here?" I pried open an eye and saw Virgil silhouetted in his bedroom doorway.

"What time is it?" I yawned.

"Four," he said, and muttered, "I can't believe it."

"A couple more hours then." I rolled over and waited.

"I believe I asked a question."

I turned back over. Virgil had turned out the light behind him, so I could now make out his features.

"I don't like being put off," I said. "Besides, I figured out what your problem is . . ."

"What problem?"

". . . and I thought you'd like to know. He's reading you."

Virgil shook his head and moved out of the room. I heard the glass door slide open and closed. I sat up and slid open the window by the bed. He was making himself comfortable on the grass-covered patio.

"From what you've said, it's the only option you haven't considered. That's why you haven't figured it out."

Virgil seemed to be having trouble getting comfortable.

"You read body language like a book, don't you," I said.

"Better."

"Why can't Titus do the same thing?"

"Because I project as well as read."

"Oh." I hadn't thought of that.

"So there's nothing for him to read except what I want him to see. And even if he isn't trying, it works on the subconscious."

"On Titus?"

"Not consistently."

That reassured me that I had the right track. So I persisted.

"Well, he's reading you somehow."

"How?"

"I don't know."

"Good night then." He rolled over. I rested my chin on my arms and watched him for a few minutes and thought. Looking out over the patio, I could make out the other quarters. The closest was just the other side of a pond, through some trees. The sight distracted me from this problem, reminding me of something else I had wondered about.

"Virgil?"

"What?" Reluctantly.

"I can't sleep."

"I can."

"What if somebody came in and raped me?"

"Wouldn't be me."

"No?"

"Call it the way I was raised if you're offended."

"I heard that you attacked a girl right over there."

"The court said otherwise."

"How did you get off?"

"I was innocent."

"It didn't sound that way to me."

"You didn't hear my version."

"I love stories."

I heard him sigh. Then he sat up cross-legged and looked toward me. He sat still for a moment, fingering his beard.

"How did you hear it?" he asked.

I told him what Iyako had reported. He interrupted at times, pointing out locations; where the Widengren people had been lodging, where Melinda had been walking, his own route home along the stream, where the attack had been reported, her escape and discovery by the doctor, and his own discovery by the doctor and body guard.

"Well?" I said.

"You know enough." He'd taken the offensive. "Figure out what happened, and I might decide you could be of some use."

I drew a blank. He gazed at me and shrugged. "I thought not," he said. Then he turned and slept. A thoughtful hour later I left for work.

Virgil had chosen a poor method of getting rid of some-one with little else to think about. I followed Virgil discreetly for a couple of days, and observed that he didn't drink, neither did he dally with the groupies; I decided he had been set up. Max Widengren's daughter had a personal doctor. When I inquired as to why I found the basis for a theory.

Melinda Widengren was a cyborg. A serious accident had left her paralyzed and deaf. Prosthetic hearing devices and spinal fusion, with a moderating computer installed, restored the losses. The doctor was not only her fiancee, but an employee of Truesight and a relative of Hawthorne.

If Hawthorne was behind it, he would exploit his capabilities. Prosthetic devices translated between neural and electronic signals. A capability to prerecord is implied, as is the ability to interrupt a direct signal and substitute a recorded one. Suppose that when they operated on Melinda, they also wired her vision. A previously staged attack could be re-corded and played back into her. For her it would be totally real.

Assuming the technical details then, the perpetrator still requires a knowledge of Sayer's habits, and some control over Melinda's habits. The doctor had both. He could use the stream and his justified presence to deceive the heat picture.

I found Virgil on his way to the casino one day and he verified my theory, though with little enthusiasm.

"And you just asked them to x-ray her and explain the excess hardware?" I asked.

"More or less."

"How come it was hushed up?"

"I wasn't in on the negotiations." He stretched and yawned. "Widengren is a Machiavellian sort."

"The doctor?"

"Word came out that he decided to practice on a penal rock somewhere."

"How does it feel to have enemies like that?"

"You claim to be on my side," Virgil said. "Just think about it."


A few days later, armed with another theory, I located Emory Titus lunching in an open market in the Shambles.

"Hello, Emory," I said cheerfully. "Remember me?"

He glanced up from a bowl of chowder, offered no sign of recollection or interest, and continued to eat.

"I've spent the night with Virgil since you talked with him again, and have gotten my guitar back. I want to thank you for your part."

The first few words got his attention. His interest grew exponentially as I spoke. He smiled warmly, took me by the arm, and led me out from among the crowded tables to a quiet spot behind the food counters. There he stood directly before me, still holding my arm firmly. Both eyes fixed on me.

"Would you repeat what you just said?"

"What?"

"You said you slept with Virgil."

"Yes."

"Say it again, as you said it before."

"I spent the night with Virgil, and have gotten my guitar back. And I want to thank you for your part."

He grinned broadly, and rocked with breathy laughter. I pulled a little with my arm, but he didn't let go. He paused in his joviality and returned his attention to me.

"And how," he said, "do you intend to thank me?"

"I have thanked you."

"Oh come now."

I pulled again with my arm, then smiled and relaxed.

"I'm in need of a proper thanks," he said with Victorian gusto.

"I could rip your throat out easily."

He began to laugh again, but gazed into my face. Then he let me go.

"Sorry. I hope you will excuse my excesses."

"Good day."

I walked away leaving him with a somber expression. I heard him chuckling before I got far.

Virgil was dressed in his usual outfit, the dark frock coat. He smiled casually on seeing me, but showed no inordinate enthusiasm.

"I think I know how he does it," I said.

"How?"

"Aren't you even interested?" He hadn't changed his stride at all since I'd caught up with him.

He shrugged, slowed, smiled, and fingered his beard. "I say again, how?"

"I'll tell you over lunch." I felt enthusiasm, but not to the point of being beyond consideration.

"I'm usually at my table now," he said, still striding on.

"You want to throw away more money? How did you do yesterday?"

"I set a record," he replied. "So tell me now, and I'll beat him."

"Not on an empty stomach." I stopped and planted my feet.

Finally, he gave in. We went to a place with heavy gray lunar stone cut and piled around us like medieval walls. A tapestry hung next to our table over one wall. It pictured a lunar mass driver flinging great buckets of ore and stone into orbit. A hearth radiated warmth. As we ate I related my conversation with Titus.

"And?"

"Well, think about it."

He stared at me.

"Titus seemed to think your going to bed with me was a great joke."

"So?"

"Okay, I'll spell it out. He seemed to think it unlikely that you had slept with me. But I'm attractive enough, so he asked again to make sure."

Virgil scowled and continued to eat.

"Then he knew that I was telling the truth, granted he put more into it than was there."

Virgil stopped eating and gave me his full attention.

"What are you getting at?"

"Just listen and think," I said. "You told me you have control enough over your own body language to misrepresent your game to an opponent in such a way that he doesn't know he is being manipulated. A conscious act of deception."

I could see the wheels turning, grinding up against the mental block. He'd taken it for granted that he couldn't be read.

"But the fact that you gave my guitar back is evidence you have an emotional reaction against that sort of thing."

"And Titus can tell if someone is telling the truth or lying." Still skeptical.

"Or at least make a good guess from your emotional state."

"PanSol jams microtremors for VSA's." He was protesting still, but looking for possibilities.

"What do you know about thermography?" I said.

"Just seeing infrared wouldn't do it."

"Not seeing infrared. Seeing a temperature map, using infrared. Emotional changes cause minute temperature changes. With computer enhancement, he sees the differences as colors."

Virgil stopped in thought. The wheels turned, strained, then ran free. "That would work," he said. He looked down again, and finished his meal.

Afterwards, we walked together towards the casino. Virgil paused in the gardens. He strolled over to a bench and sprawled upon it. I sat on the grass in front of him.

"You aren't just going to catch him," I said.

He shook his head. "Right now, Titus is seeing signs of me breaking."

"Sleeping with me."

"Other things too." He fingered his beard. "I could feed on that for a while. In the meantime, with a bio-feedback unit I could bring it under conscious control."

"If you start winning he'll know that you know."

"I only need to do it once."

"You figure on a big pot."

"I'm sure I can manage that."

"How?"

"First things first." He stood and extended a hand to help me up. "I'll go display my symptoms. I want you to go to the Shambles and price a feedback unit for me." He started away.

"What's in it for me?"

He stopped short, turning with an expression of mixed bafflement, defensiveness, and then contrition.

"Sorry, I'll get it myself. Call it square for the guitar."

"I just don't want you making assumptions about me," I said. "That's what upset me the first time we met."

He nodded and went off to the casino. It occurred to me that I ought to decide how much I liked this man. I resolved to wait for him to make a move on a personal score. Also I would see about performing in the casino. There was a small stage that was usually vacant.


I found I could pay in performing time for the extra labor due from me over Dirk. It gave me a chance to unobtrusively watch Virgil's progress. I didn't see any. The minor players began mimicking Titus' betting behavior towards Virgil and vice versa whenever possible. As time passed pots grew smaller and smaller. Although Virgil didn't lose much, except in obvious attempts to buy information, he didn't win much either.

A couple of months rolled by. I never did tell anyone exactly what had passed between Virgil and me. I'd nod and smile at whatever they guessed. I had staved off a couple of would-be romancers, and was tinkering with the idea of encouraging a couple more when Virgil asked me out to dinner.

He showed up in ordinary dress, perhaps anticipating my ordinary outfit. I didn't want him to think I was trying to impress him. Over a meal of fish and chips, the conversation rolled around to his efforts when he startled me by laughing. I looked around. Not seeing anything, I turned my best inquisitive look at him.

"Just anticipating," he explained.

I stood abruptly and started walking away. He followed quickly.

"Natalie?"

"Your success doesn't seem so inevitable to me."

"The pattern is set. When the time is right, Emory will think I'm bluffing, and he'll call."

"And that will be it?"

"Yes."

"Why?"

"Because Emory hasn't broken me. If I hock my gear, I've got plenty enough to stay on the Queen."

"And he'd cover a massive bet to do that?"

"He wasn't hired to come here," Virgil said. "He paid. He wants to be known as the best. For that, he'll do it."

I stopped walking, and turned to face Virgil. I saw again the easy confidence in his eyes.

"And you, why will you do it?" I asked softly. "To be the best?"

His expression changed to something more thoughtful, more melancholy.

"Mere survival," he said.

"There must be more to it than that."

"Why?"

"Because there are other ways to survive."

"Like what?"

"By growing things, for instance." I made a sweeping gesture with my hand to refer to other things. "You could have just turned him into security.''

"All right then, pride,'' he muttered.

"And how will they try next year?''

"Look, I'd really much rather be living elsewhere, doing something else. I applied for artist-in-residence at the dark-ride park years ago. They prefer to play games with genetics. So I've been accumulating my own gear.''

"So you plan on staying aboard the Queen forever?''

He shrugged. "They'll open up someday. For a little culture. People with non-essential talents.''

"I think it's taking longer because of you,'' I said. "Eve Brooks paints you as a living example of the evils of hedonism.''

"It's more complicated than that. Eve is a traditionalist. But she's also a bit tiffed over the public not making much of the way her husband died.''

"Sounds like you know her.''

"We're acquainted,'' he said, then continued. "The corporate lobbies consider tradition to be more profitable and stable.''

"You could go to other places. Earth.''

"I'd prefer not to be anyplace strategic.''

The way he said this last sparked a connection between the generalized decade of his tenure on the Queen, and a time of violence on Earth.

"So you're just going to wait it out?''

He nodded. We started walking again, both solemn.

"They'll be shuttling people off to Providence soon,'' Virgil said. The words hung on the air, draped over unspoken implications.

"You better make your move pretty soon then,'' I said.

"I suppose so.''

We parted a few awkward moments later.

The shuttles began arriving, taking people off the Hohmann Queen to their new homes, jobs, and mortgages at Providence, and would be doing so for several days. Iyako left on the second day. The population decline showed everywhere except in the casino. Interest ran high in the possible outcome of Virgil's duel with Titus. I finagled my way into more performing time. And I noticed a few new faces, people who had come from the city on business, and happened to have time enough to watch the game. Two in particular stood out in mind.

The first was Jerome Hawthorne himself. Of a somewhat bland physical appearance, he managed to come across as striking due to an intense personal drive, and an incredible wardrobe. He sat in on the game, never once looking at his cards. He just antied up and folded, smoked big cigars, and did a couple of other calculatedly obnoxious things to make his presence strongly felt. Virgil ignored him with great skill.

The second I met as I performed. Only a few people sat in proximity to the stage, so I played mostly to myself, sifting my feelings. On a particular occasion when I decided to sing, as a change from purely instrumental work, I was surprised to hear someone singing harmony. I fumbled and looked down to see a woman sitting at a table out of line with the game. She smiled up an encouragement, and I finished. She looked to be thirty-five, and a little taller than I, fuller bodied, but still slim. She wore her hair to shoulder length, tied back simply at the nape of her neck. Her face was comely, the forehead moon-shaped; she had well defined, but rounded cheekbones, and slight lines at her eyes and forehead. She had a graciousness and dignity that did not conceal an inward tiredness—and a conviction that she could do well despite it. We spoke at the end of the song.

"I'm surprised that anyone would know that song," I said.

"The loveliest things should never be forgotten," she replied. "You sing and play with much expression."

"Thank you." I felt appreciated for the first time since Iyako left.

"We appreciate talent out here," she continued. "What is your name?"

I told her, and volunteered the information that I'd be working the crops.

"And I'm Eve Brooks."

That stunned me, as I'd built up a completely different picture, one far easier to dislike. At the moment, a murmur rose from the tables. We both looked over to the game. Then our eyes met, communicated something, and we moved together across the room to a clear spot on the terrace.

Do you know the game of draw poker? I'll describe an example of the game. You may pick it up from that. The dealer, under the eyes of a PanSol security camera, deals five cards face down to each of five players. The first player to the dealer's left, a well dressed man brandishing a foully aromatic cigar, says "fold," and does his best to look arrogant and overpowering. The next player opens the first round of bidding. It is a small bid, a token that says, "I was there." The next man sees the bid with an equal number of chips. His face is rigid, unreadable. His presence ominous. He has won a standoff, but seeks a crown. The next player, a woman, consults her cards and a pocket computer, and also folds.

The last man has a unique aura about him. If you watch him closely as he plays, you find yourself making guesses about the strength of his hand, which invariably prove to be wrong. He ignores the cigarist so skillfully that a nearby person may fall under his influence and ignore the man too. But of late there is tension in him. All his skills, his place and his legend have been challenged. He is not willing to merely ride out the challenge, perhaps not at the expense of his dreams. He calls.

The first player draws three cards. Titus draws two. Sayer takes one. The first player makes a small bid. Titus raises moderately. Sayer sees, and raises, moving all his chips to the center of the table. The crowd murmurs, anticipating. The first player folds. Titus considers a moment. He gestures with his left hand. He gazes steadily at Sayer. He sees the bid, leaving himself only a few chips at the table. Sayer considers this, drumming his fingers on his cards.

"Will you accept an IOU?" he asks.

Titus nods.

Sayer produces a note equal to the sum value of his assets.

"Raise," he says.

Titus considers the amount, and fingers the meager look-ing stack before him.

"Will you extend the same courtesy?" he asks in his flat monotone.

"You ought to debug your program first," Sayer replies evenly.

Titus produces a note. "This is a receipt for a bit of zoo excess." He places it at the center of the table. Then he looks to Hawthorne. Hawthorne blows smoke in Virgil's direction. "And this is my promise for the balance. Call."

Titus gestures with his left hand, and his features loosen, and turn to a triumphant smile. He begins to turn his cards, gazes at Sayer, who to all outward appearances looks wor-ried, and stops short.

Sayer turns over his five cards, all clubs. A flush. Titus hasn't moved. Hawthorne reaches over, and turns the cards. Three aces.

"Should have debugged." Virgil says. He pulls in the winnings.

A murmur from the galleries grows to a roar, and general pandemonium.

Hawthorne glares at Titus.

"He did it," I said.

Beside me, Eve added, "Again," and left. Not wanting to take my guitar through the crowd, I figured I could see Virgil at the exchange shop in the Shambles.

Virgil arrived a little after I did, and had shaken most of the enthusiasts and their congratulations.

"Now what?" I asked. Virgil stepped to the counter and dumped the pile of chips. He turned to me, slipping the receipt, and Titus' note from his pocket.

"More of the same, I suppose." he replied. "Thanks for your help."

I looked into his face and tried to read it. He showed no enthusiasm. Just a kind of relaxation. Once I'd been con-cerned about how much I should like him. Pointless now. He grew awkward under my gaze.

"I haven't done much in the way of making friends for a long time," he started. Then, "When does your turn come for a shuttle?"

"Tomorrow."

He thought about that for a long moment. "It never seems like there is a whole lot of time."

"Well, there's ways, and ways of spending what you've got." I turned and started to walk out. An interruption from the clerk halted me.

"Sorry Virgil, but Emory hasn't got enough to cover this."

"You sure?"

"I could check again."

"Don't bother. Just process it."

Virgil saw me looking inquisitive. "That's all I can do right now." He stepped outside into the narrow street.

"Can you get the money?"

"Yeah, with interest. The courts will see to that. A little slice off the top of his paycheck for the next several years." He bit his lip and muttered, "I should have made sure."

"Can you pay fare now though?"

He pondered briefly. "I'll have to hock some of my gear, if I want fare and a reasonable amount of working capital." He crossed the street and paused at the window display I'd seen before. A holo image of a winged horse pranced and strutted. Next to it was an image of a creature that looked part lion, part reptile. A "sold" notice hung over it.

"How come Titus defaulted?" I asked.

"It was Hawthorne that defaulted," he replied. "Emory must have had to pay off Hawthorne for arranging things. You saw their little interchange before the bet?"

I nodded.

"Not legally binding," Virgil said. "If I'd asked for a credit check he'd have made the deposit." He paused. "I'll have to scalp a lot more innocents than usual to get my gear back," he sighed. "And I won't be able to work until then."

He gazed at the window display and fingered the receipt.

"And I'll alienate the powers more and more, close the doors."

He looked at me and fingered his beard.

"Like you said," I commented, "they'll open up someday. I don't think you should give up your chance to live your kind of life."

Virgil walked into the store. Shortly he strode out, carrying a second receipt. A "sold" notice flicked over the winged horse now too.

"A matched set," he said. "I'll see you on the shuttle. I'm going respectable."

"I just don't understand you."

We floated near a port where we could watch our approach to the shuttle dock. The Providence twin cylinders loomed up before us. Islands of life in the void. We'd just begun to match spin for the final approach.

"Did I tell you," he began, "why they always play the Blue Danube for dockings?"

"You've given up."

He laughed.

"Tell me something," I said.

"What am I going to do with a winged horse, a chimera, and a job picking up freight?"

"For starters."

"Would you do me a favor?"

I hesitated answering. Virgil was looking awfully clever.

"Peggy's wings are just decorative at present," he began. "I need you to teach her to fly."

I scowled. He knew what that meant.

"I just need her for one flight. I'll give her to you in return."

"Virgil," I mulled over what I wanted to say. "You manipulate people when you play . . ."

He furrowed his brow, and locked eyes with me.

"Do you ever use the ability with me?"

"I'm very fond of you," he said.

"That isn't what I asked." I felt a flush go over my face.

"I've never tried to get you to do anything, or lead you on."

"What have you done?"

"Concealed thoughts." He broke off his gaze. "On occasion I have desires I don't feel at liberty to express." He met my eyes again. "Does that answer your question?"

Honesty without invitation or commitment. I still didn't know what to think of him, but I agreed to take on Peggy.

Providence. The best way I can think of to give an impression of it is to describe an experience I had Earthside, during orientation. A group of thirty of us were gathered in a corner room on the seventeenth floor of the orientation center.

"I'm sure that you've all seen paintings, films, and models of O'Neill-type habitats," began our little uniformed instructor. "But I don't think you should let yourselves take the idea for granted without first being awed by it." That was all the warning we had. He turned and pointed to what we thought was a big panorama window, curving around two walls. It showed a familiar, but still spectacular view of the city.

"Imagine if you will," he said, pointing with a grand gesture to the scene before us, "taking three strips of land, about three kilometers by thirty kilometers . . ."

At that moment three sections of the city and surrounding area of that size, including ours, pulled themselves out of the ground, complete with buildings, parks, foliage, and waterways, and rose in the air.

Everyone at least jumped. Several people screamed or gasped. And those most at home with the darkride experience shouted approval.

". . . and taking them into space."

Special effects lifted us quickly, leaving the Earth to dwindle to moon-like proportions. A fellow next to me groaned and put his head between his knees.

"Then form a cylinder, joining the land with glass sections . . ."

These duly appeared. The six massive-appearing panels positioned themselves after a brief aerial ballet.

"Cap the ends. Spin for gravity. Provide mirrors to bring in sunlight."

These things were done.

"And of course air to breathe. Clouds will form at the kilometer level."

A bluish tint fell over the upward curving horizon, the overhead landed sections, and the distant cylinder end. Clouds formed into a concentric cylinder of fluff. None of us noticed the instructor leave. We just looked about till the view faded, silent and eager and sparkling, or silent and afraid.

I remembered that experience as I looked out into Providence. The lay of the land and the architecture looked different, of course. In fact, from our entry point near the axis you could see where landscaping was still under way in places. The reality of it set a harder edge to the feeling of vastness, and the feeling of vulnerability in riding a tiny bubble of life in a great sea of darkness. Even so, I wanted to get to the floor and walk as far as I could to make sure that I wouldn't bump up against a darkride screen, and find a door to normality.

Then I noticed the flyers. Several types of flycycles performed aerobatics near the axis. Many of the flyers looked lighter and speedier than those I had flown back on Earth, as if designed solely for use near the axis. A broad landing area set at the cloud level catered to them.

We descended to the floor with a ritual climb down two and a half kilometers of stairs. Then we began the hectic days of getting moved in and learning our way around to our jobs. I began my acquaintance with the farming modules haloed around the end of the city. When at last I got some free time, Virgil showed up. He asked if I wanted to meet the horse. I accepted.

On the way to a skimmer that took us across the glass to within a short walk of the darkride park, he described his work. He explained that he wouldn't have to leave Providence to chase freight due to the use of telefactors to pilot the tugs. Visual and tactile feedback systems allowed the pilots to control the actions of robots in the tugs as if the pilots were present.

"How do people treat you?" I asked.

"Like they want to ask a lot of personal questions."

"Such as, Why did you leave the Queen? And what are you going to do with the horse and chimera? And et cetera?"

"Et cetera yes, and exotics yes. They don't ask why I left the Queen. I hear that I left for a woman."

I stopped.

"People talk about you. Didn't you know?" He spoke without mockery, but no real seriousness. More an elegant amusement. I tried to put the awkwardness I felt back to him.

"Are they right?" He fielded it gracefully.

"I tend to think of us as platonic friends."

"And that's all?"

"What more could we be? We haven't spent all that much time together."

"Then why the talk?"

He shrugged. "It doesn't take much."

"What exactly do people say?"

"The usual for such things."

I chewed on that for a moment, remembering some conversations I'd had. Cursing the situation wouldn't change the taste.

"Now what?" I said.

"Nothing, with your permission," he said. "It helps me."

"How?"

"I came here to get a respectable job." He paused, leaving the thought incomplete. He had one job already, so that wasn't what he meant. And he told me that the darkride park had no use for a stop-motion artist. Something else then.

"How will the rumor of romance help you get any job?"

He smiled, pleased I was trying to figure things the hard way. "It removes any specter of defeat from my image."

And in what respectable endeavor is image most important?

"How in hell do you think you are going to get elected to the city council?"

He laughed. "Planning, preparation. Any citizen is eligible. I've targeted the social factions I'm likely to pick up."

I felt frustrated and angry and burning inside. I shook my head. "It's stupid, Virgil," I cried. "The public sees you as an outlaw. You're synonymous with decadence."

"Have you known me to be foolish?"

"Yes!"

"Generally?" He grew impassioned.

I thought about it. "No."

"I've got fame going for me already. In a couple of weeks I'm going to kill the chimera." He paused again to make me think about it.

"All right," I said. "You'll get the hunters on your side." If they could keep the killing going, they had political clout.

"Then a little while after that, I'm going on the talk show. The subject will be me. I'll enlighten the public on a few things, and announce my intention to run."

"And the horse?"

"More attention-getting—to start the active campaign. Everything should follow on inertia."

He looked confident. The kind of look that became infectious.

"Some people won't be pleased," I said.

"I expect not."

The stables and pastures were placed a convenient distance from both the darkride park and research center. The stables were built of stone and metal. The pastures were fenced in with metal posts rather than the gnarled and rotted wooden posts I was used to. Neither that alien-ness, nor that of the upward curve of the horizon quite prepared me for Peggy.

To begin with, a horse, brilliant white with a shaggy mane. She seemed streamlined to me, especially about her flanks.

At the shoulders where her wings joined, she was oddly, but strongly muscled. It was the wings though. They were big and feathered, and it looked as though she ought to be able to fly then and there. I was hooked.

Virgil stayed with me as I got to know her by walking her about the green. I agreed to help him on the stated condition that after he used her for the campaign, she was mine. I offered to help perpetuate rumors for free.

On the way home, Virgil detoured us through a hall where victors and kills from the hunts were holo displayed. Walking past the smiling figures with rifles posing over inert trophies, Virgil paused before a grim-faced man holding a spear over a hydra.

"This guy is teaching me," he said.

My plan for teaching Peggy to fly was simple. I led her around the pasture and rode her; in general getting her used to me. I measured her for a safety harness. Before long, I arranged to take her over to the freight elevators and up to the flight landing to get her used to the low-g. That got me a lot of abuse from the local clowns, especially when I took Peggy down again without testing her wings.

After I'd done that a few times, I brought her up in the harness and tethered her to a flycycle. Then I pedaled over the edge, pulling her with me. She screamed and struggled all agawk in the air, and when I brought her back she plowed into the landing like the biggest gooney ever.

By this time I had a gallery of hecklers. I constantly mumbled proverbs on self-control I hadn't bothered with since karate school. Then one day, Peggy figured out what wings are for. She got control of herself in the air, and made a sound of exaltation. I followed her till she got tired and pulled her in. The next time up, she pulled me off the landing. I helped her to a good elevation, where flight is almost effortless. She developed a marvelous sense for the corridor of low-g and a grace and exhilaration in flight.

At last I felt ready to try riding her. I ran my fingers into her mane and pulled myself to her back. Then I prodded her toward the edge. We hesitated. One of the hecklers (by now jealous admirers) offered to tether with me for safety's sake. I smiled sweetly and told him where he could find a good plate of manure. Then I urged Peggy forward. She strode, then leapt over the edge. Suddenly it was a kilometer down. I made a sharp intake of breath, and the hair prickled on the nape of my neck. Peggy worked her wings powerfully, and we rose steadily. I clutched her mane tighter, but sat straighter and laughed. Only once after that did I ever settle for a flycycle. From that moment on I began to think of her, not as a horse with wings, but a big bird with an excess amount of horse-ness.

While I was busy with Peggy, Virgil labored with his various preparations. One day he came by to chat, and invited me to the darkride park.

"How long since you've been to one?" he asked.

"Five years, I think. I got out of the habit at the university. I did have an experience during orientation." I described the experience.

"It might take some getting used to."

"How do you figure?"

"Some people have a way of forgetting how involved they got."

"Fat chance. You don't know why I got out of the habit."

"I can imagine."

The park spread over a couple of kilometers, extending to the glass on either side of the section. A park with holo displays of various kinds of animals, exotics and natural, surrounded a central complex of buildings that housed the darkrides. Many people wandered in the park. Often parents led children from animal to animal, answering millions of questions, at times holding the kids back, at times comforting the fearful.

The general nature of the passersby changed as we moved among the buildings. Courting couples, cohabs in various combinations, and clusters of young adults walked and chattered, sometimes encouraging one another to try an unfamiliar, or too familiar ride. People sat on benches talking up, or shaking off recent rides. The buildings reflected the themes of the rides they contained, and were grouped and stacked accordingly.

We took in a dozen or so, sampling the various types. Macro-type rides where we'd sit unencumbered with the illusions around us. Micro-types with the exoskel suit fitted with programmed visuals, sound, and tactile feedback allowing us to experience deep-sea diving, deep-space exploration, or combat in medieval armor. Plus variations.

We were resting on a bench after Virgil had knocked the wind from me in a medieval combat. I'd made the mistake of suggesting I take his place in the duel with the chimera if I unhorsed him. He reassured me as to his competence. Not that I hadn't gotten in a lick.

"Whose side are you on in the great darkride debate?" Virgil asked, touching his mouth gingerly. "Are they just direct access to fantasy, or . . ."

"Intersection with reality," I finished. "Definitely. Something of each one stays with you. Especially in releasing the impulse to violence at will. It changes you, for better or worse, I don't know. And being able to encounter something terrible, then just close your eyes, and sure enough it wasn't real. But there is an intersection. You do keep something."

Virgil nodded. I wondered how he felt about doing it to people. Creating a temporary reality. Someday I should ask him about solipsism.

"Dawn Patrol—Flying Circus." He pointed to a ride on the upper level of the structure across from us. "Must be one in every park ever built. Game?"

I shook my head. "Getting shot down might ruin me for Peggy. Vertigo."

He smiled. "Okay. You notice I didn't argue about keeping traces."

"I quit for a while because of it."

"I ought to get down to business anyway." He slipped a key from his pocket and fingered it. "I'll get in touch with you later." He stood and moved towards a ramp leading up to the higher levels.

"I'm in no rush to leave." I hurried along beside him. "And you've got me curious."

Virgil led the way up a couple of ramps, and across a walkway. He stopped in front of a closed darkride. The sign announced a time safari. An illustration pictured a Tyrannosaurus Rex looming over people with rifles.

"Every now and then good, concerned people put sensors on the most devious rides so they shut down if a passenger becomes too fearful." He slipped the key into the lock, opened the door and led the way in. After finding the light switch, he closed the door behind us.

"How thoughtful." I looked around. The lobby had a white on white antiseptic look. "I take it this one hasn't been castrated yet."

"Nope." He keyed open another door and stepped through. I peeked in after him. Virgil had found a switch box. The room, plainly the projection center, was crammed with several tiers of horizontal seventy-millimeter film cans. They nearly buried the projectors. Virgil flipped several switches, turned some knobs, mumbled a little, then closed the box and came out. "It's ready."

"Why this? Getting up your nerve for the chimera?"

"You got it."

"It seems a reasonable way."

"You don't have to come."

"Always, always the gentleman," I returned. "How archaic." I proceeded to open the door to the ride for him. He chuckled and walked in. I selected one of the seats in the semi-open coach. There were two large rifles mounted on the platform extending in front of the seats. Another weapon rested in a rack beside me, and another across the other side. Virgil sat opposite me, stretching out his legs. A voice came on, mixing hype with instructions. The rifles would be effective against the Rex, it said, but only at certain intervals, signaled by the sights illuminating.

"That's so they can splice alternative endings in," Virgil

commented. "I hear the last track gets very intense."

The area around the car went to a hazy gray, interspersed with rainbow flashes streaking through. Then the scene resolved into a prehistoric rain forest, teeming with life. Insects buzzed among the flora and flew through the car. The scents of exotic flowers came in on a light humid breeze and soon blended with the musk of reptiles and the water flowing nearby. Off to the right a dog-sized reptile chased something indistinct through the bush. A trachedon nearby rose suddenly to its hind legs to a three meter height, and reached with its hands to pull a fern to a bill-like mouth.

I looked back to the rear of the car. The sights continued around, even through a window in the door. The sun had set. I heard a screech overhead. I stepped out from under the half canopy in time to see a pteronodon soaring by, something dangling in its talon. A full moon shone in the dimming light.

"It's beautiful," I said. I looked back at the nearby trachedon. The beast had paused in its chewing to watch the flying dinosaur go past. I watched it fascinated. Intellectually I knew it was a small model, filmed in stop-motion, made of synthetics layered carefully over intricate armature, and painted to look like skin and hide. But it chewed and breathed. It looked at me and blinked, twitching its tail in serpentine slidings. I could smell its stink. Sensory input assaults and breaks down the borders of reality. Insistent and uncompromising. Magic.

I spoke then, for the same reason that most people speak on darkrides, an attempt to remind yourself that it isn't real, and a sure sign you've been seduced.

"This kind of thing is done in lots of parks, isn't it?"

Virgil just nodded, looking around.

A sudden stillness sent a chill through me. The trachedon stopped chewing. It turned to look across the clearing ahead of us. A gut-rumbling bellow tore through the moss-draped trees. The trachedon turned and strode past us, the size of it pressing home as it jostled up against the carriage. The tyrannosaurus broke into the open on the far side of the clearing. The massive head towered over medium-sized trees. The thick tail twitched from side to side in agitation as it shifted its weight on thighs like hydraulic wine barrels. The cruel eyes locked on us, and it roared through dagger teeth like stalactites and stalagmites neatly arranged in a red cavern.

"Nice effect," Virgil said. I was pleased that he had spoken.

"When do we shoot?" The rifle had gotten to my hands. The sights lit up.

"I planned on waiting it out," he said.

The beast glared and snapped its jaws hungrily. Not real, I thought, the gun barrel rising.

"People used to favor this one for playing chicken," Virgil went on. "A weak heart or two clued the good, concerned people." Voice steady. His knuckles white on the seat.

"Wonderful," I muttered. I put the rifle back. The sights flickered derisively.

The ground trembled with the footfalls of the beast. It loomed higher in the sky. It paused to roar again, the moon silhouetting its skull. The gun sights flickered again. The breeze carried a smell of death. Twenty meters away. The gun-sights flickered on again. Suddenly the beast made a final lunge towards us. Virgil cursed and grabbed for his gun. A great taloned foot crushed down on the front of the carriage, tilting the whole thing. I fell. The open jaws dropped, fouling the air. I heard screams in three different octaves. The head reared back with arms and legs dangling from bloody jaws. A nearby tree fell on it. The scene dissolved into gray and colors drifting.

I looked over and saw Virgil on the floor, sitting up with his back against the seats. Perspiration covered his face. He took a deep breath and looked at me, smiling weakly. I took my fingers from my mouth and muttered, "Never again." Virgil shook himself and wiped his brow.

"Now what?" I said.

"I do it again. It will be just as real. But this time I shoot.

At the last moment.''

"And in comparison," I added, "the chimera will be cuddly."

He nodded. I got up from the floor and sat.

"I'm game," I said. Between us we killed it eleven times.


The chimera spent its waking hours lurking about in a desert area a few kilometers from the park. Virgil took me to a place where they dropped food to it, a seven meter deep amphitheater-like place at the end of one of the deep gullies that meandered through the area. The highest ground was hollow, a fact made obvious by the landscaping going on further along.

"The darkride people will have three cameras going," Virgil explained. "There, there, and here."

"In spite of everything, it doesn't seem like you to be doing this."

He shrugged. "What does seem like me?"

I couldn't answer that. "It isn't too late to settle down and pilot shuttles. You could work on your art in your spare time."

He shook his head. "I've wasted way too much time already."

"You know who I feel like? Rosencrantz and Guildenstern. Unimportant and only accidentally involved."

"They were involved enough to die, even in the Stoppard version."

"Especially in the Stoppard play. They served to anti-romanticize death. You die, and that's that. Nothing. Gone. No acting and coming back in a different hat."

He stood silently for a moment.

"Virgil?"

He sighed. "Be careful?"

"Yes."


Change of scene. The amphitheater is illuminated against the progress of mirrorshift, giving the setting an unreal quality as a pool of light in the deepening darkness. The cameras are in place, each crewed by two. I stood near the third camera, arms folded as if against a chill. The crews spoke in their jargon, making sure of their equipment. A medic and a reporter, whom I recognized as Brian Carr, the talk show host, bantered on, telling Sayer stories. Idle thoughts and idle chatter ceased as the chimera entered from the gully.

It paused at the entrance to look things over. A lizard tongue flicked in and out. The shaggy mane and dusty brown fur covered the head and torso. Gray-scaled leathery hide ran over the nose, snaked tail, and the squat reptilian legs. It moved forward in a lumbering slither, rather than a feline stride. It looked more pathetic than monstrous as it moved, looking for food that wasn't there. It stopped nosing about when Virgil entered. With him there for scale, the creature took on a fearsome aspect. Three meters from head to flanks, longer with the tail. It watched him. The cameras hummed and muted directions were whispered.

Virgil moved warily, carrying a two-meter spear. A sword and dagger hung sheathed at his waist, and he wore a thick vest, heavy leggings and long gloves. He halted just inside. The creature tilted its head and roared without menace, seeming to be asking where dinner was. Virgil hefted the spear. It had a long leaf blade, and a cross-bar part way down the shaft. The creature nosed about further, then approached the gully exit, pausing a few meters from Virgil. It cried out again, then suddenly scurried forward, trying to skirt around Virgil. Virgil moved quickly, blocking its path and thrusting the spear into the creature's breast.

It scrambled backwards with a cry of fear and pain. Virgil advanced carefully. The creature moved first to one side, then the other. Then it scrambled partway up the walls, as far as its claws could gain purchase, and began to creep along toward the gully. It passed below us, but out of Virgil's reach. It breathed in great rasping gasps, nails clicking on the face of the walls.

Virgil ran ahead quickly, drew back his arm, and cast the spear. It penetrated just behind the chimera's right shoulder. It fell with an agonized cry. Virgil moved up, drawing the sword for the kill. The twitching tail bumped up against Virgil, startling him into hesitation and warning the beast. It spun around, roaring out in savage rage, lashing out with its talons. The blow caught Virgil across the chest, hurling him back five meters, leaving the vest shredded and torn and his breast gashed and bleeding.

The chimera paused then, its cry turning again to pain, for the sudden movement had worked the spear deeper in the wound. It tried to worry the spear, buried now to the cross-piece.

Virgil looked up from where he had fallen. He rolled cautiously, rose to his knees, looked to the beast, then to where the sword had fallen. He got to a crouch, the dagger glittered in his left hand. The beast snarled pain and challenge. He moved to sweep the sword up, and around as the chimera lunged. Hampered by the spear and beaten down by the sword, still it managed to close its jaws on Virgil's thigh. Virgil threw his weight forward and stabbed viciously with the long dagger, again and again. The creature stilled, its roar faded. The dagger fell from Virgil's hand, clattering to the arena floor.

I felt detached, as if watching from a silent place, kilometers distant. Slowly, as with the sensation of weight coming to you in a gradual descent from the axis, I became aware of sounds and place. I felt the veins pounding in my head, and heard the hum of the cameras and the panted breathing of the medic. Finally, Virgil screaming on and on. I whispered, "It's no darkride."

I turned and shook the medic. The crews watched me dumbly, paled. "It's no damn darkride!" They became animated all at once, and we scrambled down.

"If it hadn't been for the leggings," Virgil was saying, gesturing to his heavily bandaged limb, "it might have been bitten clean off. I'll be fine with a little care."

He sat up in the hospital bed so that he could work with the swing-out terminal placed beside him. I sat next to the bed, feeling glum and not saying anything. Virgil went to a different subject, trying to open me up.

"I've been doing research on myself for the Brian Carr interview." He waved at the terminal. "Got a lot of information sifted."

No change from my corner.

"I'm glad you came to see me," he continued. "I could use some cheering up. Eve Brooks passed through the floor this morning, comforting the infirmed. Passed me by . . . unclean, I guess."

"Virgil."

"Yeah."

"Why'd you start all of this?"

"Making conversation."

"That isn't what I mean."

"What do you mean?"

"Why'd you start back in the first place on the Queen?"

He eased back on his pillow, crossed one arm over his lap, and fingered his beard with his other hand.

"I used to be a goalie on a lunar mass catcher. Did I tell you that? For three dull years. I decided if I'm going to be doing something I don't like doing, I've got to be doing it for somebody, or something worth putting up with it for."

I thought about that. His something now was a combination of striking a blow for his politics, and revenge in an appropriate form. As to a present somebody, I didn't know.

"What was your somebody and something back then?" I asked.

"My wife and child. I figured to make enough money either to bring them up, or to get a good start on Earth someplace."

"What happened?"

"They died. Killed." He paused. "Nothing to go back to Earth for and the Hohmann Queen heading out. Once on the Queen I decided I'd had enough of chasing rocks. Thus and so. Here I be."

Virgil made a big impression on the talk show interview

with Brain Carr. He referred to his popular image as a creation of the people who emphasized and distorted the facts like a crazy mirror according to their own needs. Folklore is a mode of expression, he said. What does the entity called Virgil Sayer express? he asked, and offered up a few suggestions. Greater social mobility. Financial freedom. Access to cultural expression.

Brian Carr asked if gambling was a cultural wish-fantasy. Sayer replied that the gambling was only important as a focal point of excellence upon which to hang attitudes. People like to relate with the best, he said.

Then Virgil brought up the point that the present colony emphasis on simple living and hard work began as a response to accusations that the space habitats were islands of paradisiacal decadence for the rich, and that the builders were letting the earth rot. But now, he said, the grounders have felt the effects of the Third Industrial Revolution more widely. The traditions are no longer necessary.

Then he announced his intention to run for office.

In all the excitement, no one noticed that he didn't say a thing about himself. He overturned a pot of controversy that filled Providence to overflowing. He'd forced people to ask themselves what they really wanted. The more recently arrived were easiest to convince. He'd forced his opponents into defending the status quo without being able to deal effectively with the questions he'd raised. They attacked him as an irresponsible menace. The opposition party adopted Virgil with open arms. He looked to be in a strong position. He told me that he planned on flying Peggy the length of the city to start the active campaign.

Two hundred people milling about the flight landing, and not all of them equally adept in moving in low-g. It made interesting watching as we waited for the time of the broadcast and flight. A couple of newsmen were moving a camera in place. A steady stream of people moved around Peggy.

"There he is," Virgil said. He had his leg bundled up to protect it, and had been among the awkward on coming down to the departure point.

"Who?"

"Looked like Hawthorne."

"Where?"

"Doesn't matter, it's almost time."

"You ready?"

"Almost. I forgot something."

"What? Your pilot's license?"

"There's a name from an old myth that I want to use."

I could tell from the way he said it, glancing back towards the elevators where there was a terminal.

"You want me to look it up?"

He nodded and smiled for good measure.

"Okay," I said. "What is it?"

"A Greek myth. About a character who bridled the winged horse Pegasus and slew the chimera."

"Sounds appropriate."

"Very. He was helped by the goddess Athena."

"I believe I have been complimented." Virgil surprised me by bending over to kiss me.

"One more thing," he said. "I'm going right now, and you won't be back in time. Just wave and mouth it. I read lips."

"I can tell," I laughed.

I made my way back to the terminal. Bellerophon was the name Virgil wanted. I waved and mouthed it. Then he gave a little speech. Brief and witty, he recapped what he'd said on the interview. There was a healthy spattering of applause from those gathered. Virgil moved over and pulled himself to Peggy's back. Seconds later they were off. I felt a tinge of pride watching Peggy, and jealousy seeing her go off with someone else. Mirrorshift had progressed enough for the sky to be dusk-dark. They moved gracefully down a scanty tunnel of clouds, each wing stroke making them smaller, coriolis effect twisting them out of line.

I looked down to turn off the v.t. screen. The story of Bellerophon was before me, in my hurry I had not read it. By some accounts a son of Poseidon and so destined for a dramatic life, he'd been falsely accused of raping a king's wife, and as punishment sent to kill the chimera. Athena aided him by giving him the bridle of Pegasus. After his successes, he began to think thoughts too great for man. He aspired to a place in the city of the gods, and so mounted Pegasus, and flew to gain entry. The gods, offended by such hubris, sent a gadfly to sting his mount. He fell . . . no.

I ran. They were high in the distance, near the axis. I stumbled into a man, knocking him down, and falling.

"What do you think . . ." he started. I recognized Emory Titus. I kicked him full in the face. Then I bounded to the hanger, grabbed a flycycle and flew after Virgil.

He was far ahead, perhaps two kilometers. There were shouts behind me. I pulled up for elevation and greater speed. Most of the shouts faded. I pedaled furiously. My legs began to ache. Far below dots of light marked the population centers. I looked back to the landing once, a reef of light in a growing sea of gloom. Two flyers followed after me. I pulled away from them, gradually catching up to Virgil. Hard to see them . . . there . . .

As fatigue grew in me, I felt the first inklings of doubt. I glanced back at the pursuing flyers. Chagrin levered into my jumbled feelings. I shook myself. I was their best chance. And Titus had been there. I began counting pedal strokes against wingbeats.

"Virgil . . ." I shouted, but the distance was still too far. He hadn't looked back. Despite my closing the distance, it got harder to make them out against the dusk and cloudy backdrop. Fewer lights below.

"Oh, damn," I started to slow despite myself, muscles protesting that nothing would happen, fatigue protesting over fears.

Then I saw Peggy buck about violently in the air. Horse and rider separated, drifting apart. The floor three kilometers down.

"Virgil," I screamed.

I pedaled frantically, close enough now to hear Peggy's screams. Virgil drifted further, twisting in the air, falling so slowly. . . . but picking up speed all the while. Peggy began to get control back, and beat her wings steadily to slow her descent. Virgil in comparison fell like a stone. The clouds rushed up. He fell faster, diminishing against, and finally disappearing through the clouds.

I passed through a moment later. Only dark and silence. I pulled from my dive into a turn that pointed me back to the landing. City lights blurred and brimmed over. I rose slowly through the clouds. Two flyers overhead led Peggy back. I followed heavily.

By the time I got back, the news of Virgil's having fallen had likely gotten to everyone in the cities. A search for the body was being organized. Newspeople were on hand to question me. They were already quoting prosperity party people as saying that a reckless fool had come to a timely end.

The first thing I did was to have Peggy checked over. We uncovered a small burn. I accused Titus of putting a stinger on Peggy. Unfortunately we could produce no witnesses who could testify that they had seen Titus anywhere near my horse. He had plenty of reputable witnesses to the contrary. Also several who could testify that they had seen me assault him without provocation causing significant bodily and mechanical harm. He invited me to a lawsuit in my honor.

Sitting in detention a few days later, I got a visitor. A short portly man with dark skin named Lyle Saar. I knew him by reputation as a member of the destiny party, and instrumental in convincing them to adopt Virgil into the fold.

"Natalie Schofield?"

"That's me."

"You are in trouble."

"Trouble," I laughed bitterly. "I'll be out soon enough."

"And you'll be giving twenty percent of your pay to Emory Titus for the next twenty years." He sat next to me on the bunk. "That doesn't leave you much."

"I'll live."

"Not well."

"What's it to you?"

"I have a proposal."

"I'm listening."

"Or at least, I may have a proposal."

I stood and walked over by the bars, leaning against them.

"Depending on what?" I said.

"The results of the investigation."

"If Titus didn't do it, then Hawthorne must have."

"Hawthorne has an alibi," Saar said. "He has all kinds of witnesses. He wasn't even up at the landing."

"You sound as though the investigation was settled."

"Not yours."

"Me?"

"You proved it was no accident," Saar said. "And a crime of passion would affect the elections far less than assassination. What's going to happen when they question you?"

"Get out," I muttered.

"I'm here to help."

"So convince me."

"We want you to run for office."

I was too depressed to think of a punch line so I just snorted.

"For which," he went on, "we would pay your debt to Titus."

"Even if I were an aspiring politician, which I'm not, you just said I'm being investigated for murder." I turned and hung my arms through the bars.

"Exactly our problem," he said.

I turned and looked back at him. His expression implied that he had no ideas at all.

"Thanks for the help," I mumbled.

"With you as a masthead, we could win enough seats to bring about some changes." He paused. "Are you in the clear?"

"Look," I shouted. "I'd never have even thought of me. But Peggy's my horse, and all that's left of Virgil is a bucket of gore."

"Are you in the clear?" he said calmly. "Can we use you?"

"I don't need to be in the clear. Only the guilty need alibis."

"But Titus is in the clear. And Hawthorne wasn't there."

I remembered then. "But Virgil saw him."

"Impossible," Saar said. "He was working. Max Widengren was among the witnesses."

"Working on what?"

"I don't know."

I had an idea. Virgil saw people, not just as a face and features, but as a kinetic pattern. Suppose Virgil did recognize Hawthorne, despite his absence. I knew that Hawthorne had once tried to get to Virgil by broadcasting sensory information to a suitably cyborged person. That implied the capacity to broadcast physical commands, in effect, interrupting the brain's commands, and using a suitably wired person as a telefactor.

"Lyle Saar," I said, "Get out of here." I savored his disappointed expression. The matron came and let him out. "And when you see the sherlock who thinks I did it, have him find out who else on the landing besides Titus was a cyborg."

"Why?" He brightened.

"So they can peek inside."

"You've figured something."

"Then you can get me out of here and put Hawthorne in."

"Then we can use you."

"Somebody's always using somebody," I said. "I don't owe you if I lose."

"You won't lose."

I was right. And he was right. A bunch of council seats changed. But the biggest change was in attitude. We got rid of Hawthorne, and sent him to keep his nephew company. Titus we exported for fraudulent entry. Evangiline Brooks faded from the political scene, caught in the backlash for no good reason. We've got a symphony, a theater company, a ballet, a load of artists and performers of diverse creative modes, and a growing economy and population. We aren't yet decadent, but we are much less pious. Open. Some people left and went to homestead the rocks. I've won another election. I've been neither frustrated nor lonely, at least no more so than I could handle.

End of story.

Epilogue.

One day I took in a darkride called The Black Mountains. Inside I rode a balloon gondola up the face of a cliff, and over an ensorceled battlefield. There, among other things, I saw Zapranoth and Draffut. I asked around and found that the effects for the ride had been done locally. I sought the artist out, and visited him at his home.

"Hello, Virgil," I said.

"Hello, Natalie," he said. "Would you like to come in?"

"No."

"How is it with you then?" he asked. The beard was gone and the hair a different color, but he'd changed more deeply, or perhaps a different light brought up other facets.

"Oh, you know," I said. "Public people have no secrets."

"I knew what they were going to do."

I cleared my throat. He continued.

"I planned on it from the start, and pushed for it."

"You padded your leg with a para-foil," I said.

"The landing was still a little rough," he commented, nodding.

"How so?"

He showed me that he had a prosthetic leg.

"Oh."

"By the time I recovered sufficiently to learn of your troubles, you'd already figured the Hawthorne trick, and begun the campaign."

"You had help. A doctor, and someone to help you with a new name."

He nodded again. "I didn't want to put you in a position where you had to lie, but I tried to tell you."

"How?"

"Bellerophon."

"How?" I repeated.

"He survived the fall, and lived out his life in obscurity."

"Oh." I remembered. "I didn't read that far."

"I guessed later."

"And why this?"

"I planned differently," he paused. "I got a visitor in post-op at hospital."

Vague recollections surfaced.

"Losing the election hadn't stopped her humanitarian visits, and I'd forgotten them." His eyes glazed over momentarily at the recollection. "She recognized me, but decided not to make noise till she asked why."

"And?"

"I told her. And we talked. And somehow . . . we seemed to fit."

"I see."

"I suppose it's what I always wanted. A home and family."

In my head, a kalidostorm of feelings raged. Exhilaration, disgust, the anguish I'd known, the glory, the burden . . . and Roxanne's last words to Cyrano, Rhett's to Scarlet. I choked them all off, not sure at that moment which were true.

"Are you happy?" I finally said.

"Yes," he said softly.

"That's really all I wanted to know."

". . . I'm sorry."

". . . Whatever for?"

Call it the stuff of legends, when you hear it. And consider the sight and the setting; an inside-out world. I ride Peggy often. And someday when it no longer matters, I'll speak my knowledge.

# EDITOR'S INTRODUCTION TO:

## THE HIGH-LIFTER TRILOGY

### by Robert Frazier

*I've never met Robert Frazier, but I've a lot of sympathy for him. Poets are not highly appreciated these days, and there's almost no market at all for space-oriented poetry.*

*To make matters worse, after we accepted his poems and sent him a contract, his manuscript was misplaced; one of my assistants had the unpleasant task of telling the poor chap not only that he wouldn't be in Volume One of this series, but that we couldn't even find where we'd put his work. Believe me, that doesn't happen often here. Oh, it would if the administrative details were left to me; fortunately, for all, though, I don't usually take care of them. It was, of course, I who had lost the ms. While I was working on Volume One, but before it could be entered in the Table of Contents, it became buried in one of the archaeological strata on my desk.*

*And of course that was Frazier's first poetry sale. It would be.*

*Things all worked out, though, and since that time Frazier has sold poetry to* Isaac Asimov's, *Scott Card's* Dragons of Light *and other anthologies; so although this is his first sale, these are not his first published poems.*

# THE HIGH-LIFTER TRILOGY

**Robert Frazier**

## I. THE TITAN-O COLONY

From afar it lies as invisible
  as an evening cricket,
  and as silent as a sere desert wind.

From outside it appears child's play,
  titanium ringtoss of frost giants;
  yet it embodies all man's hopes
  cast in one die.
A maypole gyroscope,
  it balances centrifugically this carton of eggs
  and spins blindly across the rafters of space.

Inside the sky is bent,
  a strung bow,
  and you stand, wherever you are,
  at the exact bottom of the bowl of a lute.
The world is circumferential,
  yet is bound by diameters:
  spaced evenly in DNA helicals
  are spider's glide wires
  alive with shifting abacus beads;
  cylindrical trolleys on a one rail track.
Here the heavens are schizophrenic;
  as the sun rises in the east it also sets
  in the mock west,
  a purplish glow of fog.
The stars are insomniacs,
  never blinking;

only gliding like Peregrine falcons
through the center of a tubular sky.
Here the moons are many,
  like cloned streetlights
  trapped in the asylum of night.

In the null space the High-lifters fly;
  their motion is a music,
  one more movement within greater movements,
  as they attend to a symphony of stars.

## II. HIGH-LIFTER

Like a mustard seed in a gale,
  or a particle in the largest of cyclotrons,
Kia accelerates at will;
  motion is her breath,
  and she lives by her eyes, by her reflexes.
Sweeping debris from the sky,
  replacing burnt stars with soft light,
  finetuning the lunar phases;
  she rides the funnels of wind
  and the null air,
She is the Annie Oakley of the star lane;
  a drifter on the high, high plains.
  and the panhandles of control hutches.
Her sight is as keen as a rattlesnake's,
  yet her judgment is quick as a roadrunner's;
  and when she acts
  they both move in a synchronous orbit.

## III. PEREGRINA

Peregrina once met a Crewman here:
  far from the beehive confusion of the Colony,
  far from the High-lifter's cheetah fleet pace,
  where plexi-portals open like morning glories.
Naked to the eternal dawnlight of new constellations,
  naked under the dust dew of nebulae,
  the bubble was her meditation mat.

Here she puzzled her life with her partner Kia;
    or unpuzzled the classic tales
    about the colony Captain
    and the dreamtime of the Crew
    living by a different clock
    of temporal crystallizations:
    "quick years."

To most colonists these are myths.
The world is round, yes,
    but the sky is trapped in layers inside it
    and nothing Copernican lies beyond.

To Peregrina there is the sober truth
    of the starways,
    and the silent, calm touch of its aloof majesty.
Spinning at a snail's pace,
    the light cold and razorblade sharp,
    her mind unbound;
    she roams the ridgetops of imagination.
A drifter on the highest planes.
She dreams of someday seeing the TITAN-O
    from the outside
    in.

EDITOR'S INTRODUCTION TO:

DESIGNING A DYSON SPHERE

by Jack Williamson

*Jack Williamson comes from the Old Days: from before the Golden Age of science fiction. He was the second winner (Robert A. Heinlein was the first) of the Grandmaster Award of the Science Fiction Writers of America; certainly an "established" writer, making a good living at the trade. Yet when in his fifties he took his doctorate in English, writing a very readable dissertation on H.G. Wells; and he is now a college professor as well as a prolific novelist. One wonders what else he will undertake.*

*Moreover—when Jack was here for the Jupiter encounter, he met Ezekial—my friend who happens to be a Z-80 micro computer—and watched as I demonstrated how Zeke and I write stories. Six weeks later I received a letter from Jack's computer. Adaptable, that's what he is. . .*

*In fact, the only thing I don't understand about Dr. Williamson is how we suckered him into twice being President of SFWA. I mean, he already had the Grandmaster award . . . but accept he did, and Jack's two years were among the most productive and least controversial in SFWA's stormy history.*

\* \* \*

*Freeman Dyson is a fellow Director of the L-5 Society. His book* Disturbing the Universe *is a must read. He has invented so many concepts that it's hard to keep track of them all.*

*One is Dyson spheres: shells, either solid or made up of many, many objects in various orbits, surrounding stars.*

*After all, stars radiate energy; and energy is scarce. Why let it go to waste? Catch it and use it first.*

*Dyson's idea inspired Larry Niven's* Ringworld. *It also captured the imaginations of Jack Williamson and Fred Pohl, as Jack tells us.*

# DESIGNING A DYSON SPHERE

## Jack Williamson

An impossible object appears at the fringes of our galaxy,
looming out of unknown space at a sixth the speed of light.
The size of a giant star, it seems incredibly solid, not gase-
ous, and cool as a planet. Yet it's far too light to be a mass of
any possible substance. Any really solid object of its size
would be sucked into a black hole by its own gravitation.
Baffled by its riddles, the galactic observers call it Cuckoo.

It's a Dyson sphere, designed for the science fiction trilogy
I'm now writing with Fred Pohl. Outside such fiction, Dyson
spheres still belong to theory, as did positrons and neutrinos
not long ago. Yet there are exciting reasons to believe they
should exist. Though no actual observations have been confirmed, they're open for imaginative exploration.

Such probing of possible alternative worlds is half the fun
of science fiction—perhaps more than half for the writer. Yet
even so, too few writers venture as boldly as they might. Too
often we're simply informed that the new planet just happens
to be oddly Earthlike, happily provided with breathable air
and a friendly biochemistry.

The universe offers probable worlds enough awaiting exploration, actual or imagined. Our own galaxy holds perhaps
a hundred billion suns, and there's accumulating evidence
that a family of planets is formed with every normal star.
Most of them, however, will offer our spacemen a pretty
grim welcome.

We Earthfolk inhabit a pretty limited ecological niche. In
the scale of cosmic temperatures, ranging from the absolute
zero outside the galaxies to the hundreds of millions of
degrees inside the stars, our sort of life is confined to the

narrow zone where water is commonly liquid. In our own planetary family, Mars is now too cold, Venus far too hot.

We require free oxygen, which is thermodynamically unstable and therefore probably rare—our own supply is here only because the chlorophyll in plants releases it faster than it can combine again. We can only suppose, or hope, that other worlds will evolve equally helpful plants.

We require a sheltered environment, permanently protected from all sorts of common cosmic extremes—from the deadly gases in other planetary atmospheres; from the energetic ions around Jupiter, from the meteors that once bombarded the moon.

Our own Earth is an unlikely place, though precisely how unlikely we can't yet say. One star in a hundred may have a planet where we could feel at home, or one in ten thousand. The odds are still unknown, but most worlds are going to be different.

A few science fiction writers have become specialists in exotic planets. Notably Hal Clement, who has created big worlds and strange worlds, hot worlds and cold ones. Both he and Poul Anderson have written illuminating chapters on the invention of new planets and new forms of life for Bretnor's *Science Fiction: Today and Tomorrow*.

Often, of course, the writer is more intent on biological and social extrapolations than on new geologies. Ursula Le Guin's planet Winter in *Left Hand of Darkness* is about what Earth might have been at the peak of the last ice age; the absorbing innovations are in her people and their culture.

But the problems of building physically different environments does offer a stimulating mental challenge and a widened scope for all sorts of story development. The Dyson sphere that Fred and I have been designing for our new trilogy is I think the largest habitable world in all science fiction.

Freeman Dyson is a mathematician at the Institute for Advanced Study. He has suggested that our neighbor civilizations might be observable in space as points of infrared radiation, because a really advanced people might be able to trap and use all the radiation shining in every direction from their sun, allowing only waste heat to escape.

The simplest way of doing this would be to build all the metal of the planets into a swarm of sun-vaned spacecraft, moving in orbits that keep them spread in a cloud all around their sun. I have suggested this sort of thing in a novel called *The Power of Blackness*, but for the trilogy we wanted a solid wall around the star.

(Larry Niven took one step in this direction with *Ringworld*. His invention is an immense metal ring spinning around a sun, so fast that its air and its inhabitants are held against the inner surface by centrifugal force. To make the ring, he requires a very remarkable metal.)

Our own first problem was building material for the sphere. Most of the Universe is hydrogen. The heavy metals, formed only in supernova explosions, are relatively rare. At best, the stuff of any ordinary planetary system would be enough to make only a flimsy sphere.

But ours was to be a sort of cosmic ark, constructed by the common effort of all the intelligent races of an ancient galaxy, designed to carry them to safety when the galactic core explodes. Materials for it could come from many thousands, or even millions of stellar systems. Iron and its sister metals, incidentally, ought to be relatively plentiful in such an old galaxy, much of it formed by natural supernovas but more of it artificial. Very stable elements, they would be logical waste products from the most sophisticated fusion power generators. We can assume the technology not only to build such generators, but to fabricate the waste metal into extraordinary alloys.

Even given such alloys, however, there are still grave engineering problems in placing a solid shell around a star. No possible metal would be rigid enough to support itself against the gravitation of the central sun, or even against the pull of its own mass. Though a hollow sphere might be rotated fast enough to support its equatorial zone with centrifugal force, its polar regions would fall in.

The solution we found was to surround the star with

several layers of ring-shaped tubes. The tubes themselves are stationary, but they contain a heavy, low-viscosity fluid flowing fast enough to create the centrifugal force required to support the tubes and the loads above them. One set of parallel tubes holds up the "equator"—which isn't really moving—and other sets, tilted at suitable angles, support the regions near the "poles."

The tubes are also heat-engines, with the fluid driven by energy absorbed from the sun and flowing through generator stations which supply power to all the inhabited levels above. Master computers adjust the velocity of flow to fit the loads.

Cuckoo is enormous. With a radius of 86 million miles—200 times that of our sun—it's 540 million miles in circumference. The surface area is vast almost beyond imagination—some $9 \times 10^{16}$ square miles. Space enough for story action!

Though light for its size—a high vacuum in the same space might weigh more—it's heavy enough. The entire construction, including tubes and fluid, living quarters and control devices and surface armor, cargo and fuel and atmosphere, has some ten times the mass of the star inside, which in turn is heavier by half than our sun.

The shell is equivalent in weight to a plate of solid steel more than two miles thick; with the open spaces between the several levels, its total thickness is some forty miles. Massively armored, with the supporting tubes arranged in multiple layers, it is well protected from accidental damage.

With fifteen solar masses, Cuckoo has a surface gravity about one percent that of Earth. This is force enough to hold the atmosphere which has collected above the outside armor. Part of this is interstellar gas; most of it is waste oxygen and helium from nuclear power plants which use water for fuel—tanks for this fuel form vast seas on Cuckoo's surface. This oxy-helium mix is breathably dense at the lower levels and a hundred times as deep as the air of Earth.

The last link in the complex energy-chain from the inner star, carrying convective heat from the metal surface toward open space, the atmosphere of Cuckoo has its own awesome meteorology, with storm-clouds rising a thousand miles high.

Launched out of its exploding home galaxy in search of new worlds, the sphere is not only a super-planet but a supership. An immense ramjet, it uses magnetic fields created by the flow in the centrifugal tubes to sweep up cosmic gas, which is drawn past the central sun, energized, and expelled behind.

The propulsion system raised new engineering problems, the worst of them due to the fact that a star at the center of a massive hollow shell is in unstable equilibrium, so that any nudge would tend to tip it toward collision. We were able, however, to turn this dangerous instability into a means of propulsion. The solution here is to store the surplus water and centrifugal fluid in enormous tanks spaced about the sphere, with a system of pumps to empty or fill them as necessary to adjust the gravitational balances to keep the sun in place at the center of the moving globe.

This pump system and other controls are hooked to a complex net of sensors inside the sphere and on orbital satellites, and to the master computers, which are entirely automatic robot devices equipped with failsafe defenses and elaborately protected against time, accident, and vandalism.

The passengers of Cuckoo are less immune to time and change. As the sphere was completed, they left their home planets for their alloted spaces in the levels between the inmost layer of centrifugal tubes and the heavy outside armor. Most of them are still there, some still active, others surviving in various states of arrested animation.

By now the sphere has been in flight for hundreds of millions or perhaps billions of years, the remnants of its exploded native galaxy lost in the cosmos behind. Some of the races that built it are extinct; many have forgotten their origins, evolving or degenerating into wholly different orders of life, often in conflict with one another.

The outer surface was at first an endless plain of bare metal, but much of it is covered now with soil from accumulated cosmic dust and the industrial wastes dumped from the occupied levels. Plant life has evolved there, supported by the energy-flow from below through a process of thermosynthesis. These plants are often luminescent, so that vast landscapes glow with varied color. There's animal life, adapted to the low gravity and to varied local conditions of light or darkness, heat or cold, wild storms or unending calm—with no rotation and no external sun, Cuckoo had no seasonal climatic change. Most of these beings evolved on the surface, but some are migrants from below. A few are human.

Not, however, native to Cuckoo. Much fiction to the contrary, our human body can't be a cosmic norm. There are arguments, of course, that the evolution of intelligence on every world would tend to follow parallel tracks, that the logic of change would demand our bipedal shape and our erect posture, elevating the eyes and the brain and freeing the hands for tool-making. But all those arguments are rationalizations, I suspect, which overlook the chance factors that have helped make us what we are.

The human inhabitants of Cuckoo are descendants of specimens taken by a scouting ship from Cuckoo that touched Earth many thousand years ago. Escaping to the surface, they have evolved physique and culture to fit their new environment. Though still at a primitive level, they've learned to fly with crude leather-and-fabric wings.

Though we've assumed technologies for interstellar flight for our own galactic cultures as well as for the builders of Cuckoo, we've tried to respect the velocity of light as a relativistic limit to the speed of any material thing. For a solution to the problems of communication, we call on Jerry Feinberg's tachyon, the hypothetical subatomic particle whose minimum-energy velocity is infinite. Though nothing material can be sent by tachyon beam, holographic scanning of objects and even of living beings yields information that can be transmitted to produce instantaneous replicates—copies of an original that remains safe at home.

In bald outline, these have been the basic assumptions of our trilogy, the bare physical foundation for all the complex

extrapolations of culture and society and character and action
that go into the making of fiction. *The Farthest Star* is already
published. The novels to follow will continue to trace the
impacts of Cuckoo on our galaxy. The details are beyond the
scope of this paper, but I find designing such worlds a
stimulating exercise of the imagination, more exciting than
crossword puzzles or duplicate bridge. I hope readers will
enjoy the exploration of Cuckoo as much as Fred and I did the
building of it.

EDITOR'S INTRODUCTION TO:

## CONSERVATION OF MASS

### by Karl T. Pflock

*Karl Pflock has recently inherited the Chairmanship of the SFWA Grievance Committee. It's not the easiest job in the world. He took it over from Joe Haldeman, who inherited it from, ahem, your servant; I know just how much work it involves.*

*A former editor of* Libertarian Review, *Karl has, as senior editor of Arlington House, been responsible for the publication of dozens of books, many of which would have been unpublishable without his able editorial assistance.*

*They say if you want a job done, give it to a busy man. Karl is a pleasant chap, but he's nearly always too busy (he couldn't get to the VOYAGER encounter with Saturn, for example). Consequently, I've seen more of Carol Pflock than Karl; she gets to American Astronautical Society meetings and such like. The first time I telephoned Karl—we've since become good friends, but at the time I had never met him, and I think we had exchanged one letter—Carol answered as "The Resident Indian." I've forgotten the tribe, but she is apparently legally entitled to "Native American" status; as if the Pflocks, libertarians as they are, would claim any such thing. Another time I found I was speaking to Mrs. Colorado, a Mrs. America contender; hardly surprising, if you know Carol.*

*Anyway, as if the Pflocks weren't busy enough to begin with, SFWA prevailed on them to handle professional affairs*

*with the Denver 1981 World Science Fiction Convention.
And if they still haven't enough to do, why we can—*

*          *          *          *

   *At one point during the "Saturn and the Mind of Man"
symposium described in the introduction to Don Kingsbury's
story, the panelists turned to the topic of Dyson spheres.
   Then they laughed. Of course Drs. Sagan and Murray and
Morrison had already chuckled over the concept of space
colonies, so perhaps we shouldn't be surprised; but I was.
   "It will be a long time before we do that," one said.
   "Very long," said another. He laughed again. "The
protons will decay first."
   Everyone thought that very clever.*

*          *          *          *

   *Karl Pflock writes of a time in the future; a fairly far
future, but still well before the thousand billion years required for the protons to decay; a time when we have built
Dyson spheres, and thus have no shortage of energy. We do,
however, have one small problem. . .
   You may find this story annoying. That's all right. You're
intended to.*

# CONSERVATION OF MASS

## Karl T. Pflock

There was no need, of course. Chief Engineer Patt Neab would *know* the message as it came in. But the waiting was getting him down. He thought-queried the ship's computer: *Have we got the okay yet?* The response formed in his mind almost in parallel with the question. The genetically engineered alphalink center in his brain made him one with the computer; he was, in effect, talking to himself. *Nothing yet*.

"Dammit!" he said aloud. "Bloody politicians—no guts and fewer brains."

"Whajusay, Patt?" mumbled Rif Aagrad. Neab's deputy drifted nearby in the wardroom air. He was stretched out as if lying on his back, hands folded on his ample belly. He had been reading/experiencing an erotic novel via alphalink.

"Nothing, Rif. Just fretting. We've been ready to boost for more than a week. Charges, everything, set up right on schedule. Then those diddle-farts in Ring Central had to go squishy. If they don't get a move on, we're going to loose our boost window." Neab ran a strong hand over his tanned, completely blad head, then absently stroked his luxuriant blond mustache.

A wry smile grew on Aagrad's broad, dark face. "Don't you feel for the poor aborigines, Patt?"

Neab glared at his deputy. "Come on, Rif. A few million barbarians squatting on a chunk of prime mass we've got to have? Forgotten about the mass crisis? I feel for 'em alright—but not like you mean."

"Hey, take it easy. I'm with you, remember?" Aagrad cast a say-something glance at the third person in the compartment, Eleez Esmund, the ship's captain.

Captain Esmund grinned through the holo game-pieces on the table before her. "Yes, Patt, take it easy. Peers Council will give the Sanctuarists the politically necessary show of objectivity . . . then give us the go-ahead. After all, what choice do they have?"

The redheaded spacer was right, of course. "Sorry, Rif, Ellie." They smiled acceptance. "But if we miss our window . . ." Aagrad and Esmund had already gone back to their respective amusements.

Neab sighed, gently pushed off from the bulkhead behind him with the touch of a toe, and floated across the compartment toward the holo wallscreen spanning the opposite bulkhead. He hove to about a meter away from the electronic window opening onto the infinite depths beyond the ship's skin. Dominating the view was the "chunk of prime mass": a beautiful planet in quarter phase, over which they hovered in synchronous orbit. It was a gorgeous sight. But Neab saw only mass, trillions of tonnes of mass, mass that would bail mankind out of the present shortage and make possible the project that would guarantee plenty for thousands of years to come.

Funny, Neab thought, old Homo Sap seemed to live, to progress, from crisis to crisis. Almost six hundred years ago, a half-century before grandfather—how many times removed?—left Earth for the first space colony, it was an energy crisis. Now the race lives in space, and we've got energy coming out of our ears.

Now, he mused, the problem is mass. The asteroids are gone, mined out long since. The system's major moons, the terrestrial planets—nearly gone, too, mined, fed into the transmuters, raw material for the construction of the Ring's flying city-states, the manufacture of necessities and luxuries to satisfy the needs and desires of the billions who live as gods of old.

Now the problem is mass. But the solution is at hand—if the Sanctuarists don't stop us, Neab thought with a frown. Well, they won't. Ellie is right; the Council has no choice. Elbowroom is at a premium again—as it always is, eventually. The Dyson sphere *must* be built, enclosing the Sun in an envelope of solar collectors and, more important, myriads of new manmade city-worlds—living space for the burgeoning billions. And Jupiter has more than enough mass for the job. We'll drop transmuters into his atmosphere and drain him of his substance, convert it by fusion alchemy into iron, aluminum, all the elements needed.

But first things first, he thought. First we build a sphere around Jupiter. Fusion transmutation produces one hell of a lot of waste energy. It has to be contained to protect the Ring-dwellers. And we can use it, recycle it, to speed transmutation. Waste not, want not.

Neab looked at the planet hanging before him in the blackness. Five-point-nine-four-times-ten-to-the-twenty-first tonnes of raw material, he thought. More than five times what we need for the Project Big Boy containment sphere and fabrication of the transmuters and such. The rest we'll toss back down the gravity well to feed the industrial estates of the Ring. Too bad about the locals, but we told them what was coming. We offered to take them off and resettle them. It's not our fault that damn near all of them listened to their high priests and shamans, their warlords and what have you, and stayed behind. There's—

A thought cut into his musings: *Council has denied Sanctuarist petition. You are authorized to initiate mass boost.* "Hurrah!" he whooped.

Neab's shout startled Aagrad and Esmund. "What gives?" said Aagrad.

"We've got 'go,' " Neab replied. "Rif, run a program check. Ellie, prepare to get under way; give the word to the outriders."

"Will do," they chorused, unnecessarily. Their alphalink transactions with the ship's computer were already playing through Neab's mind. Everything was coming up green. *Optimum boost time, five-point-oh-six minutes from mark . . . Mark.* Five minutes! He let the data flow. No problems. *Okay, initiate boost sequence.* The acknowledgment came back at once.

Neab looked around. Aagrad and Esmund were gone, already at their stations on the bridge. He decided to stay put, watch the show on the wallscreen. He alphalinked word to the bridge and strapped down.

Any minute now, he thought. *Fifteen-point-oh-three seconds*. Nothing . . . nothing . . . Then, on the night side, very near the terminator, an eye-searing, sun-bright flare. The first boost charge.

Beautiful! Neab was exhilarated. It did not occur to him that the charge had vaporized the ancient and, to some of the doomed below, sacred ruins of Denver. Not that he would have cared had it come to mind. At long last all that mass was going to be put to good use!

# EDITOR'S INTRODUCTION TO:

## THE QUIET

### by George Florance-Guthridge

*Pflock's story won't happen. Not in six hundred years; not in six thousand, either. By the time we need Earth's mass, we'll not only be able to go to the stars—but we can, if we like, take Earth with us as we set forth.*

*Still, we do want to be careful; it would be all too easy to become as Pflock's engineer.*

*C. S. Lewis examined the problem in his essay "The Abolition of Man." Man's final conquest of nature would not be what we think: for "what we call Man's power over Nature turns out to be a power exercised by some men over other men with Nature as its instrument . . . The final stage is come when Man by eugenics, by pre-natal conditioning, and by an education and propaganda based on a perfect applied psychology, has obtained full control over himself. Human nature will be the last part of Nature to surrender to Man. The battle will then be won. But who, precisely, will have won it?"*

*That is no trivial question.*

\* \* \*

*As we were wrapping up this book—literally as I was writing the final introductions—there came in the mail a story from a former college professor turned writer. We try not to return anything unread, even when there's little chance we can use it; and as it happened, "The Quiet" came in on a weekend when I wasn't too busy; so I read it first.*

295

*Then I put it in John's box and waited.*

*He took his mail and went off; a half hour later he came back. "Just how finished is* Endless Frontier?*" he asked.*

*"Oh, pretty well done," I said wickedly. "Why?"*

*"There's this new story—"*

*And I laughed and explained that I'd already decided I wanted it.*

*Lest the scientists and engineers become too enamored of their power, they should remember that Nemesis stalks those whose pride makes them believe themselves as gods . . .*

# THE QUIET

## George Florance-Guthridge

Kuara, my son, the Whites have stolen the moon.

Outside the window the sky is black. A blue-white disc hangs among the stars. It is Earth, says Doctor Stefanko. I wail and beat my fists. Straps bind me to a bed. Doctor Stefanko forces my shoulders down, swabs my arm. "Since you can't keep still I'm going to have to put you under again," she says, smiling. I lie quietly.

It is not Earth. Earth is brown. Earth is Kalahari.

"You are on the moon," Doctor Stefanko says. It is the second or third time she has told me; I have awakened and slept, awakened and slept until I am not sure what voices are dream and what are real, if any. Something pricks my skin. "Rest now. You have had a long sleep."

I remember awakening the first time. White. Everything white. The room white, Doctor Stefanko white, a white smell, white cloth covering me. Outside, blackness and the blue-white disc.

"On the moon," I say. My limbs feel heavy. My head spins. Sleep drags at my flesh. "The moon."

"Isn't it wonderful?"

"And you say my husband, /Tuka—dead."

Her lips tighten. She looks at me solemnly. Her hand, cool hand, strokes my forehead. "He did not survive the sleep."

"The moon is hollow," I tell her. "Everyone knows that. The dead sleep there." I stare at the ceiling. "I am alive and on the moon. /Tuka is dead but is not here." The words seem to float from my mouth. There are little dots on the ceiling.

"Sleep now. That's a girl. We'll talk more later."

"And Kuara. My son. Alive." The dots are spinning. I close my eyes. The dots keep spinning.

"Yes, but. . . ."

The dots. The dots.

*  *  *

"About a hundred years ago a law was formulated to protect endangered species—animals which, unless human-kind was careful, might become extinct," Doctor Stefanko says. Her face is no longer blurry. She has gray hair, drawn cheeks, sad eyes. I have seen her somewhere—long before I was brought to this place. I cannot remember where. The memory slips away. Dread haunts my heart.

!Gai, wearing a breechclout, stands grinning near the window. The blue-white disc Doctor Stefanko calls Earth haloes his head. His huge, pitted tongue sticks out where his front teeth are missing. His shoulders slope like those of a hartebeest. His chest, leathery and wrinkled, is tufted with hair beginning to gray. I am not surprised to see him, after his treachery. He makes n/um pulse in the pit of my belly. I look away.

"Then the law was broadened to include endangered peoples. Peoples like the /Gwi." Doctor Stefanko smiles maternally and presses her index finger against my nose. I toss my head. She frowns. "Obviously, it would be impossible to save entire tribes. So the founders of the law did what they thought best. They saved certain representatives. You. Your family. A few others, such as !Gai. These representatives were frozen."

"Frozen?"

"Made cold."

"As during !gum, when ice forms inside the ostrich-egg containers?"

"Much colder."

It was not dream, then. I remember staring through a blue, crinkled sheen. Like light seen through a snakeskin. I could not move, though my insides never stopped shivering. *So this is death, I kept thinking. An awful thing, death.*

"In the interim you were brought here to the moon. To Carnival. It is a fine place. A truly international facility. This will be your home now, !U."

"And Kuara?"

"He will live here with you, in time." Again, that tightening of the lips. Fear touches me. Then she says, "Would you like to see him?" Some of the fear slides away.

"Is it wise, Doctor?" !Gai asks. "She has a temper, this one." His eyes grin down at me. He stares at my pelvis.

"Oh, we'll manage. You'll be a good girl, won't you !U?"

My head nods. My heart does not say yes or no.

The straps leap away with a loud click. Doctor Stefanko and !Gai help me to my feet. The world wobbles. The Earth-disc tilts and swings. The floor slants one way, another way. Needles tingle in my feet and hands. I am helped into a chair. More clicking. The door hisses open and the chair floats out, Doctor Stefanko leading, !Gai lumbering behind. We move down one corridor after another. This is a place of angles. No curves, except the smiles of Whites as we pass. And they curve too much.

Another door hisses. We enter a room full of chill. Blue glass, the inside laced with frost, stretches from floor to ceiling along each wall. Frozen figures stand behind the glass. I remember this place. I remember how sluggish was the hate in my heart.

"Kuara is on the end," Doctor Stefanko says, her breath white.

The chair floats closer. My legs bump the glass; cold shocks my knees. The chair draws back. I lean forward. Through the glass I can see the closed eyes of my son. Ice furs his lashes and brows. His head is tilted to one side. His little arms dangle. I touch the glass in spite of the cold. I hear !Gai's sharp intake of breath and he draws back my shoulders, but Doctor Stefanko puts a hand on !Gai's wrist and I am released. There is give to the glass. Not like that on the trucks in the tsama patch. My n/um rises. My heart beats faster. N/um enters my arms, floods my fingers. "Kuara," I whisper. Warmth spreads upon the glass. It makes a small, ragged circle.

"He'll be taken from here as soon as you've made the adjustment," Doctor Stefanko says.

Kuara. If only I could dance. N/um would boil within me. I could !kia. I would shoo away the ghosts of the cold. Awakening, you would step through the glass and into my arms.

\* \* \*

Though we often lacked water we were not unhappy. The tsama melons supported us. It was a large patch, and by conserving we could last long periods without journeying to the waterholes. Whites and tame Bushmen had taken over the /Gam and Gautscha Pans, and the people there, the !Kung, either had run away or had stayed for the water and now worked the Whites' farms and ate mealie meal.

There were eleven of us, though sometimes one or two more. !Gai, the bachelor, was one of those who came and went. /Tuka would say, "You can always count us on three hands, but never on two or four hands." He would laugh, then. He was always laughing. I think he laughed because there was so little game near the !A Ha !O Pan, our home. The few duiker and steenbok that had once roamed our plain had smelled the coming of the Whites and the fleeing !Kung, and had run away. /Tuka laughed to fill up the empty spaces.

Sometimes, when he wasn't trapping springhare and porcupine, he helped me gather wood and tubers. We dug !xwa roots and ≠koa, the water root buried deep in the earth, until our arms ached. Sometimes we hit the n=a trees with sticks, making the sweet berries fall, and /Tuka would chase me round and round, laughing and yelling like a madman. It was times like those when I wondered why I had once hated him so much.

I wondered much about that during !kuma, a hot season

when starvation stalked us. During the day I would take off
my kaross, dig a shallow pit within what little shade a ≠uri
bush offered, then urinate in the sand, cover myself with
more sand and place a leaf over my head. The three of
us—/Tuka, Kuara, and I—lay side by side like dead people.
"My heart is sad from hunger," I sang to myself all day.
"Like an old man, sick and slow." I thought of the bad
things, then. My parents marrying me to /Tuka before I was
ready, because, paying them bride service, he brought them
new karosses. /Tuka doing the marrying thing to me before I
was ready. Everything before I was ready! Sometimes I
prayed into the leaf that a paouw would fly down and think
his penis a fat caterpillar.

Then one night /Tuka snared a honey badger. A badger,
during !kuma! Everyone was excited. /Tuka said, "Yesterday, when we slept, I told the land that my !U was hungry,
and I must have meat for her and Kuara." The badger was
very tender. !Gai ate his share and went begging, though he
had never brought meat to the camp. When the meat was
gone we roasted /ga roots and sang and danced while /Tuka
played the //gwashi. I danced proudly. Not for /Tuka but for
myself. N/um uncurled from the pit of my belly and came
boiling up my spine. I was afraid, because when n/um
reaches my skull I !kia. Then I see ghosts killing people, and I
smell the rotting smell of death, like decayed carcasses.

/Tuka took my head in his hands. "You must not !kia," he
said. "Not now. Your body will suffer too much for the
visions." He held me beside the fire and stroked me, and
n/um subsided. "When I lie in the sand during the day I
dream I have climbed the footpegs in a great baobab tree," he
said. "I look out from the treetop, and the land is agraze with
animals. Giraffe and wildebeest and kudu. 'You must kill
these beasts and bring them to !U and Kuara before the
Whites kill them,' my dream says."

Then he asked, "What do you think of when you lie there,
!U?"

I did not answer. He smiled. His eyes, moist, shone with
firelight. Perhaps he thought n/um had stopped my tongue.

The next day the quiet came. Lying beneath the sand, I felt n/um pulse in my belly. I fought the fear it always brought. I did not cry out to /Tuka. The pulsing increased. I began to tremor. Sweat ran down my face. N/um boiled within me. It entered my spine and pushed toward my throat. My eyes were wide and I kept staring at the veins of the leaf but seeing dread. I felt myself going rigid and shivering at the same time. My head throbbed; it was as large as a /ga root. I could hear my mouth make sputtery noises, like Kuara used to at my breast. The pressure inside me kept building, building.

And suddenly was gone. It burrowed into the earth, taking my daydreams with it. I went down and down into the sand. I passed =ubbee roots and animals long dead, their bones bleached and forgotten. I came to a waterhole far beneath the ground. /Tuka was in the water. Kuara was too. He looked younger, barely old enough to toddle. I took off my kaross, and the three of us held hands and danced, naked, splashing. There was no n/um to seize me. No marrying-thing urge to seize /Tuka. Only quiet, and laughter.

*  *  *

"This will be your new home, !U," Doctor Stefanko says as she opens a door. She has given me a new kaross; of *genuine* gemsbok, she tells me, though I am uncertain why she speaks of it that way. When she puts her hand on my back and pushes me forward, the kaross feels soft and smooth against my skin. "We think you'll like it; and if there's anything you need. . ."

I grab the sides of the door and turn my face away. I will not live in nor even look at the place. But her push becomes firmer, and I stumble inside. I cover my face with my hands.

"There, now," Doctor Stefanko says. I spy through my fingers.

We are in Kalahari.

I turn slowly, my heart shining and singing. No door. No walls. No angles. The sandveld spreads out beneath a cloud-less sky. Endless pale-gold grass surrounds scattered white-thorn and tsi; in the distance lift several flat-topped acacias and even a mongongo tree. A dassie darts in and out of a rocky kranze.

"Here might be a good place for your tshushi—your shelter," Doctor Stefanko says, pulling me forward. She enters the tall grass, bends, comes up smiling, holding branches in one hand, sansevieria fibers in the other. "You see? We've even cut some of the materials you'll need."

"But how—"

"The moon isn't such a horrible place, now is it." She strides back through the grass. "And we here at Carnival are dedicated to making your stay as pleasant as possible. Just look here." She moves a rock. A row of buttons gleams. "Turn this knob, and you can control your weather; no more suffering through those terrible hot and cold seasons. Unless you want to, of course," she adds quickly. "And from time to time some nice people will be looking down . . . *in* on you. From up there, within the sky." She makes a sweep of her arm. "They want to watch how you live; you—and others like you—are quite a sensation, you know." I stare at her without understanding. "Anyway, if you want to see them, just turn this knob. And if you want to hear what the monitor's saying about you, turn this one." She looks up, sees my confusion. "Oh, don't worry; the monitor translates everything. It's a wonderful device."

Standing, she takes hold of my arms. Her eyes are loving. "You see, !U, there is no more Kalahari on Earth—not as you knew it anyhow—so we created another. In some ways it won't be as good as what you were used to, in a lot of ways it'll be better." Her smile comes back. "We think you'll like it."

"And Kuara?"

"He's waking now. He'll join you soon." She hugs me. "Soon." Then she walks back in the direction we came, quickly fading in the distance. Suddenly she is gone. A veil of heat shimmers above the grass where the door seemed to have been. For a moment I think of following. Finally I shrug. I work at building my tshushi. I work slowly, methodically, my head full of thoughts. I think of Kuara, and something gnaws at me. I drop the fiber I am holding and begin walking toward the opposite horizon, where a giraffe is eating from the mongongo tree.

Grasshoppers, !kxon ants, dung beetles hop and crawl among the grasses. Leguaan scuttle. A mole snake slithers for a hole beneath a ≠uri bush. I walk quickly, the sand warm but not hot beneath my feet. The plain is sun-drenched, the few small omirimbi water courses parched and cracked, yet I feel little thirst. A steenbok leaps for cover behind a white-thorn. This is a good place, part of me decides. Here will Kuara become the hunter /Tuka could not be. Kuara will never laugh to shut out sadness.

The horizon draws no closer.

I measure the giraffe with my thumb, walk a thousand paces, remeasure, walk another thousand paces, remeasure.

The giraffe does not change size.

I will walk another thousand. Then I will turn back and finish the tshushi.

A hundred paces further I bump something hard.

A wall.

Beyond, the giraffe continues feeding.

* * *

The Whites with the Land Rovers came during !ga, the hottest season. The trucks bucked and roared across the sand. /Tuka took Kuara and hurried to meet them. I went too, though I walked behind with the other women. There were several white men and some Bantu. !Gai was standing in the lead truck, waving and grinning.

A white, blond-haired woman climbed out. She was wearing white shorts and a light brown shirt with rolled-up sleeves. I recognized her immediately. Doctor Morse, come to study us again. /Tuka had said the Whites did not wonder about their own culture, so they liked to study ours.

She talked to us women a long time, asking about our families and how we felt about SWAPO, the People's Army.

Everyone spoke at once. She kept waving her hands for quiet. "Would do you think, !U?" she would ask. "What's your opinion?" I said she should ask /Tuka; he was a man and understood such things. Doctor Morse frowned, so I said SWAPO should not kill people. SWAPO should leave people alone. Doctor Morse wrote in her notebook as I talked. I was pleased. The other women were very jealous.

Doctor Morse told us the war in South Africa was going badly; soon it would sweep this way. When /Tuka finished looking at the engines I asked him what Doctor Morse meant by "badly." Badly for Blacks, or Whites. Badly for those in the south, or those of us in the Kalahari. He did not know. None of us asked Doctor Morse.

Then she said, "We have brought water. Lots of water. We've heard you've been without." Her hair caught the sunlight. She was very beautiful for a white woman.

We smiled but refused her offer. She frowned but did not seem angry. Maybe she thought it was because she was white. If so, she was wrong. "Well, at least go for a ride in the trucks," she said, beaming. /Tuka laughed and, taking Kuara by the hand, scrambled for the two Land Rovers. I shook my head. "You really should go," Doctor Morse said. "It'll be good for you."

"That is something for men to do," I told her. "Women do not understand those things."

"All they're going to do is ride in the back!"

"Trucks. Hunting. Fire. Those are men's things," I said.

Only one of the trucks came back. Everyone but /Tuka, Kuara, and some of the Bantu returned. "The truck's stuck in the sand; the Whites decided to wait until dawn to pull it out," !Gai said. "/Tuka said he'd sleep beside it. You know how he is about trucks!" Everyone laughed. Except me. An empty space throbbed in my heart.

Then the rain came. It was !ga !go—male rain. It poured down strong and sudden, not even and gentle, the female rain that fills the land with water. Rain, during !ga! Everyone shouted and danced for joy. Even the Whites danced. A miracle! people said. I thought about the honey badger

caught during !kuma, and was afraid. I felt alone. In spite of
my fear, perhaps because of it, I did a foolish thing. I slept
away from the others.

In the night the quiet again touched me. N/um uncurled in
my belly. I did not beckon it forth. I swear I didn't. I wasn't
even thinking about it. As I slept I felt my body clench tight.
In my dreams I could hear my breathing—shallow and rapid.
Fear seized me and shook me like the twig of a n≠in≠i bush.
I sank into the earth. /Tuka and Kuara were standing slump-
shouldered in steaming, ankle-deep water at the waterhole
where we had danced. Kuara was wearing the head of a
wildebeest; the eyes had been carved out and replaced with
smoldering coals. "Run away, mother," he kept saying.

I awoke to shadows. A fleeting darkness came upon me
before I could move. I glimpsed !Gai grinning beneath the
moon. Then a hand was clapped over my mouth.

* * *

Doctor Stefanko returns after I've finished the hut. She and
!Gai bring warthog and kudu hides, porcupine quills, tortoise
shells, ostrich eggs, a sharpening stone, an awl, two assagai
blades, pots of Bantu clay. Many things. !Gai grins as he sets
them down.

Later, Doctor Stefanko brings Kuara.

He comes sprinting, gangly, the grass nearly to his chin.
"Mama," he shouts, "Mama, mama," and I take him in my
arms, whirling and laughing. I put my hands upon his cheeks;
his arms are around my waist. Real. Oh, yes. So very real,
my Kuara! Tears roll down my face. He looks hollow-eyed,
and his hair has been shaved. But I do not let concern stop my
heart. I weep from joy, not pain.

Doctor Stefanko leaves, and Kuara and I talk. He babbles
about a strange sleep, and Doctor Stefanko, and !Gai, as I
show him the camp. I show him how one of the knobs makes
a line of small windows blink on in the slight angle between
wall-sky and ceiling-sky. The windows look like square
beads. There, faces pause and peer. Children. Old men.

Women with smiles like springhares. People of many races. I tell him not to smile or acknowledge their presence. Not even that of the children. Especially not the children. The faces are surely ghosts, I warn. Ghosts dreaming of becoming /Gwi.

We listen to the voice Doctor Stefanko calls the monitor. It is sing-song, lulling. A woman's voice, I think. "!U and Kuara, the latest additions to Carnival, will soon become accustomed to our excellent accommodations," the voice says. The voice floats with us as we go to gather roots and wood.

A leguaan pokes its head from the rocky kranze, listening. Silently I put down my wood. Then my hand moves slowly. So slowly it is almost not movement. I grab. Caught! Kuara shrieks and claps his hands. "Notice the scarification across the cheeks and upper legs," the voice is saying. "The same is true of the buttocks, though like any self-respecting /Gwi, !U will not remove her kaross in the presence of others except during the Eland Dance." I carry the leguaan wiggling to the hut. "Were she to disrobe, you would notice tremendous fatty deposits in the buttocks, a phenomenon known as steatopygia. Unique to Bushmen (or 'Bushwomen,' we should say), this anatomical feature aids in food storage. It was once believed that. . . ."

After breaking the leguaan's neck, I take off the kaross of genuine gemsbok and, using sansevieria fiber, tie it in front of my hut. It makes a wonderful door. I have never had a door. /Tuka and I slept outside, using the tshushi for storage. Kuara will have a door. A door between him and the watchers.

He will have fire. Fire for warmth and food and !U to sing beside. I gather grewia sticks and carve male and female, then use //galli grass for tinder. Like /Tuka did. "The /Gwi are marked by a low, flattened skull, tiny mastoid processes, a bulging or vetical forehead, peppercorn hair, a nonpragnathous face. . . ." I twirl the sticks between my palms. It seems to take forever. My arms grow sore. I am ready to give up when smoke suddenly curls. Gibbering, Kuara goes leaping about the camp. I gaze at the fire and grin with delight.

But it is frightened delight. I will make warmth fires and food fires, I decide as I blow the smoke into flame. Not ritual fires. Not without /Tuka.

I roast the leguaan with /ore berries and the tsha-cucumber which seems plentiful. But I am not /Tuka, quick with fire and laughter; the firemaking has taken too long. Halfway through the cooking, Kuara seizes the lizard and, bouncing it in his hands as though it were hot dough, tears it apart. "Kuara!" I blurt out in pretended anger. He giggles as, the intestines dangling, he holds up the lizard to eat. I smile sadly. Kuara's laughing eyes and ostrich legs . . . so much like /Tuka!

"The /Gwi sing no praises of battles or warriors," the voice sing-says. I help Kuara finish the leguaan. "They have no history of warfare. Although petty arguments are common (even a nonviolent society cannot keep husbands and wives from scrapping), fighting is considered dishonorable. To fight is to have failed to. . . ." When I gaze up there are no faces in the windows.

At last, dusk dapples the grass. Kuara finds a guinea-fowl feather and a reed; leaning against my legs, he busies himself making a zani. The temperature begins to drop. I decide the door would fit better around our shoulders than across the tshushi.

A figure strides out of the setting sun. I shield my eyes with my arm. Doctor Stefanko. She smiles and nods at Kuara, now tying a nut onto his toy for a weight, and sits on a log. Her smile remains, though it is drained of joy. She looks at me seriously.

"I do hope Kuara's presence will dissuade you from any more *displays* such as you exhibited this afternoon," she tells me. "Surely you must realize that he is here with you on a . . . a trial basis, shall we say." She taps her forefinger against her palm. "This impetuousness of yours has got to cease." Another tap. "And cease now." Her left brow lifts.

Head cocked, I gaze at her, not understanding.

"Taking off your kaross simply because the monitor said you do not." She nods knowingly. "Oh, yes, we're aware when you're listening. And that frightful display with the lizard!'' She makes a face and appears to shudder. ''Then there's the matter of the fire.'' She points toward the embers. ''You're supposed to be living here like you did back on Earth. At least during the day. Men *always* started the fires.''

''Men were always present.'' I shrug.

''Yes. Well, arrangements are being made. For the time being stick to foods you don't need to cook. And use the heating system.'' She goes to the rock and, on hands and knees, turns one of the knobs. A humming sounds. Smiling and rubbing her hands over the fire, she reseats herself on the log, pulls a photograph from her hip pocket and hands it to me. I turn the picture rightside-up. Doctor Morse is standing with her arm across !Gai's shoulders. His left arm is around her waist. The Land Rovers are in the background.

''Impetuous,'' Doctor Stefanko says, leaning over and clicking her fingernail against the photograph. ''That's exactly what Doctor Morse wrote about you in her notebooks. *She* considered it a virtue.'' Again the eyebrow lifts. ''We do not.'' Then she adds proudly, ''She was my grandmother, you know. As you can imagine, I have more than simply a professional interest in our Southwest African section here at Carnival.''

I start to hand back the photograph. She raises her hand, halting me. ''Keep it,'' she says. ''Think of it as a wedding present. The first of many.''

* * *

That night, wrapped in the kaross, Kuara and I sleep in one another's arms, in the tshushi. He is still clutching the zani, though he has not thrown it once into the air to watch it spin down. Perhaps he will tomorrow. Tomorrow. An ugly word. I lie staring at the dark ground, sand clenched in my fists. I wonder if, somehow using devices to see in the dark, the ghosts in the sky-windows are watching me sleep. I wonder if they will watch the night !Gai climbs upon my back and grunts throughout the marrying-thing.

Sleep comes. A tortured sleep. I can feel myself hugging Kuara. He squirms against the embrace but does not awaken. In my dreams I slide out of myself and, stirring up the fire, dance the Eland Dance. My body is slick with eland fat. My eyes stare rigidly into the darkness and my head is held high and stiff. Chanting, I lift and put down my feet, moving around and around the fire. Other women—my sister Di!ai, my cousin Xama, many others—clap and sing the !kia-healing songs. Men play the //gwashi and musical bows. The music lifts and lilts and throbs. Rhythm thrums within me. Each muscle knows the song. Around and around, ever dancing. Tears squeeze from my eyes. Pain leadens my legs. And still I dance.

Then, at last, n/um rises. It uncurls in my belly and breathes fire-breath up my spine. I fight the fear. I dance against the dread. I tremble with fire. My eyes slit with agony. I do not watch the women clapping and singing. My breaths come in shallow, heated gasps. My breasts bounce. I dance. N/um continues to rise. It tingles against the base of my brain. It fills my head. My entire body is alive, burning. Thorns are sticking everywhere in my flesh. My breasts are fiery coals. I can feel ghosts, hot ghosts, ghosts of the past, crowding into my skull. I stagger for the hut; Kuara and !U, my old self, await me. I slide into her flesh like someone slipping beneath the cool, mudslicked waters of a year-round pan. I slide in among her fear and sorrow and the anguished joy of Kuara beside her.

She stirs. A movement of a sleeping head. A small groan; denial. I slide in further. I become her once again. My head is aflame with n/um and ghosts. "!U," I whisper, "I bring the ghosts of all your former selves, and of your people." Again she groans, though weaker; the pleasure-groan of a woman making love. Her body stretches, stiffens. Her nails rake Kuara's back. She accepts me, then; accepts her self. I fill her flesh.

And bring the quiet, for the third time. Down and down into the sand she seeps, like !ga !go rain soaking into parched earth, leaving nothing of her self behind, her hands around

Kuara's wrists as she pulls him after her, the zani's guinea-fowl feather whipping behind him as if in a wind. She passes through sand, Carnival's concrete base, moonrock, moving ever downward, badger-burrowing. She breaks through into a darkness streaked with silver light: into the core of the moon, where live the ghosts of !kia. She tumbles downward, crying her dismay and joy, her kaross fluttering. In the center of the hollow, where water shines like cold silver, /Tuka awaits, arms outstretched. He is laughing—a shrill, forced cackle. Such is the only laughter a ghost can know whose sleep has been disturbed. They will dance this night, the three of them: !U, /Tuka, Kuara.

Then he will teach her the secret of !oa, the poison squeezed from the female larvae of the dung beetle. Poison for arrows he will teach her to make. Poison for which Bushmen know no antidote.

She will hunt when she returns to !Gai and to Doctor Stefanko.

She will not hunt animals.

# EDITOR'S INTRODUCTION TO:

## PSI-REC: OF ANABASIS AND
## BIVOUAC, THE SWARMCANTOR

### by Peter Dillingham

*I can't pretend that I always understand Peter Dillingham;
but I find myself including his work in most of my anthologies.*

*John and I agreed: this is certainly the most visually
memorable piece we've ever included; and we like it better
each time we read it—and it seems naturally to follow the
Guthridge story.*

# PSI-REC: OF ANABASIS AND BIVOUAC, THE SWARMCANTOR

## Peter Dillingham

*Poetry . . . it survives,*
*a way of happening, a mouth.*
　　　　*—W. H. Auden*

Noomen, we bivouac in great open of ruin, nest ruin of Nukeman. We bivouac at sunsink after swarm, swarm raid ransack of Nukeman nest ruin.

We bivouac in silence, always in silence.

FIRST CIRCLE: Straddlers, Swarm's twelve strongest, stockade of Straddlers around the Queen's nest, arms interlocked over each other's shoulders, heads bowed inward.

FIRST RING: Kneelers, plugs, on their hands and knees, heads bowed, stuck between the first circle's legs.

SECOND CIRCLE THIRD CIRCLE: straddling the first ring's backs. Linked circles: left arms over each other's shoulders. Interlocking circles: right arms around those in front . . .

We bivouac. Circles and rings around the Queen's nest, circles of Straddlers astride rings of Kneelers. Outward, outward. Three and one. Three and one. Linked and interlocking, pressing inward.

I Timur, once proud Straddler of the second circle, now Timur the Lame, swarm raid wounded, lowly Kneeler of the outermost rings, I Timur am cold.

Outward, outward from the center the circles loosen,
weaken. The rings sag. The night wind storms the bivouac,
and I Timur am cold. Bone cold. Pain and cold.

| | |
|---|---|
| I whisper: | tighter, press tighter! |
| Echoes: | tighter tighter |
| I whisper: | tighter, press tighter! |
| Echoes: | tighter tighter |
| I chant: | press tight! tight! tight! |
| Echoes: | tight tight tight tight |
| I chant: | tightightight |
| Echoes: | tightightightightightight |
| I chant: | tightightight |
| Echoes: | tightightightightightight |

Chant and echoes:

```
                    tight
                 tightightight
              tightight tightight
            tightightightightightight
          tightightightight tightightight
        tightightightight tightightightight
      tightightightightight tightightightight
    tightightightightight tightightightightight
   tightightightightightightightightightightight
  tightightightightight tightightightightight
 tightightightightightightightightightightightight
tightightightightightight tightightightightightight
tightightightightightight tightightightightightight
tightightightightightight tightightightightightight
tightightightightightight tightightightightightight
tightightightightightight tightightightightightight
 tightightightightightightightightightightightight
  tightightightightight tightightightightight
   tightightightightightightightightightightight
    tightightightightight tightightightightight
      tightightightightight tightightightight
        tightightightight tightightightight
           tightightightight tightightightight
             tightightightightightightight
               tightight tightight
                 tightightight
                    tight
```

Warmer, I Timur, Timur the Lame, sleep. . .

We swarm, swarm raid at sunrise after bivouac, swarm raid across war wrack of Nukeman, war waste of Nukeman.

We swarm in noise, always noise.

I chant:           raid, raiders, raid!
Echoes:          raid raid raid
I chant:           raid, raider, raid, raider!
Echoes:          raider raider raider
I chant:           raideraider

Chant and echoes:

```
                raideraideraideraider
                raideraideraideraider
                raideraideraideraider
                raideraideraideraider
                raideraideraideraider
                raideraideraideraider
                raideraideraideraider
                raideraideraideraider
                raideraideraideraider
                raideraideraideraider
                raideraideraideraider
                raideraideraideraider
                raideraideraideraider
                raideraideraideraider
              raideraideraideraideraider
              raideraideraideraideraider
           raideraideraideraideraideraideraider
           raideraideraideraideraideraideraider
         raideraideraideraideraideraideraideraider
          raideraideraideraideraideraideraider
       raideraideraideraideraideraideraideraideraider
       raideraideraideraideraideraideraideraideraider
     raideraideraideraideraideraideraideraideraideraider
     raideraideraideraideraideraideraideraideraideraider
raideraideraideraideraideraideraideraideraideraideraideraider
raideraideraideraideraideraideraideraideraideraideraideraider
raideraideraideraideraideraideraideraideraideraideraideraider
raideraideraideraideraideraideraideraideraideraideraideraider
raideraideraideraideraideraideraideraideraideraideraideraider
raideraideraideraideraideraideraideraideraideraideraideraider
raideraideraideraideraideraideraideraideraideraideraideraider
     raideraideraideraideraideraideraideraideraideraider
     raideraideraideraideraideraideraideraideraideraider
       raideraideraideraideraideraideraideraideraider
       raideraideraideraideraideraideraideraideraider
         raideraideraideraideraideraideraideraider
         raideraideraideraideraideraideraideraider
           raideraideraideraideraideraideraider
           raideraideraideraideraideraideraider
              raideraideraideraideraider
              raideraideraideraideraider
```

Subswarm, we raid, swarm raid rocks rooting Doomen from cave nests. . .

"Timur," they cry, "give us song, song of slaving, Slave Raid Song!"

I Timur chant:        slaves, enslave slaves!
Echoes:             slaves slaves slaves
I chant:             slaveslaves
Echoes:             slaveslaveslaves
Chant and echoes:

```
                    slaveslaveslaves
                    slaveslaveslaves
                    slaveslaveslaves
                    slaveslaveslaves
                    slaveslaveslaves
                    slaveslaveslaves
                    slaveslaveslaves
                    slaveslaveslaves
                    slaveslaveslaves
                    slaveslaveslaves
                    slaveslaveslaves
                    slaveslaveslaves
              slaveslaveslaveslaveslaves
        slaveslaveslaves          slaveslaveslaves
        slaveslaveslaves          slaveslaveslaves
       slaveslaveslaves           slaveslaveslaves
       slaveslaveslaves            slaveslaveslaves
      slaveslaveslaves             slaveslaveslaves
     slaveslaveslaves               slaveslaveslaves
     slaveslaveslaves               slaveslaveslaves
     slaveslaveslaves               slaveslaveslaves
     slaveslaveslaves               slaveslaveslaves
     slaveslaveslaves               slaveslaveslaves
      slaveslaveslaves             slaveslaveslaves
       slaveslaveslaves           slaveslaveslaves
       slaveslaveslaves           slaveslaveslaves
        slaveslaveslaves          slaveslaveslaves
         slaveslaveslaves         slaveslaveslaves
          slaveslaveslaves     slaveslaveslaves
            slaveslaveslaves  slaveslaveslaves
```

We bivouac in great open, great open of noman land.
We bivouac at sunsink after swarm, swarm raid slave raid.

FIRST CIRCLE, Straddlers, Swarm's twelve strongest, stockade of Straddlers around the Queen's nest, arms interlocked over each other's shoulders, heads bowed inward.

FIRST RING: Kneelers, plugs, on their hands and knees, heads bowed, stuck between the first circle's legs.

SECOND CIRCLE THIRD CIRCLE: straddling the first ring's backs. Linked circles: left arms over each other's shoulders. Interlocking circles: right arms around those in front . . .

They wait.
"Timur," they cry, "give us song, Bivouac Song!"

I Timur chant:          tightightight
Echoes:              tightightightightightight
I chant:              tightightightight
Echoes:              tightightightightightightightight
Chant and echoes:

```
                  tight
               tightightight
            tightight tightight
         tightightightightightight
       tightightightight tightightight
      tightightightight tightightightight
     tightightightight tightightightight
    tightightightightight tightightightightight
   tightightightightightightightightightightight
  tightightightightightight tightightightightight
 tightightightightightightightightightightightight
tightightightightightight tightightightightightight
tightightightightightight tightightightightightight
tightightightightightight tightightightightightight
tightightightightightight tightightightightightight
 tightightightightightightightightightightightight
  tightightightightightight tightightightightight
 tightightightightightightightightightightightight
  tightightightightight tightightightightight
   tightightightightight tightightightight
    tightightightight tightightightight
     tightightightight tightightightight
      tightightightightightight
       tightight tightight
         tightightight
           tight
```

We swarm at sunrise after bivouac, swarm toward far ruins of Nukeman, ruins like Nooman teeth, sky-biting.
We break camp in noise, always noise: hoot, whoop, tramp, stamp . . .

I Timur chant:        troop tramp trample loot
Echoes:               trample loot trample loot
I chant:              troop tramp trample loot
Echoes:               trample loot trample loot
I chant:              tramplootramploot
Echoes:               tramplootramplootramplootramploot
Chant and echoes:

```
                    tramplootramploot
                    tramplootramploot
                    tramplootramploot
                    tramplootramploot
                    tramplootramploot
                    tramplootramploot
                    tramplootramploot
                    tramplootramploot
                    tramplootramploot
                    tramplootramploot
                    tramplootramploot
                    tramplootramploot
                    tramplootramploot
                    tramplootramploot
                    tramplootramploot
              tramplootramplootramplootramploot
                tramplootramplootramplootramploot
          tramplootramplootramplootramplootramploot
        tramplootramplootramplootramplootramplootramploot
      tramplootramplootramplootramplootramplootramplootramploot
    tramplootramplootramplootramplootramplootramplootramplootramploot
  tramplootramplootramplootramplootramplootramplootramplootramplootramploot
tramplootramplootramplootramplootramplootramplootramplootramplootramploot
tramplootramplootramplootramplootramplootramplootramplootramplootramploot
  tramplootramplootramplootramplootramplootramplootramplootramplootramploot
    tramplootramplootramplootramplootramplootramplootramplootramploot
      tramplootramplootramplootramplootramplootramplootramploot
        tramplootramplootramplootramplootramplootramploot
          tramplootramplootramplootramplootramploot
            tramplootramplootramplootramploot
            tramplootramplootramplootramploot
```

Subswarm we surround runaway slaves.
"Timur," they cry, "give us song, song of killing, Kill
Song!"

I Timur chant:        maul laim maul maim
Echoes:               maul maim maul maim
I chant:              maul laim maim maul laim maim
Echoes:               maul laim maim maul laim maim
                          maul laim maim

I chant:              maulaimaim
Echoes:               maulaimaimmaulaimaim
Chant and echoes:

```
            maulaimaimaulaimaim
            maulaimaimaulaimaim
          maulaimaim maulaimaim
         maulaimaim      maulaimaim
        maulaimaimaul  maimaulaimaim
       maulaimaimaulaim laimaimaulaimaim
      maulaimaimaulaim  laimaimaulaimaim
     maulaimaimaulaimaimaulaimaimaulaimaim
    maulaimaimaulaimaim maulaimaimaulaimaim
   maulaimaimaulaimaim    maulaimaimaulaimaim
   maulaimaimaulaimaim    maulaimaimaulaimaim
   maulaimaimaulaimaim    maulaimaimaulaimaim
   maulaimaimaulaimaim    maulaimaimaulaimaim
   maulaimaimaulaimaim    maulaimaimaulaimaim
    maulaimaimaulaimaim maulaimaimaulaimaim
     maulaimaimaulaimaimaulaimaimaulaimaim
      maulaimaimaulaim  laimaimaulaimaim
       maulaimaimaulaim laimaimaulaimaim
        maulaimaimaul  maimaulaimaim
         maulaimaim      maulaimaim
          maulaimaim maulaimaim
            maulaimaimaulaimaim
```

Noomen, we bivouac at sunsink after swarm. We bivouac in great great open of wind and sand nearer far ruins of Nukeman, ruins like wounds, sky-wounds.

FIRST CIRCLE: Straddlers, Swarm's twelve strongest, stockade of Straddlers around the Queen's nest. . .

They wait.          Timur Timur Timur Timur Timur
                    Timur
They call:          Timur Timur Timur Timur Timur
                    Timur

I Timur, Timur the Lame, Swarmcantor, am called, called to the center, called to the Queen's nest . . . Queen's touch! Queen's kiss! Queen's tongue in Timur's mouth! Queen's gut drink!

I Timur chant, sing:    tightightightightightight
Echoes:               tightightightightightightightigh-
                           tightight

Chant and echoes:

```
                        tight
                   tightightight
                 tightightight tight
              tightightightightightight
            tightightightightightight tight
          tightightightightightightightight tight
        tightightightightightightightightight tight
      tightightightightightightightightightight tight
     tightightightightightightightightightightight
   tightightightightightightightightightightight tight
  tightightightightightightightightightightightight
 tightightightightightightightightightightightight tight
 tightightightightightightightightightightightightight tight
 tightightightightightightightightightightightightight tight
 tight tightightightightightightightightightightightight
 tight tightightightightightightightightightightightight
  tightightightightightightightightightightightightight
  tight tightightightightightightightightightightight
    tightightightightightightightightightightight
     tight tightightightightightightightightight
       tight tightightightightightightightight
        tight tightightightightightightight
         tight tightightightightightight
           tightightightightightight
            tight tightightight
               tightightight
                  tight
```

# EDITOR'S INTRODUCTION TO:

## OUR MANY ROADS TO THE STARS

### by Poul Anderson

*Poul Anderson might have been a scientist. He has a degree in physics, and follows the scientific literature closely. If you've spent much time with him, you'll be certain he has the brains to be a scientist, and even some of the temperament. He has patience, curiosity, and a flair for seeing that odd little fact that just doesn't fit.*

*In fact, I've often wondered why Poul didn't take the same route as Greg Benford; and I think I know.*

*Poul would hate to specialize. Certainly he follows the scientific literature in physics—but he's also devoted to biology, history, archaeology, planetary sciences, engineering . . . In fact, he's the closest thing I know to the mythical Renaissance man.*

# OUR MANY ROADS TO THE STARS

## by Poul Anderson

There are countless varieties of science fiction these days, and I would be the last to want any of them restricted in any way. Nevertheless, what first drew me to this literature and, after more years than I like to add up, still holds me, is its dealing with the marvels of the universe. To look aloft at the stars on a clear night and think that someday, somehow we might actually get out among them, rouses the thrill anew, and I become young again. After all, we made it to the Moon, didn't we? Meanwhile, only science fiction of the old and truly kind takes the imagination forth on that journey. Therefore I put up with its frequent flaws; and so does many another dreamer.

But are we mere dreamers, telling ourselves stories of voyages yonder as our ancestors told of voyages to Avalon and Cíbola? Those never existed, and the stars do; but, realistically, does any possibility of reaching them?

The case against interstellar travel traditionally begins with the sheer distances. While Pioneer 10 and 11, the Jupiter flybys, will leave the Solar System, they won't get as far as Alpha Centauri, the nearest neighbor sun, for more than 40,000 years. (They aren't actually bound in that direction.) At five times their speed, or 100 miles per second, which we are nowhere close to reaching today, the trip would take longer than recorded history goes back. And the average separation of stars in this galactic vicinity is twice as great.

If we could go very much faster—

At almost the speed of light, we'd reach Alpha Centauri in about four and a third years. But as most of you know, we who were faring would experience a shorter journey. Both the theory of relativity and experimental physics show that time passes "faster" for a fast-moving object. The closer to the speed of light, the greater the difference, until at that velocity itself, a spaceman would make the trip in no time at all. However, the girl he left behind him would measure his transit as taking the same number of years as a light ray does; and he'd take equally long in coming back to her.

In reality, the velocity of light *in vacuo*, usually symbolized by $c$, cannot be attained by any material body. From a physical viewpoint, the reason lies in Einstein's famous equation $E = mc^2$. Mass and energy are equivalent. The faster a body moves, the more energy it has, and hence the more mass. This rises steeply as velocity gets close to $c$, and at that speed would become infinite, an obvious impossibility.

Mass increases by the same factor as time (and length) shrink. An appendix to this essay defines the terms more precisely than here. A table there gives some representative values of the factor for different values of velocity, $v$, compared to $c$. At $v = 0.7\,c$, that is, at a speed of 70% light's, time aboard ship equals distance covered in light-years. Thus, a journey of 100 light-years at $0.7\,c$ would occupy 10 years of the crew's lives, although to people on Earth or on the target planet, it would take about 14.

There's a catch here. We have quietly been supposing that the whole voyage is made at exactly this rate. In practice, the ship would have to get up to speed first, and brake as it neared the goal. Both these maneuvers take time; and most of this time is spent at low velocities where the relativistic effects aren't noticeable.

Let's imagine that we accelerate at one gravity, increasing our speed by 32 feet per second each second and thus providing ourselves with a comfortable Earth-normal weight inboard. It will take us approximately a year (a shade less) to come near $c$, during which period we will have covered almost half a light-year, and during most of which period our time rate won't be significantly different from that of the outside cosmos. In fact, not until the eleventh month would the factor get as low as 0.5, though from then on it would start a really steepening nosedive. Similar considerations apply at journey's end, while we slow down. Therefore a trip under these conditions would never take less than two years as far as we are concerned; if the distance covered is 10 light-years, the time required is 11 years as far as the girl (or boy) friend left behind is concerned.

At the ''equalizing'' $v$ of $0.7\,c$, these figures become 10.7 years for the crew and 14.4 years for the stay-at-homes. This illustrates the dramatic gains that the former, if not the latter, can make by pushing $c$ quite closely. But let's stay with that value of $0.7\,c$ for the time being, since it happens to be the one chosen by Bernard Oliver for his argument against the feasibility of star travel.

Now Dr. Oliver, vice president for research and development at Hewlett-Packard, is definitely not unimaginative, nor hostile to the idea as such. Rather, he is intensely interested in contacting extraterrestrial intelligence, and was the guiding genius of Project Cyclops, which explored the means of doing so by radio. The design which his group came up with could, if built, detect anybody who's using radio energy like us today within 100 light-years. Or it could receive beacon signals of reasonable strength within 1000 light-years: a sphere which encloses a million suns akin to Sol and half a billion which are different.

Still, he does not fudge the facts. Making the most favorable assumption, a matter-antimatter annihilation system which expels radiation itself, he has calculated the minimum requirement for a round trip with a stopover at the destination star, at a peak speed of $0.7c$. Assuming 1000 tons of ship plus payload, which is certainly modest, he found that it must convert some 33,000 tons of fuel into energy—sufficient to supply the United States, at present levels of use, for half a million years. On first starting off from orbit, the ship would spend 10 times the power that the Sun gives to our entire Earth. Shielding requirements alone, against stray gamma rays, make this an absurdity, not to speak of a thousand square miles of radiating surface to cool the vessel if as little as one one-millionth of the energy reaches it in the form of waste heat.

Though we can reduce these figures a good deal if we assume it can refuel at the other end for its return home, the scheme looks impractical regardless. Moreover, Dr. Oliver, no doubt deliberately, has not mentioned that space is not empty. Between local stars, it contains about one hydrogen atom per cubic centimeter, plus smaller amounts of other materials. This is a harder vacuum than any we can achieve artificially. But a vessel ramming through it at $0.7\ c$ would release X-radiation at the rate of some 50 million roentgen units per hour. It takes less than 1000 to kill a human being. No material shielding could protect the crew for long, if at all.

Not every scientist is this pessimistic about the rocket to the stars, that is, a craft which carries its own energy source and reaction mass. Some hope for smaller, unmanned probes, perhaps moving at considerably lower speeds. But given the mass required for their life support and equipment, men who went by such a vehicle would have to reckon on voyages lasting generations or centuries.

This is not impossible, of course. Maybe they could pass the time in suspended animation. Naturally radioactive atoms in the body set an upper limit to that, since they destroy tissue which would then not be replaced. But Carl Sagan, astronomer and exobiologist at Cornell University, estimates that a spore can survive up to a million years. This suggests to me that humans should be good for anyway several thousand.

Or maybe, in a huge ship with a complete ecology, an expedition could beget and raise children to carry their mission on. Calculations by Gerald K. O'Neill, professor of physics at Harvard, strongly indicate that this is quite feasible. His work has actually dealt with the possibility of establishing permanent, self-sustaining colonies in orbit, pleasanter to live in than most of Earth and capable of producing more worldlets like themselves from extraterrestrial resources. He concludes that we can start on it *now,* with existing technology and at startlingly low cost, and have the first operational by the late 1980's. Not long afterward, somebody could put a motor on one of these.

The hardened science fiction reader may think such ideas are old hat. And so they are, in fiction. But to me the fact is infinitely more exciting than any story—that the accomplishment can actually be made, that sober studies by reputable professionals are confirming the dream.

True, I'd prefer to believe that men and women can get out there faster, more easily, so that the people who sent them off will still be alive when word arrives of what they have discovered. Is this wishful thinking? We've written off the rocket as a means of ultra-fast travel, but may there be other ways?

Yes, probably there are. Even within the framework of conventional physics, where you can never surpass $c$, we already have more than one well-reasoned proposal. If not yet as detailed and mathematical as Oberth's keystone work on interplanetary travel of 1929, the best of them seem equivalent to Tsiolkovsky's cornerstone work of 1911. If the time scale is the same for future as for past developments, then the first manned Alpha Centauri expedition should leave about the year 2010. . . .

That's counting from R. W. Bussard's original paper on the interstellar ramjet, which appeared in 1960. Chances are that a flat historical parallel is silly. But the engineering ideas positively are not. They make a great deal of sense.

Since the ramjet has been in a fair number of stories already, I'll describe the principle rather briefly. We've seen that at high speeds, a vessel must somehow protect its crew from the atoms and ions in space. Lead or other material shielding is out of the question. Hopelessly too much would be required, it would give off secondary radiation of its own, and ablation would wear it down, incidentally producing a lot of heat, less readily dissipated in space than in an atmosphere. Since the gas must be controlled anyway, why not put it to work?

Once the ship has reached a speed which turns out to be reasonable for a thermonuclear rocket—and we're on the verge of that technology today—a scoop can collect the interstellar gas and funnel it into a reaction chamber. There, chosen parts can be fusion-burned for energy to throw the rest out backward, thus propelling the vessel forward. Ramjet aircraft use the same principle, except that they must supply fuel to combine with the oxygen they collect. The ramjet starcraft takes everything it needs from its surroundings. Living off the country, it faces none of the mass-ratio problems of a rocket, and might be able to crowd $c$ very closely.

Needless to say, even at the present stage of pure theory, things aren't that simple. For openers, how large an apparatus do we need? For a ship-plus-payload mass of 1000 tons, accelerating at one gravity and using proton-proton fusion for power, Bussard and Sagan have both calculated a scoop radius of 2000 kilometers. Now we have no idea as yet how to make that particular reaction go. We are near the point of fusing deuterons, or deuterons and tritons (hydrogen nuclei with one and two neutrons respectively), to get a net energy release. But these isotopes are far less common than ordinary hydrogen, and thus would require correspondingly larger intakes. Obviously, we can't use collectors made of metal.

But then, we need nonmaterial shielding anyway. Electromagnetic fields exert force on charged particles. A steady laser barrage emitted by the ship can ionize all neutral atoms within a safety zone, and so make them controllable, as well as vaporizing rare bits of dust and gravel which would otherwise be a hazard. (I suspect, myself, that this won't be necessary. Neutral atoms have electrical asymmetries which offer a possible grip to the force-fields of a more advanced technology than ours. I also feel sure we will master the proton-proton reaction, and eventually matter-antimatter annihilation. But for now, let's play close to our vests.) A force-field scoop, which being massless can be of enormous size, will catch these ions, funnel them down paths which are well clear of the crew section and into a fusion chamber, cause the chosen nuclei to burn, and expel everything aft to drive the vessel forward, faster and faster.

To generate such fields, A. J. Fennelly of Yeshiva University and G. L. Matloff of the Polytechnic Institute of New York propose a copper cylinder coated with a superconducting layer of niobium-tin alloy. The size is not excessive, 400 meters in length and 200 in diameter. As for braking, they suggest a drogue made of boron, for its high melting point, ten kilometers across. This would necessarily work rather slowly. But then, these authors are cautious in their assumptions; for instance, they derive a peak velocity of just $0.12\,c$. The system could reach Alpha Centauri in about 53 years, Tau Ceti in 115.

By adding wings, however, they approximately halve these travel times. The wings are two great superconducting batteries, each a kilometer square. Cutting the lines of the galactic magnetic field, they generate voltages which can be tapped for exhaust acceleration, for magnetic bottle containers for the power reaction, and for inboard electricity. With thrust shut off, they act as auxiliary brakes, much shortening the deceleration period. When power is drawn at different rates on either side, they provide maneuverability—majestically slow, but sufficient—almost as if they were huge oars.

All in all, it appears that a vessel of this general type can bring explorers to the nearest stars while they are still young enough to carry out the exploration—and the preliminary colonization?—themselves. Civilization at home will start receiving a flood of beamed information, fascinating, no doubt often revolutionary in unforeseeable ways, within a few years of their arrival. Given only a slight lengthening of human life expectancy, they might well spend a generation out yonder and get home alive, still hale. Certainly their children can.

Robert L. Forward, a leading physicist at Hughes Research Laboratories, has also interested himself in the use of the galactic magnetic field. As he points out, the ion density in interstellar space is so low that a probe could easily maintain a substantial voltage across itself. Properly adjusted, the interaction forces produced by this will allow mid-course corrections and terminal maneuvers at small extra energy cost. Thus we could investigate more than one star with a single probe, and eventually bring it home again.

Indeed, the price of research in deep space is rather small. Even the cost of manned vessels is estimated by several careful thinkers as no more than ten billion dollars each—starting with today's technology. That's about 50 dollars per American, much less than we spend every year on cigarettes and booze, enormously less than goes for wars, bureaucrats, subsidies to inefficient businesses, or the servicing of the national debt. For mankind as a whole, a starship would run about $2.50 per head. The benefits it would return in the way of knowledge, and thus of improved capability, are immeasurably great.

But to continue with those manned craft. Mention of using interstellar magnetism for maneuvering raises the thought of using it for propulsion. That is, by employing electromagnetic forces which interact with that field, a ship could ideally accelerate itself without having to expel any mass backward. This would represent a huge saving over what the rocket demands.

The trouble is, the galactic field is very weak, and no doubt very variable from region to region. Though it can be valuable in ways that we have seen, there appears to be no hope of using it for a powerful drive.

Might we invent other devices? For instance, if we could somehow establish a negative gravity force, this might let our ship react against the mass of the universe as a whole, and thus need no jets. Unfortunately, nobody today knows how to do any such thing, and most physicists take for granted it's impossible. Not all agree: because antigravity-type forces do occur in relativity theory, under special conditions.

Physics does offer one way of reaching extremely high speeds free, the Einsteinian catapult. Later I shall have more to say about the weird things that happen when large, ultra-dense masses spin very fast. But among these is their generation of a force different from Newtonian gravity, which has a mighty accelerating effect of its own. Two neutron stars, orbiting nearly in contact, could kick almost to light velocity a ship which approached them on the right orbit.

Alas, no such pair seems to exist anywhere near the Solar System. Besides, we'd presumably want something similar in the neighborhood of our destination, with exactly the characteristics necessary to slow us down. The technique looks rather implausible. What is likely, though, is that closer study of phenomena like these may give us clues to the method of constructing a field drive.

Yet do we really need it? Won't the Bussard ramjet serve? Since it picks up everything it requires as it goes, why can't it keep on accelerating indefinitely, until it comes as close to $c$ as the captain desires? The Fennelly-Matloff vehicle is not intended to do this. But why can't a more advanced model?

Quite possibly it can!

Before taking us off on such a voyage, maybe I'd better answer a question or two. If the ship, accelerating at one gravity, is near $c$ in a year, and if $c$ is the ultimate speed which nature allows, how can the ship keep on accelerating just as hard, for just as long as the flight plan says?

The reason lies in the relativistic contraction of space and time, when these are measured by a fast-moving observer. Suppose we, at rest with respect to the stars, track a vessel for 10 light-years at its steady speed of $0.9\,c$. To us, the passage takes 11 years. To the crew, it takes 4.4 years: because the distance crossed is proportionately less. They never experience faster-than-light travel either. What they do experience, when they turn their instruments outward, is a cosmos strangely flattened in the direction of their motion, where the stars (and their unseen friends at home) age strangely fast.

The nearer they come to $c$, the more rapidly these effects increase. Thus as they speed up, they perceive themselves as accelerating at a steady rate through a constantly shrinking universe. Observers on a planet would perceive them as accelerating at an ever lower rate through an unchanged universe. At last, perhaps, millions of light-years might be traversed and millions of years pass by outside while a man inboard draws a breath.

By the way, those authors are wrong who have described the phenomenon in terms of "subjective" versus "objective" time. One set of measurements is as valid as another.

The "twin paradox" does not arise. This old chestnut says, "Look, suppose we're twins, and you stay home while I go traveling at high speed. Now I could equally well claim I'm stationary and you're in motion—therefore that you're the one flattened out and living at a slower rate, not me. So what happens when we get back together again? How can each of us be younger than his twin?"

It overlooks the fact that the traveler does come home. The situation would indeed be symmetrical if the spaceman moved forever at a fixed velocity. But then he and his brother, by definition, never would meet to compare notes. His accelerations (which include slowdowns and changes of course) take the whole problem out of special and into general relativity. Against the background of the stars, the traveler has moved in a variable fashion; forces have acted on him.

Long before time and space measurements aboard ship differ bizarrely much from those on Earth, navigational problems will arise. They are the result of two factors, aberration and Doppler effect.

Aberration is the apparent displacement of an object in the visual field of a moving observer. It results from combining his velocity with the velocity of light. (Analogously, if we are out in the rain and, standing still, feel it falling straight down, we will feel it hitting us at a slant when we start walking. The change in angle will be larger if we run.) At the comparatively small orbital speed of Earth, sensitive instruments can detect the aberration of the stars. At speeds close to $c$, it will be huge. Stars will seem to crawl across the sky as we accelerate, bunching in its forward half and thinning out aft.

Doppler effect, perhaps more widely familiar, is the shift in observed wavelength from an emitting object, when the observer's velocity changes. If we move away from a star, we see its light reddened; if we move toward a star, we see its light turned more blue. Again, these changes become extremely marked as we approach $c$.

Eventually our relativistic astronaut sees most of the stars gathered in a ring ahead of him, though a few sparsely strewn individuals remain visible elsewhere. The ring itself, which Frederik Pohl has dubbed the "starbow," centers on a circle which is mainly dark, because nearly all light from there has been blue-shifted out of the frequencies we can see. The leading or inner edge of the ring is bluish white, its trailing or outer edge reddish; in between is a gradation of colors, akin to what we normally observe. Fred Hollander, a chemist at Brookhaven National Laboratories, has calculated the starbow's exact appearance for different $v$. It gets narrower and moves farther forward, the bull's eye dead ahead gets smaller and blacker, the faster we go—until, for instance, at $0.9999\,c$ we perceive a starbow about ten degrees of arc in width, centered on a totally black circle of about the same diameter, and little or nothing shows anywhere else in the sky.

At that speed, $0.9999\,c$, we'd cross 100 light-years in 20 months of our personal lifetimes. So it's worth trying for; but we'll have to figure out some means of knowing where we are! Though difficult, the problem does not look unsolvable in principle.

It may become so beyond a certain velocity. If we travel under acceleration the whole way, speeding up continuously to the half-way point, thereafter braking at the same rate until we reach our goal: then over considerable distances we get truly staggering relativity factors. The longer a voyage, the less difference it makes to us precisely how long it is.

Thus, Dr. Sagan points out that explorers faring in this wise at one gravity will reach the nearer stars within a few years, Earth time, and slightly less, crew time. But they will cross the approximately 650 light-years to Deneb in 12 or 13 years of their own lifespans; the 30,000 light-years to the center of our galaxy in 21 ship years; the two million light-years to the Andromeda galaxy in 29 ship years; or the 10 million light-years to the Virgo cluster of galaxies in 31 ship years. If they can stand higher accelerations, or have some way to counteract the drag on their bodies, they can cross these gulfs in less of their own time; the mathematical formula governing this is in the appendix.

But will the starbow become too thin and dim for navigation? Or will they encounter some other practical limit? For instance, when matter is accelerated, it radiates energy in the form of gravity waves. The larger the mass, the stronger this radiation; and of course the mass of our spaceship will be increasing by leaps and bounds and pole-vaults. Eventually it may reach a condition where it is radiating away as much energy as it can take in, and thus be unable to go any faster.

However, the real practical limit is likelier to arise from the fact that we have enough stars near home to keep us interested for millennia to come. Colonies planted on worlds around some of these can, in due course, serve as nuclei for human expansion ever further into the universe.

Because many atoms swept through its force-fields are bound to give off light, a ramjet under weigh must be an awesome spectacle. At a safe distance, probably the hull where the crew lives is too small for the naked eye. Instead, against the constellations one sees a translucent shell of multi-colored glow, broad in front, tapering aft to a fiery point where the nuclear reaction is going on. (Since this must be contained by force-fields anyway, there is no obvious reason for the fusion chamber to be a metal room.) Thence the exhaust streams backward, at first invisible or nearly so, where its particles are closely controlled, but becoming brilliant further off as they begin to collide, until finally a nebula-like chaos fades away into the spatial night.

It's not only premature, it's pointless to worry about limitations. Conventional physics appears to tell us that, although nature has placed an eternal bound on the speed of our traveling, the stars can still be ours . . . if we really want them.

Yet we would like to reach them more swiftly, with less effort. Have we any realistic chance whatsoever of finding a way around the light-velocity barrier?

Until quite recently, every sensible physicist would have replied with a resounding "No." Most continue to do so.

They point to a vast mass of experimental data; for instance, if subatomic particles did not precisely obey Einsteinian laws, our big accelerators wouldn't work. The conservatives ask where there is the slightest empirical evidence for phenomena which don't fit into the basic scheme of relativity. And they maintain that, if ever we did send anything faster than light, it would violate causality.

I don't buy that last argument, myself. It seems to me that, mathematically and logically, it presupposes part of what it sets out to prove. But this gets a bit too technical for the present essay, especially since many highly intelligent persons disagree with me. Those whom I mentioned are not conservatives in the sense of having stick-in-the-mud minds. They are among the very people whose genius and imagination make science the supremely exciting, creative endeavor which it is these days.

Nevertheless we do have a minority of equally qualified pioneers who have lately been advancing new suggestions.

I suppose the best known idea comes from Gerald Feinberg, professor of physics at Columbia University. He has noted that the Einsteinian equations do not actually forbid material particles which move faster than light—if these have a mass that can be described by an imaginary number (that is, an ordinary number multiplied by the square root of minus one. Imaginary quantities are common, e.g., in the theory of electromagnetism). Such "tachyons," as he calls them, would travel faster and faster the *less* energy they have; it would take infinite energy to slow them down to $c$, which is thus a barrier for them too.

Will it forever separate us, who are composed of "tardyons," from the tachyon part of the cosmos? Perhaps—but not totally. It is meaningless to speak of anything which we cannot, in principle, detect if it exists. If tachyons do, there must be some way by which we can find experimental evidence for them, no matter how indirect. This implies some kind of interaction (via photons?) with tardyons. But interaction, in turn, implies a possibility of modulation. That is, if they can affect us, we can affect them.

And . . . in principle, if you can modulate, you can do anything. Maybe it won't ever be feasible to use tachyons to beam a man across space; but might we, for instance, use them to communicate faster than light?

Needless to say, first we have to catch them, i.e. show that they exist. This has not yet been done, and maybe it never can be done because in fact there aren't any. Still, one dares hope. A very few suggestive data are beginning to come out of certain laboratories—

Besides, we have other places to look. Hyperspace turns out to be more than a hoary science fiction catchphrase. Geometrodynamics now allows a transit from point to point, without crossing the space between, via a warp going "outside" that space—often called a wormhole. Most wormholes are exceedingly small, of subatomic dimensions; and a trip through one is no faster than a trip through normal space. Nevertheless, the idea opens up a whole new field of research, which may yield startling discoveries.

Black holes have been much in the news, and in science fiction, these past several years. They are masses so dense, with gravity fields so strong, that light itself cannot escape. Theory has predicted for more than 40 years that all stars above a particular size must eventually collapse into the black hole state. Today astronomers think they have located some, as in Cygnus X-1. And we see hypotheses about black holes of less than stellar mass, which we might be able to find floating in space and utilize.

For our purposes here, the most interesting trait of a black hole is its apparent violation of a whole series of conservation laws so fundamental to physics that they are well-nigh Holy Writ. Thus many an issue, not long ago considered thoroughly settled, is again up for grabs. The possibility of entering a black hole and coming out "instantly" at the far end of a space warp is being seriously discussed. Granted, astronauts probably couldn't survive a close approach to such an object. But knowledge of these space warp phenomena and their laws, if they do occur in reality, might well enable us to build machines which—because they don't employ velocity—can circumvent the $c$ barrier.

Black holes aren't the sole things which play curious tricks on space and time. An ultra-dense toroid, spinning very rapidly in smoke ring fashion, should theoretically create what is called a Kerr metric space warp, opening a way to hyperspace.

The most breathtaking recent development of relativity that I know of is by F. J. Tipler, a physicist at the University of Maryland. According to his calculations, not just near-instantaneous crossings of space should be possible, but time travel should be! A cylinder of ultra-dense matter, rotating extremely fast (velocity at the circumference greater than 0.5 $c$) produces a region of multiple periodic space-time. A particle entering this can, depending on its exact track, reach any event in the universe, past or future.

The work was accepted for publication in *Physical Review,* which is about as respectable as science can get. Whether it will survive criticism remains to be seen. But if nothing else, it has probably knocked the foundation out from under the causality argument against faster-than-light travel: by forcing us to rethink our whole concept of causality.

The foregoing ideas lie within the realm of accepted physics, or at least on its debatable borders. Dr. Forward has listed several others which are beyond the frontier . . . but only barely, and only to date. Closer study could show, in our near future, that one or more of them refer to something real.

For instance, we don't know what inertia ''is.'' It seems to be a basic property of matter; but why? Could it be an inductive effect of gravitation, as Mach's Principle suggests? If so, could we find ways to modify it, and would we then be held back by the increase of mass with velocity?

Could we discover, or produce, negative mass? This would gravitationally repel the usual positive kind. Two equal masses, positive and negative, linked together, would make each other accelerate in a particular direction without any change in momentum or energy. Could they therefore transcend $c$?

A solution of Einstein's field equations in five dimensions

for charged particles gives an electron velocity of a billion trillion $c$. What then of a spaceship, if the continuum should turn out to have five rather than four dimensions?

Conventional physics limits the speed of mass-energy. But information is neither; from a physical standpoint, it represents negative entropy. So can information outrun light, perhaps without requiring any medium for its transmission? If you can send information, in principle you can send anything.

Magnificent and invaluable though the structure of relativity is, does it hold the entire truth? There are certain contradictions in its basic assumptions which have never been resolved and perhaps never can be. Or relativity could be just a special case, applying only to local conditions.

Once we are well and truly out into space, we may find the signs of a structure immensely more ample.

These speculations have taken us quite far beyond known science. But they help to show us how little known that science really is, even the parts which have long felt comfortingly, or confiningly, familiar. We can almost certainly reach the stars. Very possibly, we can reach them easily.

If we have the will.

## *Appendix*

Readers who shudder at sight of an equation can skip this part, though they may like to see the promised table. For different velocities, it gives the values of the factors "tau" and "gamma." These are simply the inverses of each other. A little explanation of them may be in order.

Suppose we have two observers, A and B, who have *constant* velocities. We can consider either one as being stationary, the other as moving at velocity $v$. A will measure the length of a yardstick B carries, in the direction of motion, and the interval between two readings of a clock B carries, as if these quantities were multiplied by tau. For example, if $v$ is $0.9\,c$, then B's yardstick is merely 0.44 times as long in A's eyes as if B were motionless; and an hour, registered on B's clock, corresponds to merely 0.44 hour on A's. On the other hand, mass is multiplied by gamma. That is, when B moves at $0.9\,c$, his mass according to A is 2.26 times what it was when B was motionless.

B, in turn, observes himself as normal, but A and A's environs as having suffered exactly the same changes. Both observers are right.

| $v$ | Tau | Gamma |
|---|---|---|
| $0.1\,c$ | 0.995 | 1.005 |
| $0.5\,c$ | 0.87 | 1.15 |
| $0.7\,c$ | 0.72 | 1.39 |
| $0.9\,c$ | 0.44 | 2.26 |
| $0.99\,c$ | 0.14 | 7.10 |
| $0.9999\,c$ | 0.017 | 58.6 |

The formula for tau is $(1 - v^2/c^2)^{1/2}$ where the exponent "½" indicates a square root. Gamma equals one divided by tau, or $(1 - v^2/c^2)^{-1/2}$.

As for relativistic acceleration, if this has a constant value $a$ up to midpoint, then a negative (braking) value $-a$ to destination, the time to cover a distance $S$ equals $(2c/a)$ arc cosh $(1 - aS/2c^2)$. For long distances, this reduces to $(2c/a)$ $1n$ $(aS/c^2)$ where "1 $n$" means "natural logarithm." The maximum velocity, reached at midpoint, is $c[1 - (1 + aS/2c^2)^{-2}]^{1/2}$.

# EDITOR'S INTRODUCTION TO:

## EXPLORING INFRASTELLAR
## SPACE

### by Dr. Robert L. Forward

*Bob Forward is a scientist/executive with Hughes Research Laboratories in Malibu. He is the inventor of the Forward mass detector, a gadget that can find an airplane many miles away from its gravitational mass alone. He also likes expensive bourbon and wears the loudest vests I have ever seen.*

*Things flow in physics: not long after Poul Anderson wrote "Our Many Roads to the Stars," Bob Forward called to ask if I'd like to meet the English geometrician Roger Penrose.*

*Of course I did. Penrose invented much of black hole theory. He and his former student Stephen Hawking have between them at least as much good theory on the fundamental structure of the universe as any pair alive.*

*Since we were meeting in the Berkeley area, we also invited Poul Anderson (Karen Anderson and Bob Forward were in high school together). It was certainly a fascinating afternoon. Perose explained his "Twistor" theory. Twistors are something between an elementary physical particle and a geometrical concept; they are more fundamental than the quarks, as an example. Of course they may not exist.*

*On the other hand, they just might; and if they do, then particle physics makes sense again. Penrose's equations should be solvable to yield the various particle interactions which are driving theoretical physicists crazy just now.*

*We all listened attentively, although I'm certain that Bob Forward was the only one in the room who really understood*

*what Penrose was saying; Roger Penrose thinks on his feet,
and in the midst of presenting old ideas he gets new ones.*

*Eventually an idea came to me. "Roger," I asked. "Does
twistor theory allow faster-than-light travel?"*

*"No," he said. Then he looked thoughtful. "Well, I'm
fairly certain it doesn't. . ."*

*"It might," one of Penrose's graduate students said.
"That is, there are some fundamental transformations such
that what appear to be great distances in normal space might
be quite short in twistor space. . ."*

*Penrose looked doubtful. "Well, possibly." He didn't
look happy at all.*

*"I take it you don't believe there's any chance of faster-
than-light travel?" I asked.*

*"No," Penrose said firmly. "Well—no."*

*"I'm not so sure," said his students.*

*And there the matter rests. I've met Roger Penrose several
times since then, and the situation hasn't really changed.*

*Bob Forward, meanwhile, goes right on looking for roads
to the stars. He says we don't need faster-than-light travel.
We can manage in many other ways.*

*Now when I first met Bob Forward he was a scientist and
nothing more. Oh, true, he was in charge of far out ideas for
Hughes; but that was still* science.

*Then one day he began writing science fiction. His short
stories have appeared in prestigious magazines like* Omni,
*and his novel* The Dragon's Egg *has the most original alien
civilization since* The Mote in God's Eye. *I understand his
next novel will show how we can reach the nearer stars using
light sails. (We used that gimmick in* Mote, *of course; but
Bob Forward's book will show how it* really *could be done.)*

*He hasn't abandoned science, though. Not long ago he
sent me a copy of a very straightforward scientific publication.*

*The subject was interstellar probes.*

# EXPLORING INFRASTELLAR SPACE

## Dr. Robert L. Forward

Is there any reason for us to now consider the conduct or design of space missions beyond the solar system? If so, how should we get started?

We could talk about lots of different possible missions: Interstellar Flight, Gravitational and Relativity Experiments, SETI (Search for Extraterrestrial Intelligence), as well as many types of observational programs: Cosmological, Galactic, Near-Stellar, Infrastellar, Extrasolar, even Introsolar—going out and looking back at ourselves, snuggled up to the warming Sun (Don't forget, we developed a whole new perspective of the Earth when we went way out to the Moon and then looked back at our big, blue, floating, fragile marble). You might expect that I would have a tendency to concentrate on interstellar flight, but even I have to admit that to get to the stars, we have to cross an awful lot of wild, and black—but interesting—territory before we get there, and we might be missing something important if we didn't do a little bit of exploring on the way. So let us speculate and think—and plan—as we go about sizing up the territory from Pluto to Proxima.

If we start with a circle of 5 AU encompassing Jupiter's orbit (the part of the solar system we have only just begun to explore), and expand it an order of magnitude to 50 AU, or about 1/1000 of a light-year, we take in the entire known solar system. (How parochial that sounds!) If we expand that by an order of magnitude to 500 AU, or about 1/100 ly, we take in a few short period comets (attendants of Jupiter). If we expand that by another order of magnitude to 1/10 ly, or 5000 AU, we find—*nothing new!* If we expand that by *another* order of magnitude to 1 ly we still find *nothing!* (or at least we know of nothing out there). Only after we have expanded our circle of interest out to 10 ly do the nearest stars draw into our picture. There sure seems to be an awful lot of nothing out there (or at most a few fluff-ball comets).

## Things to Do and See On Your Way to Proxima Centauri

Just as the ancient cartographers populated the blank corners of their maps with strange beasties and dragons, so also can we (although we do it in a properly scientific and sophisticated way). Is the deep space between Pluto and Proxima empty? or is it filled with strange wonders? We know there are comets out there, we can calculate their orbits and know that they come from a comet belt out at about a light-year. *But*—there is a gap in the comet aphelion distances between 1000 and 5000 AU. What strange monster lurks out there to hurl the comets down to a scalding death around the Sun if they dare to cross its path?

Some astronomers say that there must be every size of planetoid from gram-sized pebbles to protostars sprinkled uniformly from here to there. The Sun and planets have swept up everything here, but how many are still out there? Long ago, Shapely pointed out that the process of gravitational contraction of dust and gas would form objects of all sizes, from larger than the Sun to smaller than the Moon. However, only those centers of condensation with a mass greater than about 1/10 of a solar mass would actually ignite to form a visible star. Those between 1/10 and 1/1000 of a solar mass (bigger than Jupiter, but smaller than the Sun) would not have nuclear fusion taking place in their interiors. However, they would still be heated internally by radioactive decay and gravitational contraction. Shapely called them crusted stars or self-warming planets, and postulated that life might even exist on them. He estimated that there should be ten of these Lilliputian stars for every visible star, and that one could exist at a few thousand AU, with its IR radiation undetectable by our best sensors.

Roach recently expanded on these speculations and attempted to make a quantitative estimate of the interstellar density of these Lilliputian stars. He constructed a log-log plot of the cumulative number density of objects versus their mass. At one end were the stars, and at the other end the galactic dust. An interpolated curve was used to estimate the space density of the objects of planetary mass. From this, Roach estimates that within a sphere halfway to Proxima there could be 10 objects the mass of Jupiter, 1000 of Earth size, 60,000 of Moon size, 5 million asteroids and a trillion large comets. The existence of these large numbers of large bodies cannot be yet ruled out by orbital predictions. The present state of knowledge of the observed motions of the outer planets does not even rule out a crusted star of 1/100 of a solar mass as close as 700 AU.

There seem to be a lot of things out there to look at. Let's go out there and see.

"See!" you say. "With what? There is no light out there."

I say, "Try IR for the hot ones, radio for the belted ones, radar for the reflective ones, flux meters for the magnetic ones, lightning flash detectors for the stormy ones, gravity for the massive ones, and stellar occultation for the bulky ones. But one of the things we should do is invent and develop other sensors besides these obvious ones."

"Aren't *bulky* and *massive* synonymous?" you say. No!—not if you believe in Hawking black holes, which are hot and massive, but so small they couldn't occult a microbe. Hawking holes are a new astronomical concept. They are primordial black holes with asteroidal masses but Angstrom dimensions emitting photons and particles which tunnel across their classically impenetrable gravity potential well. The smaller the mass, the hotter the effective temperature, and the faster the mass dissipates until it finally disappears in a burst of radiation. Those less massive than Phobos are already gone, but those larger have a long life yet, and are out there glowing—an incandescent speck a few Angstroms across.

There might be other things to look for out there besides

the obvious particles and fields, the dark planetoids and the black holes. In and on the dust and planetoids there may be organic material or even viable spores. If we could find a technique for looking for this organic material we could test the interstellar panspermia theory. How do we "filter" out the organic from the inorganic? With a physical "filter"?— or can we come up with a radiative equivalent by using selected laser wavelengths which excite a fluorescent response whenever the beam strikes the right organic molecular bond? More ideas are needed.

## See the Stars on Only a Million A Day

Off we go on a mission into deep space! We have a long way to go and we don't have all century to do it in. It isn't going to be easy, and it isn't going to be cheap. Fortunately, the cost can be spread out over decades, so the mission cost will come down to merely a million a day (in constantly inflating dollars). But still, a lot of thinking now will pay off in significantly lower costs later.

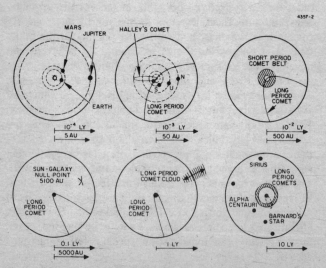

Figure 1: The scale of deep space (adapted from Hennes, et al)

First, we have to start thinking about how we are going to get out there into deep space, and do it in a reasonable time. To do this will require propulsion concepts that are significantly better than the chemical rockets starting from the surface of the Earth that we use now. There are a lot of ideas around, so let us look at some of them, and try to dream up better ones.

Long ago, Krafft Ehricke took a hard look at what you could do using the gravity whip concept to get out into deep space. It is obvious that by going out to Jupiter and using it to slingshot in toward the Sun, you could arrange a very close, very short, highly elliptical pass around the Sun. If you applied your thrust at perihelion, you could obtain significant gain factors in your ultimate escape velocity. He also found a maneuver that improved things more, a tricky Saturn-Jupiter-Sol double cushion shot. However, even with all these tricks, you still need a lot of delta V, and it has to be applied in the short period (1 to 10 days) when you are closest to the Sun. This requires many days of high thrust acceleration at 1/10 g and rapidly gets us away from present propulsion technology. You also only get significant gain factors when the perihelion is very close to the Sun, like 1/100 AU. At 1/100 AU, the 6000-degree solar disk is covering one-third of the sky, and you roast unless you have brought a comet along to hide behind.

So, since present propulsion concepts and gravity whips don't seem to do the job, what can we consider?—and which ones shall we work on in the future?

We could consider the Orion, or pulsed nuclear rocket concept. There are many versions of this, from the technologically feasible one-atomic-bomb-per-second monster to the near future laser or electron beam ignited micropellet fusion concepts that buzz along at 250 miniature explosions a second.

There are various versions of the controlled fusion rocket, including the Bussard interstellar fusion rocket ramscoop concept. However, any design of these has to wait until we find out how heavy a magnet is needed to obtain controlled fusion here on Earth.

Perhaps we should think about non-fusion versions of the ramscoop. Could we obtain better performance out of a hot hydrogen nuclear or electric-MHD rocket if we scooped up our hydrogen supply as we went along? How do you build a scoop that preferentially gathers hydrogen without a weight penalty that negates the advantage? Can you use radiation or lasers to presweep the dust and helium and gather in the hydrogen? Do the lasers have to be on the vehicle or can that job be done from Earth or an orbiting station?

How about sailing through space using a solar sail? At first, this looks like a poor idea for propulsion in deep space where the Sun is just a bright star. But if you combine it with the gravity whip concept and carry out your propulsion phase near the Sun, it begins to look much more promising.

Although we call it solar sailing, the present state of the art of solar sailing is far from the sophistication of the Clipper ships and Hobie cats of wind sailing. Wind-sailing ships can tack into the wind, because they have keels. Solar sailing is still in the dark ages—like using a blanket on a raft. Can we give the solar sail a keel?

The wind-sailing ship moves through the slippery water in one direction, the keel applies pressure to the water at right angles to that motion, while the sail feels the pressure from the wind at some other angle. When the resultant forces are added up, the wind sail can tack into the wind.

To give the solar sail a keel, we might try using the solar light as our water and the solar wind as our wind (or vice versa). A charged mesh would pass the light, but reflect the ionized solar wind. We also might try using the trapped magnetic field in the solar wind as our water and the light as our wind. To grab onto the magnetic field we can use the Lorentz force. By charging portions of the solar sail to high voltages (adding long wires will increase the self-capacitance and therefore the total charge) we can use the Lorentz force $F=q(v \times B)$, which is at right angles to the direction of the solar sail velocity and the magnetic field. I don't know whether the Lorentz keel will work for solar sail missions near the Sun, but it is an interesting concept that needs to be first checked analytically, and then checked again by tests in the real space environment.

There are other versions of the solar sail. One is to use a laser instead of sunlight. This could be used in addition to the solar thrust, or for prime propulsion, or for trajectory trim on the way out into deep space.

If it turns out that the solar sail could provide us with the propulsion that we need for a deep space mission, how do we get started? Tests of solar sail material on the upcoming LDEF, Long Duration Exposure Facility, are obvious first candidates. [The LDEF is a large cylindrical framework that will be left in space by one of the first shuttle flights and picked up eighteen months later. Trays with experiments to check on the effects of the space exposure on various materials are bolted to the main frame which supplies power, cooling, data collection, and other housekeeping functions.] What are the best sail materials? Metals and strong nontearing coated films are obvious. How about completely new

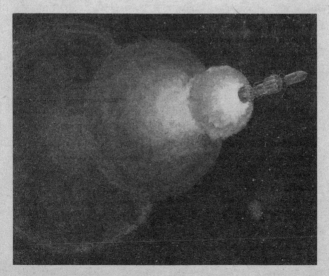

Figure 2: Nuclear pulse jet rocket (Orion concept)

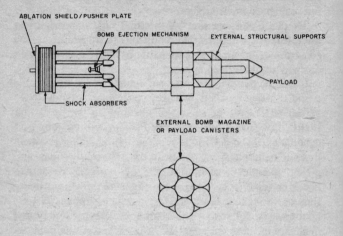

**Figure 2a: Nuclear pulse vehicle**

concepts such as a bimolecular film like a soap bubble, only with viscous glass instead of soapy water to provide the extremely thin, but self-repairing feature of a soap film? More and better ideas are needed.

After we get the propulsion to get out there, what are the other things we can do besides measure particles and fields? (I include in particles everything from an electron to a crusted star.) Some possible ideas are:

• Develop a very long base line radio interferometric capability by sending probes to different parts of the solar system. Think what a field year the radio astronomers would have with a 1000 AU base line!

• Establish a network of deep space laser communication relays to increase the data rate back from smaller probes sent out into the deeper reaches of space.

• Carry out tests of the prototype probe designs for an interstellar mission. Send the probe out to 1/10 ly, then have it come into the solar system and see if it is smart enough to find life in the solar system. If the probe is only semi-intelligent we won't tell it the answer ahead of time. If it is really intelligent, we can tell it ahead of time, and it can pretend it doesn't know while it is going through the search procedure. (We could probably trust it not to peek at that part of its mind better than we could any human raised with our wily animal heritage.)

## Probe Design for Infrastellar Exploration

In the days before the ubiquitous telegraph and newfangled telephone, the launching of a student off to a distant college to learn about the mysteries of the world was as fraught with uncertainty as a launch of a probe into deep space. You had to hope that your years of training had developed not only a routine habit pattern that would keep the traveler on course and functioning, but had also developed a strong capability of independent thought so that the traveler could cope with the uncertainties and problems that would have to be faced many miles and many days away.

In the same way, we are going to have to develop probes that can not only be programmed ahead of time with instructions and contingency plans, but also that are "intelligent" enough to function properly under circumstances or opportunities that we could not foresee and program before the mission started. The first robot probe to visit another planet was the JPL/Hughes Surveyor. The two-second time delay from Earth to Moon required minimal preprogramming and intelligence. We are already well into the multicontingency preprogrammed probe with the Viking orbiter and lander, but it is already obvious that we could use some more intelligence at the other end of our half-hour-long communication link with Mars. If it were really intelligent, the Viking lander should have known by itself that the locking pin on the arm was stuck and jiggled the arm a little until it fell out. Things will be even worse for a deep space probe, where time delays will be measured in days and months rather than minutes. Is there a way out?

First, we can hope that ongoing research will develop

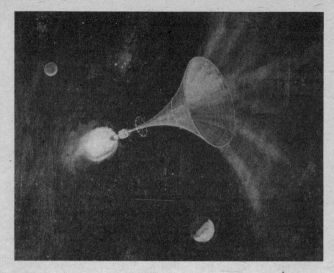

**Figure 3: Bussard interstellar ramjet**

better and better concepts for intelligent computers and that these can be incorporated into the probe design. This would be the best solution, and is one of the near term efforts that we should concentrate on. However, despite my usual extreme optimism, I don't see any significant breakthroughs in this area; just a constant, tedious, slogging, slow improvement in the average electronic IQ of computers, and I wonder whether that electronic IQ will be sufficient for the job of managing a probe by the time we want to launch it. There is no question that we ought to work in this area, and work hard, but it is also reasonable to consider alternatives.

One way of getting some intelligence in the probe is to use the present, well-developed intelligent ionic computers instead of waiting for the development of the newer electronic versions. Yes, I know they are bulky, slow, wasteful of power, unreliable, and have a rather low operational and survivability environmental range; but they *are* available, and *definitely* have the kind of intelligence that we would supply if we were there ourselves.

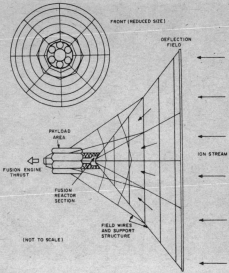

**Figure 3a:**
**Bussard interstellar ramjet**

Yes, you guessed it—what is really *wrong* with a *one-way* manned deep space probe? Is it really out of the question? Or should we seriously consider it in a really broad search for the optimum deep space probe? "But a one-way mission!" you exclaim. "Even if you could get a volunteer, the public wouldn't allow it!"

Yet—each one of us—right now—is on a one-way mission through this life. We come into life without a choice, we train for a career, and if we are lucky, we find an exciting career that we can stay in and contribute to for the rest of our working lives. Then, if it is a career like writing, law, politics, or science, which don't have an arbitrary retirement age, and which don't depend primarily on the strength of your body or the freshness of your education, we find people working at their careers with gusto until they finally die in the harness. The missions that we can plan in the deep space from Pluto to Proxima are going to take decades. They are open-ended missions, in that there is always something interesting

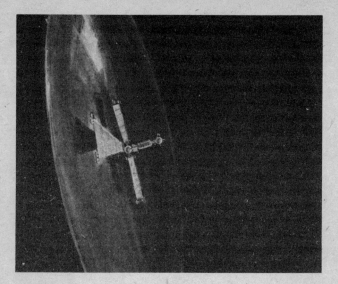

**Figure 4: 0.8 kilometer square solar sail**

left to do. In fact, these missions are well matched to the productive lifetime of a well-trained individual just starting off in a lifetime career after completing graduate education. What an exciting career! What an opportunity for immortality in the annals of science! Then, at the end, a tomb that would exceed that of King Tut's in splendor and agelessness! No, in my opinion, a one-way manned deep space probe is *not* out of the question.

Another possibility is to not have intelligence at the other end of the communication link, but instead use a system similar to that employed by the blind driver ants in the jungles. Instead of sending out a single large intelligent probe to find and bring down a giant planet out past Pluto, send out a swarm of small, preprogrammed probes. We would lose many due to trivial causes, but one or more of them is bound to stumble blindly into the target.

There are two versions of this approach. First, we could make the probes so simple and small that many would stum-

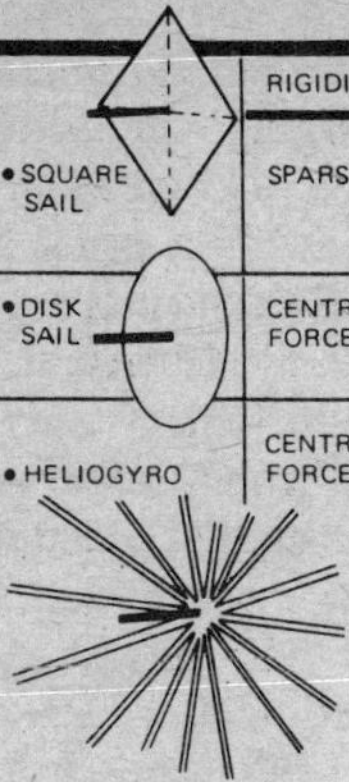

| | RIGIDIZATION | STABILIZATION | CONTROL | PERFORMANCE |
|---|---|---|---|---|
| ● SQUARE SAIL | SPARS | 3-AXIS | SOLAR PRESSURE VANES | MODERATE |
| ● DISK SAIL | CENTRIFUGAL FORCE | SPIN UNSTABLE BUT CONTROLLABLE | GAS JETS, TORQUE VANES | BEST |
| ● HELIOGYRO | CENTRIFUGAL FORCE | SPIN UNSTABLE BUT CONTROLLABLE | BLADE PITCH | INTERMEDIATE |

**Figure 4a: Types of solar sail vehicles proposed**

ble on the target, each to sample only one of the many possible characteristics. (One responding only to acceleration, another to magnetic field, another to temperature, etc.) Alternatively, the swarm could be more sophisticated, and smaller in number, with scouts out front which find a target, then send signals back to the main swarm to gather those behind it that have enough delta V to swerve toward the target ahead.

These kind of thoughts lead us to another area of thought suitable for brainstorming. How small can we make a probe? Of course, that depends upon what we are asking it to do, but suppose we only ask it to do one simple thing? How small can we make it and still get the information back from it? Can it be as small as a kilogram?—a gram?—how about a milligram?

Let me try to give an example of what might be a minimal probe. The basic structure would be a thin fiber or a fiber mesh with imbedded metallic films, wires, microcircuits and spots of radioactive isotopes. The charged particles shooting off into space from the radioisotope would leave a charge on the probe, which would leak off into space at field emission points. By proper placement of the charging radioisotopes and the discharging field emission points, currents can be made to flow in the metal coated portions of the probe and used to power the microcircuits which collect and process the data and convert it to rf signals. The rf energy is then radiated into space by the probe acting as a multielement array of electromagnetic dipoles. By tracing the probe swarm as it moves in helical paths through space, the strength and direction of the magnetic field, and possibly even the ion and particle density can be calculated. Will there be enough rf generated to get back to a relay? I don't know. Our receivers will be better then, the directionality of the beams from a multielement array will aid in antenna gain, but lose in contact time (do we really need to have constant contact with all members of a swarm?), and the bit rate to be transmitted is low.

These milligram, unintelligent probes are one extreme, a multiton, one-way manned probe is another, the typical one ton JPL deep space spacecraft such as the Mariner Jupiter-Uranus (MJU) spacecraft is what people usually settle on for their studies. I bring up these extremes to stretch our imagination for it may be that for deep space exploration, the optimum probe is not a stretched version of the Mariner Jupiter-Uranus spacecraft.

## Conclusions and Recommendations

The SETI program is getting started in a significant way in NASA because the people working on the program found a good starting point that:
- Was more than another study
- Furthered the long range goals of SETI
- Could be started with near term technology
- Had good technological fallout potential
- Didn't cost too much.

The people on the SETI program are designing and building a broad-band, multichannel spectrum analyzer to attach to Arecibo to look for SETI signals (and just incidentally improving the performance of Arecibo by 40 dB). What candidates do we have?

- Electronic intelligence research—*but*, based on developing a limited intelligence to solve the limited set of problems that will be faced in deep space exploration.
- Design and space environmental test of solar sail materials on the Long Duration Exposure Facility (LDEF).
- Engineering studies of the equipment and search strategy for the detection of planetoids and crusted stars in deep space.
- Design and test of spacecraft charging techniques and the efficacy of the magnetic keel concept, both in near Earth and near solar space.

These are just a few suggestions to help us get started; I am sure we will have many more. I fervently hope so; for I sure would like to be around to help push the launch button when

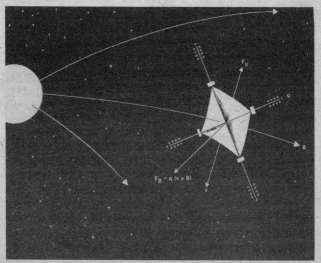

Figure 5: Charged square solar sail experiencing solar light pressure force $F_p$ and solar magnetic field Lorentz force $F_B = q (v \times B)$

the first probe sets off into deep space to blaze the trail to the stars.

## Recommended Reading and References

K. Davidson, "Does the Solar System Include Distant But Discoverable Infrared Dwarfs?", Icarus *26*, 99 (Sept 1975).

Krafft A. Ehricke, "Evolution of Interstellar Operations", AAS Joint National Meeting, Denver, Colorado, (June 1969), AAS Paper No. 69-387-1,2.

Krafft A. Ehricke, "The Ultraplanetary Probe", Proc. AAS 17th Annual Meeting, Preprint No. AAS-71-164, (28-30 June 1971); *Advances in the Astronautical Sciences—The Outer Solar System*, Juris Vagners, Ed., Vol. 29, Part II, pp. 617-679.

Krafft A. Ehricke, "A Method of High Speed Spacecraft Ejection from the Solar System", JBIS *25*, (1972).

Robert L. Forward, "Zero Thrust Velocity Vector Control for Interstellar Probes: Lorentz Force Navigation and Circling", AIAA J *2*, 885 (1964).

Robert L. Forward, "A Program for Interstellar Exploration", *Future Space Programs 1975*, Vol. II, a report of the Subcommittee on Space Science and Applications, Committee on Science and Technology, U.S. House of Representatives, Serial M (Sept 1975). (also to be published in JBIS).

S. Hawking, Monthly Not. R. Astr. Soc. *152*, 75 (1971).

A. T. Lawton, " 'Stray' Planets, Their Formation and the Possibilities of CETI", Spaceflight *16*, 18 (May 1974).

Eugene F. Mallove and Robert L. Forward, "Bibliography of Interstellar Travel and Communication", JBIS *27*, 921 (Dec 1974), JBIS *28*, 191 (March 1975), JBIS *28*, 405 (June 1975).

Eugene F. Mallove, Robert L. Forward and Zbigniew Paprotny, "Bibliography of Interstellar Travel and Communication—August 1975 Update", JBIS *29*, 494 (July-Aug 1976).

W. E. Moeckel, "Comparison of Advanced Propulsion Concepts for Deep Space Exploration", NASA TN D-6968, NTIS, Springfield, VA 22151 (Sept 1972).

F. Roach, "Astronomers' Views on UFO's", in *UFO's: A Scientific Debate*, C. Sagan and T. Page, Eds., W. W. Norton and Co., NY (1972).

C. Sagan and T. Page, Editors, *UFO's: A Scientific Debate*, W. W. Norton and Co., NY (1972).

H. Shapely, *Of Stars and Men*, Beacon Press, Boston (1958).

H. Shapely, "Crusted Stars and Self Heating Planets", Mat. Y. Fisica Teorica Seria A *14*, 69 (1962).

H. Shapely, "Life on Unseen Planets", Science Digest *53*, 59 (Feb 1963).

# EDITOR'S INTRODUCTION TO:

## SHAPES OF THINGS TO COME

### by John F. Carr

*There are two kinds of people it's hard to write introductions for: those you don't know at all, and those you know too well. John Carr falls into the latter category, having been my assistant for several years and four anthologies. I certainly wouldn't be doing these books without him.*

*John is a former schoolteacher turned rock musician turned writer. He's also starting a new publishing venture: quality editions of important works by major writers; works that ought to be published, but somehow haven't been. He's also fast turning into the authority on the late H. Beam Piper.*

*When John was editor of the SFWA Bulletin, he decided to do the best issue ever: and he certainly succeeded, getting a number of major writers to contribute to a volume on future histories. "Why that subject?" I asked him.*

*"So I can learn how to construct them. This is the issue of the Bulletin I always wanted to read, and since nobody else would put it together, I had to. . ."*

*I've seen some of John's future history, and it's intriguing. "Shapes of Things to Come" is part of it.*

# SHAPES OF THINGS TO COME

## John F. Carr

Stewart was hiding in the corridors of Diaspar when the emergency override shut off the fantasizer.

Moments later he was back in the homeshaft on Eunomia. "Stew, this is John Harvey calling," said a voice from the comboard. "I need help. Two of my rear extendors have gone dead!"

Stewart was more worried by the slight edge to John Harvey's voice than by the message. He remembered what they had taught in the C-M classes: *The ADMAP, Adept Mobile Asteroid Processor, cannot experience emotion; it can only operate within those parameters described by its program. Its only emotions are those projected by its human co-operator.*

Those words were the litany of his profession. Yet if they were true (he'd heard other, older transducers refute them) then why had he named John Harvey? He hadn't named any of the other ADMAPs in his team. Anxiety made his skin prickle.

What was wrong with having a slight attachment to an intelligent machine? They were more trustworthy than any person he had ever met. Certainly easier to take care of than a pet.

A former classmate had one told him that United Space Industries was careful never to reveal how intelligent those machines were. It would be a long time before anyone forgot the frenzied years when labs had been sacked and changers hunted down by crazed mobs. Most social scientists blamed the Genetic Pogroms of the twenties on the Neo-Fundamentalist Movement and the conservative backlash to the licentiousness of the previous two decades; a few thought the pogroms were a genetic response to divergence from human "normality." But John Harvey was a machine, not a changer. . .

Stewart patched into the com console. "What's your problem, John Harvey?"

"There is some kind of foreign object inside my hull!"

"Are your rear sensors working?"

"I can't pick up anything on the visible light spectrum and my infra-red sensors just went out."

Stewart ran his fingers over the keloid ridges on the back of his upper legs. There were only three USI transducers in this sector of the Harmondy Cluster, and maybe four or five more working for their competitors. Once he had heard his supervisor mention an Indian settlement in this sector, but the Indians kept to themselves these days and he didn't know where they were.

What could it be inside the ADMAP? An alien? No, that was nonsense. Maybe he had been living alone too long.

"Let me plug in the meta-link," he said, pulling line six out of the console and placing the gold plug into the nape of his neck. With the meta-link he became one with John Harvey; thinking his thoughts, sensing his inputs, and experiencing sensations along the entire electro-magnetic frequency range.

Not only did the increased information produce a feeling akin of that of waking up in the middle of a daydream, but the meta-link electrically strimulated the medial forebrain bundle, one of the brain's major pleasure relay stations. To Stewart the mental tickle was just the whipped cream on his spiritual pie-in-the-sky.

As the initial euphoria of first contact began to subside, Stewart began to feel the deadness of the ADMAP's dorsal extendors. Then the sonic detectors picked up multi-frequency vibrations from inside the hull/body. *Something was inside their skin!*

He was suddenly aware of the identity meld. Stewart felt his hull bristle. He shook his head to clear his mind.

An identity meld was a transducer's greatest enemy, one of

the reasons why the company mind menders picked introverted personalities for the job. According to regulations he
should break contact; but he couldn't. Not this time. John
Harvey needed him.

"What's happening to me?" bellowed John Harvey.

The ADMAP's hull shuddered. Stewart was caught in the
vortex of terror. He broke contact.

Stewart knew intellectually that crystalline brains could
not feel emotions; at least not the way colloidal forms of
intelligence could. An emotive feedback loop had been set up
between the two of them. Before his first tour of duty, they
had taken him for a visit to the Goodman Neuro-Psychiatric
Clinic where he had been shown a ward holding former
transducers who had not broken contact in time. Two rows
of men ensconced in clear homeostatic life-support pods;
they had looked like dead fish floating belly-up in plastic
baggies.

John Harvey's voice jolted him out of his reverie.

"What happened?" shouted Stewart into the mike.

"My dorsal power cable shorted out. I think it was cut. I'm
paralyzed."

"Are you picking up any more sonics?"

"No. Stew . . . most of my sensors are dead."

"Can you come back to the station?"

"No. I can't move. That cable fed directly into the ion
engines."

"How is the main power source?" The ADMAP wouldn't
last long if its pulsed nuclear motor failed. John Harvey's
cybernetic brain could live for eighteen hours on reserve
power, then . . . Machines died, no matter what the engineers thought.

"The power system is still working, but—. Stew, I think
something is trying to kill me."

Stewart knew what he had to do, but he didn't like it. He
didn't want to leave the station, but there was no way the
ADMAP could return to Eunomia without his help.

His fingers began to slowly massage the lumps of scar
tissue on his legs. He hadn't been off base in three years, not

since ADMAP #29 had been wrecked in an asteroid collision. Even an ADMAP the size of a sixty-story tall wall wasn't built to withstand the impact of a thirteen ton boulder.

Stewart could still vividly remember the five hellish days he had spent inside a skinsuit directing salvage operations. Not again! But he had no choice. A friend needed help.

He cursed and then informed the computer that he was leaving. In order to reach the outer port he had to take the lift to the surface and pass through the food domes where potatoes, soybeans, and leaf vegetables grew on vertical pullulators. This was no simple spacewalk for the robot tendors were aggressively protective of their charges.

Stewart moved stealthily through the leafy aisles, only relaxing when he reached the underground corridors that connected the domes. He was halfway through the last dome when one of the three-meter tendors, spraying fertilizer, approached with its klaxon blaring.

He managed to slither by, but not before it had soaked him with a malodorous spray. He was chilled and in low spirits by the time he reached the outer port. Except for the occasional emergency, he was less important to the smooth flow of the asteroid than even the lowly robot tendors.

After shedding his wet bodysuit Stewart put on a skinsuit and began to mull over which vehicle to travel in. The scooters were too small for both him and the wardens, the ovaloid repair bots he needed to help repair John Harvey. The shuttle was overpowered, designed for emergency use. The caterpillar, a series of interconnected modules, was the logical choice. It was slow, but roomy and dependable.

As the caterpillar left Eunomia, he watched two of the wardens as they grappled an ion engine and attached it to a large ore body. In a few minutes the smart ion engine would drive the nickle-iron mass to one of the inner Belt spacehooks where it would be catapulted to one of the Earth-Luna libration points.

In the distance he could see a large boulder of kerogen as it swung toward the asteroid. One of the homers, a spider-like mass catcher, rushed out to intercept it and stow it away. It made no difference whether he was there or not; the machines would continue to function.

The ship moved painfully slow; its ion engines would not gain any real speed until they had already reached their destination. There was little to see on the screen as the asteroids were far apart even in the densely packed Harmondy Cluster. The Ice Rush had quadrupled the non-Indian population in the Cluster, but it hadn't made much difference around Eunomia, which was several million klicks away from the ice islands.

As the caterpillar angled into the course that would take it to John Harvey, Stewart thought about the unlikely trajectory bringing him to this tiny shell in the midst of the asteroid belt. At age six his mother rented him to Boy Howdy, a family franchise specializing in pre-adolescent boys. His first three contracts had been cut short; few putative parents liked his withdrawn and restrained manner.

He could still hear Gary Don say, "Look boy, you've got the wrong attitude. People don't want no sullen snot-nosed brat; they could have their own if they did. No, they want an ideal; a boy howdy. Try and think like a dog, be loyal, cheerful, and affectionate. Otherwise, I'll have to keep sendin' you back to your mother. And you don't like that. Do you boy?"

No. His mother was unhappy when a contract—and the cash—was broken off. When he came home the drinking began, and then the beatings, with a coat hanger or her fists. Her boyfriends were worse. One of them used to make his mom put his hair up in curlers and send him out to play. He would sneak down to the basement of the old conapt and cry himself to sleep in front of the illegal incinerator.

Finally he found someone who would accept him. An old, at least he had seemed old then, professor of mathematics who had inherited a large family fortune. Stewart never had any designs on the money; it was enough that Mr. Grady accepted him. It was heaven for a boy like himself; a housekeeper who didn't speak English and a house filled with objects d'art and the memorabilia of several lifetimes. It lasted six years and died the day he broke the Ming vase.

Professor Grady never said a word; he just picked up his cane with the silver wolf's head and struck him repeatedly about the head and shoulders and, when he'd fallen down, on the back of his legs. Two days later he was back with his mom and the tall stranger she called his uncle.

He had not cared for anyone since, at least not for any body. Not that he didn't get lonely. But he had learned to cope with loneliness; it was an adversary he understood.

Except for an occasional Friendly Sally, Stewart hadn't seen another human being in five years. That was the way United liked it; they didn't make any profits by shuttling transducers between Earth and the Belt. As compensation they paid very high wages. At the end of this tour he would have enough to buy a luxury dome on the farside of Luna.

"It's moving again," said John Harvey.

Stewart checked the autopilot and was surprised to find that he was only seven hundred and sixty kilometers away. "I'll be there in fifteen minutes," he said.

He could have sworn he heard John Harvey sigh in relief.

From six klicks the ADMAP looked like a silver cigar with funnels at both ends, one larger than the other. At the front was the intake scoop which picked up small asteroids and meteors. It used its arm-like extendors to plant explosive charges on the larger asteroids. After the explosion it went around like a vacuum cleaner picking up the digestable sized chunks. The asteroid pieces were sorted by composition and processed into five ton chunks to be pulsed off to Eunomia.

At one kilometer the ADMAP appeared much less symmetrical and was cluttered with antennas and dish-shaped sensors. As the caterpillar drew even closer, he could see that two of the rear extendors were bent akimbo.

Stewart decided to board at the dorsal service hatch. He used the space sled to take him to the ADMAP. Where the service hatch should have been was a gaping hole. The edges were as smooth as sea-worn glass; someone had used a laser torch to peel open the hull.

He turned quickly, his eyes darting in all directions. All he could see was the steely starlight and the humped shadow of the caterpillar. He removed a laser torch from the sled and, after checking his tank gauge, he cautiously entered the hull.

The upper light nodes, which should have flared brightly at his approach, were dead. He turned on his helm beam. The small spear of light barely illuminated the girder-lined catwalk. Shadows loomed and bobbed before him.

Stewart felt his shoulders grow stiff with tension. At each new compartment he was forced to bend down and each time his head came up he expected to see the ADMAP's unknown assailant.

Fear began to stir his entrails. He had heard the stories about humped beasts lurking around uncharted asteroids, but he had put them in the same category as tales about the *yeti* or *Sasquatch*. Now he wasn't so sure. He knew there were Indians around somewhere, but they wanted nothing to do with miners or company workers. Just what had breached John Harvey's outer skin?

Without warning he was thrown hard against the side of the catwalk. The ADMAP shuddered again and again. His light bounced drunkenly in front of him. Several of his ribs ached as though they were broken.

Stewart tongued on his transceiver and shouted, "What's happening?"

John Harvey's voice sounded very distant. "There has been an explosion inside the hull. Near the nuclear engine."

Stewart's fingers pressed firmly against the wiry textured skinsuit covering his upper left leg. He had never heard of a pulsed nuclear engine exploding on its own, but they weren't sabotage proof. . .

"What's the power situation?"

"Bad. The engine is dead. I'm using auxiliary storage right now."

Eighteen hours. That was all the time John Harvey had. The auxiliary power system was not meant to be used. Nuclear engines didn't fail. And John Harvey's chips and circuits wouldn't be harmed when the power died.

But John Harvey would be dead. When the power was

restored, he would be a different ADMAP. The quirks that made John Harvey unique and the rapport they shared would be gone forever.

Stewart had to get to the drive station and repair the nuclear engine, or at least find out what replacements he needed to bring back from Eunomia. But first he had to stop the invader.

"Do you have any sensors that are still functioning in the drive station?"

"I do not know. I shut down all unnecessary functions when the cutoff occurred. I will test the circuits."

While he was waiting, Stewart took a deep breath. No sharp pains; maybe his ribs weren't broken, just bruised.

"One of the infra-red detectors is registering. There is a strong heat source inside the drive station."

"Is it moving?"

"No. It is stationary."

Stewart had expected that. In all probability the only thing inside the drive station was a warm corpse. At least he knew it was a person rather than a defective warden or maintenance machine.

Despite knowing where his quarry was, Stewart moved cautiously along the catwalk that followed the curvature of the ADMAP's hull like a spinal cord. There might be more than one of them.

It took ten minutes to reach the open lift that would carry him to the drive station. As he entered the lift he removed the laser torch from his service belt and held it by his side.

"Has it moved?" he asked John Harvey.

"No. The infra-red emissions have remained constant."

Whatever was down there was alive and possibly dangerous. When the lift reached the compartment above the drive station, he could see where the metal floor had buckled and warped. He lifted the laser and squeezed the handle tightly.

Stewart checked the skinsuit's radiation strip as the lift entered the drive station. The strip was still clear; he expelled a lung full of air.

The floor of the drive station was chaotic. Shards of metal

and debris littered the floor. The nuclear engine, about the size of an elcar, was still intact. Some of the casing was bent and it was lopsided.

He looked around for the body. There was nothing but smashed machinery.

Stepping off the lift he saw something move. He walked cautiously toward the pile of rubble with his laser in hand. He tongued his suitcom's frequency modulator. There was no response, except for an occasional static crackle.

Then a fat tentacle pushed its way out of the rubble. It fell limply before he could fire his laser.

Stewart held his laser out waiting for it to move. His mouth felt like he had been sucking vacuum. When it was obvious that the tentacle was harmless, he picked up a long piece of metal and began to move the debris from around the snake-like appendage.

Within minutes a general outline of the beast began to appear. It was vaguely turtle shaped with squat tentacles instead of flippers. It didn't appear to have on a pressure suit, or any field that his instruments could discern. He wondered if it might be an unknown Belt lifeform.

*Then he saw the face!*

Despite the large beak and scales it was human. The way the hair on the back of Stewart's neck stood out was proof of that. The thing moved and the eye membrane receded, exposing a large milky orb.

He broke out into a cold sweat. It was a changer. One of the illegal form-changed humans. Simultaneously he was engulfed with revulsion and hatred. Only the unexpectedness of John Harvey's voice prevented him from killing it.

"Stew, what is it?"

"A *changer*." He could taste bile at the back of his throat. Now he knew what the sociobiologists meant by "intruder reaction." He felt an instinctive desire to kill the deviant.

Other animals didn't hesitate to kill the unfit, freak, or changeling. Why should humans be any different? But they were. They had the ability to alter and channel their basic

drives and behaviors. Within minutes Stewart had his mindless rage and disgust under control.

He forced himself to approach it again, even though he was
shaking inside. There was a rich orange residue of blood on
its hump, but he couldn't bring himself to touch it. He used
the metal probe to turn it over; it was surprisingly light.

In the center of its large hump he saw a deep gash dusted
with orange crystals. It looked like it was dying. But he had to
find out where it came from and why it attacked the ADMAP.

Each compartment of the asteroid processor was capable
of being sealed off so normal air pressure could be obtained.
Stewart walked over to the lift and checked the door panels.
They appeared okay. He hit the manual override switch and
began to turn the handwheel. It took almost ten minutes
before the door shut with a satisfying bump.

The roof was buckled and the side panels were bent, but he
couldn't find any leaks. He opened the aircock and felt a firm
pressure against his hand.

When the air pressure was high enough that his voice no
longer squeaked, Stewart turned off the air. Without the
blowers and purification system the air wouldn't stay fresh
for long, but it would give him enough time to ask his
questions—that was if the changer could live in an oxygen
environment?

The fresh air revived the changer and it gave several croaks
as though to clear its throat.

"Who are you?" asked Stewart.

The changer spoke as though its beak were full of gravel,
but he could make out most of the words. "I am known as
Dives Backwards. My people are the Cheyenne."

The Indians were form-changing! No wonder they had
been so secretive. But why attack the ADMAP? He had never
heard of them attacking machines, although on occasion they
had run off solitary prospectors or company scouts.

"Why have you done this?" he asked, pointing at the
nuclear engine.

"Your machines are devouring our homeland. It is time
for a . . . cleansing, as our medicine men call it."

"That's mad. There's enough mass in the Harmondy Cluster to last all of us a thousand years."

"Yes, but the ice will be gone in fifty!"

Water, the river of life, thought Stewart. Too expensive to pump up from Earth's deep-gravity well and rare other than on the distant moons of Jupiter and Saturn. Except in the Harmondy Cluster where its discovery had sparked off an Ice Rush.

"On Earth," continued Dives Backwards, "we thought there was enough for us and the whites. We were wrong. The white man devoured the land as the locust strip the prairies. This time we will not wait until it is too late. . ."

This means war, he thought, suddenly energized. He had to tell the company. Or did they already know?

The Indian's body shook with each new cough, and red spittle began to trail down one side of his beak.

"What's wrong?"

When the coughing stopped, Dive Backwards answered, "My deep lung is bleeding inside. I cannot stop it."

"You seem to be breathing all right."

"My shallow lung was not injured."

The shallow lung must be for breathing in a normal atmosphere and the deep lung for storing oxygen in deep space like an air tank, thought Stewart.

"I shall die soon," said Dives Backwards. "I have only one request."

"What's that?"

"That you remove me from this souless beast and let me die in free space."

Dives Backwards' simple plea moved him as no cry for help or mercy could. Stewart saw himself as a humane person and knew he had met another, even though disguised in filth.

John Harvey's voice broke into his thoughts. He put back his helm to communicate in privacy. In a few minutes he had explained the situation.

"What will you do?" asked John Harvey.

"I don't know. I'll have to talk with him further."

"Dives Backwards, how long can you hold out?"

The Indian sighed. "In this air eight, maybe ten hours. I have some control over the bleeding. Outside, less than an hour."

"I can get you back to my station in under eight hours. My medical facilities are the best."

"Thank you, but they would do little good. I need access to a shape-changing device to bind my wounds. There is one at our village, but it is far away."

"How far?"

"Thirty thousand klicks."

At maximum acceleration, using most of his reaction mass, Stewart could make it in less than eight hours. It would be chancy and he would have to depend upon the Indians' gratitude for mass to get back to the station. There would be little welcome if he arrived with a corpse.

And he would have to abandon John Harvey. There would be no time to return to Eunomia for another nuclear engine, not even if he used the shuttle.

The Indian was long, over two and a half meters, not counting its tentacles. He wondered if he could get its body outside.

"I would like to help you, Dives Backwards, but it would cost a friend his life."

The Indian looked at him, his milky eyes seeming to turn transparent. "Your friend lives inside this machine?"

Stewart nodded.

"I do not share your feelings, but I understand your loneliness."


Inside his cabin, Stewart was alone with his thoughts. Dives Backwards rested inertly on a cot beside him, deep in the trance that the changers used when traveling in space. His breathing was almost nonexistent. Stewart still didn't understand why he had left John Harvey. Nor had the ADMAP reproached him; although possibly it didn't understand Stewart was deserting it.

It had been a hellish job maneuvering the large Indian through the narrow catwalks. Without the souless wardens he would never have made it. He wondered what the Indian would think when he recovered, if he recovered.

The remainder of the journey was quiet; the only sound was an occasional gurgle as Dives Backwards took another shallow breath. Their reception was low key. One minute nothing, the next someone tapping against the outer hull.

He let the new changer inside and found that his "intruder reaction" had almost disappeared. The changer identified himself as Echohawk. He was polite and listened to Stewart's story. Then Echohawk explained that he would have to be blindfolded to enter the village.

It hit Stewart that the Indians might have to dispose of him. With what he knew about the asteroid's location, anyone could find it. Sweat beaded on his forehead and floated away like the air bubbles of a drowning man in the null-gravity cabin.

They removed his blindfold inside one of the asteroid's wormholes. The village was not what he had expected; he hadn't thought it would turn out to be almost a twin to his own station. Nor were all the people changers. Most of the Indians were dressed the same as any other group of Belt hoppers. As they passed through an intersection he saw why everything looked so familiar; it was a former United Space Industries station. The UPI insignia was still engraved on one of the stoney walls.

He wondered how many other outposts had been lost and never reported. What had happened to their crews?

His thoughts came to a halt when the changer brought him before a tall Indian. The man looked ageless and his amber eyes were like bottomless pools. A man could get sucked into them.

"Why did you spare Dives Backwards, Demon Mover?" asked the Indian.

Stewart shook his head. "I don't know."

The Indian seemed to look into his soul.

He nodded lamely.

"I do not like you or any of the others who run the

machines that eat our land and ice.''

Stewart squirmed under the Indian's gaze, then turned away. It was only a job, he wanted to blurt. But he knew how pathetic that sounded, even to himself. It wasn't anything personal against the Indians. It had been the discovery of ice that had turned the Cluster from a minor mining operation into a boom belt. And it would continue until someone managed to move one of Saturn's ice-moons into a Lunar orbit, or the ice ran out.

Stewart began to speak.

''There is nothing you can say. What is wrong is wrong. We have learned. Once we trusted and let others steal our homeland, the ground, the trees, the mountains, the lakes, the sky, and even the buffalo. We were forced to journey to this desolate land to make new homes. We will not be forced out again.''

''But you can't win,'' Stewart found himself saying. ''They own worlds. They will bring soldiers by the thousands to kill your people if you try to stop them. I know them,'' he added, thinking of how callously they used people like himself. Casting them into institutions when they were all used up.

The Indian nodded grimly. ''Well they may. But this time they will have to kill all of us. We will not live on reservations again. And this time we have the Void People. Many of our young people have grown tired of living like grubs in the ground. I laud their courage.''

''But how?''

''If you wish to leave there are some questions you must not ask.''

Stewart felt his heart quicken.

''What do you want of me?'' he asked, his voice strained. Afraid that he might make a mistake that would cost him the freedom so newly promised.

''Your word that you will tell no one of what you have seen here today.''

''Is that all? How will you know if I talk?''

"I will know." said the Indian flatly, as though that were all the answer he would need.

Stewart realized it was enough. If they thought he might talk, he would not be leaving. It was that simple.

"But, who are you?"

"I am John White Bull, Chief of the Cheyenne. Father of Dives Backwards."

The trip back to Eunomia was the longest journey Stewart had ever made. Never had he felt so alone. When the Caterpillar passed John Harvey, he tried to raise the ADMAP on the ship's communicator. But there was no answer, not even on the broadest beam.

For the first time, since he was ten years old, Stewart tried to cry, but the tears would not come. His eyes were as barren as his whole life had been.

It was then he decided to turn back. No one had ever needed him before, but they did. The Indians might not know it: but they would find out. Just as he had learned.

# THE ENDLESS FRONTIER AND
# THE THINKING MACHINE

### by Hans P. Moravec

*I have a certain reputation for being politically conservative but technologically progressive—as if either of those terms meant anything. (If you want a one-line summary of my political philosophy, it comes from Robinson Jeffers: "Long live freedom, and damn the ideologies!") But certainly I have not recently been accused of anti-technological bias.*

*Yet there come in the night these worms of doubt . . .*

*Whenever I talk to the Artificial Intelligence (AI) people, I get ambiguous feelings: on the one hand, I hear stories of the marvellous accomplishments which we will have Real Soon Now; and on the other, I see that they haven't the foggiest clue to how to get a machine to "understand" anything: that is, they can create a program that can correct your spelling, but not your grammar, because much of grammar is so inprecise that one finally must turn to "you know what I mean". . .*

*And machines haven't got close to knowing anything.*

*This is not to say they won't. I am aware of the fantastic progress in Large Scale Integrated Circuits, which make possible even smaller, faster, and more complex computers. And yet—I see that Joe Weissenbaum's "ELIZA" program, which simulates a rather silly non-directive psychotherapist of the Rogerian school, is among the best of the "human emulator" or "smart" programs; and I understand Dr. Weissenbaum's contempt for many of the fantastic claims of the AI community.*

It's an intriguing question. Is "the operation called understanding" somehow fundamentally different from other concepts? Is "you know what I mean" forever beyond the reach of programmers? Sure, machines can do things people have never done; but Stanford's robots still·haven't built their Heathkit color television set, much less "understood" electronics. Can one believe they'll do the one but never the other?

There's a second problem with AI: how far do we want to go with it? Could the anti-technology people be right? Is AI the step that abolishes Man? Is it time to smash the machines?

First: at the moment, robots and machines don't take over many jobs that ought to be done by people. Those who would reject what automation has done to the present day want, so far as I can see, to preserve the most mind-stultifying and dehumanizing jobs we know of. Jobs like adding up columns of figures, knowing that someone else has added them before you, and another person will add them again after you're done . . . There's damned little glamour in most of the jobs a machine can do, because machines at present are very stupid.

Second: we are getting close to decision time. It won't be long before machines can do jobs as well as or better than morons: and then what do we do with the morons and half-wits?

I have a bit of experience in this. Many years ago I worked for a large company which had a horrible problem with turnover among mini-plug solderers. It was easy to see why. Soldering mini-plugs is boring, repetitious, exacting, and not very rewarding. It required careful attention to detail and painstaking care, but almost zero intelligence: you didn't even have to be able to read.

It paid very well, and was thus a desirable job among electronic assembly workers; but they could stand it only so long before either going back to their old jobs, or leaving the company entirely. The turnover was costing a fortune.

It didn't take long to see the problem: because this was a

*"critical item"*, *the personnel department insisted on a fairly high minimum IQ for the job. And of course they had the right idea, but they had the sign wrong: they should have insisted on a* maximum *level of intelligence. After all, the job didn't take brains, just a careful temperament—*

*The upshot was that on my advice they began to hire mentally retarded people for the job—and they turned out to be very good at it. They took a bit longer, but they were always careful. They were proud to be able to contribute to the aerospace industry; to have important jobs. Unlike robots, they* cared.

*So far there is no robot which can solder mini-plugs without human assistance; and the last time I spoke with an AI industrial designer, he said "You don't appreciate just how smart a moron is until you try to design a robot." But that will change, and soon enough robots will be able to do jobs that could be done by the useless and unwanted. . .*

*Of course not very many companies will even consider the useless and unwanted for repetitive, dull, but important work; so perhaps it's not so bad after all.*

*What do you do when it's your job the robot is after?*

\* \* \*

*Not long ago, Marvin Minsky posed a serious problem: what kind of system might be used to send* milligram *payloads to the stars? Minsky, founder of the Artificial Intelligence Laboratories at MIT, seriously believes that within decades we will be able to build* tiny *devices, no larger than a pinhead, which would store enough information to be able to take random materials and construct machinery; duplicate themselves; and eventually build, if not a star-ship, then at least a transmitter capable of reporting back to Earth on conditions found at, say, the planets of Rigel or Tau Ceti.*

*Contrasted with the present state of the art you might think that ludicrous; yet there seems to be no* theoretical *reason why it cannot be done. "If you can send up whole gram payloads," Minsky says, "then it's a lot easier—"*

*Query: is that what we mean by exploring the stars? To send off fly-specks that duplicate themselves and launch other probes to go to other places and duplicate themselves again and so forth, ad infinitum?*

*The point, I hope, is made. Should there be limits to the growth of Artificial Intelligence?*

\* \* \*

*Hans Moravec was formerly a graduate student under John P. McCarthy of Stanford. McCarthy, you will recall, is the chap who bought the Heathkit color TV to be assembled by a robot; and he hasn't at all lost faith in AI's ultimate capabilities.*

*Neither has Hans Moravec. This essay deserves quite a lot of attention.*

# THE ENDLESS FRONTIER AND THE THINKING MACHINE

## Hans P. Moravec

The first modern computers, appearing in the late 1940's, offered unprecedented opportunities for experiments in complexity. They raised the hope in influential scientists like John von Neumann and Alan Turing that the ability to think, our greatest asset in dealing with the world, might soon be understood well enough to duplicate. Our minds might be amplified just as our muscles had been by energy machines.

Computers have become vastly more capable since then, but are still much stupider than people in most areas. Not for lack of trying. The last decade, in particular, has seen thousands of people years devoted directly to making them smarter. Much effort has been expended on computer programs which do mathematics, computer programming and common sense reasoning, are able to understand natural languages and interpret scenes seen through cameras and spoken language heard through microphones and to play games humans find challenging.

There's been some progress. Arthur Samuel's 20 year old checker program occasionally beats checker champions, and chess programs have played at good amateur (class B) level for nearly as long. In August of 1978 a chess program written by David Slate and Larry Atkin of Northwestern University won one serious game and tied another against David Levy, a chess International Grandmaster. It happened in a tournament to settle a 1968 bet between Levy and several computer scientists that a computer couldn't beat him within a decade. Levy won the tournament and the bet, but by a narrower margin than he expected. An earlier version of the Northwestern program won the Minnesota Open Chess Championship in March 1977, earning a chess rating in the expert range. The program owes much of its success to the computer it runs on, a CDC Cyber 176. Executing 14 million instructions per second it is about 10 times faster than prior machines used to play chess.

A ten year effort at MIT has gathered specialized knowledge about algebra, trigonometry, calculus and related fields from many sources into a wonderful program called MACSYMA. MACSYMA manipulates symbolic formulas the way pocket calculators manipulate numbers. With it a person can, for instance, solve a differential equation without thinking about the mechanics of doing an integral in the same way that someone with a pocket calculator can find the quotient of two numbers without knowing about long division. MACSYMA has been used by many to solve problems that would otherwise have been left untouched.

Other semi-intelligent programs showing up in the real world can understand simplified typewritten English about restricted subjects, make elementary deductions in the course of answering questions and interpret spoken commands chosen from hundred word repertoires. Some can do simple visual inspection tasks, such as deciding whether or not a screw is at the end of a shaft.

Computers are at their worst trying to do the things most natural to humans, like seeing, hearing, language and common sense reasoning. Large portions of our nervous systems are dedicated to these skills, and computers are unlikely to match human performance until they can process as much data as the neural centers. I calculate that a typical present day computer is a million times less powerful than a human brain. The computer can perform a million simple steps per second, but the 40 billion neurons in a brain can switch a thousand times in the same interval. The spectacular, continuing evolution of microelectronics should make the requisite power available at great cost in a decade, and inexpensively by the end of the century.

In addition to being powerful enough, a computer able to

perform like a human must be properly programmed. Just how long before the right programs are written is a matter of controversy. Many critical experiments can't be done now because computers are too small and too slow. I feel that infusing an adequately powerful machine with near-human intelligence is not as hard as some guess.

Evolution has independently produced moderate intelligence several times, indicating that it develops naturally and does not require improbable leaps. The difficulty can be gauged by the evolutionary timescale. 300 million years passed between the invention of the neuron and development of the worm, a similar period between worms and dumb vertebrates, and 300 million more between vertebrates and us. Our technology has paralleled nature in many respects. It had developed electronic switching by 1920, electronic computers by 1950, and semi-intelligent machines by 1980. By analogy we ought to have truly smart machines by 2010.

Human equivalent computers will have a profound effect on the nature and pace of space colonization. People are not built to live in space, but must be supported by massive, Earth simulating machinery to remain healthy. Robots can be made without this handicap. Tiny space probes cruise unprotected through the Solar System, their functioning unimpaired by vacuum, radiation and temperature extremes. Machines with these advantages and with human or above human intelligence have an overwhelming edge in space industrialization. We may be able to keep up, but only by profoundly changing ourselves.

## Natural Intelligence

My optimism about the future of intelligent machines is based partly on the evolutionary record. Nature holds the patents on high intelligence. It invented it not once, but several times, as if to demonstrate how easy it was.

A billion years ago, before brains or eyes were invented, when the most complicated animals were something like hydras, double layers of cells with a primitive nerve net, our progenitors parted company with the invertebrates. Now both clans have intelligent members.

Cephalopods are the most intellectual invertebrates. Most mollusks are sessile shellfish, but octopus and squid are highly mobile, with big brains and excellent eyes. Evolved independently of us, they are different. The optic nerve connects to the back of the retina, so there is no blind spot. The brain is annular, a ring around the esophagus. The green blood is circulated by a systemic heart oxygenating the tissues and two gill hearts moving depleted blood. Hemocyanin, a copper doped protein related to hemoglobin and chlorophyll, carries the oxygen.

Octopus and their relatives are swimming light shows, their surfaces covered by a million individually controlled color changing cells. A cuttlefish placed on a checkerboard can imitate the pattern, a fleeing octopus can make deceiving seaweed shapes coruscate backward along its body. Photophores of deep sea squid, some with irises and lenses, generate bright multicolored light. Since they also have good vision, there is a potential for high bandwidth communication.

Their behavior is mammal-like. Octopus are reclusive and shy, squid are occasionally very aggressive. Small octopus can learn to solve problems like how to open a container of food. Giant squid, with large nervous systems, have hardly ever been observed except as corpses. They might be as clever as whales.

Birds are vertebrates, related to us through a 300 million year old, probably not very bright, early reptile. Size-limited by the dynamics of flying, some are intellectually comparable to the highest mammals.

The intuitive number sense of crows and ravens extends to seven, compared to three of four for us. Birds outperform all mammals except high primates and the whales in ''learning set'' tasks, where the idea is to generalize from specific instances. In mammals generalization depends on cerebral cortex size. In birds forebrain regions called the wulst and the hyperstriatum are critical, while the cortex is small and unimportant.

Our last common ancestor with the whales was a primitive rat-like mammal alive 30 million years ago. Some dolphin species have body and brain masses identical to ours, and have had them for more generations. They are as good as us at many kinds of problem solving, and can grasp and communicate complex ideas. Killer whales have brains seven times human size, and their ability to formulate plans is better than the dolphins', who they occasionally eat. Sperm whales, though not the largest animals, have the world's largest brains. Intelligence may be an important part of their struggle with large squid, their main food.

Elephant brains are five times human size. Elephants form matriarchal tribal societies and exhibit complex behavior. Indian domestic elephants learn over 500 commands, and form voluntary mutual benefit relationships with their trainers, exchanging labor for baths. They can solve problems such as how to sneak into a plantation at night to steal bananas, after having been belled (answer: stuff mud into the bells). And they never forget (really).

Apes are our 10 million year cousins. Chimps and gorillas can learn to use tools and to communicate in human sign languages at a retarded level. Chimps have one third, and gorillas one half, human brainsize.

## Nervous System Size and Intelligence

Animals exhibiting near-human behavior have hundred billion neuron nervous systems. Imaging vision alone requires a billion. The smartest insects have a million brain cells, while slugs and worms make do with a thousand, and sessile animals with a hundred. The portions of nervous systems for which tentative wiring diagrams have been obtained, including nearly all of the large neuroned sea slug, Aplysia, the flight controller of the locust and the early stages of vertebrate vision, reveal neurons configured into efficient, clever, assemblies.

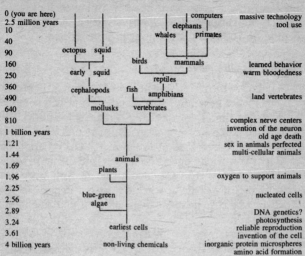

| Time before present | Representative Creatures | Significant events |
| --- | --- | --- |
| 0 (you are here) | computers | massive technology |
| 2.5 million years | elephants | tool use |
| 10 | whales   primates | |
| 40 | | |
| 90 | octopus   squid | |
| 160 | birds   mammals | learned behavior |
| 250 | early   squid | warm bloodedness |
| | reptiles | |
| 360 | cephalopods   fish   amphibians | |
| 490 | | land vertebrates |
| 640 | mollusks   vertebrates | |
| 810 | | complex nerve centers |
| 1 billion years | | invention of the neuron |
| | | old age death |
| 1.21 | | sex in animals perfected |
| 1.44 | | multi-cellular animals |
| | animals | |
| 1.69 | plants | |
| 1.96 | | oxygen to support animals |
| 2.25 | | |
| 2.56 | blue-green | nucleated cells |
| | algae | |
| 2.89 | | DNA genetics? |
| 3.24 | | photosynthesis |
| | earliest cells | reliable reproduction |
| 3.61 | | invention of the cell |
| 4 billion years | non-living chemicals | inorganic protein microspheres |
| | | amino acid formation |

**FIGURE: Highlights in the evolution of terrestrial intelligence. The distance along the edge of the tree is proportional to the square root of the time from the present. This seems to space things nicely.**

## Measuring Processing Power

The vertebrate retina has been studied extensively. Its 20 million neurons take signals from a million light sensors and combine them in a series of simple operations to detect things like edges, curvature and motion. Then image thus processed goes on to the much bigger visual cortex in the brain.

Assuming the visual cortex does as much computing for its size as the retina, we can estimate the total capability of the system. The optic nerve has a million signal carrying fibers and the optical cortex is a thousand times deeper than the neurons which do a basic retinal operation. The eye can process ten images a second, so the cortex handles the equivalent of 10,000 simple retinal operations a second, or 3 million an hour.

An efficient program running on a typical computer can simulate a retinal operation in about two minutes, for a rate of 30 per hour. Thus seeing programs on present day computers seem to be 100,000 times slower than vertebrate vision.

## Another Measurement

To compare the processing power of brains and computer programs more generally, note that devices which compute (or think) do things unexpectedly. Predictable entities like rocks do no computation, pocket calculators do a little, bees do a lot, and humans do even more. By this criterion the amount of computing done by a device is in the mind of the beholder. If you were very good at mental arithmetic and could predict a calculator's answer before it gave it, the calculator would do no real computation for you, and might as well be a rock.

Information theory can make this idea precise. If an entity in a given state can change to one of N next states with equal probability, the information in the transition, which I will call the Compute Energy, is given by

$$\text{Compute Energy} = \log_2 N$$

where N is the number of next states. The measure is in binary digits, bits. Similarly the total compute energy of the entity is the log of the number of distinct states it can ever be in. Some people call this the memory size.

A machine that computes faster is more powerful than a slower one. Compute Power is found by dividing the compute energy of a state transition by the time required for the transition.

$$\text{Compute Power} = \frac{\log_2 N}{t}$$

The units are bits/second.

Slightly more complicated formulas, which give lower values, apply if the transitions probabilities and times are not all equal.

These measures are highly analogous to the energy and

power capacities of a battery. The compute power and energy of a system of two or more independent machines is the sum of the individual powers and energies. A device with a high power, able to reach a moderate number of states in a short time, can yet have a low energy, if the total number attainable in the long run is not high. Speeding up a machine by a factor of n increases the power by the same factor. A completely predictable system has zero power and energy.

## Computer Power

The PDP-10 computer used by many researchers obeys simple instructions at the rate of one million per second. An instruction contains one of $2^5$ different commands, involving one of $2^4$ accumulators and one of $2^{18}$ memory locations, most of these combinations resulting in distinct next states. This gives a Compute Power of

$$\frac{\log_2(2^5 \times 2^4 \times 2^{18}) \text{ bit}}{10^6 \text{ sec}} = 27 \times 10^6 \ \frac{\text{bit}}{\text{sec}}.$$

The power is reduced because different instruction sequences can result in the same outcome and increased by information flowing in from high speed storage devices connected to the computer for a net of about $10^7 \ \frac{\text{bit}}{\text{sec}}$.

The power is also limited by the total compute energy, which is about $10^7$ bits. The PDP-10 could execute at its maximum effectiveness for one second before reaching a state which could have been arrived at more quickly another way. Connecting the computer to the external world can increase this time indefinitely.

## Brain Power

Making a number of simplifying assumptions, the human brain has 40 billion neurons, each able to change state 1000

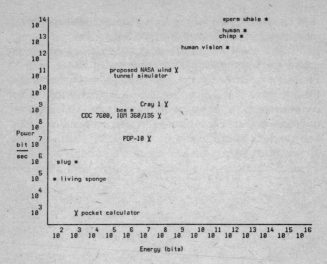

**FIGURE: Compute Power and Energy of various devices. Scales are logarithmic. The Cray machine is an extremely fast and large scientific computer. The NASA simulator would probably be a general purpose computer 100 times as powerful as the biggest existing machines. It has not been designed yet.**

times a second. Considering the space of all possible interconnections of these 40 billion (treating this as the search space natural evolution had, in the same sense that all possible programs are available to someone trying to make a computer smart), we note that the number of combinations reachable from a given state is $2^{40} \times 10^9$, giving a compute power of

$$\frac{40 \times 10^9 \text{ bit}}{10^3 \text{ sec}} = 40 \times 10^{12} \quad \frac{\text{bit}}{\text{sec}}$$

which is about a million times more than a PDP-10 program. This ratio agrees with the visual system calculation, because the visual cortex is about ten percent of the brain.

We got our figure by comparing all possible brain interconnections with all possible PDP-10 programs, measuring the relative computational richness of the media available to nature and a programmer. We concluded that a million PDP-10's would be needed to support a program that thinks like a human. But a computer can be reprogrammed more conveniently than a brain can be rewired, and this is a source of hidden power. The human-equivalent program on a million machine system could be replaced by single-minded programs to play superhuman chess or blindingly solve differential equations, an option not available with a real human.

This generality has a price. The PDP-10 computer is just one instance of all possible ways of connecting its components. The extra options give the raw circuitry about 1000 times the compute power of the finished computer.

But there's a tradeoff between efficiency and design effort. It's much easier, faster and cheaper to write a program than to build a circuit for a complex function. Computer instructions do useful things with few unexpected side effects. In circuit design the basic operations are more primitive, and the side effects many. A program that can be written in a few days by one person may take months to implement in special hardware. It's for this reason that the best machine chess player is a general purpose computer rather than a special gadget. I imagine that the first near-human machines will similarly be implemented on general purpose computers, and converted later into more efficient hardware.

## The Growth of Processing Power

A millionfold increase in processing power seems a tall order, but the gap is not quite as wide as our simple analysis implies.

PDP-10 computers, still used, are a decade old. Today's similarly priced machines are ten times as fast. And for ten million dollars one can buy scientific computers with more than 100 times the speed. 10,000 of these supercomputers operating together with the right program should be as intelligent as a human. At a hundred billion dollars, it's an offer easily refused.

The cost of computing has dropped steadily since the 1950's by a factor of ten every five years. Each price drop expanded the market and fueled further advances. In the last few years computers have crept into the consumer area, disguised as calculators, watches, smart appliances and automotive electronics.

Computer use will continue to expand in the forseeable future. The conventional applications of micro-computers will continue to grow. Calculators and computer games will merge with television and the phone system to become a universal information utility, giving bidirectional access to the world's knowledge.

Until now assembly line robots have been deaf, blind and very dumb. Like the sorcerer's apprentice's broomsticks, they repeated a sequence of motions over and over, oblivious to the world. Computers, seeing through cameras and feeling with switches and strain gauges, are beginning to provide the senses and the sense robots have lacked. As they become more capable and cheaper, and human labor becomes more expensive, they will be increasingly in demand. Not only the number of computers, but the capability of each one, will grow.

Homes are less structured than assembly lines, and home robots are more difficult to make, but they will appear, and be in great demand, when computers become smart enough. They will be cheap partly because other robots will assemble them.

Outer space is prime grazing land for machinery. Robot mines and robot factories making more robots on the moon or in the asteroids ought to be a fast growing and lucrative investment, once the machines are good enough.

Integrated circuit technology is nowhere near its physical limits, and the science to support a few decades of continuing improvement already exists. In production are new semiconductor techniques, $I^2L$, ten times as efficient as older TTL, and super fast D-MOS, CCD for large sensors and fast bulk memory, and magnetic bubbles for mass storage. The new 65K memory chips use V-MOS, where transistors trade depth in the silicon for surface area, pointing towards much denser three dimensional circuits. The structures on IC surfaces are becoming smaller than one micron, and electron beams and X-rays are displacing longer wavelength light in their manufacture.

Industrial and university labs are full of potential major improvements. Exotic semiconductors like gallium arsenide can be made into IC's several times faster than silicon. Thermal disturbances show up as electrical noise, and the amount of energy needed to unambiguously signal a circuit is proportional to its temperature. Cooling semiconductor circuits to liquid nitrogen temperatures allows them to deal with much smaller signals, and consequently be smaller and less power hungry, and up to 100 times faster. If we go to 4 degree absolute liquid helium temperatures, even more astounding things are possible. A Josephson junction gate is a superconducting logic element in which the magnetic field of one current can switch off another supercurrent tunneling through a very thin insulator. The transition takes as little as a picosecond, 1000 times faster than existing semiconductors. Josephson junctions use 1000 times less energy per switching function than neurons.

New discoveries, unpredicatable in detail, will further fuel the fire. Magnetic monopoles weighing 1000 protons, as yet undiscovered because they are so massive and hard to make, could drastically expand our options. Matter made of monopole atoms would be extremely dense and strong, and solid state magnetic circuits could be millions of times faster than conventional electronics. The lowest transition in a magnetic atom is so energetic that monopole wire would magnetically superconduct at the plasma temperatures of conventional matter.

The cost of computing will continue to fall, by a factor of 10,000 in the next 20 years, and a ten million dollar general purpose computer powerful enough to be programmed for human equivalence will exist by the 21st century. But that's not the whole story.

In measuring the processing power of the PDP-10 we assumed it could do nothing but obey its instructions. Processing power expresses the possibilities per unit time, and this restriction was expensive. If we instead think about rewiring the computer's circuitry, the number of options is much greater, and the processing power is about 1000 times as large. Or, carrying it to absurdity, if we considered how the atoms of the PDP-10 could be reconfigured, the compute power would be astronomical.

Hardware design is becoming more automated. Most new computers, and all new integrated circuits, were designed with the help of other computers. Programs exist that make printed circuit or IC patterns from circuit diagrams, and others can simulate designs and check for errors. As computers get smarter these automatic design aids will get better, and the complexity bounds on special hardware will rise.

Some specialized operations useful for human equivalence are already in hardware. Hughes has built an IC that locates edges in TV images a hundred times faster than typical programs. Some air traffic control systems have associative memory units able to look up data dozens of times more quickly than an unaided computer. Within twenty years this kind of development, coupled with the general cost reductions, should allow human equivalent machines costing a year's salary.

Even before then idiot savant machines like the Northwestern/CDC chess computer mentioned earlier, better than humans at a few things, though stupider on the whole, will be slaving for our short term well being, and long term obsolescence. It has already begun.

## The Future

What happens when increasingly cheap machines can replace humans in any situation? What will I do when a computer can write this article, and do research, better than me? These questions face some occupations now. They will affect everybody in a few decades.

By design, machines are our obedient and able slaves. But intelligent machines, however benevolent, threaten our existence because they are alternative inhabitants of our ecological niche. Machines merely as clever as human beings will have enormous advantages in competitive situations. Their production and upkeep costs less, so more of them can be put to work with given resources. They can be optimized for their jobs, and programmed to work tirelessly.

Intelligent robots will have even greater advantages away from our usual haunts. Very little of the known universe is suitable for unaided humans. Only by massive machinery can we survive in outer space, on the surfaces of the planets or on the sea floor. Smaller, intelligent but unpeople, devices will be able to do what needs to be done there more cheaply. The Apollo project put people on the moon for forty billion dollars. Viking landed machines on Mars for one billion. If the Viking landers had been as capable as humans, their multi-year stay would have told us much more about Mars than we found out about the moon from Apollo.

As if this weren't bad enough, the very pace of technology presents an even more serious challenge. We evolved with a leisurely 100 million years between significant changes. The machines are making similar strides in decades. The rate will quicken further as multitudes of cheap machines are put to work as programmers and engineers, with the task of optimizing the software and hardware which makes them what they are. The successive generations of machines produced this way will be increasingly smarter and cheaper. There is no reason to believe that human equivalence represents any sort of upper bound. When pocket calculators can out-think humans, what will a big computer be like? We will simply be outclassed.

Then why rush headlong into the intelligent machine era? Wouldn't any sane human try to delay things as long as possible? The answer is obvious, if unpalatable on the surface. Societies and economies are as surely subject to evolutionary pressures as biological organisms. Failing social systems wither and die, to be replaced by more successful competitors. Those that can sustain the most rapid expansion dominate sooner or later.

We compete with each other for the resources of the accessible universe. If automation is more efficient than hand labor, organizations and societies which embrace it will be wealthier and better able to survive in difficult times, and expand in favorable ones. If the U.S. were to unilaterally halt technological development, as a vociferous minority urges, it would soon succumb either to the military might of the Soviets, or the economic success of its trading partners. Either way the social ideals which led to the decision would become as unimportant on the world scale as the opinions of the religious cults.

If, by some evil and unlikely miracle, the whole human race decided to eschew progress, the long term result would be almost certain extinction. The universe is one random event after another. Sooner or later an unstoppable virus deadly to humans will evolve, or a major asteroid will collide with the earth, or the sun will go nova, or we will be invaded from the stars, or a black hole will swallow the galaxy.

The bigger, more diverse and competent a culture is, the better it can detect and deal with external dangers. The bigger events happen less frequently. By growing sufficiently rapidly it has a finite chance of surviving forever. Even the eventual collapse or heat death of the universe might be evaded or survived if an entity can restructure itself properly.

The human race will expand into the solar system soon, and Gerry O'Neill's little Earths will be part of it. But the economics of automation will become very persuasive in space even before machines achieve human competence.

I visualize immensely lucrative self-reproducing robot factories in the asteroids. Solar powered machines would prospect and deliver raw materials to huge, unenclosed, automatic processing plants. Metals, semiconductors and plastics produced there would be converted by robots into components which would be assembled into other robots and structural parts for more plants. Machines would be recycled as they broke. If the reproduction rate is higher than the wear out rate, the system will grow exponentially. A small fraction of the output of materials, components, and whole robots could make someone very, very rich.

The first space industries will be more conventional. Raw materials purchased from Earth or from human space settlements will be processed by human supervised machines and sold at a profit. The high cost of maintaining humans in space insures that that there will always be more machinery per person there than on Earth. As machines become more capable, the economics will favor an ever higher machine/people ratio. Humans will not necessarily become fewer, but the machines will multiply faster.

When humans become unnecessary in space industry, the machines' physical growth rate will climb. When machines reach and surpass humans in intelligence, the intellectual growth rate will rise similarly. The scientific and technical discoveries of super-intelligent mechanisms will be applied to making themselves smarter still. The machines, looking quite unlike the machines we know, will explode into the universe, leaving us behind in a figurative cloud of dust. Our intellectual, but not genetic, progeny will inherit the universe. Barring prior claims.

This may not be as bad as it sounds, since the machine civilization will certainly take along everything we consider important, including the information in our minds and genes. Real live human beings, and a whole human community, could be reconstituted if an appropriate circumstance ever arose. Since we are biologically committed to personal death, immortal only through our children and our culture, shouldn't we rejoice to see that culture become as robust as possible?

*An Alternative*

Some of us have very egocentric world views. We anticipate the discovery, within our lifetimes, of methods to extend human lifespans, and look forward to a few eons of exploring the universe. We don't take kindly to being upstaged by our creations.

The machines' major advantage is their progress rate. We evolve by DNA + nucleated cell + sex + personal death, they develop by the much faster intelligence + language + culture + science + technology technique. If we could somehow learn the new way, we might be able hold our own.

Genetic engineering is an option. Successive generations of human beings could be designed by mathematics, computer simulations, and experimentation, like airplanes and computers are now. But this is just building robots out of protein. Away from Earth, protein is not an ideal material. It's stable only in a narrow temperature and pressure range, is sensitive to high energy disturbances, and rules out many construction techniques and components. Anyway, second rate superhuman beings are just as threatening as first rate ones, whatever they're made of.

What's really needed is a process that gives an individual all the advantages of the machines, at small personal cost. Transplantation of human brains into manufactured bodies has some merit, because the body can be matched to the environment. It does nothing about the limited and fixed intelligence of the brain, which the artificial intellects will surpass.

## Transmigration

You are in an operating room. A robot brain surgeon is in attendance. By your side is a potentially human equivalent computer, dormant for lack of a program to run. Your skull, but not your brain, is anaesthetized. You are fully conscious. The surgeon opens your brain case and peers inside. Its attention is directed at a small clump of about 100 neurons somewhere near the surface. It determines the three dimensional structure and chemical makeup of that clump nondestructively with neutron tomography, phased array radio encephalography, and ultrasonic radar. It writes a program that models the behavior of the clump, and starts it running on a small portion of the computer next to you. Fine wires are run from the edges of the neuron assembly to the computer, providing the simulation with the same inputs as the neurons. You and the surgeon check the accuracy of the simulation. After you are satisfied, tiny relays are inserted between the edges of the clump and the rest of the brain. Initially these leave brain unchanged, but on command they can connect the simulation in place of the clump. A button which activates the relays when pressed is placed in your hand. You press it, release it and press it again. There should be no difference. As soon as you are satisfied, the simulation connection is established firmly, and the now unconnected clump of neurons is removed.

The process is repeated over and over for adjoining clumps, until the entire brain has been dealt with. Occasionally several clump simulations are combined into a single equivalent but more efficient program. Though you have not lost consciousness, or even your train of thought, your mind (some would say soul) has been removed from the brain and transferred to a machine.

In a final step your old body is disconnected. The computer is installed in a shiny new one, in the style, color and material of your choice. You are no longer a cyborg halfbreed, your metamorphosis is complete.

Advantages become instantly apparent. Your computer has a control labelled *speed*. It had been set to *slow*, to keep the simulations synchronized with the old brain, but now you change it to *fast*. You can communicate, react and think a thousand times faster. But that's just a start.

The program in your machine can be read out and altered, letting you conveniently examine, modify, improve and extend yourself. The entire program may be copied into similar machines, giving two or more thinking, feeling versions of you. You may choose to move your mind from one computer to another more technically advanced, or more suited to a new environment. The program can also be copied to some future equivalent of magnetic tape. If the machine you inhabit is fatally clobbered, the tape can be read into a blank

computer, resulting in another you, minus the experiences
since the copy. With enough copies, permanent death would
be very unlikely.

As a computer program, your mind can travel over information channels. A laser can send it from one computer to
another across great distances and other barriers. If you found
life on a neutron star, and wished to make a field trip, you
might devise a way to build a neutron computer and robot
body on the surface, then transmit your mind to it. Nuclear
reactions are a million times quicker than chemistry, so the
neutron you can probably think that much faster. It can act,
acquire new experiences and memories, then beam its mind
back home. The original body could be kept dormant during
the trip to be reactivated with the new memories when the
return message arrived. Alternatively, the original might
remain active. There would then be two separate versions of
you, with different memories for the trip interval.

Two sets of memories can be merged, if mind programs
are adequately understood. To prevent confusion, memories
of events would indicate in which body they happened.
Merging should be possible not only between two versions of
the same individual but also between different persons.
Selective mergings, involving some of the other person's
memories, and not others, would be a very superior form of
communication, in which recollections, skills, attitudes and
personalities can be rapidly and effectively shared.

Your new body will be able to carry more memories than
your original biological one, but the accelerated information
explosion will insure the impossibility of lugging around all
of civilization's knowledge. You will have to pick and
choose what your mind contains at any one time. There will
often be knowledge and skills available from others superior
to your own, and the incentive to substitute those talents for
yours will be overwhelming. In the long run you will remember mostly other people's experiences, while memories
you originated will be floating around the population at large.
The very concept of *you* will become fuzzy, replaced by
larger, communal egos.

Mind transferral need not be limited to human beings. Earth has other species with brains as large, from dolphins, our cephalic equals, to elephants, whales, and giant squid, with brains up to twenty times as big. Translation between their mental representation and ours is a technical problem comparable to converting our minds into a computer program. Our culture could be fused with theirs, we could incorporate each other's memories, and the species boundaries would fade. Non-intelligent creatures could also be popped into the data banks. The simplest organisms might contribute little more than the information in their DNA. In this way our future selves will benefit from all the lessons learned by terrestrial biological and cultural evolution. This is a far more secure form of storage than the present one, where genes and ideas are lost when the conditions that gave rise to them change.

Our speculation ends in a super-civilization, the synthesis of all solar system life, constantly improving and extending itself, spreading outwards from the sun, converting non-life into mind. There may be other such bubbles expanding from elsewhere. What happens when we meet? Fusion of us with them is a possibility, requiring only a translation scheme between the memory representations. This process, possibly occurring now elsewhere, might convert the entire universe into an extended thinking entity, a prelude to even greater things.

EDITOR'S INTRODUCTION TO:

SONGS OF A SPACEFARER

by Judith R. Conly


It's hard to judge poetry, so I generally go by what John and I like and have done with it; but once in a while we get corroboration.

Ms. Conly sent "Songs of a Spacefarer" on the recommendation of Roger Zelazny; and I'm enormously grateful to both of them. If Moravec sings of man's potential accomplishments, Conly tells of man's future.

# SONGS OF A SPACEFARER

## Judith R. Conly

### I

### The Parting

You are the victim of the nights we did not share:
    the suspended nights, unblessed by any moon,
    before the full-sphere audience of moving stars,
    within the clear black sky that knows neither cloud nor
    wind.
Because you have not touched the varied glories
    that people the all beyond your global borders,
    nor lain beneath a radiant rainbow of suns,
    you content yourself to die within your air-shelled egg.

### II

### The Comet

At first the comet seemed no larger,
    slipping distantly among the distant stars,
    than a burning minnow in a pebbled brook of ink.
Its indifference tantalized and beckoned
    to our impromptu curiosity,
    and our own small fiery tail stalked it
    like a restless bee would court an eagle.
Relinquishing the sentience of free travel,
    we joined the lumbering unrebellious rubble

in its will-less careless worship
of the almost-sun-bright force
that was made no less
by contrast-banishing proximity.
But then we, the firefly independent of the flame,
tired of violent passive light without answers,
returned to the page-cool dark of space
and the stars like waiting question marks.


III


The Repair


One of the random shots from the dark
had struck with unminded accuracy,
so they sent me forth to pit my training
against the heartstopping splinter's wound.
Clad in metal and assurances and air,
with only crafted fire to arm my manipulations
that try to counteract uncaring time and chance,
I venture my timorous exit
from the independent shell of metal and air.
Seeing me grounded only by an unalive umbilicus,
the vastness without walls or direction
grants my mission barely the temporal nod
its completion requires and demands;
then the mewling witless terror,
the impact of such an imposing nothing
on the almost infinitely finite consciousness
impels my forcedly cautious flight.
So, acknowledging the abashed offspring,
the womb resorbs the ill-considered birth
into the depanicking light of warm-enclosed security.

## IV

### The Death

Your final stillness contains and ingathers
   a shadow of the absolute cold
   that awaits us on the other side
   of our outclosing double shell
   that is cast in metal and in spirit.
We felt secure in the ship-like shelter
   of the smile that represented you—
   but we still follow our ship-clad course,
   while the heart-woven garment
   that was your contribution to our immortality
   has ravelled to become your shroud.
We do not mourn for you,
   but rather for the disarming weakness,
   the new-found inability of man-born light
   to banish the annihilating dark.

## V

### The Nova

It was not made by man,
   and yet it held some flaw
   that made its steadfast heart
   of trusty boastful fire
   falter within its body of ellipses.
The pensive creatures it sheltered
   —symbiotes or parasites—
   forewarned by the signals
   of its too-great generosity,

flew out, like panicked spores
  in search of new and safer soil.
Alone, abandoned, unseeing,
  it spread an excess of its life-blood,
  like a moronic benificent deity
  who spattered obliterating paint
  across the filled dark canvas of its sky.


## VI


### The Spacefarer


Even when I was too young to demand true answers
  you found your place in the day sky of my eyes.
I spent many baking or frosty nights, watching,
  listening to the soul-ache, my first and only child,
  conceived in wordless eloquent curiosity
  borne through patience-losing years and studies,
  brought to light in the pin-pricked darkness,
  to suffer the fate of a realized dream.
I sought the solitude of a candle-filled endless night
  that contains and separates the other lives,
  the intrusive thoughts, the unwanted words,
  from my exquisite isolation that sings like a single bell
  in the congregationless midnight cathedral.
I found, in place of the still-born child,
  a family of strangers, closer than kin,
  bound by a dream that goes beyond flesh,
  beyond words and their acts, beyond the star-cleft
  emptiness.
We are stronger than our skin of flesh and metal,
  for we carry and share a spectrum of suns and lands

that lends us legends as we craft our immortality
and interweave our destinies of water and air,
leaving shadows that gather color of their own,
until they outshine the substance that cast them.

EDITOR'S INTRODUCTION TO:

REDEEMER

by Gregory Benford

*Greg Benford is another of the new breed of SF writers: those who do science as well as write about it. A professor of physics at the University of California at Irvine, he recently spent a semester as a visiting lecturer in England. There's a faint possibility that he could be the first Hugo winner to be a Nobel laureate. Greg's new novel* Timescape *could only have been written by a scientist; it conveys the excitement of scientific investigation better than anything I've ever seen. It's also a whacking good story.*

*So is this one, which tells of tragedy and triumph in the endless frontier.*

# REDEEMER

## Gregory Benford

He had trouble finding it. The blue-white exhaust plume was a long trail of ionized hydrogen scratching a line across the black. It had been a lot harder to locate out here than Central said it would be.

Nagara came up on the *Redeemer* from behind, their blind side. They wouldn't have any sensors pointed aft. No point in it when you're on a one-way trip, not expecting visitors and haven't seen anybody for seventy-three years.

He boosted in with the fusion plant, cutting off the translight to avoid overshoot. The translight rig was delicate and still experimental and it had already pushed him over seven light years out from Earth. And anyway, when he got back to Earth there would be an accounting, and he would have to pay off from his profit anything he spent for overexpenditure of the translight hardware.

The ramscoop vessel ahead was running hot. It was a long cylinder, fluted fore and aft. The blue-white fire came boiling out of the aft throat, pushing *Redeemer* along at a little below a tenth of light velocity. Nagara's board buzzed. He cut in the null-mag system. The ship's skin visible outside fluxed into its superconducting state, gleaming like chrome. The readout winked and Nagara could see on the sim board his ship slipping like a silver fish through the webbing of magnetic field lines that protected *Redeemer*.

The field was mostly magnetic dipole. He cut through it and glided in parallel to the hot exhaust streamer. The stuff was spitting out a lot of UV and he had to change filters to see what he was doing. He came up along the aft section of the

405

ship and matched velocities. The magnetic throat up ahead
sucked in the interstellar hydrogen for the fusion motors. He
stayed away from it. There was enough radiation up there to
fry you for good.

*Redeemer*'s midsection was rotating but the big clumsy-
looking lock aft was stationary. Fine. No trouble clamping
on.

The couplers seized *clang* and he used a waldo to manu-
ally open the lock. He would have to be fast now, fast and
careful.

He pressed a code into the keyin plate on his chest to check
it. It worked. The slick aura enveloped him, cutting out the
ship's hum. Nagara nodded to himself.

He went quickly through the *Redeemer*'s lock. The pumps
were still laboring when he spun the manual override to open
the big inner hatch. He pulled himself through in the zero-g
with one powerful motion, through the hatch and into a
cramped suitup room. He cut in his magnetos and settled to
the grid deck.

As Nagara crossed the desk a young man came in from a
side hatchway. Nagara stopped and thumped off his protective shield. The man didn't see Nagara at first because he was
looking the other way as he came through the hatchway,
moving with easy agility. He was studying the subsystem
monitoring panels on the far bulkhead. The status phosphors
were red but they winked green as Nagara took three steps
forward and grabbed the man's shoulder and spun him
around. Nagara was grounded and the man was not. Nagara
hit him once in the stomach and then shoved him against a
bulkhead. The man gasped for breath. Nagara stepped back
and put his hand into his coverall pocket and when it came out
there was a dart pistol in it. The man's eyes didn't register
anything at first and when they did he just stared at the pistol,
getting his breath back, staring as though he couldn't believe
either Nagara or the pistol was there.

"What's your name?" Nagara demanded in a clipped,
efficient voice.

"What? I—"

"Your name. Quick."

"I . . . Zak."

"All right, Zak, now listen to me. I'm inside now and I'm not staying long. I don't care what you've been told. You do just what I say and nobody will blame you for it."

" . . . Nobody . . . ?" Zak was still trying to unscramble his thoughts and he looked at the pistol again as though that would explain things.

"Zak, how many of you are manning this ship?"

"Manning? You mean crewing?" Confronted with a clear question, he forgot his confusion and frowned. "Three. We're doing our five year stint. The Revealer and Jacob and me."

"Fine. Now, where's Jacob?"

"Asleep. This isn't his shift."

"Good." Nagara jerked a thumb over his shoulder. "Personnel quarters that way?"

"Uh, yes."

"Did an alarm go off through the whole ship, Zak?"

"No, just on the bridge."

"So it didn't wake up Jacob?"

"I . . . I suppose not."

"Fine, good. Now, where's the Revealer?"

So far it was working well. The best way to handle people who might give you trouble right away was to keep them busy telling you things before they had time to decide what they should be doing. And Zak plainly was used to taking orders.

"She's in the forest."

"Good. I have to see her. You lead the way, Zak."

Zak automatically half turned to kick down the hatchway he'd come in through and then the questions came out. "What—who *are* you? How—"

"I'm just visiting. We've got faster ways of moving now, Zak. I caught up with you."

"A faster ramscoop? But we—"

"Let's go, Zak." Nagara waved the dart gun and Zak

looked at it a moment and then, still visibly struggling with his confusion, he kicked off and glided down the drift tube.

\* \* \*

The forest was one half of a one hundred meter long cylinder, located near the middle of the ship and rotating to give one g. The forest was dense with pines and oak and tall bushes. A fine mist hung over the tree tops, obscuring the other half of the cylinder, a gardening zone that hung over their heads. Nagara hadn't been in a small cylinder like this for decades. He was used to seeing a distant green carpet overhead, so far away you couldn't make out individual trees, and shrouded by the cottonball clouds that accumulated at the zero-g along the cylinder axis. This whole place felt cramped to him.

Zak led him along footpaths and into a bamboo-walled clearing and the Revealer was sitting in lotus position in the middle of it. She was wearing a Flatlander robe and cowl just like Zak. He recognized it from a historical fax readout.

She was a plain-faced woman, wrinkled and wiry, her hands thick and calloused, the fingers stubby, the nails clipped off square. She didn't go rigid with surprise when Nagara came into view and that bothered him a little. She didn't look at the dart pistol more than once, to see what it was, and that surprised him, too.

"What's your name?" Nagara said as he walked into the bamboo-encased silence.

"I am the Revealer." A steady voice.

"No, I meant your name."

"That is my name."

"I mean—"

"I am the Revealer for this stage of our exodus."

Nagara watched as Zak stopped halfway between them and then stood uncertainly, looking back and forth.

"All right. When they freeze you back down, what'll they call you then?"

She smiled at this. "Michele Astanza."

Nagara didn't show anything in his face. He waved the pistol at her and said, "Get up."

"I prefer to sit."

"And I prefer you stand."

"Oh."

He watched both of them carefully. "Zak, I'm going to have to ask you to do a favor for me."

Zak glanced at the Revealer and she moved her head a few millimeters in a nod. He said, "Sure."

"This way." Nagara gestured with the pistol to the woman. "You lead."

The woman nodded to herself as if this confirmed something and got up and started down a footpath to the right, her steps so soft on the leafy path that Nagara could not hear them over the tinkling of a stream on the overhead side of the cylinder. Nagara followed her. The trees trapped the sound in here and made him jumpy.

He knew he was taking a calculated risk by not getting Jacob, too. But the odds against Jacob waking up in time were good and the whole point of doing it this way was to get in and out fast, exploit surprise. And he wasn't sure he could handle the three of them together. That was just it—he was doing this alone so he could collect the whole fee, and for that you had to take some extra risk. That was the way this thing worked.

The forest gave onto some corn fields and then some wheat, all with UV phosphors netted above. The three of them skirted around the nets and through a hatchway in the big aft wall. Whenever Zak started to say anything Nagara cut him off with a wave of the pistol. Then Nagara saw that with some time to think Zak was adding some things up and the lines around his mouth were tightening, so Nagara asked him some questions about the ship's design. That worked. Zak rattled on about quintuple-redundant failsafe subsystems he'd been repairing until they were at the entrance to the freezing compartment.

It was bigger than Nagara had thought. He had done all the research he could, going through old faxes of *Redeemer*'s prelim designs, but plainly the Flatlanders had changed things in some later design phase.

One whole axial section of *Redeemer* was given over to the freezedown vaults. It was at zero-g because otherwise the slow compression of tissues in the corpses would do permanent damage. They floated in their translucent compartments, like strange fish in endless rows of pale, blue-white aquariums.

The vaults were stored in a huge array, each layer a cylinder slightly larger than the one it enclosed, all aligned along the ship's axis. Each cylinder was two compartments thick, a corpse in every one, and the long cylinders extended into the distance until the chilly fog steaming off them blurred the perspective and the eye could not judge the size of the things. Despite himself Nagara was impressed. There were thousands upon thousands of Flatlanders in here, all dead and waiting for the promised land ahead, circling Tau Ceti. And with seventy-five more years of data to judge by, Nagara knew something this Revealer couldn't reveal: the failure rate when they thawed them out would be thirty percent.

They had come out on the center face of the bulwark separating the vault section from the farming part. Nagara stopped them and studied the front face of the vault array, which spread away from them radially like an immense spider web. He reviewed the old plans in his head. The axis of the whole thing was a tube a meter wide, the same translucent organiform. Liquid nitrogen flowed in the hollow walls of the array and the phosphor light was pale and watery.

"That's the DNA storage," Nagara said, pointing at the axial tube.

"What?" Zak said. "Yes, it is."

"Take them out."

"What?"

"They're in failsafe self-refrigerated canisters, aren't they?"

"Yes."

"That's fine." Nagara turned to the Revealer. "You've got the working combinations, don't you?"

She had been silent for some time. She looked at him steadily and said, "I do."

"Let's have them."

"Why should I give them?"

"I think you know what's going on."

"Not really."

He knew she was playing some game but he couldn't see why. "You're carrying DNA material for over ten thousand people. Old genotypes, undamaged. It wasn't so rare when you collected it seventy-five years ago but it is now. I want it."

"It is for our colony."

"You've got enough corpses here."

"We need genetic diversity."

"The System needs it more than you. There's been a war. A lot of radiation damage."

"Who won?"

"Us. The outskirters."

"That means nothing to me."

"We're the environments in orbit around the sun, not sucking up to Earth. We knew what was going on. We're mostly in Bernal spheres. We got the jump on—"

"You've wrecked each other genetically, haven't you? That was always the trouble with your damned cities. No place to dig a hole and hide."

Nagara shrugged. He was watching Zak. From the man's face Nagara could tell he was getting to be more insulted than angry—outraged at somebody walking in and stealing their future. And from the way his leg muscles were tensing against a foothold Nagara guessed Zak was also getting more insulted than scared, which was trouble for sure. It was a lot better if you dealt with a man who cared more about the long odds against a dart gun at this range than about some principle. Nagara knew he couldn't count on Zak ignoring all the Flatlander nonsense the Revealer and others had pumped into him.

They hung there in zero-g, nobody moving in the wan light, the only sound a gurgling of liquid nitrogen. The

Revealer was saying something and there was another thing bothering Nagara, some sound, but he ignored it.

"How did the planetary enclaves hold out?" the woman was asking. "I had many friends—"

"They're gone."

Something came into the woman's face. "You've lost man's *birthright?*"

"They sided with the—"

"Abandoned the planets altogether? Made them unfit to *live* on? All for your awful cities—" and she made a funny jerking motion with her right hand.

That was it. When she started moving that way Nagara saw it had to be a signal and he jumped to the left. He didn't take time to place his boots right and so he picked up some spin but the important thing was to get away from that spot fast. He heard a *chuung* off to the right and a dart smacking into the bulkhead and when he turned his head to the right and up behind him a burly man with black hair and the same Flatlander robes and a dart gun was coming at him on a glide.

Nagara had started twisting his shoulder when he leaped and now the differential angular momentum was bringing his shooting arm around. Jacob was already aiming again. Nagara took the extra second to make his shot and allow for the relative motions. His dart gun puffed and Nagara saw it take Jacob in the chest, just right. The man's face went white and he reached down to pull the dart out but by that time the nerve inhibitor had reached the heart and abruptly Jacob stopped plucking at the dart and his fingers went slack and the body drifted on in the chilly air, smacking into a vault door and coming to rest.

Nagara wrenched around to cover the other two. Zak was coming at him. Nagara leaped away, braked. He turned and Zak had come to rest against the translucent organiform, waiting.

"That's a lesson," Nagara said evenly. "Here's another."

He touched the keyin on his chest and his force screen flickered on around him, making him look metallic. He

turned it off in time to hear the hollow boom that came rolling
through the ship like a giant's shout.

"That's a sample. A shaped charge. My ship set it off two
hundred meters from *Redeemer*. The next one's keyed to go
on impact with your skin. You'll lose pressure too fast to do
anything about it. My force field comes on when the charge
goes, so it won't hurt me."

"We've never seen such a field," the woman said unstead-
ily.

"Outskirter invention. That's why we won."

He didn't bother watching Zak. He looked at the woman as
she clasped her thick worker's hands together and began to
realize what choices were left. When she was done with that
she murmured, "Zak, take out the canisters."

*  *  *

The woman sagged against a strut. Her robes clung to her
and made her look gaunt and old.

"You're not giving us a chance, are you?" she said.

"You've got a lot of corpses here. You'll have a big
colony out at Tau Ceti." Nagara was watching Zak maneuver
the canisters onto a mobile carrier. The young man was going
to be all right now, he could tell that. There was the look of
weary defeat about him.

"We need the genotypes for insurance. In a strange ecology there will be genetic drift."

"The System has worse problems right now."

"With Earth dead you people in the artificial worlds are
*finished*," she said savagely, a spark returning. "That's why
we left. We could see it coming."

Nagara wondered if they'd have left at all if they'd known
a faster than light drive would come along. But no, it
wouldn't have made any difference. The translight transition
cost too much and only worked for small ships. He narrowed
his eyes and made a smile without humor.

"I know quite well why you left. A bunch of scum-lovers.
Purists. Said Earth was just as bad as the cylinder cities, all

artificial, all controlled. Yeah, I know. You flatties sold off everything you had and built *this*—'' His voice became bitter. "Ransacked a fortune—*my* fortune."

For once she looked genuinely curious, uncalculating. "Yours?"

He flicked a glance at her and then back at Zak. ''Yeah. I would've inherited some of your billions you made out of those smelting patents.''

"You—"

"I'm one of your great grandsons."

Her face changed. ''No.''

"It's true. Stuffing the money into this clunker made all your descendants have to bust ass for a living. And it's not so easy these days.''

"I . . . didn't. . ."

He waved her into silence. "I knew you were one of the mainstays, one of the rich Flatlanders. The family talked about it a lot. We're not doing so well now. Not as well as you did, not by a thousandth. I thought that would mean you'd get to sleep right through, wake up at Tau Ceti. Instead—'' he laughed—''they've got you standing watch.''

"Someone has to be the Revealer of the word, grandson."

"Great grandson. Revealer? If you'd 'revealed' a little common sense to that kid over there, he would've been alert and I wouldn't be in here.''

She frowned and watched Zak, who was awkwardly shifting the squat modular canisters stenciled GENETIC BANK. MAX SECURITY. ''We are not military types.''

Nagara grinned. ''Right. I was looking through the family records and I thought up this job. I figured you for an easy setup. A max of three or four on duty, considering the size of the life support systems and redundancies. So I got the venture capital together for time in a translight and here I am.''

"We're not your kind. Why can't you give us a chance, grandson?"

"I'm a businessman."

She had a dry, rasping laugh. "A few centuries ago everybody thought space colonies would be the final answer. Get off the stinking old Earth and everything's solved. Athens in the sky. But look at you—a paid assassin. A 'businessman'. You're no grandson of *mine*."

"Old ideas." He watched Zak.

"Don't you see it? The colony environments aren't a social advance. You need discipline to keep life-support systems from springing a leak or poisoning you. Communication and travel have to be regulated for simple safety. So you don't get democracies, you get strong men. And then they turned on *us*—on Earth."

"You were out of date," he said casually, not paying much attention.

"Do you ever read any history?"

"No." He knew this was part of her spiel—he'd seen it on a fax from a century ago—but he let her go on to keep her occupied. Talkers never acted when they could talk.

"They turned Earth into a handy preserve. The Berbers and Normans had it the same way a thousand years ago. They were seafarers. They depopulated Europe's coastline by raids, taking what or who they wanted. You did the same to us, from orbit, using solar lasers. But to—"

"Enough," Nagara said. He checked the long bore of the axial tube. It was empty. Zak had the stuff secured on the carrier. There wasn't any point in staying here any longer than necessary.

"Let's go," he said.

"One more thing," the woman said.

"What?"

"We went peacefully, I want you to remember that. We have no defenses."

"Yeah," Nagara said impatiently.

"But we have huge energies at our disposal. The scoop fields funnel an enormous flux of relativistic particles. We could've temporarily altered the magnetic multipolar fields and burned your sort to death."

"But you didn't."

"No, we didn't. But remember that."

Nagara shrugged. Zak was floating by the carrier ready to take orders, looking tired. The kid had been easy to take, too easy for him to take any pride in doing it. Nagara liked an even match. He didn't even mind losing if it was to somebody he could respect. Zak wasn't in that league, though.

"Let's go," he said.

\*   \*   \*

The loading took time but he covered Zak on every step and there were no problems. When he cast off from *Redeemer* he looked around by reflex for a planet to sight on, relaxing now, and it struck him that he was more alone than he had ever been, the stars scattered like oily jewels on velvet were the nearest destination he could have. That woman in *Redeemer* had lived with this for years. He looked at the endless long night out here, felt it as a shadow that passed through his mind, and then he punched in instructions and *Redeemer* dropped away, its blue-white arc a fuzzy blade that cut the darkness, and he slipped with a hollow clapping sound into translight.

\*   \*   \*

He was three hours from his dropout point when one of the canisters strapped down behind the pilot's couch gave a warning buzz from thermal overload. It popped open.

Nagara twisted around and fumbled with the latches. He could pull the top two access drawers a little way out and when he did he saw that inside there was a store of medical supplies. Boxes and tubes and fluid cubes. Cheap stuff. No DNA manifolds.

Nagara sat and stared at the complete blankness outside. *We could've temporarily altered the magnetic multipolar fields and burned your sort to death,* she had said. *Remember that.*

If he went back she would be ready. They could rig some kind of aft sensor and focus the ramscoop fields on him when he came tunneling in through the flux. Fry him good.

They must have planned it all from the first. Something about it, something about the way she'd looked, told him it had been the old woman's idea.

The risky part of it had been the business with Jacob. That didn't make sense. But maybe she'd known Jacob would try something and since she couldn't do anything about it she used it. Used it to relax him, make him think the touchy part of the job was done so that he didn't think to check inside the stenciled canisters.

He looked at the medical supplies. Seventy-three years ago the woman had known they couldn't protect themselves from what they didn't know, ships that hadn't been invented yet. So on her five year watch she had arranged a dodge that would work even if some System ship caught up to them. Now the Flatlanders knew what to defend against.

He sat and looked out at the blankness and thought about that.

\* \* \*

Only later did he look carefully through the canisters. In the lowest access drawer was a simple scrap of paper. On it someone—he knew instantly it must have been the old woman, or somebody damned like her—had hand printed a message:

If you're from the System and you're reading this on the way back home, you've just found out you're holding the sack. Great. But after you've cooled off, remember that if you leave us alone, we'll be another human settlement someday. We'll have things you'll find useful. If you've caught up with *Redeemer* you certainly have something *we* want—a faster drive. So we can trade. Remember that. Show this measure to your bosses. In a few centuries we can be an asset to you. But until then, keep off our backs. We'll have more tricks waiting for you.

\* \* \*

When he popped out into System space the A47 sphere was hanging up to the left at precisely the relative coordinates and distance he'd left it.

A47 was big and inside there were three men waiting to divide up and classify and market the genotypes and when he told them what was in the canisters it would all be over, his money gone and theirs and no hope of his getting a stake again. And maybe worse than that. Maybe a lot worse.

He squinted at A47 as he came in for rendezvous. It looked different. Some of the third quadrant damage from the war wasn't repaired yet. The skin that had gleamed once was smudged now and twisted gray girders stuck out of the ports. It looked pretty beat up. It was the best high-tech fortress they had and A47 had made the whole difference in the war. It broke the African shield by itself. But now it didn't look like so much. All the dots of light orbiting in the distance were pretty nearly the same or worse and now they were all that was left in the system.

Nagara turned his ship about to vector on the landing bay, listening to the rumble as the engines cut in. The console phosphors rippled blue, green, yellow as Central reffed him.

This next part was going to be pretty bad. Damned bad. And out there his great grandmother was on the way still, somebody he could respect now, and for the first time he thought the Flatlanders probably were going to make it. In the darkness of the cabin something about the thought made him smile.

# DEAR MR. PRESIDENT

## Jerry Pournelle

After the election of 1980, I was asked to present my views to the Space Policy Committee for the incoming administration. The article following was a large part of my presentation.

Mr. Ronald Reagan
President of the United States
1600 Pennsylvania Avenue
Washington, DC 20500

> "Once to every man and nation
> Comes the moment to decide."
> James Russell Lowell, Anglican Hymnal #519

Dear Mr. President,

Ask the average American the precise moment when he last felt really proud of the nation, and chances are high that he'll say "July 20, 1969, at about 4 PM Pacific Daylight Time." Nearly everyone remembers where he was on that day, and many have never lost the thrill of that moment. "Tranquility Base here. The Eagle has landed."

A properly designed space policy could win back that lost pride—and make a profit in the bargain.

Until a few years ago, the US had a positive balance of payments. Our largest export was high technology. Now, like other under-developed nations, our major export is agricultural products. We had technology for export because we invested in technology; now we have used up that investment, and there is no cutting edge to our technology development.

NASA's most remarkable achievement may have been to

419

make mankind's greatest achievement look dull. It is fashionable in anti-technology circles to denigrate the benefits of the space program. "Teflon frying pans," the scoffers say; but in the real world, we got computers, firefighting methods, medical instruments, communications systems, techniques for fabricating large glass fibre structures, automated quality control procedures, and a host of other things now taken for granted.

Another benefit was development of a methodology for managing the most complex task in human history. Before Apollo, D-Day held that record.

Perhaps the most important benefit was recruiting bright young men and women into science and engineering disciplines. Space had glamour, and many went to engineering schools in order to participate in the space program. Without such attractions, it becomes more difficult to induce young people to undertake that arduous training that modern technological leadership demands.

It is clear that good high technology research does not cost money. You always get your money back. Usually you make a large profit. A vigorous space program is important in high technology development.

* * *

In 1871, France lay prostrate, as Bismark erected his new German Empire across the corpses of French dreams. It would be hard to exaggerate the depth of French despair. Then, in 1889, Alexandre-Gustav Eiffel built the tallest structure in the world; and France had pride again. The Eiffel tower wasn't useful, and at the time it certainly wasn't thought pretty; but nothing remotely like it had ever been done. Twice as high as St. Peter's or the Great Pyramid, built with almost contemptuous ease, it stood as a monument to the new France, and remained the tallest building in the world until the completion of the Chrysler Building in 1930.

In 1981, the United States does not lie prostrate, but many citizens are demoralized because we have no sense of national purpose. The American people have too often been told there is no solution to the problems facing us; that we must share the misery and equitably distribute the poverty, because we can do nothing else.

This is nonsense; yet there is a grain of truth in the counsels of despair. So long as we live on Only One Earth, we must inevitably come to the time when our non-renewable resources are gone. In a small closed system such as a single planet, we may not agree on the limits to growth—but we all must admit there *are* limits.

The Earth is just too small and fragile a basket for the human race to keep all its eggs in. Some day we will lose the Earth. Probably not soon. Cosmic disasters are inevitable, but the chances that one will happen in any given century are fairly small. Over the long haul, though, we will lose the Earth, to a comet collision, or to the exploding Sun, or to a new Ice Age, or to any of a dozen other unlikely-sounding catastrophes. By that time we must be able to survive without Earth. History will bless the men and nation who took the first steps to give humanity a home other than "Only One Earth."

\* \* \*

In summer of 1980, I took part in a high-level NASA planning study held at Pajaro Dunes near Santa Cruz. For a full week some of the most creative minds in the space community considered "bold new missions for the 25-50 year time frame." During the last two days, Administrator Robert Frosch took part.

I have recently been at JPL where I have been privileged to be among the first humans on Earth to see detailed pictures of Saturn. It was a thrilling experience. It also provided me an opportunity to confer with dozens of space experts from all over the nation. Following that, I called colleagues across the country. My question was simple enough: what are the best things we can do in space? What should be our long-term goals, and what should we do this afternoon?

A surprising consensus emerged.

First: everyone agrees that the Halley Comet Intercept
Mission is worthwhile. It is also URGENT. Unless some $20
million is put into the FY82 budget, there is no chance that
the mission can fly. That $20 million buys an option to
something unique in our lifetimes. It would be silly not to
take that option; if later you decide the mission is not worthwhile, you can cancel it.

The Halley Comet Mission is one of pure science. There is
no likely commercial payoff, and very little research and
development will be done. It is a relatively safe mission, well
within JPL's proven capabilities. It is important largely because of the stimulus it will give to the science teams. It is a
race we can win, a fight fixed in advance, one of the few
things we can do that the Soviets cannot. In addition, the
returns from the mission will be spectacular, with high entertainment value for the public.

As an aside: one should not neglect the entertainment value
of space. A full third of the projected benefits of Grand
Coulee Dam were "recreational". At a *per capita* cost lower
than the price of admission to a movie, the public gets a show
that could not be bought anywhere else.

The Halley Mission will help demonstrate that we have not
lost our technological superiority to the Soviets—whose
space spectaculars will mature in the 1984-88 time frame. It
is well worth $20 million to preserve the Halley option.

The balance of the space program will cost a lot more. The
investment is justified, but it is not small. The outline below
presents both long-term and intermediate goals.

1. It is clear that we could have a Lunar colony within this
century; and that such a colony could be made self-
sustaining. There is disagreement over when we could send
up the first colonists—would they be on the Moon before
1990—and, secondly, over when the colony could become
self-sustaining. (Basic supplies such as power and oxygen
are plentiful on the Moon; but just how small can a closed

ecology be?) A Lunar Colony makes a desirable long-term space goal, because it makes use of the capabilities developed by Apollo; and it has the intrinsic appeal of the settling of a new frontier. It would be an appreciable step toward insuring that no single accident or disaster could exterminate the human race.

2. There is immense potential profit in space industries. At the moment, we know of no single space-made product that is sufficiently profitable to support not only its costs of manufacture, but also the "housekeeping" costs of a space station; but we do know of at least a dozen products which would be profitable if the basic space "industrial park" existed, so that the industry paid only its own costs.

If a space industrial facility existed, it would be profitable; and it would bring private enterprise into space.

3. Building a space industrial facility gives us experience in large orbital construction techniques. These skills are vital for both military and civilian space activities.

4. The industrial facility has already been designed by large aerospace companies under the general title of "Space Operations Facility." This name has little power to inspire public acceptance. The President of one of the larger Star Trek clubs suggests "Starbase One".

Aerospace engineers closely associated with the project are agreed that construction of an operational space base is (given operational Shuttle) a three to four year task; but that the administrative and decision cycle of NASA as presently organized would add at least three years to that.

Starbase One could be minimally operational, with a crew aboard, by summer of 1984; and this can be accomplished without wasteful crash programs. This would require cooperation among aerospace companies.

Given intelligent management, there is no reason why Starbase One could not be sufficiently complete to allow on-site inspection by a high-ranking official in fall of 1984. Vice President Bush has been suggested.

5. Starbase One would provide support for civilian industries in space, but it is also a logical step toward construction

of Lunar colonies. Indeed, once industries are well established in space, the laws of physics dictate that we go to the Moon as the most economical source of many raw materials including oxygen. Thus the space facility leads us toward a genuine escape from ''Only One Earth''—but without committing us to any kind of Lunar timetable.

6. The Soviet Union is certain to have a very large space facility in operation by 1985; a facility much larger and probably more spectacular than the proposed Starbase. However, Starbase One gives us at least a chance of countering the inevitable Soviet claims to mastery of space (and to being the world's most powerful nation). Although one probably should not plan space missions solely to ''beat the Russians'', the psychological effects on our diplomacy cannot be ignored.

Starbase One is, of course, an Earth-observation facility which passes over the Soviet Union every two hours. The Soviet trawler fleet provided Soviet intelligence agencies with a great deal of information; it also makes money from its fishing activities. Starbase One could also aid intelligence while making profits. Why should the Russians have all the fun?

7. Construction of Starbase One is compatible with completion of the Large Space Telescope by summer of 1984. An orbital telescope can provide photographs of Jupiter nearly as spectacular as those sent back by the Voyager spacecraft. It has big scientific utility combined with lots of color and flash and public appeal.

8. In addition to Starbase One, we should immediately open a program office for Solar Power Satellites. This ought to be funded at about $50 million a year.

The Solar Power Satellite (SPS) system is, like nuclear fusion, a ''far-out'' technology. Unlike fusion, SPS is known to work. It may not work economically, but it can't fail to produce electricity. Moreover, our best evidence to date is that SPS really is competitive with other systems. After all, coal will require some 5 billion tons a year before 2000—and we don't have the rail net to carry it. I have never seen firm estimates of the total cost of coal—or any other "conventional" energy system, but if one takes into account transport and environmental factors, the "incidental" costs will not be small. As an example, the sludges produced by stack gas scrubbers are LARGER than the original coal put into the boiler; disposal of all that cancerous stuff (stack-scrub sludge is really horrible goo) cannot be cheap.

SPS provides insurance against technological disaster. SPS *can* produce the electricity needed to run the country; it *may* be the cheapest way. It is likely to be competitive in cost. Best of all, once we have the SPS option, we can *know* that our worst problems only cost money which we spend in our own country. We don't have to go to war or sell the nation on the installment plan.

If we want SPS later, it is cheaper to start now; crash funding is not only wasteful, but also detrimental. There is a maximum level a new start can absorb; after that, you're hiring anything that walks up the steps. Beginning a program office now will save a great deal of money later if we go with the SPS option. If we do not buy SPS, the $50 million a year spent will not all be wasted, since much will go for research. It will prove to have been cheap insurance.

9. SPS requires capability for construction of large devices in orbit. Starbase One develops that capability. Thus Starbase One contributes to the SPS option.

10. There are two routes to SPS. The NASA "standard" study spends some $25 billion (over 4-7 years) in research and development, then invests some $50-60 billion in a fleet of Heavy Lift Vehicles (HLV). Thus the first SPS power station costs some $100 billion dollars (and delivers about as much power as we presently get from Grand Coulee Dam). The *second* SPS will cost an additional $11 billion. Each new SPS would be marginally cheaper, since we would already have the Fleet of HLV and the R&D would be done.

The other route has been proposed by David Criswell, formerly of the Lunar and Planetary Institute (and winner of a Proxmire Golden Fleece due to Criswell's commendable zeal for protecting the lunar soil samples brought back by

Apollo). Dr. Criswell believes we can build SPS with Shuttle, without the enormous investment in the HLV Fleet. His method envisions going to the Moon first and building SPS largely from Lunar materials.

The Criswell method has more risks than the "standard" SPS program as envisioned by NASA. It has some cost advantages, and of course puts us on the Moon fairly early in the program. It is an option which ought to be studied. Fortunately it costs very little to keep the option alive.

Note that Starbase One is a highly desirable step toward building SPS on the Criswell plan; and that opening a $50 million/year program office for SPS will let us examine both the HLV and the Moon-first methods of building SPS.

11. The Pajaro Dunes mission planning study group produced excellent results. This group ought to be institutionalized: that is, there are great advantages to periodic meetings of an *outside* advisory group composed in large part of people who are uninterested in NASA jobs, and who get together at, say, semi-annual intervals. It should also have a semi-annual standing appointment with the NASA Administrator.

The Pajaro Dunes study was funded through the University of Santa Clara, which provided support services and secretariat. This is an excellent system, in that it keeps bureaucratic involvement to a minimum, and makes use of eager young people.

Such a group, to include engineers, scientists, science writers, and indeed science fiction dreamers, can do yeoman service at almost trivial costs.

You might even consider forming such a group to report yearly to you on new developments in all fields of science and technology. If nothing else you'd find it stimulating. Many of us get paid pretty well for our lectures and essays—meaning that someone out there finds them entertaining as well as instructive.

In conclusion: nothing is cheap; but our only chance to

improve productivity is to invest in new technology. Technological research needs a focus, a cutting edge to attract bright new people. Space serves that role admirably.

It is the historic mission of government to build roads to new frontiers and protect early settlers. This is as true in 1981 as it was in 1781.

You have a unique opportunity. It may not come again to any man or nation.

# AFTERWORD

## Jerry Pournelle

As I write this, the space program is again in trouble. It is not that the new administration is unfriendly to space and technology; far from it.

But inflation is serious, and what a high official of the Office of Management and Budget told me is true: "The Government has no money. All we have is authority to borrow money at 20% interest. Man, we're broke!"

He went on to point out that of the 700+ billion dollar budget, only about $30 billion was anywhere that he could get at it. The rest was in "entitlements", programs that couldn't be cut—not merely for political reasons, but because they were firmly embedded in the law. The courts won't allow the President anything like the leeway he needs.

This is no place to examine our very recent tendency to glorify the courts. (Andrew Jackson, you will recall, said "John Marshall has made his decision. Now let him enforce it.") Let us concede the arguments.

In which case it is doubly vital that we have a vigorous space program. If you're going to spend more—far more— than you have, you had better INVEST SOMETHING too. With wise investments you stand some chance of getting enough money to cover the other debts you're running up. Indeed, ten to twenty billion a year on space (less than 3% of the national budget!) has the potential of generating enough income to pay for all the untouchables in the rest of the budget. Add another ten to twenty billion for other high-technology research and development, and we have a chance of economic survival. Without those investments—

Without them, we MUST eventually cut back on those entitlements, with what effect on the political health of the Republic I am not sure.

\* \* \*

We must go to space. Or so think I. If you believe likewise, let them know in Washington. Tell your Congressman, your Senators, and your President. Tell them in your own words, and not just once, but monthly. They're already sympathetic there; we only have to let them know that space has a vocal and enthusiastic constituency, people who're willing to speak up for the future.

Tell them before it's too late.

# FRED SABERHAGEN

| | | |
|---|---|---|
| ☐ 49548 | **LOVE CONQUERS ALL** | $1.95 |
| ☐ 52077 | **THE MASK OF THE SUN** | $1.95 |
| ☐ 86064 | **THE VEILS OF AZLAROC** | $2.25 |
| ☐ 20563 | **EMPIRE OF THE EAST** | $2.95 |
| ☐ 77766 | **A SPADEFUL OF SPACETIME** | $2.50 |

## BERSERKER SERIES

Humanity struggles against inhuman death machines
whose mission is to destroy life wherever they find it:

| | | |
|---|---|---|
| ☐ 05462 | **BERSERKER** | $2.25 |
| ☐ 05407 | **BERSERKER MAN** | $1.95 |
| ☐ 05408 | **BERSERKER'S PLANET** | $2.25 |
| ☐ 08215 | **BROTHER ASSASSIN** | $1.95 |
| ☐ 84315 | **THE ULTIMATE ENEMY** | $1.95 |

## THE NEW DRACULA

The *real* story—as told by the dread Count himself!

| | | |
|---|---|---|
| ☐ 34245 | **THE HOLMES DRACULA FILE** | $1.95 |
| ☐ 16600 | **THE DRACULA TAPE** | $1.95 |
| ☐ 62160 | **AN OLD FRIEND OF THE FAMILY** | $1.95 |
| ☐ 80744 | **THORN** | $2.75 |

**A ACE SCIENCE FICTION**
P.O. Box 400, Kirkwood, N.Y. 13795

S-12

Please send me the titles checked above. I enclose _____.
Include 75¢ for postage and handling if one book is ordered; 50¢ per
book for two to five. If six or more are ordered, postage is free. California, Illinois, New York and Tennessee residents please add sales tax.

NAME_____

ADDRESS_____

CITY_____ STATE_____ ZIP_____

# H. BEAM PIPER

| | | |
|---|---|---|
| ☐ 24890 | **FOUR DAY PLANET/LONE STAR PLANET** | $2.25 |
| ☐ 26192 | **FUZZY SAPIENS** | $1.95 |
| ☐ 48492 | **LITTLE FUZZY** | $1.95 |
| ☐ 26193 | **FUZZY PAPERS** | $2.75 |
| ☐ 49053 | **LORD KALVAN OF OTHERWHEN** | $2.25 |
| ☐ 77779 | **SPACE VIKING** | $2.25 |
| ☐ 23188 | **FEDERATION (5¼″ x 8¼″)** | $5.95 |

**ACE SCIENCE FICTION**
P.O. Box 400, Kirkwood, N.Y. 13795

S-10

Please send me the titles checked above. I enclose _____.
Include 75¢ for postage and handling if one book is ordered; 50¢ per book for two to five. If six or more are ordered, postage is free. California, Illinois, New York and Tennessee residents please add sales tax.

NAME_____

ADDRESS_____

CITY_____STATE_____ZIP_____

Classic stories by America's most distinguished and successful author of science fiction and fantasy.

| | | |
|---|---|---|
| ☐ 12314 | **CROSSROADS OF TIME** | $1.95 |
| ☐ 33704 | **HIGH SORCERY** | $1.95 |
| ☐ 37292 | **IRON CAGE** | $2.25 |
| ☐ 45001 | **KNAVE OF DREAMS** | $1.95 |
| ☐ 47441 | **LAVENDER GREEN MAGIC** | $1.95 |
| ☐ 43675 | **KEY OUT OF TIME** | $2.25 |
| ☐ 67556 | **POSTMARKED THE STARS** | $1.25 |
| ☐ 69684 | **QUEST CROSSTIME** | $2.50 |
| ☐ 71100 | **RED HART MAGIC** | $1.95 |
| ☐ 78015 | **STAR BORN** | $1.95 |

**ACE SCIENCE FICTION**
P.O. Box 400, Kirkwood, N.Y. 13795          S-02

Please send me the titles checked above. I enclose _____.
Include 75¢ for postage and handling if one book is ordered; 50¢ per book for two to five. If six or more are ordered, postage is free. California, Illinois, New York and Tennessee residents please add sales tax.

NAME_____

ADDRESS_____ _____

CITY_____STATE_____ZIP_____

# MORE TRADE SCIENCE FICTION

Ace Books is proud to publish these latest works by major SF authors in deluxe large format collectors' editions. Many are illustrated by top artists such as Alicia Austin, Esteban Maroto and Fernando.

| | | | |
|---|---|---|---|
| Robert A. Heinlein | Expanded Universe | 21883 | $8.95 |
| Frederik Pohl | Science Fiction: Studies in Film (illustrated) | 75437 | $6.95 |
| Frank Herbert | Direct Descent (illustrated) | 14897 | $6.95 |
| Harry G. Stine | The Space Enterprise (illustrated) | 77742 | $6.95 |
| Ursula K. LeGuin and Virginia Kidd | Interfaces | 37092 | $5.95 |
| Marion Zimmer Bradley | Survey Ship (illustrated) | 79110 | $6.95 |
| Hal Clement | The Nitrogen Fix | 58116 | $6.95 |
| Andre Norton | Voorloper | 86609 | $6.95 |
| Orson Scott Card | Dragons of Light (illustrated) | 16660 | $7.95 |

*Available wherever paperbacks are sold or use this coupon.*

**ACE SCIENCE FICTION**
P.O. Box 400, Kirkwood, N.Y. 13795

Please send me the titles checked above. I enclose _____.
Include 75¢ for postage and handling if one book is ordered; 50¢ per book for two to five. If six or more are ordered, postage is free. California, Illinois, New York and Tennessee residents please add sales tax.

NAME_____

ADDRESS_____

CITY_____ STATE_____ ZIP_____

S-15

# Gordon R. Dickson

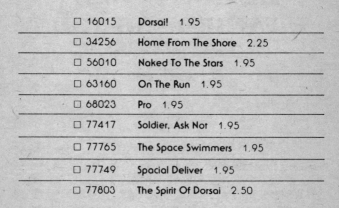

| | | |
|---|---|---|
| ☐ 16015 | Dorsai! | 1.95 |
| ☐ 34256 | Home From The Shore | 2.25 |
| ☐ 56010 | Naked To The Stars | 1.95 |
| ☐ 63160 | On The Run | 1.95 |
| ☐ 68023 | Pro | 1.95 |
| ☐ 77417 | Soldier, Ask Not | 1.95 |
| ☐ 77765 | The Space Swimmers | 1.95 |
| ☐ 77749 | Spacial Deliver | 1.95 |
| ☐ 77803 | The Spirit Of Dorsai | 2.50 |

Available wherever paperbacks are sold or use this coupon.

---

**ACE SCIENCE FICTION**
P.O. Box 400, Kirkwood, N.Y. 13795

Please send me the titles checked above. I enclose _____.
Include 75¢ for postage and handling if one book is ordered; 50¢ per
book for two to five. If six or more are ordered, postage is free. California, Illinois, New York and Tennessee residents please add sales tax.

NAME_____

ADDRESS_____

CITY_____STATE_____ZIP_____

## FAFHRD AND THE
## GRAY MOUSER
## SAGA

| ☐ 79176 | SWORDS AND DEVILTRY | $2.25 |
| ☐ 79156 | SWORDS AGAINST DEATH | $2.25 |
| ☐ 79185 | SWORDS IN THE MIST | $2.25 |
| ☐ 79165 | SWORDS AGAINST WIZARDRY | $2.25 |
| ☐ 79223 | THE SWORDS OF LANKHMAR | $1.95 |
| ☐ 79169 | SWORDS AND ICE MAGIC | $2.25 |

*Available wherever paperbacks are sold or use this coupon*

**ACE SCIENCE FICTION**
P.O. Box 400, Kirkwood, N.Y. 13795

Please send me the titles checked above. I enclose $_____.
Include 75¢ for postage and handling if one book is ordered; $1.00 if
two to five are ordered. If six or more are ordered, postage is free.

NAME_____

ADDRESS_____

CITY_____STATE_____ZIP_____

# Current and Recent
# Ace Science Fiction Releases
# of Special Interest, As Selected
# by the Editor of <u>Destinies</u>

Poul Anderson, ENSIGN FLANDRY . . . . . . . . . **$1.95**
FLANDRY OF TERRA. . . . . . . **$1.95**
THE MAN WHO COUNTS. . . . . **$1.95**
James Baen, THE BEST FROM GALAXY,
VOL. IV. . . . . . . . . . . . . . . . . . . . . **$1.95**
Donald R. Bensen, AND HAVING WRIT . . . . . . **$1.95**
Ben Bova, THE BEST FROM ANALOG . . . . . . . **$2.25**
Arsen Darnay, THE KARMA AFFAIR . . . . . . . . . **$2.25**
Gordon R. Dickson, PRO (illustrated) . . . . . . . . . **$1.95**
David Drake, HAMMER'S SLAMMERS . . . . . . **$1.95**
Randall Garrett, MURDER AND MAGIC
(fantasy). . . . . . . . . . . . . . . . . **$1.95**
Harry Harrison, SKYFALL. . . . . . . . . . . . . . . . . **$1.95**
Keith Laumer, RETIEF AT LARGE . . . . . . . . . . **$1.95**
RETIEF UNBOUND. . . . . . . . . . **$1.95**
Philip Francis Nowlan, ARMAGEDDON 2419 A.D.
(revised by Spider Robinson) . . . . . . . . . . . **$1.95**
Jerry Pournelle, EXILES TO GLORY . . . . . . . . **$1.95**
Spider Robinson, CALLAHAN'S CROSSTIME
SALOON . . . . . . . . . . . . . . . . . **$1.75**
Thomas J. Ryan, THE ADOLESCENCE OF P-1 **$2.25**
Fred Saberhagen, BERSERKER MAN. . . . . . . . **$1.95**
THE HOLMES/DRACULA FILE
(fantasy) . . . . . . . . . . . . . . . . **$1.95**
LOVE CONQUERS ALL . . . . **$1.95**
AN OLD FRIEND OF THE
FAMILY (fantasy). . . . . . . . . **$1.95**
THE ULTIMATE ENEMY . . . . **$1.95**
Dennis Schmidt, WAY-FARER . . . . . . . . . . . . . **$1.75**
Bob Shaw, SHIP OF STRANGERS . . . . . . . . . . **$1.95**
VERTIGO. . . . . . . . . . . . . . . . . . . . . **$1.95**
Charles Sheffield, SIGHT OF PROTEUS . . . . . . **$1.75**
Norman Spinrad, THE STAR-SPANGLED
FUTURE . . . . . . . . . . . . . . . . . **$2.25**
G. Harry Stine, THE THIRD INDUSTRIAL
REVOLUTION (science fact) . . . **$2.25**
Ian Watson, MIRACLE VISITORS . . . . . . . . . . . **$1.95**

# POUL ANDERSON

| | | |
|---|---|---|
| 78657 | **A Stone in Heaven** | $2.50 |
| 20724 | **Ensign Flandry** | $1.95 |
| 48923 | **The Long Way Home** | $1.95 |
| 51904 | **The Man Who Counts** | $1.95 |
| 57451 | **The Night Face** | $1.95 |
| 65954 | **The Peregrine** | $1.95 |
| 91706 | **World Without Stars** | $1.50 |

*Available wherever paperbacks are sold or use this coupon*

**ACE SCIENCE FICTION**
P.O. Box 400, Kirkwood, N.Y. 13795

Please send me the titles checked above. I enclose _____.
Include 75¢ for postage and handling if one book is ordered; 50¢ per book for two to five. If six or more are ordered, postage is free. California, Illinois, New York and Tennessee residents please add sales tax.

NAME_____

ADDRESS_____

CITY_____STATE_____ZIP_____

# Ursula K. Le Guin

| | | |
|---|---|---|
| 10705 | **City of Illusion** | $2.25 |
| 47806 | **Left Hand of Darkness** | $2.25 |
| 66956 | **Planet of Exile** | $1.95 |
| 73294 | **Rocannon's World** | $1.95 |

*Available wherever paperbacks are sold or use this coupon*

**ACE SCIENCE FICTION**
P.O. Box 400, Kirkwood, N.Y. 13795

Please send me the titles checked above. I enclose _____.
Include 75¢ for postage and handling if one book is ordered; 50¢ per
book for two to five. If six or more are ordered, postage is free. California, Illinois, New York and Tennessee residents please add sales tax.

NAME_____

ADDRESS_____

CITY_____STATE_____ZIP_____